Finding Lenny

STANLEY L. WITKIN

This is a work of fiction. All characters, organizations, and events portrayed in this novel are either products of the author's imagination or are used fictitiously.

Copyright © 2022 by Stanley L. Witkin

All rights reserved. No part of this publication may be reproduced in whole or in part, or stored in a retrieval system, or transmitted in any form or by any means, electronic, mechanical, photocopying, recording, or otherwise, without written permission of the author, except for the inclusion of brief quotations in a review.

For information regarding permission, please write to:
info@barringerpublishing.com
Barringer Publishing, Naples, Florida
www.barringerpublishing.com

Design and layout:
Linda S. Duider, Cape Coral, Florida

Cover illustration:
Frannie J. Joseph, Charlottesville, Virginia
http://www.instagram.com/franniejsart

ISBN: 978-1-954396-23-4
Library of Congress Cataloging-in-Publication Data
Finding Lenny / Witkin

Printed in U.S.A.

For Joshua
1977 - 2020

We are not simply in the universe; we are part of it. We are born from it. One might even say we have been empowered by the universe to figure itself out—and we have only just begun.

> ~ Neil deGrasse Tyson

As you get older, I think you get less willing to buy the latest version of reality.

> ~ Leonard Cohen

FINDING LENNY

PART ONE

Chapter One

For as long as he could remember, Lenny thought of himself as different. Not in an obvious way you could point to. He didn't look markedly different from other people or behave in ways that drew attention to himself. Lenny's difference was rooted in his sense of being off-center, of seeing the world from outside the frame.

As a child, this sense was inchoate and unnamed. "Why do you draw people upside down?" a teacher would ask.

"I don't know," little Lenny would answer sheepishly. Because he didn't. Later in life, with education and experience, he would describe himself with words that fit his circumstances. When his difference won him praise or affection, he might view himself as creative or quirky. If a romantic partner ended the relationship claiming he was too weird, then neurotic or screwed-up might seem the best fit.

Interwoven among the good and the bad times were periods of self-interrogation where he would question whether this whole "I'm different thing" was a myth to protect himself from feelings of inadequacy and a lack of self-confidence. *Do I really diverge from the norm, or do I just want to believe I am unique? Don't most people feel a sense of me-ness that sets them apart? If so, doesn't that mean my sense of difference is no difference at all? That I'm just another 'Joe' wishing to be special? On the other hand, might this very analysis be a sign that I am different? After all, how many people raise such questions or give them serious consideration? Or am I grasping at straws, trying to make something out of nothing? But maybe—*

And so it went, on and on in an increasingly dizzying spiral of questions and counter-questions until he became too exhausted to maintain his train of thought.

"I should write this stuff down," he mutters as he gets up from his chair and heads toward the refrigerator. But he doesn't, despite knowing that within the next few minutes these thoughts, which seemed so insightful, would be forgotten. Instead, he browses the shelves hoping to find a surprising morsel to eat, another unlikely prospect since he knows what is there.

Lenny Isaacson has lived in this condo a little over fourteen years, ever since he and his spouse, Sally, separated and eventually divorced. They were married a long time: twenty-eight mostly discordant years. Afterward, with the benefit of distance and hindsight, he found neither the duration nor quality of the relationship surprising.

They came from starkly different backgrounds. Sally was from Jackson, Mississippi, the only child in an ever-aspiring upper-middle-class family. Her father was an attorney more interested in pursuing big paydays and winning the favor of the local gentry than seeking justice. Her mother was a housewife, pretending to be a lady of the manor. Sally's childhood was spent in a large antebellum-style home with extensive gardens dotted with magnolia and live oak trees sheathed in Spanish moss. Behind the house was a swimming pool. Raised in the manner of a debutante, she was instructed in the rules of social etiquette and the traditional Christian morals of Southern belles.

Lenny grew up in New York City, the son of working-class, Jewish, Eastern European immigrants. His family—mother, father, and younger sister—occupied a two-bedroom apartment on the third floor of a five-story tenement populated primarily by other recent immigrant families. The building was located on a wide boulevard teeming with cars, buses, and people. Lenny's childhood environment was concrete and asphalt with a few trees, bushes, and postage stamp lawns constituting 'nature.' The only pool he knew was Barney's Pool and Billiards Hall down the block.

As recent arrivals to the U.S., Lenny's parents were content to have steady employment—his father as a salesman and his mother as an office clerk—and a barely living wage. Any aspirations they had for upward mobility rested with their children. Like many Jewish parents of their generation, their hope for Lenny was to be a 'professional man,' preferably a medical doctor which they believed would protect him from antisemitism. Instead, to their dismay, he rebelled against their pressure to achieve, dashing their hopes that he would attain a more affluent economic status. So, when his life took a surprising turn and he became a serious student culminating in earning a PhD, which meant he could be called 'doctor,' they were overjoyed.

Lenny and Sally met as college students in Wisconsin, a location where each felt contentedly distanced from their families. There was an immediate physical attraction enhanced by the allure and novelty of their divergent backgrounds. Youthful fantasies, naïve expectations, and the treacly sentiment of budding romance led to a whirlwind courtship. Three months after meeting, ignoring threats of exile from both sets of parents, they married.

Their honeymoon phase lasted almost five months until both graduated and began working, Lenny as a child welfare worker and Sally as a junior executive for an advertising firm. As their lives settled into more pragmatic and routine rhythms, their differences lost their appeal and became sources of contention they were ill-equipped to address. Unresolved issues and resentments multiplied into a repetitive cycle of conflict, indifference, and reconciliation. Each life change or attempted life change—Lenny returning to graduate school, moving to Vermont where Lenny was offered a faculty position, trying unsuccessfully to have a family—brought new conflicts and resentments.

Despite resolving to leave the relationship numerous times, Lenny could never muster the courage or energy to do so. Instead, he engaged in a charade of believing things would get better.

Hope is a powerful emotion. It can incite certain actions and prevent others. For Lenny, it meant clinging to anything hinting of positive change and avoiding the upheaval of leaving and facing his insecurities about being alone. Each crisis of confidence would evoke the declaration, "This is it. I'm out of here," until his anxiety about going from the known, however bad, to the unknown would hold him in place.

What finally enabled him to overcome this impasse was a confluence of events that generated more anxiety about staying than leaving. Most significant was anxiety about growing old, he would soon turn fifty-five, exacerbated by his father's recent death at seventy-nine. More than other birthdays, this one evoked reflection about where he had been, where he was going, where he wanted to go, and the time he had left to do so. Fifty-five to seventy-nine did not feel like a long time.

Will my fate be to grow old feeling trapped and unhappy until I die? The prospect seemed likely and intolerable. It was the loss of hope.

Sally appeared stunned by his declaration that their marriage was over. Although she had to have known their relationship was floundering, it didn't mean she thought it would end. She pleaded with him to stay. Listening to her entreaties for another chance and promises to change, Lenny teetered on the edge of renouncing his words. He managed to resist, convincing himself to jump into the abyss before it was too late while praying his parachute would open.

* * *

Lenny's apartment is modest and nondescript: a living room, dining area, galley kitchen, bedroom, and bathroom. It is sparsely furnished with second-hand furniture and a few things he salvaged from the divorce: a well-worn, gray, chenille sofa, two bookcases bordering a TV, a contemporary-looking, dark leather chair with an ottoman—his one extravagance—and a small rectangular wooden kitchen table with four chairs, two that matched. His bedroom consists of a dresser, a queen-sized bed, a nightstand, a wooden worktable where he keeps his computer, another bookcase, and a mauve rocking chair, with an upholstered seat cushion and back.

Decorating is not Lenny"s strong suit; in fact, he is often barely conscious of his surroundings. He would never be mistaken for a

Feng Shui follower unless there was some hidden meaning in the haphazard placement of furniture, scattered books, and papers. The apartment had good light which his few plants—two peace lilies and a spider plant—purchased for their hardiness and alleged air-purifying qualities, undoubtedly appreciated. Rounding out his décor were some framed photos, posters, and paintings: nature scenes, some abstract art, and a print of Van Gogh's *Starry Night*. It wasn't much, but it worked for him.

Now he was on the cusp of seventy; a number that seemed surreal. He remembered turning twenty and calculating his age in the year 2000. Fifty-one! How old it seemed back then. Yet, now having surpassed it by almost two decades, his fifties felt like a time of relative youth. Even his current age with its minor infirmities and daily aches felt younger than he imagined it would be. In fact, he found it difficult to think of himself as old. Physically, he couldn't deny that the balding, wrinkled man with a gray beard and mustache he saw in the mirror looked old, but beneath his outer appearance was a more youthful self. The disconnect between what he saw and how he felt was disquieting and hard to reconcile, so he mostly avoided looking.

He wondered if others saw him as he saw himself. Was his mirror image a composite of how he believed others, past and present, saw him? As a retired social work professor, he was familiar with the idea of the self as a social construct first expressed as the 'looking glass self' by the sociologist Charles Cooley in 1902. Cooley believed we imagined how we appeared to others and based on those beliefs, how they judged us. These perceptions formed our self-image. Since what we imagined could be incorrect, there was no true self in an objective sense. Lenny found this persuasive, but the disunity he experienced still bothered him.

Is this an example of the difference between intellectual understanding and lived experience? Maybe I would feel differently if I wasn't alone and shared my life with someone who saw me as I hoped to be seen. His mouth tightens. *Jeez! What are the chances of that happening?*

He feels himself slipping but can't find a foothold. *Will I wind up a lonely old man, eating canned vegetables and frozen dinners while gazing forlornly at photos of my youth? Hold on, I am an old man! The future is now.* Some lines from a poem by the Beat poet, Gregory Corso, appear:

> what if I'm 60 years old and not married,
> all alone in a furnished room with pee stains on my underwear
> and everybody else is married! All the universe married
> but me!

Although marriage wasn't his goal, here he was, almost a decade older and alone. Still, he reasoned, being alone by oneself was better than being alone together as was the case with Sally. And who knows, maybe he would find someone with whom to share his remaining years. He waves his arm as if swatting away a bug. "Enough of this maudlin self-pity," he says aloud while going to the sink and splashing water on his face.

* * *

These tête-à-têtes with himself were typical for Lenny. Sometimes, during these periods of self-interrogation and apprehension, he wondered whether his retirement three years ago from his professorship at the university left him with too much unstructured time. On the other hand, he was grateful to no longer prepare for classes, endure unnecessary meetings, and deal with the petty yet often vicious politics of the academy. For several years before his retirement, he watched with consternation how the lengthening shadow of neoliberalism with its emphasis on the primacy of the market, the promotion of extreme individualism, and oppressive managerial oversight eroded the university's primary function of higher education in favor of producing so-called knowledge workers for the capitalist economy. He was glad to be out, yet after thirty-five years as an academic, the university was more home than any other place.

Lenny was proud of his career in social work, a field that concerned itself with the betterment of society. Even so, he sometimes questioned whether he had chosen the right field. His penchant for philosophical musings, analytical inquiry, and conceptual fishing expeditions made him an outlier among his social work colleagues. Social workers are doers. They eschew immersion in abstract, theoretical endeavors when there is so much to *do*. People are hurting. They need help now.

He empathized with this position, particularly with those on the front lines of service provision. Despite believing social workers would benefit from a more critically analytical perspective, he felt a political kinship with the field, especially its commitment, even if more in words than deeds, to serving people who were marginalized and oppressed. "What other field has such a mandate?" he would ask students. Sure, other 'helping professionals' like psychiatrists or psychologists could choose to work with these groups, but if they did, it was an act of supererogation—an individual choice—not a professional obligation.

* * *

Lenny liked the students' desire to help others and make the world a better place. Whether expressions of youthful idealism, naivety, or a strong moral compass, he admired their courage to act on their beliefs.

His favorite course was Human Behavior and the Social Environment, required of all graduate students in their first semester. Most arrived expecting to hear lectures emphasizing human development across the lifespan as was traditional in this course. Instead, Lenny presented an intellectual framework that considered beliefs and values as historical, cultural, and social expressions, learned and maintained through relationships. Consistent with this framework, his teaching approach, apart from a few spontaneous lectures, resembled a Socratic dialogue focusing on critical thinking and questioning, but without the goal of reaching consensus. For students socialized to be passive learners or not to color outside the lines, this approach coupled with the unconventional content was unnerving.

Right from the start, Lenny stirred things up by challenging students' taken-for-granted beliefs. His last course was typical. Following brief introductions, he asked, "Who believes we possess an authentic, inner self—a real you?"

Most raise their hands.

"And what is the source of your belief?"

This elicits shrugs and statements like: "Experience"; "My therapist"; "Feedback from people I trust."

"And what do these sources have in common?"

"They involve other people?" says a tentative voice in the back of the room.

"Right," answers Lenny. "We learn about ourselves from relationships with others." Seeing puzzled looks, he adds, "Consider this. If you were the only human on Earth, how would you know you are a person?"

A young woman in the front row wearing a green, University of Vermont sweatshirt says, "How could I *not* know?"

"Yes. It seems so obvious," says Lenny, "But where would you have learned the concept 'person'?"

She squinches her face thinking. Then she smiles and says, "Maybe from a talking frog?"

Amid some titters, Lenny smiles back, happy that she's lightened the mood in the room.

"Very creative, but aside from talking frogs, my point is that it is through relationships with others that we learn what it means to be a person. Personhood is a social creation. Thinking of yourself as an autonomous, separate being with an inner essence is not innate knowledge, nor is it a timeless, globally consensual belief. Rather, it's a recent Western creation.

"Let's consider an alternative. What if we adopted a relational stance in which our sense of self was fluid and multiple, changing according to the context we were in and the people we were with? What difference would that make in our lives? These are the kinds of questions we will be exploring during the semester."

The previous levity has dissipated, and the class response is underwhelming: blank stares, head scratches, fidgeting, and a few fleeting smiles.

Lenny sighs. *Thank goodness this is a required course.*

As the semester proceeds, some students warm to Lenny's approach while others remain baffled or upset. By mid-semester, Lenny's relentless interrogation of accepted beliefs inevitably leads an exasperated student to ask if he thought *anything* was true.

"I do," he would answer earnestly. "Accepting certain beliefs as true is necessary to function as a society." Then adding the caveat, "but by true, I mean reasonably justified, not a reflection of a transcendent reality. It's why we need to contextualize truths and ask true for whom, when, and where? Remember, when you create 'the true,' you also create 'the not true' that can undermine the credibility of important but unpopular views. We see this most glaringly when truths in the Western world are considered universal, justifying their imposition on everyone else."

Lenny pauses to give students a chance to digest his minilecture. "Questions?" he implores, hoping for some response, even pushback, which will show engagement with these ideas. When, as often happens, there is silence, he tries making his position more concrete and relevant to their interests.

"Let's apply this viewpoint to the concept of childhood."

He throws out a bunch of questions he hopes will generate discussion. "Is a child a person of a certain age, physical characteristics, or abilities? Are children little adults or distinct beings? Do they possess innate wisdom or are they blank slates? Are they angelic beings or possessed by demons?"

He regards the class expectantly. Eventually, if he manages to refrain from talking, a student will venture a response that initiates a conversation among them.

"A child is someone who has not reached puberty."

"But that would make the ending of childhood different for everyone."

"Legally, I think a child is someone under the age of 14."

"Doesn't childhood end at 18?"

"No, you're confusing child and minor."

"According to Piaget, it ends at adolescence."

"Children are innocent. How could they not be?"

"It's not true if you believe in original sin."

"That's religion, not science."

"What does innocence even mean? Children have not had time to be corrupted."

"But aren't babies born with certain temperaments or innate tendencies?"

It's a lively discussion and Lenny compliments them on their participation. He articulates what he hopes they now understand. "How childhood is understood will be influenced by many factors such as culture, history, and social context. Which understanding—truth—is accepted will justify different practices. Some, like corporeal punishment, which might be considered child abuse today, were once viewed as appropriate, even necessary. As society changes so do our views."

Questioning the taken for granted and accepting uncertainty was an uphill struggle for students trying to find their way into a new profession. Techniques, how-to prescriptions, and bedrock categorizations seemed a more certain path to professional success. Lenny understood this and was sympathetic to their struggles but believed shaking things up was necessary if they were to be agents of social change.

What Lenny asked of his students he asked of himself. For him, the so-called postmodern condition—ambiguity, fragmentation, contradiction, and uncertainty—was lived experience that he grappled with daily. He thought of his friend, Irving, who had been censured by his university, the academic equivalent of excommunication, for refusing to conform to requirements he considered intellectual tyranny. Irving believed challenging standard practices was a way to unmask the absurdities and dangers hidden in institutional traditions and regulations. As he explained it to Lenny, 'I wanted to abandon words like research, method, measurement, truth, and order as the foundation of their education and replace them, to the horror of my colleagues, with words such as *wonder, perspective, uncertainty, creativity,* and *chaos.*'

Lenny admired Irving's courage to act on his beliefs. He considered his own approach to teaching more nuanced but also recognized it as a rationalization for avoiding confrontation and possible sanctions. During such times of reflection, he would alternate between chiding himself for his timidity—cowardice felt too harsh—and justifying his way of doing things.

* * *

Lenny's empathy for his students stemmed from memories of his own student years. Were his anxieties so different from the present cohort? Like many of them, he had yearned for answers to questions he could not articulate. Of course, the times were different. It was the sixties and young people were being urged to turn on, tune in, and drop out. Mild psychotropic substances like marijuana and hashish, easy to obtain, offered a way to probe the enlightened consciousness being promoted. For Lenny, however, the lure was more about 'spacing out' and temporarily forgetting his insecurities and worries, than tuning in. With his stoner friends, he could do or say inane things without fear of embarrassment or the need for explanation. It seemed harmless and if not enlightening, fun.

What he didn't anticipate was the change from innocuous goofiness and giggles to something more perilous. He began ingesting amphetamines. This was a high that made him feel and act like a different person, the bold, assertive Lenny he fantasized about. Despite annoying teeth grinding and falling into deep doldrums when 'coming down,' these drug-fueled interludes of anxiety-freedom were hard to resist.

He started hanging out with people who used drugs intravenously, more for numbing their minds than expanding them. They repeatedly invited him to partake in their habit, offering 'freebies' to get him started. Although watching his friends sink into their drug-induced euphoria held some allure, it was offset by his fear of losing control and his awareness that these were dangerous and highly addictive substances. The peer pressure continued but whenever he edged closer to their urgings of "just give it one try," a red flag would appear, warning that if he crossed that line, he might not be able to return.

Psychoactive drugs were not the only route to expanded consciousness being explored during this time. Eastern spiritual practices, featured in the writings of influential literary figures like Jack Kerouac and Allan Watts were being rediscovered as a path to true happiness. For many, these practices symbolized a form of rebellion against what they viewed as the superficiality and decadent materialism of the West. Buddhist and Hindu spiritual icons like the Buddha, Krishna, and Vishnu, long relegated to an esoteric realm of recondite knowledge, were capturing young people's interest. On their coattails came numerous gurus, yogis, and other spiritual guides. Some like Maharishi Mahesh Yogi, the inventor of transcendental meditation, attained pop-star status after being endorsed by the Beatles. For acolytes, traditional prayer and religious ceremony were replaced by practices like meditation, and the *Bible,* by books like the *Bhagavad Gita.* Instead of contemplating heaven and hell after death, the focus now was on karma and reincarnation.

Around this time, Lenny encountered, through chance or providence, some people who were devotees of a Persian-born spiritual master, now living in India, named Meher Baba who claimed to be the Avatar of the age, or God incarnate. At other times, Lenny might have shrugged this off as a case of *folie de grandeur* or megalomania; however, he couldn't help but notice the devotees he met seemed kind and happy, not desperate and scared like him.

Lenny was introduced to Baba in Florida by a guy named Zachariah he met in the apartment complex where he was living as a student. Zachariah looked to be in his early thirties. He was of average height, thin, with an olive complexion, short black hair, and lucent, light gray eyes. What set him apart, however, was an enigmatic 'presence,' a sense of being Lenny could not describe but felt. Zachariah moved with effortless grace, like he was dancing. He would appear at Lenny's door without notice, and upon entering, perform some mundane task like washing the dishes left from the previous evening, When the job was done, he would leave. All without a sound.

Lenny tried engaging Zachariah in conversation, curious to learn more about this peculiar man. His efforts were met by polite but succinct responses that left Lenny feeling like he was making little headway. Then one morning, after opening the door in response to Zachariah's now-familiar knock, he handed Lenny a book and said, "read this," and left.

No longer shocked by Zachariah's eccentricities, Lenny glanced at the cover. *God Speaks* by Meher Baba. *That's a modest title*, he thought chuckling to himself. Coming from Zachariah, however, it piqued his interest and he opened the book. The first thing he saw was a photo of a smiling, middle-aged man with dark hair and a large mustache reclining on what looked like a tiger skin rug. He wore a white sari and around his neck was a flowered lei. To Lenny, he looked more like an Italian barber than a deity. This time he laughed out loud exclaiming, "This is God? Maybe I should stop smoking so much dope."

Turning to the next page, he read the book's dedication: "To the universe—the illusion that sustains reality." He found himself staring at the sentence not sure what to make of it. Then, despite a strong sense of incredulity, or because of it, he decided to read the book.

Several hours later, he learned that Meher Baba claimed our earthly life was an illusion (called Maya) and, in reality, we were infinite consciousness. Baba used the metaphor of an infinite ocean to explain this. According to him, our corporeal selves were like drops in the ocean. Although inseparable from the ocean, we have forgotten this and identify as the drop rather than the ocean. This separation was the basis for what he termed the 'illusion of reality'. Transcending this veil of illusion was the purpose of creation and required evolving back, an involution, over many lifetimes, to our source of infinite consciousness. When Baba claimed he was God, he meant he had achieved this consciousness, and although in a physical body, he experienced himself as infinite.

Lenny also learned that Baba's appearance on earth at this time was the latest in a succession of 'god realized' beings such as Buddha, Jesus, and Mohammed. According to Baba, these spiritual masters all brought the same underlying message of love and infinite consciousness to humanity, expressing it in a way appropriate to the historical period and part of the world in which they appeared. Rather than continue this tradition of preaching the same timeless truths, Baba's mission, this time around, was to be a spiritual catalyst, or as he put it, 'I am here not to teach, but to awaken.' Since there was nothing new to say, Baba took a vow of silence communicating sparingly through hand gestures interpreted by a close disciple, and occasionally, using an alphabet board where he would fluidly point to letters.

Lenny labored through the book. These ideas were so beyond his ken that at times he felt like he was reading an elaborate mythology. Also, many redundant passages made the reading tedious. As he persevered, an incipient understanding of the meaning and ultimate purpose of existence presented in the book began to form. Finally reaching the section titled "Conclusion," he felt a sense of achievement. However, rather than tying the book's ideas together into some spiritual epiphany, Baba's closing message was while he hoped the book satisfied the reader's intellectual curiosity, what we call God is ineffable and beyond the mind's capacity to grasp, so any such understanding would at best be partial and misleading.

Lenny didn't know what to think. Did Baba just undermine everything he had struggled to understand? He felt confused, frustrated, and a bit taken in, yet inexplicably drawn to this strange man with the deep, kind eyes and alluring smile.

He wanted to know more.

He wanted nirvana.

He signed on.

As Lenny became further acquainted with Baba, he found other aspects of his message attractive. In contrast to conventional religions, Baba did not moralize ('There is no bad, only lesser degrees of good'). Rather than scaring followers with threats of purgatory or preternatural wrath, he focused on living a life that would generate good karma and support the journey towards god realization. Baba opposed drug use, not because it was a moral evil, but because it distracted you from the spiritual path. So, Lenny gave it up—a decision he later looked back on as possibly lifesaving. He also adopted a healthier lifestyle becoming a vegetarian, again not because of any edict, but because the other 'Baba lovers,' as they were called, were vegetarian. He enjoyed the communal meals of large salads and freshly baked bread where they would discuss how to better follow Baba's example of selfless service to others and spiritual detachment from material life.

These were good times. He felt healthier than ever and was

part of a community that seemed to model the highest callings of humanity. It was enough for him to suspend disbelief and focus on becoming a disciple.

He soon learned the spiritual path was not without challenges. The ideals of detachment, selflessness, and a constant spiritual focus often felt out of reach. When he transferred to the University of Wisconsin, he felt isolated from the supportive community he had joined. In his new environment, he was just a guy with weird beliefs. How long would it be before he returned to the way he was before? Feeling desperate to recreate the community he had in Florida, he put a notice in the school newspaper announcing the formation of a group to study the teachings of the spiritual master, Meher Baba. To his delight, he received twelve responses. Four had heard of Baba, the rest were simply curious. This group became the nucleus of a new spiritual community.

Lenny immersed himself in his studies and Meher Baba. His new community provided a place to feel different *and* accepted. He increased his efforts to make Baba the focal point of his life, repeatedly conjuring up his image while pretending to listen to his professors' lectures.

Near the end of the semester, he received a call from a woman who said she was visiting the area and was interested in attending a meeting. After giving her the time and place, Lenny asked if she had ever attended any Baba-related activities. She laughed and said, "I think a few since I have been a Baba-lover for about twenty years and lived at his ashram in India for several months."

Lenny's jaw dropped, and for a few moments he could only gaze at the phone in awe. The opportunity to meet someone this close to Baba, someone who had been in his physical presence, seemed, well, divine. He managed to stammer his enthusiastic welcome and immediately afterward contacted everyone in the group with the exciting news.

* * *

Lorraine Harrington was a middle-aged woman of petite stature who carried herself with warmth and grace. At the meeting, she regaled the group with stories of her encounters with Baba, his often life-changing effect on people who met him, and descriptions of his life in India. At the next meeting, she informed the group that she had written to Baba about the group's excellent work and had just received a response in the form of a telegram from Baba himself. A palpable ripple of anticipation accompanied by hushed but audible 'oohs' filled the room. Mrs. Harrington, as we called her, proceeded to read the telegram, but all Lenny heard was one sentence:

"I send my love to Lenny."

The moment she spoke these words, he levitated. For an incomprehensible time, defying all laws of physics, he observed himself and the others from about fifteen feet off the ground.

It was exhilarating.

Afterward, he was reluctant to talk about the experience. However real it felt to him, he knew others might see it differently, as self-deception or hallucination rather than a spiritual experience. But for Lenny, there was no ambiguity about what happened. Questions he had previously pondered resurfaced with new importance. Was the dimension we call spiritual as real as the physical? Was everyday existence an illusion, as Baba claimed, a mirage of finiteness and separation? Was this life merely a waystation on a journey toward infinity?

Questions aside, for the next several weeks, the euphoric afterglow of his experience infused his waking hours before fading into an enduring memory. Outwardly his life stayed much the same. He still went to classes, hung out with friends, and tried to meet women. Nor did his anxieties and insecurities magically vanish. He was still Lenny, a young man trying to navigate his way through life, but with a sense of wonder that would never leave.

Then Baba died. Lenny was distraught despite Baba himself having previously communicated that his physical death was merely 'dropping his body.' With Baba physically gone, Lenny wondered if his message would survive.

It did, but to his dismay, the initial response was an uptick in the production and sales of Baba-related paraphernalia like buttons with Baba's picture and bookmarks with his quotations. This commercialization was a turnoff, and he decided his relationship with Baba would henceforth be personal rather than public. He stopped going to the meetings and withdrew from the community of Baba lovers.

Over time, Baba became a cherished part of his historical record. He remained grateful for having encountered Baba and the impact it had on his life. There was goodness in the world and the possibility of a higher purpose. Less obvious but significant was the invitation to live in a liminal space, in the interstices between the material and the spiritual world where the rules and standards of traditional society were not paramount. *Maybe, just maybe*, Lenny thought, *such a place could be home.*

FINDING LENNY

Chapter Two

Lenny is sitting in a booth in the Holy Grounds coffee shop waiting for his friend, Jerry, to arrive. The shop's retro décor reminds him of the haunts of his younger days in New York's Greenwich Village like the Café Wha? and Caffe Reggio on MacDougal Street. *They were turbulent times,* he thinks, *but you knew you were alive.*

Fast forward more than forty years and he's a retired professor. Who would have guessed? It was a circuitous route in which different, loosely connected contingencies nudged him toward his life's journey. Was it coincidence that his academic questioning of accepted beliefs and advocation for a radical shift in understanding was a secular version of what he learned from Meher Baba? Or that he was attracted to philosophers like Ludwig Wittgenstein, a tortured genius who revolutionized ideas about logic and language? There was a parallel between Wittgenstein's belief that questions about the meaning of life were not answerable by philosophy and Meher Baba's position on the futility of trying to achieve an intellectual understanding of God. Lenny remembers the feeling of déjà vu when after struggling through Wittgenstein's treatise *Tractatus Philosphicus,* he came to his famous concluding passage

'That whereof we cannot speak, thereof we must remain silent.' There was a thread running through this tapestry that was more than chance.

Glancing up, he sees Jerry enter the café. Lenny waves and Jerry walks toward the booth. Seeing that Lenny already has his coffee, Jerry makes a detour to the counter. As usual, Jerry is smartly dressed in a natty, blue, button-down collar shirt and tan chinos. He is tall, a little over six feet, and on the thin side; his friendly, blue eyes framed by a clean-shaven face topped by medium-length, brown hair with distinguished-looking gray peeking out on the sides. He projects an image of fitness and well-being that makes him look younger than his sixty-one years.

Consistent with his appearance, Jerry lives an upper-middle-class lifestyle reflecting many actual or imagined societal norms: married, two kids, house in the burbs, a late model SUV, and a middle-of-the-road Democrat. He plays tennis, jogs, and is an avid alumnus of his university. Unlike Lenny, Jerry is still actively employed as a financial analyst for a consulting firm.

On the surface, Lenny and Jerry seemed like strange bedfellows, but the relationship worked. For Lenny, Jerry was a willing sounding board for his sometimes unconventional or half-baked ideas. He was a good listener, kind, and nonjudgmental, enabling Lenny to think out loud without fear of condemnation. Jerry seemed comfortable in his own skin and never took their disagreements personally. As Lenny got to know him better, he also came to value Jerry's thoughtfulness and how his questions helped clarify his thinking.

For his part, Jerry enjoyed hearing about Lenny's intellectual conundrums and his philosophical take on things. Lenny's animated way of speaking and off-beat sense of humor was a pleasant diversion from his typical interactions At first, hesitant to contribute his thoughts to their mostly one-sided conversations, Jerry saw that Lenny appreciated his queries and viewpoints helping him feel more like a participant than an observer.

They've been meeting at the Holy Grounds coffee shop semi-regularly for the past few years. The staff was friendly, the coffee excellent, and there was no pressure to vacate their booth, making it a perfect venue for their chats.

On this day, Lenny is drumming his fingers on the table and fidgeting, a sure sign something is troubling him.

"Are you ok?" asks Jerry, concern in his voice.

Lenny grimaces. "Maybe my age is starting to get to me, but I've been thinking a lot about death lately."

"You're not so old."

"Kind of you to say, Jerry but I have a lot more years behind me than in front. What's that saying, 'No one gets out of this life alive?' Death is unfathomable, still, we want to know what it is."

Jerry nods in assent. "I guess it's one of life's unanswerable puzzles, which is probably why we keep trying to figure it out. But I can see that's not enough for you, so tell me what you've been thinking about."

Lenny shakes his head as if trying to clear out some cobwebs. "Let's assume death is nothingness. When alive, we are sentient, when dead, there is nothing. We don't know we're dead so experientially there is no 'other' to being alive. All we know is life. Ergo—Lenny liked using words like ergo—death exists only when we are alive. It is a happening of life. For those who are dead, nothing has happened."

"I don't believe most people think about it that way," offers Jerry.

"No, they don't," Lenny agrees. "We don't like the idea of not having consciousness. It's hard to conceptualize nothingness. In fact, it's impossible. Nothingness is ineffable, like God. Even people like Buddhists who claim to experience nothingness contradict themselves as soon as they tell us about it. My guess is if they experienced nothingness, we would never know it. They would be silent about it. The best we can do is imagine nothingness, but then it becomes somethingness."

"Uh, huh," says Jerry trying to make sense of Lenny's reasoning. "Could that be what beliefs about an afterlife and reincarnation are about? Attempts to deny the finiteness of life by extending it beyond death?"

"Good questions," says Lenny impressed by Jerry's logic. "There's a child psychiatrist at the University of Virginia, Jim Tucker, who researches children who claim to have lived past lives. I know it sounds far out, but he's come up with some interesting findings that are difficult to explain away. Stuff like young kids—as young as two!—who claim to have been some obscure historical figure. In some of these cases, it took Tucker's research team many hours to locate and gather information about the person to determine the accuracy of the child's report. These were not children of scholarly parents who could have done the research and then prepped their children. And even if they could, why would they do so?"

"Interesting," says Jerry giving Lenny a chance to pause and drink some of his coffee. "I never heard about this."

"It's not exactly mainstream news," says Lenny. "But it gets better. Tucker describes cases where the children have a distinctive mark on their body matching the place where their alleged former self incurred a mortal wound. He's also found children who spoke in the foreign language of their alleged past-life person! Coincidence? Fake? Possible, but highly unlikely. However, I don't think the scientific establishment or society in general can take this research seriously. The ramifications would be too great."

"What do you mean?" asks Jerry.

"Consider this. If reincarnation was real, it would be a mortal blow to materialism and undermine Western religious doctrines. How would ordinary folks cope with this knowledge?"

Jerry rubs his chin, mulling over Lenny's questions. "That's difficult to answer because it's hard to imagine any proof of reincarnation could be indisputable. Look at politicians. They can spout alternative versions of anything, even facts. You could claim we need air to breathe and if it was not in someone's political interest, he would find a way to punch holes in it. As for reincarnation, unless remembering your past lives was common and people could draw on those memories in some obvious way, or if there was exact DNA matching between the dead and the living, it would still feel like faith. I doubt there would be a major shift in beliefs."

"I agree," says Lenny. "People have an amazing capacity to ignore or reinterpret information they find unsettling or clashes with strongly held beliefs. There's probably no such thing as an ironclad argument that would be accepted by, or apply to, everyone. Even science involves interpretation. Evidentiary claims that don't conform to certain assumptions about reality will be considered outside the boundaries of science and not evidence at all. Preserving reincarnation as the province of spirituality or religion keeps it a question of faith and easy to marginalize.

"Humor me for a bit and assume you found the claims of Tucker conclusive. What would change for you?"

"Hmm, that's a tough one. I would have to rethink some of my beliefs."

Jerry pauses and straightens his collar. "It feels too big for me to tell you specifically what I would do. It would take a lot of thought, maybe prayer. Would I live my life differently? I don't know. Sorry, Lenny, but it's difficult to believe I wouldn't harbor some uncertainty or at least find a way to retain important beliefs."

"Tell me more," says Lenny curious about Jerry's response.

"For example, why couldn't reincarnated people still go to heaven or hell? Or maybe the person you get reincarnated as is a kind of heaven and hell. It seems there would always be room for reinterpretation or doubt."

Lenny shrugs his shoulders in resignation. "There is, but perhaps we are quicker to doubt some ideas more than others, particularly ones that threaten to disrupt our accepted ways of thinking."

"Maybe," says Jerry. Rather than continue to debate Lenny's point, he says, "This is interesting stuff. I remember some law of physics about energy not being able to be created or destroyed, only transformed. If we are energy, then I guess it is conceivable we could continue in some form after death."

Lenny's eyes widen like a child receiving a wished-for gift. "Right!" he exclaims. "If we think of consciousness as energy, then consciousness never dies. It is non-corporeal. Interestingly, there's a common belief within Eastern mystical traditions that we are infinite consciousness and our material life is an illusion."

"That sounds like something from your Meher Baba days," says Jerry recalling previous discussions with Lenny about his adventures with Eastern mysticism.

"I guess it does, but I'm just pointing out the similarity between secular science and certain spiritual traditions. They're saying much the same thing but in different languages. I once heard Eckhart Tolle, you know, the 'be here now' guy, say that consciousness never separates from its source; it only believes it is separate. Consciousness, soul, spirit—same things using different words. Who knows, maybe we are witnessing the eventual integration of the spiritual and the scientific."

As Jerry listens, he has a flash of insight about why he enjoys these conversations. They're unique and stimulating. His other friends do not broach these subjects and if they do, they conform to, or argue for, conventional thinking. These roads less traveled meanderings with Lenny just do not happen with anyone else. *Lenny may be a bit eccentric, but he gets me thinking.*

Inspired by his little epiphany, Jerry plunges back into the conversation. "An interesting similarity. Perhaps accepting that life simply ends is too stressful for most people to hold. But what you're proposing goes beyond the limits of science. Since we can't test these views, they are speculative. I remember believing in the afterlife and the glory awaiting me if I met the standard of goodness prescribed by the church and ultimately, judged by God. I'm still a believer, but I now understand such beliefs, religious or philosophical, are different from those grounded in scientific proof. Wouldn't it make more sense to just accept you will die and while you are here, try to live the best life you can?"

Lenny's brow knits in concentration. "I don't see how living your best life and grappling with what happens when you die are mutually exclusive. As I said, when I'm alive that's my reality and I want to live it in accord with my values."

"Ok," replies Jerry, "but what about the perspectives of people who are dying?"

"What about them?"

"It's often said that when you are on your deathbed there is unusual clarity about the life you have lived. Actions taken, or not taken, choices about career and family, may look different from the perspective of near death. There's a lot to learn from this."

Lenny takes another sip of coffee now cold. He looks around the coffee shop before turning back to Jerry. "It's true you might see past actions in a different light . . . but why should we accord death bed reflections more significance than reflections at other times? Maybe what we hear is candor, the imminence of death negating past rationales. Or perhaps it's regret about the outcomes of our choices. Does that make these declarations wiser or more perceptive? I think it's an open question."

When Jerry doesn't immediately respond, Lenny continues. "Alternatively, could it be these alleged insights are a way of trying to cope with our impending death, a *mea culpa* offering toward whatever will happen next? Making decisions in hindsight is different from making decisions in the present. The context is different. So why privilege the former?"

"As usual, you've raised some interesting questions," says Jerry. "It's a lot to consider and sort out. I'm going to need some time to think about it."

"I know, I know. I should get a life," replies Lenny thinking it's Jerry's polite way of saying he's had enough. "Maybe the topic is occupying my thoughts because I am getting closer to 'the event'" (Lenny draws scare quotes in the air). "Anyway, I appreciate your forbearance with my ramblings."

Jerry smiles which Lenny interprets as an ok to continue. "Can I share one more thought on this topic?"

"Sure," says Jerry amicably.

"To the extent the deathbed narrative is an expression of regret—I wish I had done X instead of Y, chosen the right fork instead of the left—it's also an exercise in second-guessing and sometimes self-flagellation. Once you've made a decision, you can never know what the consequences would have been had you done something different.

"Remember the movie, *Mr. Destiny*, with Jim Belushi in which he makes the final out for his high school baseball team in their championship game by striking out with the bases loaded?"

"I vaguely remember seeing it."

"Well, in the movie, after having his dream of greatness crushed, the Belushi character goes on to live a conventional life: married to a loving woman, a couple of kids, so-so job, et cetera."

"Was that movie about me?" Jerry says with a grin.

"Ha, ha," chuckles Lenny. "Your life is far more nuanced and complex than a character in a Hollywood movie. Plus, you would have at least hit a single."

"Thanks. I appreciate your faith in me."

"You're welcome, I know it's a silly movie, but it makes a point. Belushi makes a deal with the devil, played by Michael Caine, and gets to live that pivotal moment over, this time hitting a home run. He becomes a local hero and winds up marrying the head cheerleader and working for her wealthy father. It's a Hollywood movie, so he winds up hating his life despite its material success and pining for the kind of life he had before.

"Lightweight for sure, but it illustrates the 'if only' fantasy many people hold. Obviously, not all decisions work out as we hope, but that doesn't mean a different decision would have turned out any better. And what a shame to be on your deathbed and spend the little time you have left wallowing in regret. Still, I understand wanting the chance to do life over, especially if we feel unhappy. It reminds me of a song by Loudon Wainwright III."

"Who?" says Jerry.

"Loudon Wainwright III," repeats Lenny as if everyone knows who he is. The song is about the wish to have a do-over. Lenny sings a line, "'And the second time around I'm gonna get it right.' Regrettably, unlike the song or the movie, there are no do-overs, at least none that we know of."

"Maybe not," says Jerry stretching his arms. "Well, professor, I think you've filled my brain enough for one day. How about if we table this for now and enjoy another coffee? Maybe go a little crazy and get a bagel."

"Great idea," says Lenny. "All this talk has made me hungry. You listened, so I'll buy."

Chapter Three

Gerald (Jerry) Finner, Lenny's friend and confidant, hailed from St. Paul, Minnesota. Jerry's father was an executive at the 3M corporation, overseeing their adhesives and tapes division. His mother was a kindergarten teacher until giving birth to Jerry, their first child. Three years later, Daniel was born. Jerry was the proverbial big brother, watching over Daniel and passing on lessons he had learned.

The family was close and comfortable, living in one of the many large, Victorian-era homes along Summit Avenue. Jerry was a popular kid, a good student, and a natural athlete. School, sports, friends, and family—particularly hanging out with his little brother—occupied his time. He was happy and carefree. Until one snowy winter day, when Daniel, then nine, was killed by a hit-and-run driver and everything came crashing down.

His family was devastated. For Jerry, there was an added sense of guilt that he should have been there to prevent what had happened. For the next six months, he was morose and withdrawn. His parents and friends stuck by him and he began to see a school counselor. Eventually, he managed to resume what outwardly resembled his former life; however, the trauma of what happened never left him.

His sense of security and safety shattered, he compensated by becoming very ordered, trying to make his days as predictable as possible. As he matured, he learned to partition his life, keeping that part of his past in a hidden compartment not visible to others.

His high school years were uneventful. He ran cross-country, played on the basketball team, and was a solid B+ student. Only his parents and those who knew him well were aware of the subtle changes that had taken place since Daniel's death, but they accepted them without comment.

In his senior year, he met Katie Edmonson and was immediately smitten. Besides being smart and beautiful, Katie carried herself with confidence and purpose that he found alluring. Like Jerry, she was athletic although her sport was swimming.

Katie's initial impression of Jerry was of a shy, polite, and handsome boy. Having grown up in a somewhat chaotic household with three other siblings, she liked Jerry's calm demeanor, organized manner, and athleticism. Their courtship proceeded from high school to the University of Minnesota. After graduation, with a teaching degree in hand and Jerry with an MBA, they decided to marry.

They had two children, Emily, and two years later, Danny. Their initial plan was to remain in Minnesota not far from their families. However, a lucrative job opportunity for Jerry and a desire to live somewhere new that would be a good place to raise their children brought them to Vermont.

Overall, Jerry was happy with his life. He was comfortable financially, devoted to his family, a dutiful Lutheran, and an upstanding member of the community. His days were ordered and predictable, never veering too far from the script for a white,

Christian, upper-middle-class family. However, as he grew older, he found himself thinking more about the meaning of life, and whether what he was doing was truly worthwhile. This is where meeting Lenny seemed fortuitous. For Lenny, such issues were not peripheral, occasional disturbances in an otherwise calm sea of existence; they were the stuff of his everyday experience. This was both attractive and scary to Jerry. It was an opportunity to explore some big picture questions, but also carried the specter of surfacing hidden anxieties or discontents he wasn't sure he wanted to address.

Jerry met Lenny at the local gym where they were taking a spinning class, a form of exercise using stationary bikes. Being the oldest members of the class created an affinity between them. Jokes about their aches and pains and keeping up with the twenty-somethings in the class led to sharing a post-workout coffee which evolved into their coffee shop meetings.

Despite spending much of his time listening, Jerry found their get-togethers meaningful. He understood that his receptivity to Lenny's endless questions and meandering monologues was part of the quid pro quo of their relationship: Lenny was airborne, he was grounded.

There were other aspects of their relationship he enjoyed. Beyond Lenny's philosophical predilections, he wanted to make the world a better place. He agreed with this aim, even when disagreeing with Lenny's critique of conventional ways of thinking. Jerry considered himself a realist. There was a pre-existing reality that science was progressively revealing. In contrast, Lenny thought of himself as postmodern viewing reality as fluid and socially constructed.

Their differences extended to their appearance. Jerry tended toward oxford button-down or chambray shirts, sometimes accompanied by stylish V-neck or crew neck sweaters. He wore chino-type pants, usually tan or navy, and casual but fashionable shoes. In contrast, if Lenny wore a shirt with a collar, Jerry would wonder whether he was going to some special event. A t-shirt or sweatshirt, sometimes ratty, jeans and sneakers was his uniform.

Beyond their attire, Jerry was clean-shaven while Lenny had a mustache and scraggly beard. Jerry had a full head of hair, smartly coiffed; Lenny was bald on top and had a ponytail. Jerry wore contacts and had no facial jewelry; Lenny wore round, rimless glasses and had a diamond stud in his left ear.

These differences were not lost on Lenny who joked that a person in the coffee shop might think Jerry was a social worker meeting with his client. But it worked and that's what mattered.

* * *

A week has passed. Lenny and Jerry are back in Holy Grounds. They order their coffees, black for Jerry, Lenny's with cream and sugar. After exchanging pleasantries, Lenny says, "I enjoyed our talk last week. It helped me extend my thinking."

"Glad it was helpful."

Lenny continues. "Remember how we talked about how difficult it would be to believe reincarnation was real despite supporting evidence?"

"Uh, huh."

"That got me thinking more generally about belief change and the limits of scientific evidence to produce such change. Think about it." Lenny pronounces this last sentence as one word 'thinkaboutit,' a regression to the Brooklyn accent of his youth and a sign he is excited.

"How many people discard strongly held beliefs based solely on scientific data? Not many," he says before Jerry can respond. "If you want a good example, just look at the issue of climate change."

"It's certainly a disputed topic," says Jerry, "although it shouldn't be since the science is clear."

"It seems that way," says Lenny. "But if you want to change people's beliefs it will take more than presenting them with scientific data. Beliefs don't exist in isolation. They are tied to a constellation of other beliefs and relationships. It's hubris to think people will reject their trusted sources of information in favor of one they mistrust. Whether we like it or not, science is only one among multiple sources of information used to form beliefs and commitments. Unless we recognize this, we are going to have limited success changing anyone's mind."

"Yes, but how do you get people to recognize that science is superior to opinion?"

"I don't think it's as clearcut as that. Whether it's superior or not will depend on the subject.

"If I want to know about spirituality or a work of art, should I consult scientists?"

"Ok, good point," concedes Jerry. "But in matters like climate change I am not going to ask my minister whether or not it is real."

"I agree. But even in this case, we need to be careful not to dichotomize science and opinion as if the latter is the only alternative. There are many ways of knowing."

Warming to their exchange, Jerry says in a feisty tone, "There are, but they wouldn't be objective."

Lenny intertwines his fingers and cracks his knuckles like he's warming up for a competition. "What is objectivity but a claim to a kind of truth not influenced by humans. But it's people who do research, produce data, interpret them, and communicate to others. We've created a scientific culture that has generated its own problems by declaring its ultimate superiority and assuming people will obediently follow its dictates. It's wishful thinking rather than how folks operate."

"If you can't convince people that climate change is a threat based on scientific data, we're in trouble," Jerry asserts. "What's the alternative?"

"There's no simple answer or we wouldn't be in the situation we are now in. What we shouldn't do is insist that anything with the imprimatur of science be unquestionably accepted. It results in dividing people into believers and non-believers, further entrenching each side. We don't have to disregard the science, but to respect that people make judgments and decisions within a social context and to engage with them from that perspective.

"Look, Jerry," says Lenny in a more conciliatory tone. "I agree with you on the dangers of climate change. And when I hear the dogmatic arguments of climate deniers, it's frustrating as hell. But if you listen closely, it's not the data per se that's the primary point of contention, but who they believe is behind the production of the data—the government."

Jerry says, "Most deniers are politically conservative."

"Right. They are highly suspicious of official statistics and fearful of government control. To them, the actions being proposed to combat climate change represent a government intrusion into their lives they find frightening. Presenting them with research data and doomsday predictions demanding a change in their way of life only exacerbates their suspicions and fears."

"So, if you were in charge, what would you do?" asks Jerry.

Lenny takes a deep breath and sings, "If I were king of the foreeeest," imitating the Cowardly Lion in the *Wizard of Oz*. A few people in the café turn around. Jerry doesn't move as if any reaction will suck him into the alternate reality on the other side of the booth. Lenny, oblivious to it all, smiles and goes on.

"I would drop the notion that deniers must accept our argument as if there is no context to it. There's always context. Next, I would create the possibility of dialogue by communicating that their position is neither stupid nor irrational, reassuring them that although responding to the climate crisis will require change, it won't take away their freedoms. I would appeal to things we all care about like our families. Our aim would be connection and understanding instead of an adversarial us-versus-them orientation. This is a crisis of government more than science."

Jerry grimaces. "True. There's gridlock around so many important issues that it's probably worth trying something different . . . as long as we don't dismiss science as a vital source of knowledge."

"I agree that science is important, yet it can't be immune from critique. Like any knowledge system, science depends on certain assumptions and has limitations, for instance, on questions of values. Critiques help us see where it is useful and where it is not. Unfortunately, science has become such an authoritative rhetorical force that invoking it tends to silence other perspectives."

"Rhetorical force? You're losing me, Lenny. Remember, I'm your friend, not your colleague or student."

"Sorry," says Lenny sheepishly. "I've been speaking academese for so long that I sometimes forget it is a minority language, unintelligible to most people. Let me explain.

"Suppose you are arguing with someone about the effectiveness of a medical treatment, or the value of different types of parental discipline, or how birth order affects later achievement. It doesn't matter. At some point, in support of their position, the other person says, 'Well, according to science . . .'

"As soon as you hear 'science' you are likely to pause and listen attentively to what follows. More important is how this assertion limits your responses. Let's say you're arguing about the birth order issue. You don't believe it is important but your interlocutor . . . the other person, says, 'According to scientific research firstborn children are higher achievers than later-born siblings.' What can you say to counter or cast doubt on her claim?" As he speaks, Lenny looks like he's conducting an orchestra, waving his arms, and squirming in his seat.

Jerry considers Lenny's question for a long moment. "I guess if I didn't agree with the research I could say so."

"Right," says Lenny, his volume rising. "But what would be the basis of your disagreement? If you disagree without an equally authoritative justification, it would be considered mere opinion against science, and you would lose."

"What if I cited other research supporting my position?" offers Jerry.

"That could be effective, but for most people, identifying counter research would be a slim possibility. Your credible options are limited. The words 'science' and 'research' have what I called rhetorical force—authority—that makes the other's position difficult to counter. "And," Lenny adds triumphantly, "that is why we must be able to critique them."

"This is dense," says Jerry playfully wiping his hand across his brow. "I may need to order pie with my coffee to keep my head in the game." Then more seriously, "If I understand what you are saying, you think science is important but too powerful especially when it comes to issues outside of its expertise like values. Calling something science shouldn't mean uncritical acceptance."

"Good summary," replies Lenny impressed with Jerry's ability to cut to the quick of his loquacious argument. "Science is a valuable way of understanding, but it's neither infallible nor can it address all issues," he says, reiterating his central points. "And," he adds pointing towards Jerry with his index finger, "We need to remember scientific claims not only discover but generate our realities."

"Hmm," says Jerry reading Lenny's nonverbal gesture. "Why do I have the feeling you want me to ask you to elaborate on what you just said."

"You're a great shill," says a smiling Lenny. "Consider this. In the U.S., the most authoritative source of psychiatric disorders is a book called the *Diagnostic and Statistical Manual of Mental Disorders*, DSM for short, published by the American Psychiatric Association. It first came out in 1952 and listed about 106 disorders. Since then, there have been four updated editions, each adding new disorders. The latest addition has around three hundred disorders, an increase of almost 200%!"

Lenny pauses to let this sink in. "What do you think Jerry? Was this huge increase the result of scientific discoveries? Millions of people living with previously undiagnosed mental disorders?"

Jerry hesitates, looking bewildered. "No?"

"No," repeats Lenny declaratively. "What actually happens is a committee of psychiatrists, many of whom have ties with drug companies, decide what new disorders to include in the next edition of the DSM. As some critics have pointed out, based on the current DSM criteria, much of the population at some time in their lives could receive a diagnosis."

"But isn't it true," says Jerry, "that people suffer from, umm, mental problems? You know, things like depression, anxiety, or even worse? Shouldn't we try and help them?"

"Definitely," says Lenny. "The issue is not whether people suffer, but how we understand that suffering. As the late psychiatrist, Thomas Szasz, argued, people have problems in living and they should be able to seek help, but that doesn't mean they have a psychiatric disorder. Despite using medical terminology to describe these conditions, there are no specific biological markers—no blood tests or x-rays—that reveal the presence of a disease. For many people, a more likely explanation for their stress and suffering would be social stigmatization, oppression, and poverty."

Jerry's mouth pulls slightly to the left and he half closes one eye. "Okay, but what about the research on peoples' brains that show these problems are linked to chemical imbalances? I saw a *Ted Talk* on neuroimaging, and it was pretty convincing. You could see the areas of the brain being activated—by different colors on the scan—in response to different psychological states. Isn't that biological proof?"

"No offense, Jerry but *Ted Talks* are like show and tell sessions,

Readers Digest versions of complex topics. Yes, many have jumped on to the neuroscience bandwagon, but it is far from straightforward." Lenny feels a lecture coming on and reminds himself that this is not a monologue. He tries to be succinct.

"Being in an MRI machine is not exactly a typical occurrence, so we have to be cautious about generalizing from that experience to everyday life. Also, how we label an emotional state is far from exact. Are you depressed, sad, melancholy, unhappy, regretful? There's a lot of wiggle room."

He pauses to make sure Jerry hasn't tuned him out. *Is he still with me? He looks attentive.*

"Two last points about why this biological trend is attractive," he says before being able to stop himself. "If biology is the cause of our problems, then we are absolved from responsibility. We can blame our genes, neuro pathways, or biochemical processes. Secondly, if my problems are medical, then I might be able to cure them with a pill which the pharmaceutical industry is only too happy to provide."

Before Lenny can go further, Jerry's pie is served. He eagerly dives in, less because of hunger than to suspend their conversation and give himself time to ponder Lenny's words. After a few bites and some coffee to wash it down, he says, "Are you saying there's a conspiracy to get us to take more drugs?"

"Conspiracy might be too strong a word, but remember, these are multibillion-dollar, for-profit companies whose primary goal is profit, not social betterment. The more problems they can claim their drugs cure, the more money they make.

"The combination of the DSM and the trend towards biological explanations of mental disorders encourages the use of psychotropic drugs as a primary treatment. Did you know that one in six adults and about ten percent of children take these drugs?"

"No, I didn't," answers Jerry.

"Some of these kids are energetic, distractible, and highly creative, but they are labeled as noncompliant, diagnosed—ADHD is a favorite—and given drugs to pacify them so they won't disrupt the boring, regimented school curricula they are forced to endure." Lenny clenches his fist like he's about to bang it on the table.

"We have an epidemic Jerry, not of mental disorders, but of psychotropic drug use!"

"ADHD?" says Jerry calmly, trying to tone things down.

"Oops. It stands for Attention Deficit Hyperactive Disorder. Thank goodness when I was a kid these drugs weren't yet in use, or I could have easily been diagnosed with ADHD. I was fidgety, had a short attention span, doodled a lot—still do—and to quote my teachers, showed little effort. Fortunately, my parents were not psychologically sophisticated and took a straightforward approach to my difficulties: 'Do better or you'll be punished.' I'm not recommending their approach, but if I had to choose between it and getting drugged, I would take their discipline every time."

Jerry's head is spinning. "Hold on a minute, Lenny. There may be some overuse of medications with kids, but we shouldn't throw out the baby with the bathwater. After Katie's father died, she was very depressed. She was given some meds, I think it was Zoloft, and it seemed to help."

"Glad to hear it. I am not criticizing you or Katie for taking medication to help with a problem. Millions are doing it. What I am suggesting is that we need to look more closely at the reasons for the huge increase in psychiatric disorders, how we treat them, and the implications for how we live. When primary care docs are prescribing anti-depressants, we have a problem."

Lenny runs his hand through his sparse hair and sips his lukewarm coffee. "What happened to understanding human life as consisting of highs and lows, successes and failures, pleasure and pain? Nowadays not feeling happy—whatever that might mean—can suggest a psychological problem. Normal life has been medicalized and converted into disorders and syndromes.

"What's really sad is we've reached a point where we do this to ourselves. Psychological jargon has become so infused into everyday language that we use it to assess how we are feeling and to identify whether something is wrong. Are you feeling sad? It may be depression. Is your child argumentative? It could be a sign of oppositional defiant disorder. Are you grieving too long? You may have a mood disorder. It's scary."

Lenny is energized. His eyes widen as he leans toward Jerry like he's expecting him to leap up and scream, "We have to do something, Lenny!" Instead, Jerry resumes eating the rest of his pie as if he and Lenny were discussing the weather. This seems to deflate Lenny and he sits silently with his hands folded in front of him.

Jerry finishes his pie washing the last bite down with the rest of his coffee. "I never thought of it that way. But isn't trying to reduce unhappiness a good thing?"

"Yes," says Lenny happy to get a response, "but it depends on how you go about it. We are living in a time of cosmetic psychopharmacology. People take meds not only because they are ill, but because they want to improve their image, their self-esteem, or their chances of imagined happiness. What they don't realize, or don't want to realize, is the potential harm this practice is causing them. Ironically, their actions contribute to the very problems that require taking drugs as a response. It's a vicious cycle."

Jerry nods in acknowledgment. Although intrigued by Lenny's concern, he wonders why he gets so worked up about it. *Why dwell on this stuff?* he thinks. *You can't live as if everything is bad or threatening. Sure, things could be better, but overall life is pretty good. I'm Lenny's friend and expressing these thoughts out loud seems important to him, but I think this is enough now.*

Careful not to encourage further elaborations or new tangents, he says, "You've given me much to think about Lenny but I promised Katie that I would help her clean out the garage and I'm already late."

Lenny sighs as if he read Jerry's thoughts. "I'm sorry for going on so long. I tend to get caught up in these issues. Please give Katie my apologies."

"No need," says Jerry rising from the booth. "See you next week?"

"Great. I'll try not to be so long-winded."

Sure, Jerry thinks. *And the cow will jump over the moon.*

Chapter Four

Lenny decides to walk home from the coffee shop to reflect on his conversation with Jerry. As usual, it didn't resolve anything, but expressing his thoughts aloud and responding to Jerry's queries helped refine his thinking. In the past, he would have considered these ideas as fodder for a professional journal article, but since retiring he no longer feels motivated to write in that restricted format nor to produce something read only by other academics. *This is a time to express my creativity,* he thinks. *Try writing something accessible and interesting to a broad audience, like a memoir, or a novel.*

Continuing to walk while contemplating how to begin such a project, he suddenly is aware of a guy sitting on the sidewalk a few feet in front of him. Like many 'street people,' he looks as if he has seen better days. Long, scraggly brown hair and an unruly mustache and beard frame his angular face. His eyes are deep-set and slate gray, his nose prominent. His clothes hang loosely on his thin body: a dark green, threadbare T-shirt and well-worn jeans ending in what looked like hiking boots on the verge of falling apart with his next step. Lenny guesses him to be about fifty, although it was hard to tell.

As he's deciding whether to stop and give him some money, he notices a sign leaning on the wall behind him.

YOU MUST NOT ASK FOR SO MUCH

Something about it sounded familiar, but he can't put his finger on it. Curious, he stops and asks, "What does your sign mean?"

Instead of speaking, the man turns his sign around revealing the words,

WHY NOT ASK FOR MORE?

Again, the words feel vaguely familiar.

"Where did you find these lines?" asks Lenny thinking they were not original.

This time the man glances up at Lenny. His eyes have a faraway yet inviting look. In a sonorous voice, he says, "Floating through the ether."

"What does that mean?" Lenny asks, befuddled by his response.

"What do you want it to mean?"

"I don't want it to mean anything," answers Lenny starting to feel like he's wasting his time trying to converse with this guy. "I was asking because I was curious about why you made a sign with those statements."

"How do you know I made this sign? Perhaps, I pilfered it from the local evangelical church."

"Did you?"

"What would it mean if I did? Can you steal from a church?"

Answering his questions with other questions is starting to bug Lenny. He can't decide if he is an unbalanced eccentric, an arcane mystic, or simply playing a game of leading him in circles for his own amusement. Whoever he is, there is something about him that keeps Lenny talking. He decides to try a more straightforward approach.

"What's your name?"

"You can call me Ezekiel."

Finally, an answer. "Like the prophet?"

"You must not ask for so much," says Ezekiel, repeating the words on his sign.

Lenny sighs. Coming on the heels of his conversation with Jerry, he's finding this exchange exhausting. He decides he's heard enough.

"It was nice talking with you Ezekiel, but I need to go. Have a nice day."

"Do you have a dollar?"

"Sure," says Lenny. He takes out his wallet and hands him three. "Here's a little extra for the conversation."

Ezekiel takes the money and tucks the bills into his pants pocket. Lenny turns and begins walking away when he hears, "I thought you liked ambiguity."

Lenny stops. How would he know? It feels too personal to be random. He is tempted to go back and ask Ezekiel why he said this but decides he doesn't have the energy to open what might be a can of worms. Without responding, he resumes his way home, picking up his pace as he walks.

* * *

Opening his apartment door, Lenny is greeted by the familiar sounds and welcoming displays of his dog, Sisu, expressing, as always, his delight at seeing him. *Unconditional love is a powerful force.*

Sisu's name (pronounced See-Su) comes from a Finnish word

that in English means something like grit, determination, or strength of will, qualities embodied by his little Cairn Terrier mix. Surviving on the streets of San Antonio, Texas, where he was found must have taken *sisu* and intelligence.

Lenny learned the word *'sisu'* during one of his many trips to the University of Lapland in Rovaniemi Finland. His initial visit, almost sixteen years ago, came about because of a surprising invitation to present a lecture at the university. Lenny had never heard of Rovaniemi and knew little about Finland or Lapland, so before accepting the invitation he did some research. He learned that Lapland, or *Sápmi* in the language of the indigenous Sámi people, was a geographical region lying within the arctic circle, the name for the southernmost latitude where at different times of the year the sun stays below and above the horizon for twenty-four hours. Lenny also read that Finnish Lapland had more reindeer than people and was one of the best places to view the aurora borealis, the Northern Lights. Situated by the arctic circle, Rovaniemi was called the gateway to Lapland. It sounded exotic and exciting and he eagerly agreed to participate in what seemed like a once-in-a-lifetime opportunity.

The trip was long but uneventful. Arriving at Rovaniemi, a prominent sign informed him this was 'Santa's official airport,' a proclamation further accentuated by information about 'Santa Claus Village' where the mythical man allegedly lived. *It's too bad I don't have some young children to share this with*, he thought with some remorse.

En route to his hotel, he passed several modestly sized homes of functional design, not the more medieval and Renaissance styles that he, like most Americans, associated with Europe. Later, he learned Rovaniemi had been destroyed during WWII by the retreating German army so most of its buildings were constructed post-1945. Its current design was the work of Finland's most famous architect, Alvar Aalto, who used the head of a reindeer as the blueprint of the city. It was clear he wasn't in Kansas anymore.

Arriving at his hotel, Lenny checked in, trudged up to his room, collapsed on the bed, and fell almost immediately to sleep.

He awoke to daylight and bird songs. His first thought was that he had overslept his morning appointment at the university and bolted out of bed. However, when he checked the time he was shocked to see it was a little after three a.m.—his first experience of the midnight sun.

Jet lag and sunlight made the rest of his 'night' mostly sleepless, but after rousing himself with some strong, Finnish coffee, he managed to get to the university on time and meet his hosts. He was greeted warmly and happy to discover that to varying degrees they all spoke English since he did not know a word of Finnish. Even accounting for language differences, Finns were relatively taciturn. Small talk was uncommon. The ubiquitous 'How are you?' so automatic upon greeting someone in the U.S. was rare. When it was expressed—usually by someone visiting from the U.S.—it was just as likely to be met by a blank expression than the equally automatic 'fine.' For Lenny who was talkative and tactile, adapting to this cultural tendency required in-the-moment awareness and restraint.

Also new to Lenny was the Finnish custom of sauna, one of the few Finnish words to be imported into the English language although the Finns pronounced it more like sow-na. Lenny had been to saunas before at health clubs in the U.S., but compared to the Finnish sauna, what he had experienced in the U.S. was better described as sitting in a hot room. In Finland, sauna was a cultural experience, an integral part of Finnish life. Almost every home had a sauna. In fact, Finland has more saunas per capita than anywhere in the world. Even prisons had saunas!

Whereas saunas in the U.S. required covering towels or bathing suits, Finns were naked. Nudity did not have the sexual connotation it did in the U.S. The ubiquity of sauna exposed Finns from childhood to naked bodies varying in age and appearance. As a result, nudity was natural and physical differences accepted.

After overcoming his initial hesitancy, Lenny came to embrace the sauna ritual. He reveled in the heat, the profuse sweating that followed, and feeling what he imagined were toxins seeping out of his skin. He loved when water was poured over the hot rocks on top of the sauna stove to create steam, what the Finns called *löyly*, and the rush of warmth it produced. And most of all, he loved what he called the post-sauna glow when for a short time, all was right with the world. Knowing he could experience such peacefulness was revelatory and something Lenny never forgot. He tried to capture his feelings in a poem he called Ode to Sauna.

I enter your home
my nakedness formal attire
You embrace me
Soothing heat and hypnotic löyly
become my world
Stripped of pretense and posturing
I experience singular clarity

my thoughts unobstructed by the
pulls of the outside world
emotions pacified by the melodies
of the crackling wood
Having entered as a caterpillar
I emerge a glistening butterfly
at one with a world I have never seen

* * *

Lenny's Finnish hosts were gracious and modest, quietly attending to his needs and striving to make his visit pleasant and interesting. One morning, he was invited by two Finnish colleagues on an outing outside of the city. After driving nearly two hours north, they stopped at what looked to Lenny as a random spot along the road; however, for Erkki and Päiviö, it was a discernible trailhead. They followed an indistinct path through pine and white birch until arriving at a modest, rustic cabin set in a small clearing. Erkki informed him it was the former home of an artist friend, now deceased.

After a meal of smoked reindeer, cheese, and cloudberries—a slightly tart, amber-colored, raspberry-shaped fruit considered a delicacy—Lenny wandered off into the forest. When he was out-of-sight of the cabin, he stopped to absorb his surroundings. The silence enveloped him. No sounds of distant cars, the occasional airplane or even bird songs. Surprisingly and paradoxically, he began to 'hear' the silence, a non-sound cloaking him in ethereal calm. *Am I hearing the murmur of the trees? An ever-present, vibrational language lost to the cacophony of human activity?* Whatever it was, the effect was spellbinding. A haiku-like poem by Leonard Cohen appeared.

> *Silence*
> *And a deeper silence*
> *When the crickets hesitate*

This is the space where the crickets hesitate.

* * *

Only after returning to the U.S. did Lenny fully realize the calming influence of the Lapland environment. Entering the noisy, bustling terminal at JFK airport, he could feel tension reinhabiting his body. He became acutely cognizant how its constancy in his life rendered it imperceptible. It was valuable yet disconcerting information. *Holy shit,* he thought, *I am one wound up dude.*

This epiphany motivated Lenny to return to Finland as often as he could. With each visit, he grew more appreciative of this small, socially progressive country. As a social work academic, he was impressed with Finland's sense of collective responsibility for the well-being of its citizens as embodied in its generous social welfare programs, its free university education, and universal daycare.

His only frustration was his inability to learn Finnish beyond a small vocabulary. This wasn't for lack of trying. Unlike the Indo-European languages spoken across most of Europe, whose roots included English, Finnish was part of the Finno-Ugric language group. This meant most words had no similarity to their English counterparts. If you were trying to find a pharmacy in Italy or Spain, you would recognize '*farmacia*,' in France, '*pharmacie*,' but in Finland. '*apteekki*' would not be helpful.

Pronunciation also was difficult. Words are accented on the

first syllable and could be very long. Finns rolled their r's in a way he could not master, eventually deciding it was anatomically impossible for him. Although most Finns spoke English, he always felt language was a barrier keeping him from the full immersion in Finnish culture he sought. Still, he was grateful to have had this experience.

How many New York Jews get to hang out in Santa Claus land?

Chapter Five

Lenny's Finland reveries are interrupted by thoughts of his encounter with Ezekiel. *Why is this guy still in my head? Is it because he did not fit the stereotype of a homeless person? His puzzling sign? How his responses to my questions invite me to engage in some kind of self-examination?*

As always, Lenny has many questions, but now he wants answers. The next day he returns to where he left Ezekiel to see if he can learn something more. But he is nowhere in sight nor is there a trace he had ever been there. Puzzled, Lenny asks nearby shopkeepers if they recalled seeing anyone resembling Ezekiel, but no one did. Feeling befuddled and a bit unmoored, he finds himself questioning whether Ezekiel was real. *Was I experiencing an elaborate hallucination? Could I have unknowingly ingested some psychotropic substance or can't remember having done so?* The possibilities seem remote.

I need to talk with someone with whom I can process what is going on without being judged.

He calls Jerry.

* * *

FINDING LENNY

Two hours later, Lenny and Jerry are in their familiar booth with their coffees.

"Thanks for coming on such short notice," says Lenny.

"No problem. I was working from home. You sounded a bit stressed on the phone. Is everything ok?"

"Yes, but something strange happened the other day after we met that has thrown me into a tailspin. I've been thinking about it to the point where I no longer know if I am making sense. I figured expressing my thoughts out loud to someone might help sort it out."

Lenny pauses before adding with a wry smile, "I guess you won the prize."

Jerry returns the smile. "I had a feeling this would be my lucky day. Tell me about it."

"Walking home from the coffee shop after we met, I noticed a guy sitting on the sidewalk who I assumed was a homeless person. He had this sign next to him with words that sounded familiar, so I stopped and tried talking with him. That's when things got weird."

"How so?"

"Instead of directly responding, he talked in a way that reminded me of Zen Koans."

"Zen Koans? I don't know what you mean."

"A Koan is a question or anecdote used by Zen Buddhist teachers to help their students gain insights into the nature of existence."

"Like a parable?"

"Sort of, but Koans tend to involve dialogue. Also, the questions raised by Koans are often unanswerable, creating doubt. This is done purposefully to disrupt ingrained ways of thinking and to generate a state of openness beyond mind—a kind of deep intuition."

"Can you give me an example?" asks Jerry still perplexed.

Lenny replays the encounter in his mind. "When I would ask him a question, he would answer with another question, sometimes questioning my question. It was like he was toying with me, purposely talking in Koans to get me to think differently."

Jerry decides not to pursue this further. Instead, he asks, "What did the sign say?" Lenny recites the words on each side.

"Doesn't ring any bells for me," says Jerry.

"I haven't been able to figure out where I saw or heard those lines, but I feel it will come to me." He shakes his head disconsolately. "The whole episode bothered me to the point where I decided to go back to where I saw him and try to get some answers. But when I got there the street was empty. I asked some shopkeepers if they'd seen anyone resembling him, but no one had. It was like he was never there. That's when I started to wonder if I was losing it."

Jerry sips his coffee. He looks up at Lenny. "If anyone has lost it, I'd bet on him. I'll concede what you described sounds strange, not your typical encounter with a homeless person. On the other hand, is it possible you are reading more into what he said than was intended? Isn't it more likely these were just the comments of someone a bit out-of-touch and had nothing to do with you?"

Lenny considers this for a few seconds. "If you mean I'm acting like someone who sees Jesus's face after spilling coffee on a bedsheet, I don't think so. Something about him seemed, I don't know, authentic."

"Perhaps it's what made the experience so unsettling," offers Jerry. "But it might just mean he's a good actor. It's a useful talent for a panhandler."

"Maybe so, but I wish I could have found him. Who knows, perhaps he'll show up. I just have this nagging feeling this was not a chance encounter."

"Well," says Jerry, "it seems you have three choices." He holds up one finger. "Continue ruminating over the meaning of your encounter." Two fingers. "Keep searching for him." Three fingers. "Forget the whole thing and move on."

Typical Jerry, getting right down to the nuts and bolts, thinks Lenny. He lets out a resigned sigh. "Your last option is probably best. As you said, it was a strange encounter, but it's over and he's gone. Maybe at some point I'll be able to take something away from it, but I'm not going to dwell on it."

"Sounds like a plan," says Jerry feeling good that he helped Lenny resolve this.

"Thanks," says a grateful Lenny. I knew talking with you would be helpful."

* * *

Lenny tries to resume his pre-Ezekiel life. Over time, the impact of the interaction becomes less intrusive. He decides to try writing a novel to redirect his energy in a creative direction. Although a firm believer in the maxim that writers write, meaning you wrote something, good or bad, every day whether you felt like it or not, he struggled to maintain such a schedule. It was difficult to extract himself from an academic mindset and believe he could write something of interest to a broad readership. He tried countering these obstacles by telling himself it was the writing not the outcome that was important. Creative expression was inherently positive, the rest didn't matter. But then he would think, *Who am I kidding? Of course, I want people to read what I write . . . and like it.* In the end, he decides his best strategy is to repeatedly and resolutely tell himself to keep plugging along. He appropriates a line from a song about gardening as his mantra: "Inch by inch, row by row."

* * *

Taking on the challenge of fiction writing is a fertile supplement to Lenny's contracted range of activities since retiring. Without the demands and pulls of academic life, most of his time was now spent at home, reading, attending to online correspondence, listening to music, watching movies or sporting events, and periodic exercise. When he left his apartment, it was usually to meet with Jerry, occasionally other friends or former colleagues, walk Sisu and do necessary chores. He thought about getting out more but was unable to deviate from the rut he had carved. So, when he was downtown picking up groceries and noticed a poster for a folksinger who would be performing that evening at a local club, he stopped to check it out.

What caught his eye was a comment that the performer, Gideon Morse, was a singer/songwriter in the style of Leonard Cohen. A photo showed a thin, middle-aged man wearing a brown sport coat and wide-brimmed hat, holding a guitar. Lenny felt a vague sense of recognition. Had he seen him before? The name was not familiar, but as an admirer of Leonard Cohen, he was intrigued enough to go to the show.

* * *

The club was a restaurant that converted itself into a music venue on the evenings it would host musicians. Despite the makeshift nature of the setting—folding chairs and a portable sound system—it had decent acoustics and an intimacy conducive to folk music. Arriving early to get a seat near the stage, Lenny looked forward to the concert.

Showtime arrives. Following a brief introduction, Gideon walks out on stage to applause from the approximately fifty people in the audience. He is tall and slender, casually dressed in jeans, a dark pullover shirt, and a brown, wide-brimmed hat. After thanking the club for inviting him and the audience for coming, he says, "Like many people, I was deeply touched by Leonard Cohen's poetic reflections on life, love, and spirituality, and his poignant commentaries on the state of the world."

Lenny whispers to himself, "Me too."

Gideon continues. "This is a song, an ode really, that I wrote for Leonard Cohen shortly after his death. It's called "Song for Leonard."" He picks up his guitar from the stand on his right, strums a few introductory chords, and begins to sing.

> "I hear you singing Leonard
> in a voice that goes down deep
> below the caves of solitude
> where men can freely weep
> where women hold the dreams
> that fill our deepest sleep
> I hear you singing Leonard
> it never sounded so sweet
> I hear you singing Leonard
> of the angst that keeps us down

the vacuous days, the endless nights
the lies that serve the crown
where your sentence is determined
by a jury dressed as clowns
I hear you singing Leonard
I embrace the sound

> When we sat at the table
> I thought I'd be able
> to learn what I needed to say
> but the words that were spoken
> only showed I was broken
> a pilgrim who had lost his way

I hear you laughing Leonard
another irony exposed
resurrection, forged perfection
the miracle bought and sold
and although a gun lies in my hand
I can't find any bullets to load
I hear you laughing Leonard
I should laugh too I suppose
I hear you singing Leonard
like a swamp song in the night
whispers, innuendos
shifting shadows, fading light
and somewhere in the distance
a bush is burning bright
a sacrament revealing
the words you must recite

> And the swan on the river
> could not deliver
> the rose with its petals opened wide
> Still you searched for its beauty
> as if you had a duty
> to discover where beauty resides
> And Boogie Street is empty
> the storefronts are all bare
> their shades are lowered to the sills
> there's no movement in the air
> then from a distant tower
> I hear that soft refrain
> the bell is cracked but light gets in
> we shall be whole again"

"We shall be whole again," Lenny repeats to himself. "I hope so." He did not feel whole. Not in the sense of being broken, but like something was missing or hidden. He loved the line 'the bell is cracked, but light gets in' that Gideon appropriated from Cohen's song, "Anthem." In the original, it went 'there's a crack in everything, that's how light gets in.' To Lenny it meant there was no need to pursue perfection; rather, it is our imperfect selves with all our warts, blemishes, and shortcomings that enable us to receive the light, to move toward transcendence. If only he could remember this.

Not only were the lyrics reminiscent of a Leonard Cohen song—Gideon had incorporated some of Cohen's imagery—but his melody and voice also were Cohen-like. For Lenny, the effect was magical, and he hoped to acquire the lyrics so he could further ponder their significance.

As he watched the performance, he again had the sense that he had seen Gideon before, like when he first saw the poster. Something about his eyes felt familiar . . . and then it came to him. They were the eyes of Ezekiel.

This can't be real! He shouts inwardly. Caught between wanting to flee and run up to the stage for a closer look, he grabs the sides of his seat and forces himself to remain stationary. He tells himself what he had imagined about Gideon's eyes was just that, his imagination.

He tries to refocus on the performance. As Gideon continues his Cohen-inspired repertoire, Lenny feels himself calming down. Then Gideon sings a line about 'floating through the Ether,' the same words Ezekiel had uttered during their interaction. It was too much.

The room grows smaller.

'I need to leave,' says a panicky voice.

Another voice counters. '*No. You need to speak with Gideon, otherwise you will never know.*'

Somehow, he manages to remain through the first set. A twenty-minute intermission is announced. Lenny notices Gideon standing by a small table in the corner of the room.

This is your opportunity.

A caution appears. *He'll think you're a weirdo.*

And a rebuttal. *The time to act is limited. You must take the chance.*

Quelling further self-debate he walks over to the table.

"Great songs," he says trying not to sound nervous. "I especially liked Song for Leonard."

"Thanks," replies Gideon. "It was one of those rare songs that write themselves, where I feel more like a conduit than a creator.

I hope it captured some of what Leonard Cohen's songs meant for me and others."

"It did for me." Then gathering his courage, he clumsily blurts out, "You remind me of someone I know. A guy named Ezekiel." When he says the name, Lenny carefully observes Gideon for a sign of recognition but sees nothing.

"Oh, is he a performer?" asks Gideon.

"Not that I'm aware of. Just an interesting guy."

Gideon thinks for a few seconds. "I don't know anyone by that name, but I could use a prophet in my life," he says with a slight smile.

Lenny is quiet. He is mesmerized by Gideon's eyes and the timbre of his voice. He decides to push it further.

"I know this might sound weird, but do the words 'you must not ask for so much' and 'why not ask for more' mean anything to you?"

Gideon looks at him in a way Lenny fears means he's gone too far. But before he can apologize, Gideon says, "Sure. They're from an early Leonard Cohen song, "Bird on a Wire." I sing it sometimes."

Lenny staggers backward, shaken that Ezekiel was using lines from Leonard Cohen.

"Are you ok?" asks Gideon, a look of concern on his face.

"Sorry. I just got dizzy for a moment. I think I'll sit back down. Thanks for chatting."

Walking back to his seat the song's first two lines appear.

Like a bird on a wire,

like a drunk in a midnight choir,

I have tried in my way to be free.

Is that what this is about, a search for freedom? Or is this all a dream?

*　*　*

The concert ends. Driving home, Lenny tries to put his troubling questions aside focusing instead on the concert. Gideon's second set featured songs about relationships, again in a poetic, Cohen-like way. Lenny finds himself singing a verse from one of them.

> "Who will join you at the window
> When the sun rises on the lake?
> Who will offer you some comfort
> when your heart's about to break?
> Yet you spurn the hand that reaches out
> with words that are opaque
> a prisoner of dreaming
> from which you fear you might awake."

The words trigger thoughts about the complex role of relationships in our lives, in his life, how they shape our identities and provide our greatest pleasures and pains yet remain a mystery.

His thoughts meander back through time to his pubescent consciousness of romantic relationships with its excitement and uncertainty. The excitement stemming from romantic fantasies of pop culture; the uncertainty from not having a clue what to do about it. Life took on a new dimension for which he felt unprepared. Suddenly, it seemed, peer interactions were no longer dominated by sports but by crude talk of girls and sex. And if the bravado of his friends could be believed, he'd been left behind. Without a reliable source of information, his reality was shaped by pop music themes of longing, heartbreak, and bliss. Accompanied by his guitar, he would sing, 'Let It Be Me,' 'Oh Donna,' and 'I Love How You Love

Me' with a naïve yearning devoid of life experience.

At school, he would daydream about different girls in his class but refrain from approaching them for fear of being rejected or making a fool of himself. The one time he attempted to act on his desires, subtly inching toward Donna Feinberg who he thought was the most beautiful girl he had ever seen, his skyrocketing anxiety triggered hiccups which abruptly terminated further advances and added a new worry to his list of anxieties. Although he did not understand it at the time, he was rehearsing a pattern of fear and avoidance that survived as a cautionary whisper whenever approaching potential intimate encounters.

Despite these early struggles, Lenny remained a hopeless romantic. But romanticism at this age was not the same as when he was younger. In contrast to his naïve adolescent wallowing in rock and roll dreams of unfettered love and devotion, now he was embarrassingly aware of how often his fantasies still mirrored pop culture and led to superficial, misguided judgments about potential relationships. It also accentuated the disconnect between the physical changes of aging and his self-image. This was painfully evident when he had to remind himself that the real or imagined glances of younger women were not flirtations but a polite acknowledgment to an old guy looking in their direction.

With these thoughts tumbling around in his brain, he arrives at his building. Remembering that Sisu has been alone for several hours, he abandons his reverie and fetches him for their evening walk.

Well, that was an unexpected diversion, he thinks. *Lucky, I didn't drive into a tree.*

Chapter Six

Saturday, nine a.m., Lenny and Jerry are at their usual *lieu de reunion*—the Holy Grounds coffee shop. Since it was a weekend, the shop had fewer customers grabbing a coffee and something to eat on their way to work. Today, most patrons were locals, leisurely drinking their beverage of choice while reading, looking at their phones, working on their laptops, or like Lenny, chatting with a companion.

After purchasing their coffees of choice, they take their seats and proceed to the exchanging pleasantries and inquiring about their respective well-being phase of their greeting ritual.

"How have you been?" asks Lenny.

"I've been good," replies Jerry. "Busy with work and the kids' activities."

"Danny still playing soccer?" Danny was Jerry's fifteen-year-old son who, according to Jerry, was a gifted athlete.

"Yeah, he's on the school team. Doing very well. We go to the games whenever possible. They're a lot of fun."

"How about Emily? Wasn't she getting into painting?"

"That's right, she loves it. She's even thinking of being an art major when she goes off to college next year. You should see some of her work. She's quite talented."

"I'd love to," says Lenny, realizing that he knows comparatively little about Jerry. What are the issues that trouble him or that he thinks deeply about? He considers probing for more information but decides it would feel too forced. Better to wait for the right moment.

"How about you?" inquires Jerry. "Anything new happen since we last met?"

Lenny wastes no time. "Something did." He describes his encounter with the folksinger, Gideon, concluding with, "This is becoming too weird. I'm thinking I should go for a brain scan."

"It is weird," says Jerry with his usual calm, "but couldn't it be explained by coincidence? I often see people who look like someone I know. Is it possible this Ezekiel character has been on your mind and it's causing you to notice similarities you might ordinarily have overlooked?"

"You think I'm making this up?" asks Lenny, sounding a bit indignant.

Jerry quickly responds. "No. I'm not discounting what you said. I'm just suggesting there may be other less disturbing explanations."

"True," says Lenny somewhat placated. "But I don't think I conveyed my experience very well. There was more to it, a feeling of recognition that felt unequivocal."

Jerry nods. "Do you think the experience was some kind of message?"

The question surprises Lenny. Jerry did not typically go down such metaphysical roads. *Maybe I've been underestimating him.*

"Hmm. I'm not sure," says Lenny. "Assuming Ezekiel is a real person, he couldn't have had any knowledge of me. It could be that the strangeness of the encounter stirred something within me that I've yet to figure out. On the other hand, if there *was* a connection between Ezekiel and Gideon then I am in unchartered territory. What I do know is that Gideon's songs got me reminiscing about how my early relationship experiences were shaped by pop culture and peer influences and how they set the stage for my later ones."

"It's hard to shake those early experiences," says Jerry. "I still remember the first time I fell in love, or thought I did, when I was fifteen."

Lenny's about to jump in with his own story when he remembers what he just told himself about not knowing Jerry. He waits for him to continue.

"When I think about it now," says Jerry, "it seems superficial."

Lenny nods. "Life experiences can change how we think about things. My experience was feeling trapped between having strong attractions and being afraid to act on them," says Lenny forgetting to prompt Jerry to elaborate.

"What were you afraid of?" asks Jerry tabling his own story.

"Rejection. Looking foolish for not knowing what I thought was common knowledge." Lenny lowers his eyes as if even decades later he still finds the topic painful.

Lenny's emotional self-disclosure has them focusing on their coffees. Jerry breaks the silence.

"But eventually you managed to have relationships."

"True, but the critical voices of my early experiences continued to echo. To stave off my demons I adopted a persona of a caring, sensitive man who would help others overcome their issues."

"Sounds like an admirable way to be," says Jerry.

"Perfect for a future social worker," says Lenny with a wry smile. "Yes, it was easy to rationalize, but it was still a guise that assumed an inequality, the helper and the helped—a poor foundation for a long-term, intimate relationship. Hence, my previous marriage."

"So you married for the wrong reasons?" says Jerry succinctly expressing what he thought Lenny was saying.

"You might say that. The relationship was complementary, but not positive. We each got something we needed from the other, me to be a savior, she in need of saving. This interdependence kept us together, but unhappy. I became a connoisseur of hope, believing change would come even as things were getting worse. It was not sustainable."

Lenny looks around the shop and shifts in his seat. *Talking about this can't be easy for him,* thinks Jerry. What he can't tell is whether Lenny was reacting to painful memories, feeling regret about how he had acted, or both. He thinks about his marriage and feels fortunate to have met Katie.

"Ending the relationship must have been a difficult and distressing decision, but it seems like you've gained some important insights about yourself," says Jerry, trying to nudge the conversation in a positive direction.

"Yes," agrees Lenny. "I realized that my self-image as a kind, romantic, helpful partner, while having its good points, was also a cover for my insecurities. It not only led to problems with my choice of partners but with how my relationships evolved."

"How they evolved? Not sure I know what you mean."

"I mean the relational norms and expectations that developed. Think of intimate relationships like improvisational jazz duets. They begin with a general idea of the song; however, what it becomes will depend on the musicians' responses to each other's interpretation of the melody. If they can successfully coordinate their interactions, developing and adhering to certain mutual understandings, the melody will work. If not, there will be dissonance.

"Similarly, when beginning a relationship, the couple have a general idea of how it is structured, how it will work, and what to expect, but what it actually becomes will depend on their ongoing interaction, their attempts to influence the 'melody' "—Lenny mimes scare quotes again—"and their responses to the other's attempts."

"Interesting, but I think I got lost in the 'chorus,' " says Jerry also miming scare quotes in an attempt to jokingly let Lenny know he's not being clear. "Can you be a little more specific?"

Lenny scratches his head trying to think of a better way to explain what he's trying to say.

"Relationships require people to coordinate their actions. Decisions are made, not always explicitly, about how to be together. Things like how to resolve conflicts, who is responsible for various tasks, who initiates sex, and so on. They also come to less obvious understandings like what certain words mean, what behaviors will or will not be tolerated, and what rituals must be observed. Over time, these pushes and pulls function like the rules of the relationship."

"Interesting," says Jerry, trying to decide whether his relationship fits with Lenny's musical analogy. "I agree that at the beginning of a relationship people have certain expectations, or maybe hopes, about what it will be like. They also form beliefs about each other and how they will fit together. And if that fits with their experience, they might commit to one another by getting married. At least that's what Katie and I did."

"I agree," says Lenny, "but even with those criteria, the couple's lived experience is still waiting to be enacted. And in our rapidly changing world, some of those assumptions or understandings we thought existed may no longer hold requiring re-negotiation and accommodation. It can be challenging, especially if, as often happens, the understanding has never been spoken aloud. For example, when a woman in a traditional androcentric, er, male-oriented, relationship wants it to be more equal, this sets the stage for conflict."

"Do you think that's why more people get divorced than in the past?"

Lenny squinches his eyes. "Hold that thought. I have to pee."

Jerry uses the break to stretch his legs and get a refill of coffee. *Another interesting conversation with Lenny. A bit too abstract as usual but food for thought.*

Lenny returns. "Okay, now I can answer your question without distraction. In our parents' generation spousal roles and responsibilities were relatively clear. People knew and accepted social norms about marriage. 'Til death do us part' was taken more literally. Today things are more fluid and ambiguous requiring couples to negotiate how to coordinate their actions and adapt to change. We also have become more me-oriented which lessens commitment. Finally, laws and attitudes have changed so obtaining a divorce is easier and does not carry stigma. Remaining in a long-term, committed relationship is not easy."

Jerry takes a moment to digest what Lenny has said. "Are you suggesting we would be better off returning to more traditional roles?"

Lenny shakes his head. "Not at all. Traditional relationships were unequal, favoring men over women. Also, marriages may have been more stable, but they were not necessarily happy."

Jerry decides to check out how the conversation relates to his marriage. "Let me see if I understand what you are saying. When Katie and I got married, we had a general idea about what being a husband and a wife meant to us, but we didn't know how, or if, it would change over time—certainly not after we had children."

"Right," says Lenny, happy his ramblings were making sense. "It's like an internal marriage script gets activated when we utter the words 'I do.' The script combines cultural norms and beliefs about marriage and what it means to be a spouse. These meanings reflect what we've observed about married couples, particularly our parents, although depending on their relationship, such meanings may be difficult to accept. Relationships are neither static nor are our ideas about them. What we mean by husband and wife has changed. In fact, given the number of non-married people in committed, intimate relationships, those terms may one day be obsolete."

"I see your point," says Jerry. "When Katie and I married thirty-three years ago, we had more traditional expectations about what it meant to be a good husband and wife than we do now. In hindsight, we were naïve to expect things to stay the same."

"As the saying goes, 'life happens,'" interjects Lenny. "Some of these happenings like having children, may be planned and some like an illness or injury or job change may not, but in both cases, it's hard, if not impossible, to know what their impact will be on your relationship. The very process of living brings new realities, understandings, values, and interests into play." Hearing himself, Lenny wonders if his intellectualizing is also a way to avoid confronting his ongoing struggles with relationships.

As if reading his thoughts, Jerry says, "You make relationships sound exhausting. Has all this thinking turned you off to relationships? Is that why you are single now?"

Taken aback by the timing and directness of Jerry's questions, Lenny blurts out, "Wow, you're going for the jugular today," simultaneously thinking how defensive he sounds.

"Sorry. I was just interested in how your thoughts on relationships affected your own life."

Lenny drinks his coffee to give himself time to recover and collect his thoughts. He leans slightly forward.

"It's ok. They're good questions. My analyses may be accurate but they are intellectual exercises. Actual relationships are more involved. To be honest, I don't think I've fully outgrown the trauma of my early years, or ever will. My perception about my own and others' physical attractiveness, my fears about rejection, and my yearning to love and be loved in the most romantic ways are infused with who I am."

"I guess life is always a work in progress," offers Jerry.

"Well said. We have experiences and we try to make sense of them. This sensemaking in turn affects further experiences, and so it goes. That's why having friends like you with whom I can have authentic dialogue is so important. Otherwise, I'm just talking to myself, something I already do too much."

Jerry smiles.

Chapter Seven

A few blocks from Lenny's apartment is a small, arts cooperative called The Loft. Besides providing a venue for local artists to display and sell their work, The Loft hosted a variety of events ranging from wine tastings to open mikes. Lenny particularly enjoyed the latter with its eclectic mix of performances—poetry, music, even occasional stand-up comedy—and performers. All were amateurs, and he admired the courage it took to get up in front of an audience, some for the first time, and display their artistry. This admiration was shared by the audience, always magnanimous and gracious regardless of the level of talent.

Part of Lenny's attraction to open mike nights was his secret desire to perform. He played the guitar most of his life although his skill level never advanced beyond being an adequate accompanist to his vocals. Despite his mother's wish that he take piano lessons ("you have piano fingers," she would say), his persistent childhood entreaties to learn the guitar won out. They signed him up for lessons from a retired club date guitarist who taught him to play the songs of his parents' generation. He was happy with this at first, enjoying the praise of his parents who would sing along to "Bye

Bye Blackbird" and "The Sidewalks of New York." As he grew older, however, his interests turned to more contemporary music of the early rock & rollers like Buddy Holly and Elvis, so he discontinued his lessons. Later, he got swept up into the folk revival of the '60s which is where, as a musician, he has remained.

The burgeoning folk scene and its link to the Civil Rights movement and Vietnam war protests appealed to Lenny's inchoate but growing social consciousness. His youthful ideals were roused by singer-songwriters who condemned illegitimate wars, racial and social injustices, and the superficiality of contemporary life. Feeling part of a community devoted to righting the wrongs of the world was energizing and inspired Lenny to try writing songs. His early attempts were heartfelt but clunky, expressing in tortured rhyme, his adolescent outrage about injustices and his vision of a better world. He dreamed of sharing his songs with others, picturing himself as an emergent Bob Dylan. He would watch open mike nights at different clubs judging his talent in comparison to the performers. Afterward, he would vow to sign up for the next session, but as the time grew near and his performance anxiety increased, he would invariably decide it was not the right time.

Still, he kept writing songs, attending performances and dreaming. Once, despite his reclusive nature, those dreams seemed on the verge of coming true. Through the connections of a friend and fellow folksinger, he was invited to audition for a major record company. His first impulse was to refuse, but he knew if he did, he would always wonder about what might have been. So, he pushed through his anxiety and kept the appointment.

The audition took place in a Manhattan office building where the company was located. Lenny and his friend were met by John, the record company representative. After exchanging some pleasantries, John asked Lenny to play him one of his songs. Lenny, in full Dylan mode, decided to play his most recent one, a five-minute, one E minor chord stream of consciousness rant against the war. Lenny belted it out with passion and outrage fueled by his nineteen-year-old sense of injustice.

> "Airplane soars, bombshell roars
> Don't call it a war, needs more blood and gore
> Tho' it's rotten to the core, it's happened before
> and is happening again
> So you send more men
> From all over they came, with different names
> All taking aim at those who look the same
> The ones we've been told to blame
> for communism's flame
> burning brightly
> So don't take it lightly
> You gotta be strong because the fight will be long
> And the people will mourn those who are gone . . ."

And on and on with barely an intake of breath.

John listened politely. When Lenny finished, he complimented him on his voice but made it clear that he was looking for something with more commercial potential. To the young Lenny, immersed in the topical folk song movement, this was asking him to sell out—go the way of Tin Pan Alley—which he brusquely refused to do.

Years later, Lenny would look back on the experience and smile at his youthful zeal and decidedly unpragmatic judgment. He set aside his dreams of a musical career, limiting his performances to friends and his songwriting to the occasional flash of inspiration. Still, he got vicarious pleasure from attending open mike nights at The Loft and seeing the dreams of other generations on display.

* * *

Lenny was looking forward to spending a few hours in the upbeat atmosphere of The Loft. He arrived early to ensure he could get a seat near the performers. Occupying an old storefront, The Loft was a large, rectangular room filled with an assorted collection of tables and chairs and a small makeshift stage. The walls were adorned with an eclectic collection of works by local artists, most expressing commentaries on social issues. At a counter in the back, patrons could purchase coffee, tea, soft drinks, local wines, and craft beers.

About ten minutes after settling in, the first performer, a twenty-something woman with short, red hair, a nervous smile, and Goth style apparel is introduced. She recites poetry about the mystical qualities of nature in a style reminiscent of, but hardly equal to, the poet, Mary Oliver. She is followed by a young guitar-playing man who sings songs of legendary Delta blues greats like Robert Johnson and Sun House. Adopting a gravelly tone, he belts out,

"I got rambling, I got ramblin' on my mind

I got rambling, I got ramblin' on my mind

Hate to leave my baby, but you treats me so unkind"

Lenny appreciates his earnestness but can't help noticing how his effort to project an image as a down-and-out rambler is belied by his baby face and soft hands. The image evokes memories of his own comical attempts to fit into the folk music scene by adopting the persona of a hard traveling drifter. A verse from a song by the Israeli folksinger Ron Eliran pops into his head.

> *I wanna sing a song about a chain gang*
> *And swing a twelve-pound hammer all-the-day*
> *And how I'd like to kill that captain*
> *And how a Black man works his life away*
> *But . . . What do you do if you're young and white and Jewish?*
> *And you never swung a hammer in your life*
> *And you never called 'Water Boy' early in the morn*
> *And the only chain is the chain that's on your bike*

He smiles. That was him.

The performances continue. In typical fashion, regardless of their quality, the audience of about forty people is attentive and receptive, rewarding the performers with hearty applause. Lenny enthusiastically joins in grateful for this brief reprieve from his recent angst.

Feeling thirsty, he decides to get a beer. As he walks to the counter, he is surprised to see Jerry's daughter, Emily, in the crowd. They had met a few times when he had been to Jerry's home. Emily favored her mother in appearance: medium height, slim build, long brown hair, and a captivating smile. He found her to be bright and pleasant. She was curious about his work telling Lenny she was considering social work as a possible career, combining it with her interest in art.

He considers going over to her and saying hello, but she's

engaged with friends so he decides not to make contact. However, as he is looking in her direction Emily looks up and sees him. She waves and Lenny returns the gesture.

The next act is beginning so Lenny returns to his seat. Approaching the microphone is a man with long, scraggly, blonde hair who looks to be in his early thirties. He is wearing jeans and a T-shirt with the words 'I brake for marsupials' printed over a picture of what Lenny imagines is the Australian outback. He is holding a sheet of paper containing a poem he begins to recite. Lenny finds it sophomoric but earnest, sort of an existential rumination on nature and life.

> "Where do the rainbows go when the sun hides behind the clouds?
> Where is the moonbeam's glow when it is covered by a shroud?
> Put your hands on a tree, put your fingers in the soil, put your . . ."

The poet pauses mid-phrase, his performance interrupted by a commotion near the club's entrance. Lenny turns toward the sound. He sees a lot of movement but is unable to make out the source. Then, a loud bang, like a car backfiring reverberates through the room. Instantly, the buoyant atmosphere vanishes and erupts into pandemonium with chairs and tables tumbling and people scattering in all directions. More bangs. The panic is tangible. The unthinkable forces its way into Lenny's mind.

*　*　*

Turning his head towards where the sounds are loudest, he sees, to his horror, a man with a rifle yelling and shooting indiscriminately at people frantically scrambling for cover. He feels like he is dreaming yet acutely awake. His heart beats madly as his sympathetic nervous system kicks into high gear. Without conscious thought, he throws himself on the ground as the screams and chaos intensify.

Frozen in place on the floor, Lenny becomes aware the gunshots are getting closer. *Oh, God. I'm a dead man.* Intense urges to scream, run, and pray, all vie for ascendancy. Unable to decide in the seconds available to him, immobility wins out. He lies as still as possible, feeling like an ostrich hoping to be ignored by a stalking tiger while trying to quell his quaking limbs.

Out of his half-opened eyes, he sees the shooter's feet moving slowly past his body. As he lifts his leg to take another step, Lenny, for some reason he will never understand, reaches out, grabs his ankle, and yanks it upwards with all his strength. Taken by surprise, the shooter tries unsuccessfully to catch his balance and falls taking a table and a couple of chairs with him. As he hits the ground the rifle is jarred from his hands. Momentarily unarmed, he is pounced on by several people who begin pummeling him.

Whether Lenny lost consciousness or entered a dissociative state was never clear to him, but the next thing he knew police were everywhere, dragging away a semi-conscious, bloodied, and handcuffed man.

An eerie silence fills the room, intermittently broken by sobs, cries for help, and entreaties to the fallen to hang on. Lenny has not moved, his mind and body unable to process what has happened. Then he remembers Emily, and wills himself to his knees to see if she's ok. Sifting through the devastation he notices two paramedics working feverishly over what appears to be the body of a young woman. A sense of foreboding floods through him. Inching forward while squinting to get a better look, his worst fear is realized. It's Emily. *Oh God, no.* He cannot make out her wounds, but it is clear she is badly injured.

I need to call Jerry.

He pulls his cell phone out of his pocket. Fortunately, Jerry's number is on speed dial otherwise he doubts whether his shaking hand would be able to press the correct numbers. After two rings, Jerry answers.

"Jerry, it's Lenny," he says in a trembling voice.

"Hi, Lenny. What's up?"

"I am at The Loft, the arts cooperative downtown."

"I know the place. Coincidentally, I think Emily was planning to go there tonight. Is everything ok?"

A bolt of anguish courses through Lenny's body. *How do I say this?*

"Jerry, if you're standing, please sit down," he says knowing his words are likely to set off alarm bells. He takes a breath. "It's, it's . . . about Emily."

"What do you mean?" says Jerry his apprehension clear.

"There's been a, a, shooting. You need to come."

"What?" Jerry shouts. "What are you saying, Lenny? Is Emily hurt?"

"Yes," he whispers trying to hold back sobs. "Just come . . . now."

Jerry disconnects and Lenny collapses to the floor. It is then that he notices blood near the bottom of his shirt. *How did that get there?* He touches the spot and winces in pain. Was he shot without knowing it? Given his state of shock, anything is possible. Still, compared to others in the room his injury is minor, so he decides not to bother the paramedics.

He moves toward Emily. There is an oxygen mask over her face and she appears to be unconscious. A paramedic is applying bandages to her chest while another administers an IV. Lenny involuntarily shudders.

A stretcher appears and Emily is lifted onto it. As they begin moving her to the exit, a panic-stricken Jerry bursts through the door and begins looking frantically around the room. When he sees his daughter on the gurney he cries out, "Emily!" and rushes toward her. A paramedic intercepts him but Jerry brushes him aside. Lenny can hear Jerry talking to her although he cannot make out the words. She is unresponsive.

Lenny feels like he is watching a movie; it is too bizarre to be real. He wants to let Jerry know he is there, but they are out the door and into an ambulance before he can get close. He surveys the room. The devastation is staggering: overturned tables and chairs, broken glasses, bottles, clothes, and other debris are strewn everywhere. And the blood, so much blood. But worst of all are the wails, cries, and whimpers, an otherworldly dirge forming a ghastly backdrop to the focused but desperate movements of medical personnel and the stunned and dazed looks of those who escaped injury.

Lenny is not sure what to do. He feels like he might vomit. His side hurts and his head is throbbing. Afraid he might faint if he stays any longer, he decides to leave, return home, and tend to his wound.

The two blocks to his apartment are slow and painful. He concentrates on putting one foot in front of the other. By the time he arrives, he's exhausted.

He opens his door to Sisu bounding toward him with his usual enthusiastic greeting, but quickly sensing something is wrong, he backs off. Lenny tries to reassure him and manages to take him out front to pee.

Back inside, he heads to the bathroom to assess the extent of his injury. Gingerly removing his shirt, he gazes in the mirror. There's a nasty-looking bruise on his forehead above his left eye. *That explains my headache.* Looking down he sees a long and moderately deep cut along his side, but thankfully it is not a bullet wound. Typically squeamish about such things, compared to what he just witnessed this is like a shaving nick. *Perhaps, I landed on something sharp when I dove to the floor.* Whatever the cause, the important thing was to get patched up. He wasn't sure if he needed stitches but decides to treat it himself using butterfly bandages to keep the wound closed. Afterward, he stumbles to his bed, lies down, and, utterly depleted, swiftly falls into a deep sleep.

* * *

Lenny is lost. He is in a strange city. Tall, austere-looking buildings loom menacingly over him. Twisty streets recede into darkness. A dystopian sense of foreboding infuses him. *I need to get home*; he thinks and starts walking in what he hopes is the right direction. However, walking is not easy on the ground's spongy foundation and he is wary of falling. As he plods along, the cityscape suddenly changes into what looks like his childhood neighborhood in New York City.

"This isn't my home anymore," he says aloud. "I'm going to find a local and ask for directions." He spots a middle-aged man sitting outside a café reading a newspaper. He's wearing a gray, pork pie hat and a dark blue blazer with flap pockets and side vents, a style popular in the 1950s. Lenny walks up to him.

"Excuse me. I wonder if you could give me directions."

The man looks up from his newspaper. Immediately, Lenny realizes this was a mistake. He has a sinister look and a maniacal smile like one of those evil clowns in horror movies.

"Yes, I can help you," he says in a reedy voice that bespoke evil.

Fear spikes up Lenny's spine. Before the man could say another word, Lenny starts running, his only aim to get as far away from him as possible. He keeps going until his lungs can no longer sustain his body's demands. As he waits for his heaving to subside, he looks around to get his bearings. What he sees gives him chills: desolate, pothole-riddled streets strewn with garbage and lined by crumbling shells of burnt-out buildings. There is no sound save for the moaning of the wind and the scurry of rats mulling around something Lenny did not want to look at.

Everything about the place shouts danger. "I have to get out of here," he wails in desperation. He spins in circles desperately searching for an exit from this horrific wasteland but without success. Panic overtakes him and he begins to feel faint. Struggling to maintain consciousness, he hears what sounds like chimes playing somewhere in the distance. The soft, melodic tones beckon: 'This way to safety. This way to safety.'

Like a drowning man spotting a boat, he wildly waves his arms and screams, "I'm coming. I'm coming."

And awakens.

* * *

The Zen alarm clock by Lenny's bed is playing its gentle, flowing water wake-up music. For several minutes, he stares at the ceiling while gradually extracting himself from the tendrils of his dream and its echoes of terror. Then looking around the room to confirm he is, in fact, in his apartment, he turns off the music.

Being lost has been a recurrent theme in Lenny's dreams since childhood, a consequence, he believed, of his mother's incessant warnings about the myriad dangers lurking everywhere in the world. Exacerbating this sense of pervasive danger was his absence of a sense of direction which meant if he got lost, he could not find his way back. It bewildered Lenny how some people claimed to *like* getting lost and did so on purpose. Their excitement at exploring the unknown and their confidence in their ability to return to familiar territory were foreign to him. He realized he might be missing out on some interesting experiences, but tackling this particular issue was not at the head of his 'personal issues to be addressed' queue.

Lost in thought, it takes him a while to register something pressing against his arm. Glancing to his side, he sees Sisu pushing his nose against him, his not subtle way of letting Lenny know it was time to take him out. *Dogs certainly regulate your life*, he thinks. For Lenny, this was beneficial. It helped get him out of bed, dressed and walking outside even on mornings like this when he did not want to. He gently swings his legs over the side of the bed, puts on his socks, and makes his way to the bathroom. His wound hurts, but he ignores it. After performing his morning ablutions, he checks the weather, puts on the appropriate clothes, harnesses Sisu, and heads outside. It would be a brief outing given his condition, but good for both.

Despite their well-trodden route, Sisu always found new smells to explore and places to mark. The day was sunny with a slight breeze that warmed Lenny's face. He reminded himself to stay in the present by taking in his surroundings—the houses, the trees, the morning songs of birds, the people—and allow himself a brief respite from the upheaval in his life.

After walking about fifteen minutes, they reach the midpoint of their circular route and begin heading back home. For Lenny, this also was the point at which the veneer of peacefulness from being outdoors could no longer hold back the impact of the previous day's events. Thoughts about what happened and could have happened start flowing.

Who was this maniac? How many were killed? And how many injured in ways that will change their lives forever? It's unfathomable. And for what?

It could have been me!

Poor Emily. I hope she's going to be alright.

The simultaneous, contradictory sense of unreality and undeniable reality persisted. *I need to find a way to sort things out. Should I contact Jerry? No, his focus needs to be on Emily, not me. What should I do?*

He continues traipsing toward home on automatic pilot. A tug on the leash turns his attention to Sisu who is veering to his left. He glances in that direction but sees nothing.

"What is it Sisu? Do you see something I don't?"

Wanting to return home, he tries to keep Sisu on their circular path to the apartment. Sisu, however, has other ideas and continues tugging in the other direction. *Poor guy hasn't been out much. Probably just wants to walk a little further.* He reluctantly relents and follows Sisu's lead. After another block, Sisu again turns to the left. Thinking they are walking in a wider loop toward home Lenny follows. *Who's walking whom?* he chuckles to himself.

Entering a new street, Lenny looks ahead. He stops in his tracks. It's Ezekiel once again sitting on the sidewalk next to a sign.

Jesus, he's back.

Lenny slowly approaches. Ezekiel looks similar to when he first encountered him: unkempt hair and beard, worn jeans and boots, and a frayed T-shirt, although its design was different. This one was dark blue with a mandala, an eight-pointed, yellow star-like form surrounded by a grayish square. His sign leans against a lamppost beside him.

EVERYBODY KNOWS THAT THE DICE ARE LOADED

This time Lenny recognizes the words as from another Leonard Cohen song. He guesses the other side will have the song's next line:

'Everybody rolls with their fingers crossed.'

He finds himself wondering if the message is meant for him. *Are the 'dice' really loaded? Is everything already written and all we can do is hope our 'roll' comes up sevens?*

"Hello, Lenny," says Ezekiel, interrupting his speculation.

He's startled to hear Ezekiel address him by name. *Did I ever tell him my name?* Unnerved, Lenny says, "Where have you been?"

"Around."

"I see you have a new sign. Let me guess; the reverse side says, 'everybody rolls with their fingers crossed.'"

"Are your fingers crossed?" asks Ezekiel.

Unexpectedly, Ezekiel's words trigger images of The Loft followed by a torrent of emotions. Lenny feels woozy. He blurts out, "I don't have time for this!" then turns and begins walking away.

"What do you have time for, Lenny?" comes Ezekiel's fading voice.

With tears trickling down his cheeks, Lenny repeats the question to himself as he continues walking.

What do I have time for?

PART TWO

Chapter Eight

A vortex of thoughts and feelings whirl around Lenny. Images of yesterday's carnage appear like lightning bursts followed by an ominous rumble of fear. Ezekiel's questions float by: 'Are you rolling with your fingers crossed? What *do* you have time for?'

He runs his hand over his head. "Am I going crazy?" he shouts to the empty room. Desperate to quiet the chaos, he sits in his favorite chair, the old rocker with the cushioned seat, and puts on his noise-canceling headphones. Connecting it to his phone, he locates his playlist on a music app and selects "Cantus Arcticus" by the Finnish composer Einojuhani Rautavaara. It's an orchestral work in which recorded sounds of birds indigenous to Northern Finland are intermingled with musical instruments, mostly horns and woodwinds. Closing his eyes and gently rocking, Lenny is soon transported to Lapland and its peaceful environs. He dozes off.

When he opens his eyes, it is quiet, the music having long ended, but it did its job. His internal pandemonium has eased. He realizes what he experienced at The Loft was inconceivable. Of course, he knew attacks happened and people were injured and killed but experiencing such an event was entirely different. He now saw his previous understanding as a sanitized, palatable version of what actually occurs. The recognition of mortal danger, the speed and unpredictability at which things are happening, the sounds and the blood, overwhelm the mind and the senses. He thought about all the school shootings and couldn't imagine what it must be like for the children in these situations and the post-trauma reverberations they would experience.

Lenny knew he wouldn't be able to shake off these feelings but would need to find a way to deal with them. He gets up from his chair wincing from the smarting in his side and slowly walks to the kitchen where he makes himself some coffee. While it is brewing, he puts some oat cereal in a bowl with 2% milk and a sliced banana. As is his habit when eating breakfast, he takes out his iPad and opens a site for the local news. Predictably, yesterday's shooting dominated.

Reading the coverage, Lenny is struck by the superficiality of the reporting. At best, it was a two-dimensional rendering of a three-dimensional experience. Numbers and facts: the place, the time, the number of dead and injured, and the identity of the shooter. Missing were the cries, the gun shots, the chaos, and the fear. He searches the names of the victims hoping to learn about Emily but finds nothing.

When he's finished reading, it dawns on him there was no mention of anyone tripping the shooter. *Probably wasn't noticed in all the mayhem.* He's ok with this. Sticking out his arm without forethought was not an act of bravery, but more like instinct. If he had thought about it, he doubts he would have done anything. It would be inappropriate for him to receive recognition or praise.

The disparity between the news reports and his experience leads him to wonder how such accounts, read daily by millions of people, shape our reality. He recalls a passage from an old book by John Steinbeck called *Log from the Sea of Cortez* in which he describes his experience during an ichthyological research expedition in Baja, California, with his friend, Ed Ricketts, a marine biologist. Lenny often used the passage with students to illustrate the difference between the realities documented in research reports and those of lived experience. He goes to his bookshelf, takes out the book, and turns to the page which he had previously marked with a small post-it note.

> The Mexican Sierra (a fish) has 17 plus 15 plus 9 spines in the dorsal fin. These can be easily counted. But if the Sierra strikes hard on the line so that your hands are burned, if the fish sounds and nearly escapes and finally comes in over the rail, his colors pulsing and his tail beating the air, a whole new relational externality has come into being—an entity which is more than the sum of the fish plus the fisherman. The only way to count the spines of the Sierra unaffected by this second relational reality is to sit in a laboratory, open an evil-smelling jar, remove a stiff colorless fish from the formalin solution, count the spines and write the truth. . . . There you have recorded a reality which cannot be assailed—probably the least important reality concerning either the fish or yourself. It is good to know what you are doing. The man with his pickled fish has set down one truth and has recorded in this experience many lies. The fish is not

that color, that texture, that dead, nor does he smell that way.

Steinbeck's second relational reality with the fish was an apt analogy for what he read. The newspaper report was one reality, but in its reductionism were 'many lies.' He feels a new appreciation of the alienation people who experienced such trauma might feel reading such reports. How could someone who had not been through a similar experience understand what it was like to be at The Loft? How could *he* process what happened? He had no answers.

If his experience at The Loft taught him anything it was that nothing could be taken for granted and disaster could erupt in the most unlikely places. Yet, it would be impossible to live a productive or fulfilling life looking for potential dangers under every rock and around every corner. Somehow you had to be vigilant without allowing it to rule your life. He thought of the saying, commonly heard among his aging peers, that all we have is today. Like many clichés, there was truth in it. But living in the present, as many new-age gurus advised, was challenging.

He remembers a favorite sociology professor from his undergraduate days who contended humans are the only animals who live their most intense experiences in the realm of possibility. It stuck with him at the time and now seemed even more prescient. If anything, as the German sociologist, Ulrich Beck, declared, we are living in a 'risk society' where potential danger is lurking everywhere.

The irony is that as science and technology have become more sophisticated in their attempts to predict and control, the result has been to expand our sense of risk, not diminish it. We worry about things like the cleanliness of our drinking water, the additives in our food, even the air we breathe. Thanks to the media's daily reminders of the perils waiting to strike, the world seems increasingly unpredictable and uncontrollable. Anxiety has become the backdrop of our lives and disasters like what happened at The Loft concretize and magnify these fears.

Railing against his analysis he tells himself, *Yes, life might be fragile and unpredictable, but I will not become a victim. I still have volition and I will exercise it to make choices.*

Ezekiel's question resurfaces: 'What do you have time for?' As Lenny ponders its meaning for him, a favorite song appears, something that often happens. He softly sings a verse.

"I have no time for the veils of violence.

I have no time for walls without release.

I have no time for the smiles of tyrants.

I have all the time in the world for peace."

This is how I must try to live.

Chapter Nine

Jerry felt like he was dreaming. In the blink of an eye, his routine, satisfying life had vanished and been replaced by a living nightmare. All because of a single, deranged person. How could it be? Yet, he could not deny the in-your-face reality of the hospital room where Emily, looking small and frail, was lying as medical personnel performed their tests and life-sustaining protocols. Every time he looked at Emily, he felt tears welling up. His usual stoicism and composure when confronted with difficulties was overmatched by the magnitude and unimaginable turn of events. *How could this be?* his brain kept screaming over and over. Feeling helpless, he turned to his only available option: prayer. And so, he prayed, silently and fervently, for his daughter's recovery.

When Emily was brought into the emergency room, Jerry had no idea if she would survive. The scene was chaotic as other gunshot victims were also being treated. Thankfully, the gravity of Emily's condition was quickly recognized, and she was triaged into a room where a team of people began examining her wounds while hooking her up to an IV and oxygen. As Jerry stood there watching and trembling, the medical team decided to prep Emily for surgery.

A woman who looked young enough to be Jerry's child introduced herself as Dr. Green, the attending physician. She explained they needed to remove the bullet, stop the bleeding, and repair the damage right away if Emily was going to have a chance. Pulling himself together long enough to give consent, Jerry started signing the permission forms with a shaking hand. At that moment, Katie burst into the room.

* * *

Katie was visiting friends when Jerry called. As soon as she heard his voice, she knew something was terribly wrong.

"Jerry, what's the matter?"

"It's Emily," he replied trying unsuccessfully to keep his voice from cracking. "She's been hurt."

"What do you mean?" says Katie her volume rising.

Jerry desperately tries to figure out how to best communicate what happened but realizes there is no sugarcoating this. "As you know, Emily was at The Loft. Some guy came in with a gun and started shooting." Fighting to keep his composure but unable to, he sobs, "She was shot."

"SHOT!" Katie screams. Then in a quiet, trembling voice, "Is she . . ."

"She's alive," Jerry interjects, but you need to come to the university hospital emergency room right away."

"Oh God! I'll be right there." The line goes dead.

Hearing her scream, Katie's three friends rush over to her. "Katie," one says with alarm, "what's wrong?"

"Emily's been shot," answers Katie in a voice that sounds to her like it is coming from another person. Drifting into shock, Katie feels like she has walked into a wall. She is dazed and despite the emergency nature of the situation, she is having trouble moving. One of her friends, recognizing Katie's emotional state would make her a hazard on the road, springs into action and says she will drive her to the hospital. Katie numbly accepts and they leave.

After what feels like an eternity, they arrive at the emergency entrance. Mumbling "thanks" as she opens the car door, Katie runs into the ER, identifies herself, and asks where her daughter is being treated. She's given directions and a minute later enters the room. It takes her a moment to make sense of what was happening. Emily is lying on a bed with medical staff hovering. Although nonresponsive, one of them talks to Emily telling her what they are doing or are about to do. That same person, whom Katie presumes is the ER doc, directs the actions of the others.

Suddenly, the full force of what has happened closes in on her to the point where she isn't breathing. She extends her arm to the wall to keep from falling. At the same time, Jerry sees her and rushes over.

"Katie! Thank God you're here," he sobs, reaching out to hug her. She lifts her free arm. "Jerry. I'm dizzy. Can I sit somewhere?"

"There's a chair right here," he replies, quickly recovering and helping her sit. "Let me get you some water."

While waiting, Katie takes some deep breaths. She tells herself she needs to be fully present for Emily and not be sidetracked by fear. Jerry returns with a bottle of water which she eagerly drinks. Feeling more grounded she shifts her focus to dealing with the situation.

Jerry provides a brief report about what happened. Although shocked by what he tells her, she is now laser-focused and files the information away to a place that will not interfere with being present for her daughter. Katie asks the attending physician who has turned toward them for her assessment of Emily's condition. As expected, it is serious. She has a gunshot wound to the chest and a possible concussion. She has also lost a lot of blood. Nevertheless, given her age and general health, the doctor is guardedly hopeful pending the outcome of the surgery.

She turns to Emily. Cracks begin appearing in her calm façade. She wants to scream 'Why?' and to hold Emily and protect her, but from what? The harm has already been done. Assuming Emily gets through surgery, her role will be to do everything possible to support her recovery.

* * *

The surgery takes about three hours, the equivalent of three days for Katie and Jerry. They are mostly silent during the waiting time, still too stunned and anxious to talk about what had happened. They sit, hold hands, and utter hopeful platitudes for each other and themselves like 'she'll be ok' and 'she's strong.' When the surgeon finally appears, they both attempt to assess the meaning of her facial expression while preparing for the worst. Bracing, they hear her say, "The surgery went well. We were able to remove the bullet and stop the bleeding."

For Katie and Jerry, her words are like the uplifting joyfulness of Mozart's overture to "The Marriage of Figaro" playing in their hearts and bringing tears of relief. As they clutch each other and thank God, the doctor continues, "However"—the music stops—"her condition is serious. She lost a lot of blood, has two broken ribs and a concussion from her head hitting the floor after she was shot. She was fortunate the bullet embedded in the sternum and never entered the chest cavity, but as a precaution, we are going to place her in the ICU for a few days until we are confident she is out of danger."

"Can we see her?" Katie asks.

"As soon as she is out of recovery, a nurse will take you to her room. It will be at least another hour or so this would be a good time to get something to eat or drink."

"Thank you so much, Doctor," says Jerry with Katie nodding her assent.

She leaves and they are alone again. Neither has much of an appetite, but they like the idea of coffee. Jerry volunteers to get it while Katie stays in the waiting room in case they are called earlier than expected.

Returning with coffees in hand, Jerry passes two nurses in conversation. He hears one of them say, "She was in the wrong place at the wrong time."

"It's sad," the other responds. "A nice young woman enjoying an evening out and because of some crazy asshole she ends up fighting for her life."

Chance? Jerry thinks. *Is that what it comes down to? Emily's life may end or be irrevocably changed because of bad luck? Is the kind of person you are or how you live irrelevant?* An image from his past flickers in the background of his consciousness. It doesn't fully register, but he shudders involuntarily.

Thank goodness, I have Katie. Despite her fear, grief, and shock, she was functioning, at least outwardly, a lot better than him. She seemed to understand they needed to transcend the avalanche of emotions in order to assess information from the medical staff and make informed decisions about Emily's care. Watching Katie deal with the situation filled his heart with love and admiration, and gave him the strength to join with her in addressing these painful but necessary tasks.

* * *

Their first reactions on seeing Emily was relief—she was alive—coupled with immense sadness and fear. Although they would have sacrificed their own lives to ensure her recovery, there was not much they could do other than keep a vigil by her bedside. Emily did not appear to be conscious but they spoke to her anyway, repeating "we love you" and "you are going to be ok." Then they would turn away and cry softly.

The next day is spent watching, praying, and talking with medical staff. Then just before seven o'clock in the evening, Emily opened her eyes. At first, Jerry and Katie are silent, not sure if Emily knew where she was or if she was cognizant of what had happened. But before they can decide, Emily turns her head slightly in their direction and in a barely audible voice says, "Where am I?"

Hearing those three whispered words makes them want to dance and applaud but fearing they might overwhelm Emily, they rein in their euphoria and softly tell her where she is and how she got there carefully choosing their words so as not to unduly alarm her, something they find difficult to do without lying. As a compromise, they tell Emily a redacted version of the events, omitting what they believe would be the most upsetting details. It was hard to know how Emily was processing what they were saying. She didn't react in any demonstrable way, but for now, it seemed to suffice.

Katie and Jerry maintain their bedside vigil scrupulously searching for signs of improvement. After watching Emily sleep for an hour, Jerry stands and goes into the hallway to stretch his legs and fortify himself with coffee. It's quiet save for the soft beeping of monitors and the chatter of staff at the nurses' station. Nearing the visitors' lounge, he feels his phone vibrating in his pocket. He has not been answering calls, but this one is from Lenny so he answers.

"Hi Jerry, it's Lenny. I'm calling to check in on Emily. I hope she is going to be ok."

It was good to hear Lenny's voice. He was grateful Lenny had alerted him about Emily and wanted to thank him.

"Thanks for calling, Lenny, and for contacting me from The Loft. If you hadn't done so there's no telling when we would have heard about her."

"You're welcome. I only wish it wasn't such bad news. How is she doing?"

"Her prognosis is guarded but positive. She had emergency surgery and thank God, they were able to remove the bullet."

Lenny can hear the stress and exhaustion in Jerry's voice. *What a nightmare.* "What is her condition now?"

"She's stable but still critical. She's in the ICU and getting 'round the clock care. The medical staff has been great. We're hopeful but cautious." His composure unraveling, he adds, "I know you're not religious Lenny but pray for Emily."

"I will," says Lenny. *What difference does it make if I believe or not. It only matters that Jerry believes.*

"How are you and Katy and Danny holding up?"

"It's been rough. To say this was unexpected would be a gross understatement. Your child shot? Nothing prepares you for this. Emily and Katy are very close so it hit her extra hard. But we're a tight-knit family and supporting each other."

"You have a great family, Jerry. Is there anything I can do?"

"Thanks, but for now just keep us in your prayers. If anything comes up, I'll let you know."

"Would it be alright for me to check in again in a couple of days?"

"Yes, that would be fine. Er . . . Lenny, sorry but I've got to go."

"Ok," says Lenny feeling like he might have talked too long. "Hang in there my friend. I will be in touch."

Jerry goes to the Keurig machine and brews a cup of coffee. As he waits, he reflects on the phone call and realizes he hadn't asked Lenny about himself. Absorbed in his personal worry and grief he had overlooked how Lenny might have been affected by what happened. Had he been injured? It must have been traumatic. He considers calling him back but feels too depleted to do so. The immediate situation demands all his energy. He tells himself the next time they speak he will ask him about his experience and how he is coping.

At some point, I too will need to process what happened and what it means for my life going forward. And when I do, Lenny is the person I want to talk with.

Returning to the hospital room with two coffees, he sees Katie still sitting next to Emily's bed holding her hand. There's a half-smile on Emily's face that fills him with joy. He walks over to her bedside. "Hello, my Emily." She makes eye contact and blesses him with a slightly bigger smile. At that moment, he knows she will be ok.

Chapter Ten

Emily begins to recover. On day three, the medical staff determines she has improved sufficiently to be transferred out of the ICU to a regular care floor. If her progress continues, she could be discharged in another three days. Although full recovery would take several weeks, she could recuperate at home.

In contrast to her cautiously optimistic physical prognosis, Emily's emotional healing was less easy to predict. She remembered little of what happened other than being at The Loft and having a vague awareness of some sort of commotion. Her next memory was opening her eyes, feeling confusion and pain, and seeing her mother at her bedside. Although her parents filled her in on the circumstances that led to her being in the hospital and subsequent surgery, for Emily these were shadow events, disconnected from conscious memory.

After returning home, she did research to try to fill in the gaps. Newspaper reports helped some but also confronted her with the grislier details omitted in her parents' account. She was shocked by the carnage: six dead, eleven wounded. According to the reports, the number would have been higher had the shooter not tripped and been restrained by several patrons who held him until the police arrived.

She read about the perpetrator; a young man named Jeremy Larsen who had ties to various hate groups. A police photo showed an unremarkable-looking man in his early twenties, clean-shaven with short brown hair. His eyes had a blank stare and there were noticeable bruises on his face presumably from the fall and pummeling he received at the club. To Emily, his nondescript appearance made him scarier. *He could be anyone.* Although he was being held on multiple murder charges and possibly hate crimes, police spokespersons had not provided a clear motive for what he did. Most speculated it was connected to his belief that the people who frequented The Loft were primarily Jews, Blacks, and Communists who, in his deranged mind, were a threat to decent, white Americans.

How sick, Emily thought. She despaired the current state of society where mass shootings were becoming almost commonplace. But it was not surprising given a president who refuses to condemn these violent groups, and a partisan Congress and supreme court unwilling to provide a counterbalance to the executive branch. *So much for the separation of powers. It's no wonder so many young people feel cynical and alienated. Add to this a popular culture that glorifies violence and easy access to guns and you get incidents like The Loft. After I'm well, I'm going to get involved with groups pushing for social change. I'll bet there will be some at the university. Maybe I'll even work on getting Mom, Dad, and Danny to be more socially active,* a thought that brought a slight smile to her face.

Pain in her chest pulls her from these hopeful thoughts and

surfaces feelings of vulnerability, fearfulness, and reluctance to leave the house. She looks around her room at the reminders of happier times. Next to her bed is a family photograph taken a few years ago during a trip out West. They were at Cannon Beach, a beautiful town on the Oregon coast. She remembers the wildness of the Pacific Ocean, the hypnotic movement of the surf, the sounds of sea birds, and the occasional sighting of a seal. She sees herself running along the sand with Danny, laughing and untroubled. She sighs. *So many happy memories.* Tears form in her eyes as she realizes such carefreeness no longer seemed possible.

She wonders what will happen after her physical injuries heal. Will she be able to resume the life she had before? The future felt uncertain and scary. Despite her fuzzy recollection of what happened at The Loft, the last two nights were marked by terrifying dreams of which she could recall only screaming and fear. Was this to be her life now? A tormented and reclusive young woman struggling to get through each day? She prayed it would not be the case.

* * *

Since returning home, Emily had received numerous texts from friends unaware she had been injured, asking why she's been absent from school. She also heard from friends who had been at The Loft expressing their concern and wondering how she was doing. It felt good to know she had people in her life who cared about her, but she was not ready to correspond with them. She did not have the energy and any sort of venturing out, even virtually, felt too risky. For the time being, remaining at home with her family was all she could manage.

As she is ruminating on these thoughts, she becomes aware of tapping on her door followed by her mother's soft voice, "Emily, are you awake?"

"Yes, Mom."

"Can I come in?"

"Sure."

"Hi, sweetheart. How are you feeling?"

Her mom looks so tired. *I'm not going to overburden her.* "Not too bad, although my head still hurts. Is it time for me to take more of those pain pills?"

"About another fifteen minutes," answers Katie. "Is it ok if I sit with you for a bit?"

"That would be nice."

Katie and Jerry could see Emily's struggles were not confined to her injuries. However, while she was healing, they would just continue being loving and positive and not push her to talk about anything she did not initiate. Taking Emily's hand, Katie says, "I know you are struggling Emily, and feel scared about the future, but I want you to know you will get through this and that Dad and I will be with you all the way."

"Thanks, Mom," says Emily, managing a feeble smile. While grateful for her family's support, she didn't need them to keep repeating the same lines of encouragement. As much as she loved them, her sense of uncertainty and pervasive anxiety were not assuaged by their optimistic outlook. She was scared and in pain and glossing over it did not make it go away.

"Just take all the time you need, sweetie, and let us know if there's anything we can do."

Katie's desire to help her daughter, to make it all ok, consumed her, but she felt woefully inadequate. Her maternal instincts told her to tell Emily she loved her, that she had her unconditional support, and she believed things would get better. Now it was Katie's turn to look around the room taking in mementos of her daughter's life from happier times: ribbons and trophies from sporting events, her artwork, photographs, and souvenirs from family vacations. Each memento indexed years gone by yet sitting here it felt like an instant.

Emily's voice returns her to the present.

"Mom, do you think I can have that pain pill now," says Emily closing her eyes and thinking, *how much time will I need before I become normal again? Forever?*

Chapter Eleven

Jerry is struggling. Without warning, his assumptive world shattered. He had taken for granted life would continue on its current trajectory, scripted by society for educated, middle-class people like him. Now it was in shambles.

Or was it? He tells himself to be rational. Emily will heal and things will return to normal. Life will go on as before. But a lingering doubt scratches at his consciousness telling him things have irrevocably changed and he's going to have to figure out how to realign his life to accommodate those changes. And deeper still is the ominous sense, that like with his younger brother, he failed once again.

He carries this internal struggle through his waking hours and even into his dreams which have become uncharacteristically dark and foreboding. Worrying about Emily, worrying about Katie and Danny, worrying about what was happening to life as he knew it while trying to maintain a façade of the calm, optimistic father, and husband, depleted his emotional resources.

Gradually, it became clear he could not undo what had happened and life had changed. But what would it become? The question frightens him. Changes were afoot, but where they would lead seemed unknowable. He tells himself that he needs to guide his family out of this nightmare but is unsure how to even help himself. He knew he could share his feelings with Katie, but she too was struggling and he did not want to increase her emotional load. He could think of only one good option.

I'll call Lenny.

* * *

"Hello?" says a sleepy Lenny.

Hearing Lenny's voice, Jerry realizes he has forgotten he's been out of bed since the middle of the night. He checks the time; a few minutes before six in the morning.

"Hi Lenny, it's Jerry. Sorry for calling so early."

"Jerry!" Lenny exclaims, his sleepiness replaced with alarm. "Is everything alright?"

"Yes. I didn't mean to wake you. I haven't been sleeping well and lost track of the time. I can call back later."

"No, no, it's ok," says a relieved Lenny. "I'm an early riser. Glad you called."

Dismayed by yet another reminder of how much he was off his game, he nevertheless finds Lenny's voice comforting.

"I'm not surprised you're having trouble sleeping. You've had the rug pulled out from under you."

When Jerry doesn't respond he asks, "Um . . . so how is Emily?" feeling his blood pressure rise with each word.

"She's not out of the woods, but she's making progress."

Lenny lets out a long exhale realizing he had been holding his breath in expectation of hearing something catastrophic. He manages to say, "That's wonderful news. You must have all been so worried."

"We still are, but it's good to have her home and to be able to care for her."

"You're all going to need some time to recover from what happened."

"True. It has thrown my life into chaos . . . which is why I called."

I knew there was something.

"I think it would be helpful to talk this through. Would you be willing to meet?"

"Definitely," replies Lenny without hesitation. "Just let me know where and when."

"How about tomorrow at ten at The Grounds."

"Works for me. See you then."

I hope I can be helpful. I'll have to work on being a better listener.

Then another thought intrudes. *I didn't get shot, but I would have appreciated some acknowledgment that I too might be struggling.*

Well, that was self-centered. Maybe I am hurting more than I want to admit. I can't fall into an exclusive helper role again. I'll need to find a way to address my own needs too.

* * *

Lenny wants to know more about Jeremy Larsen, the person who brought such pain and suffering to so many people. He goes to his computer and googles his name. He gets over 20,000 hits. Adding conditionals to his search, he finds the only Jeremy Larsen arrested for a mass shooting. More digging reveals Jeremy was from a small town in Iowa called Centerville, the hub of a dairy farming community. He also learns Jeremy spent most of his formative years in the foster care system, following the murder-suicide of his parents when he was seven.

Jeremy's biological father had been an accountant for a farm equipment firm until he got caught skimming money from his employer to support his drinking and gambling habits. While out on bail awaiting trial, he embarked on a drinking binge resulting in a deadly confrontation with his wife and his suicide.

Seven-year-old Jeremy was in the house at the time and is believed to have witnessed the deaths. A neighbor who heard the gunshots called the police who found the couple sprawled in their bedroom. Their son, still in pajamas, was curled in a fetal position sobbing softly on the living room floor.

Lenny pauses thinking how horrific the experience must have been for little Jeremy. *It's not surprising he was so troubled. I wonder if he was aware that he was reproducing the same kind of horror for others. I doubt it.*

After the death of his parents, there was an attempt to place Jeremy with relatives. Unfortunately, his parents had so estranged themselves from other family members that no one was willing to take Jeremy into their home. The only alternative was foster care.

Soon after his first placement, Jeremy started manifesting signs of emotional disturbance: flat affect interspersed with angry outbursts, nightmares, and behavior problems at school. After four months, his foster parents asked that he be removed. And so began a succession of foster homes culminating in his placement in a residential treatment facility where he remained until age eighteen when he 'aged out' of the system.

Jeremy was described as a loner who was socially ostracized by his peers. Former teachers portrayed him as bright but disengaged and moody. A foster parent who claimed Jeremy had killed their parakeet, characterized him as a cauldron always on the verge of boiling over. In Lenny's experience, these were all signs of a deeply troubled youngster with the potential for violence. *Of course,* he tells himself, *hindsight is always 20-20.*

Jeremy's story was sadly familiar to Lenny who had worked in the child welfare system before becoming an academic. He noticed from some photos that Jeremy seemed below average height and had a slight physique. *A small kid with poor social skills; the perfect target for acting out and bullying peers.*

Reading about Jeremy surfaces memories of Lenny's first post-graduate job working with adolescent boys in a residential treatment facility euphemistically called 'The Children's Home.' Formerly an orphanage, the facility's centerpiece was a late 19th century, ornate, Italianate-style mansion in vogue during that period. By the time Lenny worked there, it had fallen into disrepair to the point where it should have been condemned. The residents had been relocated to newer, one-level brick cottages; however, the old building still housed some staff offices and two 'classrooms'—bedrooms during the orphanage days—for those boys judged unable to participate in the public school system, usually for behavioral reasons. Lenny had been assigned to one of these classrooms, a dreary, ten-by-twelve-foot room with institutional green walls and one small window. It was the antithesis of an environment conducive to learning or the promotion of self-esteem—precisely what these boys did not need.

Despite their youth, many of the residents had appalling life stories of abuse and neglect. That they survived at all was a measure of their strength, but they paid a price: lack of trust, a negative self-image, anger, and a host of social-psychological issues. For many, survival also meant developing extreme types of coping like dissociation and unsavory forms of manipulation ranging from compulsive lying to threats of physical harm.

Fresh out of college, Lenny's idealism was no match for their con artist skills which sometimes left him licking his wounds after learning what he thought was progress was him being scammed. The most challenging kids were the quiet ones who were like dormant volcanoes, compliant on the surface but ready to erupt without warning. And when they did, the fury that poured forth could be shocking.

Helping these kids to accept they were now in a safe environment and there were more constructive ways to deal with their challenges was difficult, requiring patience, persistence, and consistency. Also, for boys like Jeremy who were slight of stature and socially awkward, the environment of the treatment center was *not* safe and they continued to suffer abuse. This made it nearly impossible to develop a trusting relationship.

Lenny lasted two years before the demands and stress of the job became too much for him. The final straw came when he tried to break up a fight between two of the boys and wound up getting hit over the head with a chair. Ten stitches and a throbbing headache later, he decided he had enough. Still, he felt sad knowing this option was not available to the residents.

* * *

We are first and foremost social beings. Hostile environments, rejection, and social exclusion make people like Jeremy vulnerable to the lure of groups that embody their alienation and anger. In return, these groups provide a rationale for their circumstances, relationships, acceptance, and a sense of purpose. It's a complementary but dysfunctional relationship.

 Lenny felt conflicted about Jeremy. He had sympathy for Jeremy's traumatic childhood and dreadful life. He was not born a killer. How would he have turned out if his life circumstances had been different? At the same time, he held him responsible for his actions. What he had done could never be condoned or rationalized. *What kind of society turns innocent children into killers? This is the larger tragedy,* thought Lenny. Hidden behind the myths of American exceptionalism and the sanctity of the nuclear family, thousands of children are neglected, abused, and subject to horrors often at the hands of their parents or others they trust. For Jeremy, like the children at the treatment facility, survival came at a cost not only for him but for his victims. *Just a terrible tragedy on so many levels,* he thinks shaking his head, *and with no ending in sight.*

Chapter Twelve

Lenny is anxious about meeting with Jerry. He wants to support his friend in whatever way he can but worries his own reaction to the shooting might get in the way. Typically, Jerry would be the person with whom he would process his unresolved issues, but this situation was anything but typical. He would have to find someone else.

Arriving at the Holy Grounds coffee shop, Lenny sees Jerry already seated in their usual booth in the back. As he approaches, he notices Jerry looks haggard. His always clean and pressed clothes are wrinkled and there is a stain on his shirt. Lenny blinks hard to make sure his eyes are not deceiving him. They're not. Jerry's face has the stubble of several days' growth, there are bags under his eyes, and his expression alternates between distraction and pain.

Unnerved by Jerry's appearance, Lenny begins cautiously. "It's good to see you Jerry and to know Emily is going to be ok."

Jerry grimaces as if trying to appear normal but not quite succeeding. "Good to see you too. I just wish it could be under different circumstances."

Hearing the pain in Jerry's voice reminds Lenny that the victims of Jeremy Larsen's actions went well beyond the physically injured.

The extent of the social and psychological impact would never be known but would show up in other guises like depression, divorce, and even suicide. He didn't think such consequences were inevitable; there are always some who rise from the ashes of adversity and find new meaning in their lives but they are the minority. And his friend is hurting.

"I can't imagine the nightmare you all have gone through," says Lenny. "I know it's a cliché, but time does heal." Tangentially addressing Jerry's appearance he adds, "For now, it's important to remember to take care of yourself even while you are caring for others." *Yes, Lenny, take your own advice.*

"You may be right about time," says Jerry, ignoring Lenny's other comment, "but it doesn't feel like that. I still can't believe what happened. Sure, as a parent I worry about my kids and the things that could happen to them, but never this."

Jerry twists his napkin. He feels like he's reliving the past. Another failure to protect someone he loves. He wants to talk with Lenny but doesn't know how. A tense silence settles over them. Then without looking up Jerry murmurs, "I'm a jumble of emotions. I'm sad and worried about Emily, but there's also Katie and Danny. They're struggling too. And . . ."

He pauses in a way Lenny feels presages something important.

"And . . ." Jerry's fingers curl into fists, his mouth contorts, and his eyes have a venomous look Lenny has never seen or could imagine seeing.

"And I'm angry, *really angry* at that fucking psychopath who did this."

Lenny is dumbstruck by Jerry's rage. He's never even heard

him curse before. It's like he is being channeled by an apoplectic version of himself. Unsure how to respond, he tries redirecting the conversation.

"Your feelings are understandable. It's an overwhelming situation. But update me about Emily."

It's an awkward segue but seems to transform Jerry's wrath into sadness.

In a low, tortured-sounding voice, Jerry says, "She's a strong person, but this was overwhelming. Her physical wounds will heal, but it's the emotional damage I am most worried about. When I sit with her, she tries to put on a good face, but I can see how she is struggling to make sense out of what happened."

Holding back tears he adds, "It breaks my heart."

Lenny knows there are no magic words that will return their lives to how it was before The Loft, but he can offer sincerity and friendship. "I am so sorry, Jerry. You're probably right about Emily. Trying to find meaning in a random act is important for her and all of you, but it's difficult and takes time.

Many years ago, a close friend of mine was killed in a freak accident when a balcony railing he was leaning against, collapsed. To me, my friend was a paragon of virtue, someone who exemplified the kind of caring, sensitive, and compassionate life I wished I could live. Then suddenly for no good reason, his life was snuffed out. How could that be? I kept asking myself. Was there no justice in the universe? Is daily life just a spin of some cosmic roulette wheel? It took me a long time to come to terms with this."

"What helped you?" asks Jerry.

"For me, it was accepting that every day numerous things

happen we cannot control. Some are consequential for our lives and some are not. Their meaning and impact are influenced by our time of life, our location, our history, and our relationships, but we still have choices about how to respond."

Listen to me. Dispensing didactic advice as if Jerry could put his feelings aside and rationally figure out how to feel better. Do I really believe this will help him, or is it my way of maintaining emotional distance from my unresolved issues related to the shooting?

He tries amending his advice. "This helped me in the long run, but at the time of the accident, I was too distraught to think it through in this way. I guess I'm trying to give you the benefit of my hindsight."

Continuing to twist his now spiral-shaped napkin, Jerry does not look relieved.

"What about God? How could a loving, omniscient God allow such a thing to happen to a sweet, kind, innocent girl like Emily? I feel betrayed. I've done my best to be a good Christian. I try to follow the Golden Rule, not perfectly, but who does? And the result? My daughter's life is nearly destroyed."

Lenny knows his typical analytic take on things is not what Jerry needs. *Maybe something physical like going for a run would help, or something that appeals to his religious beliefs, like talking with a spiritual advisor.* With that last thought in mind, he says, "Are you familiar with Harold Kushner's book, *When Bad Things Happen to Good People*?"

"I've heard of it, but never read it," replies Jerry, sullenly.

"Kushner is a rabbi whose son died at fourteen of progeria, a disease that causes premature aging. The book, which came out a few years after his son's death, is about his struggle with suffering, evil, and God."

"Yeah, so?" says Jerry looking impatient or possibly irritated.

Lenny is taken aback by his so un-Jerry-like response but decides to ignore it and continue.

"Kushner asks the same question you did. How could God allow good people to be subject to such misfortune and suffering? After much contemplation, he comes to the position that God is not omniscient. There are laws of nature and human volition, and God doesn't control the everyday occurrences of our lives.

"For Kushner, there is no inherent meaning in the things that happen, rather we give them meaning by how we respond to them. We can't change the past, but we can decide how to go on. I have the book at home if you're interested."

"Perhaps another time. I don't think I'm there yet. I feel too full of sadness, anger, and . . . this might sound weird, but even guilt at not being able to prevent what happened."

"Not weird at all," says Lenny sympathetically. "It's not uncommon to cycle through a range of emotions. Eventually, you will be able to move on even if it doesn't seem like that now. For the present, it may be best to focus on caring for Emily, your family, and yourself. It's all interconnected. Just as you are kind to them, be kind to yourself."

Jerry nods, his torment seeming assuaged by Lenny's advice. "I know you're trying to help, Lenny, and I appreciate it. Thanks for talking with me."

Lenny feels relieved by the shift in mood although not convinced he was very helpful. He says "Let's do it again next week or earlier if you want. Just let me know."

"Ok." Jerry gets up and leaves, his napkin in shreds.

* * *

Lenny remains in the booth. He looks across the table at Jerry's napkin, an artifact of his emotional state. He's worried but doesn't know what else he can do. Inserting himself into Jerry's life can be counterproductive if the support he is offering does not match what he needs. He recalls when he was mourning his friend and a well-meaning colleague kept offering advice about how to cope when all he wanted was someone to listen.

I need to let Jerry be the guide. But what if he's so distraught he doesn't know what he wants? Thank goodness, he has his family. Something like this can bring a family closer or it can tear them apart. I hope it's the former.

A wave of fatigue passes through him, *God I'm tired. I should take some of my own advice about self-care. I'm scared, I'm sad, and barely able to concentrate for any length of time. But unlike Jerry, what troubles me most is what could have happened to me. I could have died!*

His hands shaking, Lenny gets up and leaves.

* * *

Lenny feels the need to speak with someone about his own experience at the Loft and its repercussions. He's already ruled out Jerry and his other close friends are too far away to provide the face-to-face encounter he desires. *Should I talk with a therapist?* It's an option, but one he feels ambivalent about. *I don't want my experience to be converted into psychological categories.*

He recalls a psychologist, Stuart Gifford, whom he met at a university-sponsored event for present and former faculty. They had an enjoyable conversation and Gifford impressed him with his insights on various social issues.

I'll give him a call. What's the worst that can happen? If I see him and it doesn't feel right, I just won't return.

Knowing any delay will lessen the chances of following through, Lenny finds his number and calls. He gets Gifford's voice mail assuring him that his call is important and will be returned as soon as possible followed by the ubiquitous option to leave a message after the beep.

"Hello er . . . Stuart—*Should I have said Dr. Gifford?*—this is Lenny Isaacson. I don't know if you remember me. We met about a year ago at a university function in the alumni building. We talked about book projects we were considering. Um . . . I'm calling now about a different matter. You undoubtedly heard about the recent shooting at The Loft. Well, I was there. Fortunately, I escaped injury but the experience has been emotionally challenging. I think it could be helpful to talk about it, so I'd like to make an appointment to see you. Hope to hear from you soon."

While waiting for a return call, Lenny makes himself something to eat and feeds Sisu. About an hour and a half later, his phone rings.

"Hello, is this Lenny Isaacson?"

"Yes."

"This is Stuart Gifford returning your call."

"Thanks for getting back to me. Do you remember me?"

"I do. And I remember enjoying our conversation. In your message you said you were at The Loft when the shooting happened.

"Yes, I was."

"It must have been very frightening. An experience like that can be overwhelming, so I'm glad you called. I had a cancellation for tomorrow at 10 a.m. Are you available then?"

"I am. See you tomorrow."

Ok, that's done. For a moment he feels good about following through, then his ambivalence about seeing a therapist resurfaces.

Will examining myself through a narrow lens of psychological concepts be helpful or harmful? Also, the relationship is inherently asymmetrical—the expert and the person with a problem—a contrived, commercial transaction that buys me a limited time to talk.

On the other hand, I might be judging Gifford prematurely. Perhaps initially meeting as colleagues at the university will somewhat equalize the relationship.

True, we were peers in that situation, but in therapy I am the client and he is the therapist.

Ok, so what's the alternative? If not a therapist or a friend, then who can I talk to?

When no answer appears, he decides to give himself a break and take a shower. Besides cleaning up, which will make him feel better, he's had some of his best ideas when standing under streaming hot water.

Ten minutes into the shower, Lenny begins to relax. He closes his eyes and lets his mind drift. However, rather than taking him to some island paradise, he returns to his internal dialogue.

What is the risk of seeing Gifford?

Not much, wasted time, him saying things that upset me.

Then why do I feel so anxious about it? Am I'm afraid he'll diagnose me and by doing so create another problem? After all, he is a psychologist.

But really, are you going to cede so much authority to him at your first meeting? You're spending one hour, fifty minutes actually, with this guy. Nothing is risk-free. Changing your mind and not keeping the appointment could also become a problem.

So, what are the upsides?

How about the obvious? That talking to him will be helpful. It's why I called in the first place.

Ok, I'll keep the appointment.

* * *

Lenny rises early. After completing his morning routines, he tries to pass the time before his appointment by reading but has trouble focusing. He opens a solitaire game on his tablet and mindlessly plays one game after another. Finally, about thirty minutes before his appointment and feeling restless, he leaves. The office is only a fifteen-minute drive, but he rationalizes that you can't predict unexpected traffic or parking problems. Neither occurs and he arrives early.

Gifford's practice is housed in an unremarkable, three-story brick building, one you might find in Anywhere, USA. Not wanting to walk in early lest he appear desperate, Lenny sits restlessly in his car for a few minutes before entering. He locates the office on the directory in the lobby. It's one flight up and he takes the stairs. He enters a small waiting room that like the building is nondescript: four standard, blue fabric chairs with wooden frames, a low, horizontal table scattered with magazines ranging from *National Geographic* to

Sports Illustrated, and some stock nature prints on the wall. There's no receptionist so Lenny takes a seat.

A minute or two before his appointed time, a door opens and Dr. Gifford appears. "Hello, Lenny," he says with a smile. "Come on in."

Gifford looks like Lenny remembers him: mid-fifties, about 5'10", average build, dark, medium length hair thinning on top, and clean-shaven. He's neatly but casually dressed: khaki pants and a lightweight tan V-neck sweater over a light blue shirt. The office is of moderate size. There's a desk with a computer against an inner wall towards the back, a couple of chairs facing a three-person leather couch framed by two small end tables in front. On one table there's a digital clock and on the other a box of tissues. A window on the side wall opposite the door has a view of the parking lot.

Gifford sits in one of the chairs and gestures for Lenny to take a seat. Always conscious of status differences, Lenny chooses the opposite chair rather than the couch. "So, you were at the Loft when the shooting occurred. That must have been frightening," says Gifford repeating what he said on the phone.

"Yes, it was," says Lenny thinking, *He starts with an obvious statement I will agree with. Isn't that what salespeople do?* Then before going any further, he catches himself. *Stop being so critical or you'll undermine this before giving it a chance.*

"It's the kind of thing you can't imagine ever happening to you, so when it does it's both horrific and surreal."

"Can you elaborate?" asks Gifford.

Lenny shrugs. "It's hard to reduce the feeling to words. I could see someone was shooting people. Yet, despite reading about these things and knowing they happen, the in-the-moment experience was unimaginably different. Like one part of me couldn't register what was happening and that I could be injured or killed, but another part went into survival mode and took over."

Gifford nods. "Were you injured?"

"Only some scrapes and bruises."

"That's fortunate given the number of injuries and fatalities. Can you tell me more about what happened, how the events unfolded, and your reaction to them?"

Lenny takes a deep breath. He realizes he hasn't told anyone his version of the shooting and wonders how much detail he should go into, what he should emphasize, what he should leave out. He's aware Gifford has a pad in his lap and is holding a pen. His internal voice returns. *This isn't good, I'm already editing what I will say. Just talk and see what happens.*

Lenny describes the events beginning with his decision to go to the Loft. He tells Gifford about the moment he became aware something unusual was happening, hearing screams, and seeing a person with a gun shooting people. He describes how he dove to the ground and lay there praying he would be spared and how without thinking he grabbed the gunman's ankle causing him to fall and drop his gun allowing others to subdue and hold him until the police arrived.

He recounts seeing Emily when he first arrived and then later after she had been badly wounded. His voice quavers when describing watching the paramedics working on her, then calling Jerry, and seeing him burst into the room as they were taking Emily to the ambulance. Finally, he tells of his decision to walk home feeling dazed and how he's been trying to cope ever since.

While he's talking, Gifford occasionally nods and takes notes. He wishes he could see what Gifford considers noteworthy. *Will he reconstruct a psychological narrative from these notes?*

When Lenny stops, Gifford thanks him for sharing his experience. "It's understandable you find yourself struggling with memories and feelings related to the event. It would be more worrisome if you were feeling nothing at all. Can you tell me about how you're feeling now?"

"My thoughts and emotions are in flux," says Lenny. "One moment I feel scared, then lucky, then apprehensive, then confused. I keep seeing images of dead and injured people and the shock and terror on the faces of those present. I'm also worried about Emily and my friend Jerry; he's having a hard time coping with what happened to his daughter."

Paraphrasing, Gifford says, "You're sorting through a lot of thoughts and feelings, trying to process what happened, and worrying about your friend and his daughter." He pauses and Lenny nods affirmatively.

"It's a lot to manage. Have you been able to sleep, okay?"

"Pretty much. I think at this point my exhaustion overcomes my anxiety although I've had some scary dreams." He notices Gifford making a note.

"That wouldn't be unusual. As you probably know, dreams are our mind's way of processing experience. They can also be a way of working through problems. There's a view called threat stimulation theory that proposes dreams are a way of preparing us to deal with threats and dangers."

"Yes, but they're not only about what happened, It feels like old stuff being dragged up," says Lenny who proceeds to tell him about the dream of being lost.

Again, Gifford makes a note. "Dreams are tricky to interpret. They're fraught with symbolism and don't necessarily follow rational timelines. When you're distraught or have had a traumatic experience, those feelings can be expressed in multiple ways including themes from your past. Some people think recurring themes like being lost suggest unresolved issues that reappear when you are experiencing stress."

"Sounds reasonable," says Lenny, although interpreting dreams seems a bit like crystal ball readings.

Returning to what happened at The Loft, Gifford says, "You mentioned tripping the shooter. I don't recall reading any mention of you. Did you tell anyone about your part in this?"

"No."

"How come? It sounds like you risked your life to save others."

"I wouldn't frame it that way. I acted without thinking. There was no plan or intent on my part. Until I make sense of it myself, I don't feel comfortable going public and risk being portrayed as someone I am not. I want to stay in control of my image."

Gifford writes in his pad. "Is feeling in control important for you?"

Boing! A red flag goes up for Lenny. *Here we go*, he thinks, his anxiety rising. *I said a loaded word, 'control,' and now I will have to walk back from all the psychological baggage it suggests.*

"No, it's not a big issue," responds Lenny hoping to end this line of questioning.

"Uh-huh," says Gifford making a quick note.

He must use a kind of shorthand that allows him to reconstruct what was said.

"Are there other things related to the shooting you want to discuss at this time?" asks Gifford.

Glad for the opportunity to change the subject, Lenny says, "Well, I'm not sure this is central, but I did some checking on the shooter. Maybe it's the social worker in me, but he had quite a troubled childhood, something I am all too familiar with through my previous work in child welfare. Reading about him reminded me of kids I worked with who grew up never knowing love or trust. This makes them very vulnerable to the appeals of extremist groups. The promise of belonging plus the chance to express your anger at real or imaginary others is a lure many cannot resist."

"I agree. Has that understanding influenced how you feel about him?" Gifford says, returning the focus to Lenny.

"Yes, along with my anger I feel sad. I believe he is responsible for what he did, but in a different way he too was a victim. In the larger sense, we are all responsible."

Gifford nods but doesn't follow up, asking instead how Lenny was taking care of himself since the Loft. Lenny talks about doing things he finds relaxing like listening to music and walking Sisu. He keeps his responses brief not feeling ready to divulge too much personal information.

Near the end of the session, Gifford asks if Lenny thinks his anxiety, nightmares, and flashbacks might be symptoms of PTSD.

An even bigger red flag appears.

This time he responds forcefully. "No. What I'm experiencing are the consequences of a highly unusual and extremely frightening experience."

"I agree," says Gifford earnestly. "But it is precisely those kinds of experiences—the ones that go beyond our coping resources—that lead to PTSD. I hear your reluctance to consider this, but there are advantages to identifying what is going on."

"That would depend on whether you are correct," answers Lenny, feeling defensive. "But I would prefer you not presume it is true for me."

Appearing to acquiesce, Gifford backs off from this line of questioning, although not from his note taking. Still, Gifford's possible diagnosis has Lenny wondering how his words are being interpreted.

He recalls a research study done in the early 1980s in which eight people purposefully tried to get themselves admitted to psychiatric hospitals. They all claimed the same symptoms, hearing voices that said 'empty, nothing, and thud,' chosen to mimic an 'existential psychosis,' a condition that did not exist. Beyond these voices, they were truthful about their life histories. All were admitted with serious diagnoses such as schizophrenia. Once on the ward, the pseudo patients dropped all symptoms; however, this did not result in their expeditious release. Rather, they learned when you are in an 'insane place' anything you do or say can be interpreted as supporting your diagnosis. When one of them took notes for their research about what they observed, it was recorded in their chart as 'patient engages in note-taking behavior' as if this was a symptom of a bigger problem.

Should I ask Gifford if I could see his notes? Would my request be interpreted as a kind of paranoia? He decides it's not worth the trouble.

The session ends with Gifford saying he was glad Lenny called and that he believes further sessions could be helpful.

Feeling ambivalent Lenny says, "How about two weeks from now? I need some time to reflect."

They make an appointment.

*　*　*

Lenny drives out of the parking lot mulling over the session. It felt good to express his thoughts and feelings aloud, but he needed more than a sounding board. And Gifford's suggestion that he might have PTSD was off-putting. Ever wary of the medical model, Lenny believed labeling his experience in such a way could shut out other, less pathologizing explanations and lead him in a direction he did not want to go.

Gifford's likable and smart, but is talking with a therapist my best alternative? Perhaps I can find someone with whom I could have an authentic relationship rather than one that is contrived or commercial. Someone not tied to a particular way of understanding but who can see things from multiple perspectives. Someone whose life experience enables them to understand pain and how to move on from it. Someone who can offer wisdom rather than psychology.

His route home takes him past the Holy Grounds coffee shop. Seeing it elicits a craving for their great coffee, much better than what he drinks at home. Like a horse following a well-trodden trail, he turns left into the parking lot.

Opening the heavy, rustic, wooden door he notices there are relatively few customers. *Must be the hour. Too early for the lunch crowd.* Out of habit, he gravitates toward his usual booth near the back and is surprised to see it occupied by a single male nursing a beverage. He peers more closely while trying to be inconspicuous. The man appears to be mid-fifties, pale-complexioned, clean-shaven, with short brown hair and tortoise shell glasses. Lenny notices the sleeves of his blue, button-down oxford shirt are fastened with shiny gold cufflinks. He is about to sit in a different booth when the person looks up and makes brief eye contact. He immediately thinks of Ezekiel but dismisses it as a figment of his overactive imagination.

Get a hold of yourself, Lenny! This guy is smartly dressed and well-groomed, definitely not a street person. Nevertheless, instead of sitting, he walks to the bathroom, a route that takes him past the back booth. As he passes, he steals a glance. There's a certain likeness but . . .

"Hello Lenny," says a familiar voice.

He freezes mid-step. It's him.

Lenny does an about-face. "Ezekiel?" he says in disbelief. On top of everything else he's been dealing with, it is too much to process. The room wobbles and he fears he might fall. He manages to sit down opposite Ezekiel. *Maybe I do have PTSD.*

Still not quite believing his eyes or ears, Lenny stares at him. Ezekiel returns his eye contact and smiles as if meeting like this is a common occurrence.

Lenny stammers, "You . . . you look so different!"

"Did you assume I would always look the same?"

"I . . . I guess I did. When we first met, I assumed you were homeless. You were sitting in the street. You were panhandling. Your clothes were dirty. You looked disheveled. What happened?"

Ezekiel considers Lenny with a kind but piercing gaze. "What are assumptions but attempts to impose order on our lives and reduce uncertainty. Would you like some coffee?"

The juxtaposition of these two sentences is further discombobulating. Wanting some distance, he says, "Yes, I'll get some," and without waiting for a reply, he stands and walks to the counter. Unable to shake the feeling this encounter is not real, he glances back at the booth. Ezekiel is still there. H*ow did he go from a bedraggled street person to the person I now see?*

Returning to the booth, Lenny asks again, "please tell me what brought about this change in you."

"Are we not protean beings, shifting, changing, enacting, and reacting?" Ezekiel pauses. "And what of the changes in you?"

Lenny reminds himself that he's not in a typical conversation that follows the implicit rules of social interaction such as when you ask someone a question, they answer you. Although Ezekiel's way of relating can be maddening, it is thought-provoking.

Just go with it and see where it leads.

"Have you heard about the shooting that happened a couple of days ago at the club in town called The Loft?"

"I was there," responds Ezekiel with a pained expression.

Lenny's eyes grow wide. "What"? "You were there?"

"Yes, and it was brave of you to grab the shooter's ankle. You saved many lives."

Feeling like he's on an emotional tilt-a-whirl, Lenny stares at Ezekiel who maintains his serene demeanor. Finally, somewhat rhetorically, Lenny says, "You saw me?"

Ezekiel nods.

"That was nice of you to say but I don't believe bravery had anything to do with it. I just reacted. Since you were there, you know the situation was terrifying. I often feel like I am still there reliving the fear and panic."

"And now you are here and in-between is an abyss," says Ezekiel in a tone somewhere between a statement and a question.

Ezekiel's words evoke a vision of sliding down the side of a mountain. The walls are steep but peppered with tree limbs every few feet. Lenny reaches out hoping they will halt his fall but gravity and his momentum prevent him from getting a firm hold. He glances down at a ribbon of river far below. Vertigo sweeps over him and he turns away.

I need to grip a branch or find a foothold, something to stop falling long enough to gather my thoughts and find a way back to level ground.

As he continues to slide, additional tree limbs sprout from the cliff face. A few are flowering. He senses these are the ones he needs to grab. But how to maneuver in their direction? *Should I let go and hope my fall will take me near one of these branches? Should I continue grabbing onto whatever is nearest my reach?* Time is running out.

His desperation verging on panic, he hears Ezekiel's voice. "Stay calm and breathe. There is a way."

And with those words echoing in his mind, Lenny is suddenly back in the booth. *Holy shit! What just happened? Did I black out or what?* He looks across to ask Ezekiel, but he is not there.

"Ok, don't freak out," he says without realizing he is talking aloud. "He's probably getting a refill or in the bathroom. Just chill and wait a bit."

Ten minutes go by. His composure is fading. He does a visual sweep of the shop but there is no sign of him. Anxiety seeps in.

Was he even here? he thinks, his calmness evaporating.

Get a grip Lenny!

He nurses his coffee, looking at its light brown color and creating swirls with his spoon. After one more look around, he leaves.

*　*　*

Driving home questions colonize his thoughts. *Who is Ezekiel? Is he even a real person? Could he be some sort of elaborate hallucination, my personal shape-shifting pooka like Harvey, James Stewart's invisible rabbit friend from the movie? Or maybe I have a brain injury from my fall at The Loft. Or I have developed some variant of one of those rare misidentification syndromes like Fregoli delusion and who I see as Ezekiel is actually someone else. I am too old to become schizophrenic, aren't I?*

I need to hold it together long enough to sort this out.

Entering his apartment, Lenny is grateful for Sisu's predictable, enthusiastic greeting which now feels grounding. Although too fatigued to match his bouncy exuberance, Lenny greets him warmly adding, "Do you want to go out?" which elicits whirling dervish-like circles and yips so high-pitched he expects to hear howling from all dogs within a mile radius.

He decides to go to a nearby park that has nice walking paths and a little pond frequented by ducks, always a source of excitement for Sisu. It's a beautiful day and Lenny finds himself regaining some semblance of calm. He takes time to admire the blooming pink, red, and white azalea bushes along the path, one of the few flowers he can identify. Judging by Sisu's relentless sniffing, marking, and tail wagging, he is happy to be out.

Lenny marvels at Sisu's sense of smell. What must the world be like when your nose is your principal sense organ? He remembers watching a show on public television where a prominent canine researcher claimed a dog's sense of smell is at least 10,000 times more acute than humans. In the same show, another researcher compared this olfactory prowess to detecting one rotten apple in a barrel that held two million. Dogs have even been reputed to be able to smell diseases like cancer in people.

A dog, thinks Lenny, *experiences a reality not accessible or even comprehensible to people. Who knows what images a dog might see when it is smelling something, assuming it sees an image at all. Maybe it 'sees' in an olfactory way. Could my experience with Ezekiel be similar? Could I be sensing something not visible to others? Yes, there are all kinds of psychological explanations for my seeing Ezekiel, but why should I privilege these over other possibilities? Maybe I've unconsciously tapped into the mystical third eye? But wait, why I am assuming that Ezekiel is not an actual flesh and blood person? It's certainly a more parsimonious explanation. Being unusual does not necessarily mean not real.*

A tug on the leash jars Lenny from his contemplation. They are by the duck pond which means Sisu is in lunge mode. If he was off leash, it's uncertain whether he would chase them or do something harmful but having no desire to find out he keeps Sisu firmly tethered.

Lenny has a lot to think about. He walks over to a tall evergreen and touches one of the leaves. He's surprised by its prickly texture. He wonders how old it is and the changes to the land it has witnessed. *This tree is a good model for how to deal with change. Slow down, endure, and turn towards the sun.* He sits down near the base, loops Sisu's leash around his wrist, and closes his eyes.

"It's an eastern red cedar," says a nearby voice.

Lenny opens his eyes and sees a wizened-looking man standing next to him. Surprisingly, Sisu did not warn Lenny of his approach and is calm around him. He is small and thin, with dark weathered skin and long, grey hair held back by a purple bandana.

"I didn't know that," says Lenny. "It must be old given how tall it is."

"More than one hundred and fifty years, I'd say. Older even than me." He grins showing a few gaps between his teeth.

"I hope it's not lonely," says Lenny gesturing to the open space around it.

The man surveys the area. "It once had more tree companions, but it still supports many communities."

"What do you mean?"

"The wildlife that eats its twigs and foliage, the sanctuary it provides for the birds who return the favor by spreading its seeds. It's a harmonious arrangement."

"We could learn from them," says Lenny thinking about recent events.

"Yes, there is much we could learn if we would slow down and appreciate their wisdom. The Cherokee people believed the cedar— *a-tsi-na tlu-gv* in their language—was made from the spirits of the ancestors." He gazes upward with a look of reverence. "We should venerate these trees."

Lenny is moved by the wisdom of his words and grateful for learning about the tree. "Thank you for educating me. I don't think I will ever look at a red cedar in the same way."

"We must all learn to see differently," says the man sounding Ezekiel-like. Before Lenny can react, he says, "Peace be with you," then turns and walks slowly across the grass.

Lenny stares in wonder. He feels calmer than he has for some time. *Maybe this was the therapy I needed.*

He starts back home.

* * *

Sitting at his computer, Lenny writes down what he remembered from his conversation with Ezekiel.

'What are assumptions but attempts to impose order and reduce uncertainty.'

'Are we not protean beings?'

'How have you changed?'

'Now you are here and in-between is an abyss.'

He also writes about his vision of falling and upon opening his eyes, Ezekiel, or who he thought was Ezekiel, being gone.

He looks at what he wrote, then continues.

'Was my encounter with Ezekiel a way of helping me understand how I am making sense of what happened? To help me reclaim volition and take me out of freefall? Or could it all be the ravings of a disturbed man?'

Uh, oh, I'm going down a rabbit hole again.

The buzzing of his cell phone interrupts his thoughts. The caller ID is not familiar, but it's a local number so he decides to answer.

"Hello," says a young-sounding, female voice. "Is this Dr. Leonard Isaacson?"

"Yes," he answers hesitantly.

"Hello, Dr. Isaacson. My name is Ashley Lee. I'm a reporter for the *Daily Chronicle*. I understand you were at the Loft at the time of the shooting and I'm wondering if I might talk with you about it."

What the hell? How did she know this?

"Who told you I was at the Loft?"

"Your name came up as I was talking to people who were there. I guess someone recognized you."

Feeling wary, he asks, "What specifically do you want to talk with me about?"

"I'm interested in getting different perspectives about what happened from people who were actually at The Loft, what they experienced and how they are dealing with it: a deeper more nuanced perspective than the initial reports."

Lenny quickly considers the pros and cons of allowing himself to be interviewed. His inclination has been to avoid the spotlight, even social media, and he's not sure he wants his presence at The Loft to be made known in this way. On the other hand, this might be an opportunity to broaden people's understanding of why such events have been occurring.

Several seconds pass. "Dr. Isaacson, are you there?"

With a start, he says, "Yes, yes, I'm still here. Just trying to decide. Er . . . ok, we can talk, but no guarantees. If I don't like how it's going, I walk," thinking that came out harsher than he intended.

Ashley seems unfazed. "Great. Where would you like to meet?"

"How about the Holy Grounds coffee shop?" says Lenny

thinking that he might as well go somewhere familiar, give himself a home-court advantage.

"Do you know where it is?"

"I do," replies Ashley, and a meeting is arranged for the next day at ten.

Chapter Thirteen

Lenny googles "Ashley Lee." He learns she graduated fourteen years ago from Syracuse University with a major in communication and media studies. A few years later, she earned a master's degree in journalism from American University in Washington, DC. She has been working at the *Chronicle* for about four years. Although satisfied with her credentials, he counsels himself to be cautious.

He arrives at Holy Grounds a few minutes past ten still feeling uncertain about agreeing to meet. *Remember, if I don't like how it's going, end it.*

Entering the coffee shop, he spots a petite, attractive Asian woman, mid-to-late thirties, standing a few feet inside the doorway. She has shoulder-length, straight black hair and round, wire-frame glasses. Her attire is professional: a black blazer over a maroon top and matching black pants.

They make eye contact.

Ashley extends her hand. "Hello, Dr. Isaacson. I'm Ashley Lee. Nice to meet you."

"Hello," says Lenny deciding to forgo introducing himself as Lenny in favor of keeping things more formal. They order drinks, a regular coffee for Lenny and a cappuccino for Ashley and settle into a booth.

"I appreciate your agreeing to talk to me," says Ashley. "I imagine dealing with what happened cannot be easy."

Treading cautiously, Lenny responds with a nod. He feels distracted by her attractiveness and reminds himself she does not see him as a peer but an elder. *Focus Lenny!*

Ashley continues. "As I said on the phone, I am doing a story about the people who were at The Loft during the shooting. I believe a first-person perspective is the best way to inform others about what it's like to be in such a scary situation. Also, I want to report on how people who were not injured are coping with the experience."

"Ok," says Lenny as a way of telling her to continue.

"Do you mind if I tape our conversation?" Ashley says placing her cell phone face up between them on the table. Lenny had anticipated this request and was ready with his requirements.

In what he hopes is a friendly but firm tone, he says, "Before I answer, and before you turn that on, there are certain conditions you must agree to if we are to have this interview. First, I assume anything I say is on the record. So, no off-the-record asides. Second, I need to know a little more about you." Despite his preliminary research, he wanted to hear how she presented herself. "Third, if I don't think a question is appropriate, I will not answer. If you persist, I will terminate the interview."

While he is speaking, Ashley's face remains impassive. "Ok," she says, "that seems reasonable." Should I begin by telling you a little about me?"

Disarmed by her ready acquiescence to his demands—he was half-expecting the interview would not take place—he says, "Sounds good."

After confirming what he had read about her education, Ashley continues. "I feel like I've been doing journalism most of my life. I started out writing for student publications in high school and then at the university. After graduation, I worked as a reporter at two different small-town newspapers before taking my current position at the *Chronicle* a little more than four years ago."

As she is speaking, Lenny is forming the impression of a bright, earnest young woman, but knowing his vulnerability to the halo effect, he asks, "What is it about journalism that inspires you?"

Without missing a beat, Ashley says, "I love hearing peoples' stories and writing about them in a way I hope is faithful to the teller. Stories are the primary way readers learn about the world and themselves."

"Like what?" Lenny inquires.

"It could be many things, but an important one would be learning about the lives of other people, especially those who are not like them, not just pedantically, but in a more in-depth, nuanced way. I believe this kind of learning can help readers become more tolerant and respectful of differences."

Lenny is sold. He couldn't have said it better if he had scripted her answer himself.

"Was that, ok?" Ashley asks with a captivating smile.

"That's great. Thank you," Lenny answers, now also smiling. He is again aware of how easily, despite his age, he is smitten by attractive, intelligent, and charming women.

Admonishing himself, he thinks, *Will I always be a perpetual adolescent? What was it that ageless baseball pitcher, Satchel Paige, once said, 'How old would you be if you didn't know how old you are?' Good question. Depending on the relationship I can be any of the ages that I have experienced.*

"Dr. Isaacson? Are you ok?" Ashley's voice ends his excursus on aging.

Embarrassed—*she must think I'm a doddering, old guy with the attention span of a turnip*—he mumbles, "Sorry, I guess I got lost in thought."

"No problem," says Ashley still smiling. Picking up on their last thread she continues, "Do you have more questions of me, or shall we proceed with the interview?"

"Yes, let's begin."

Ashley repositions her phone closer to Lenny to get a clear recording. "I'd like to hear about how you experienced what happened, how you have been dealing with it, and any other thoughts you would like to share.

"How about starting with why you went to The Loft, what the atmosphere was like and how you knew something unusual was happening. Then if it's ok, I'd like to know how you became aware of the presence of the gunman. What did you feel and do? Finally, what has it been like for you since?"

"Ok. I agree that approaching this chronologically will make it easier to understand."

He begins. "It seemed like a typical evening. I'd been there before and enjoyed the entertainment. I like the variety of talent levels and admire the courage it takes to perform in front of an audience."

Ashley interjects. "I agree. I don't think I would be brave enough to perform."

"What would you do if you did?" asks Lenny curious about Ashley's other talents.

Ashley twiddles her napkin and lowers her head a bit. "Mmm . . . I don't know, maybe read a poem."

"By whom?"

"I think Mary Oliver. I love her poems about nature and how they often end with a profound statement or question. My favorite is "The Summer Day" where she observes a grasshopper in the intricate and beautiful way only Mary Oliver can and then ends the poem with the lines:

> "Doesn't everything die at last, and too soon?
> Tell me, what is it you plan to do
> With your one wild and precious life?'"

She recites the words with such earnestness and depth of feeling that Lenny momentarily forgets the purpose of their meeting. Ashley is more grounded and says in a playful voice, "Wait a minute, I thought I was doing the interviewing."

Lenny's cheeks flush. "Yes, of course," he intones, recovering. Then, adding in jest, "However, if you ever tire of your day job, you might consider performance art." What he doesn't reveal is the poignancy of those lines to his current situation. He wonders if Ashley's choice of a poem is a coincidence or if he unconsciously revealed something about himself that she sensed.

"I'll keep it in mind," says Ashley with a chuckle. "Now back to your experience."

Before meeting Ashley, Lenny was ambivalent about whether to tell her about tripping the shooter. *What is likely to happen if I do?* he had asked himself. *How would she respond and write about it? And what would be the public reaction?*

He had experienced his so-called fifteen minutes of fame as a young assistant professor when his research on marital relationships got picked up by the Associated Press. Suddenly, he was getting calls from radio stations all over the U.S. wanting to interview him. Excited by the interest in his research, he followed up on the requests.

His first interview did not go as expected. Rather than talk about his research, he was treated like a glorified advice columnist.

Radio Host: "Good morning listeners. We are here with Dr. Leonard Isaacson to talk about marriages, good and bad. Dr. Isaacson, what are the characteristics of a healthy marriage, and what suggestions would you give couples whose relationship is not up to snuff, so to speak?"

This type of questioning turned out to be typical. As an aspiring social scientist whose research was still in process, he was reluctant to offer generic advice to couples. Instead, his responses were vague and hedged in conditionals.

"It's hard to generalize to all relationships. The dynamics of relationships can vary. If a couple is unhappy with their relationship they should try communicating with their partner. If that doesn't improve things, they should seek professional help."

He was a boring guest. As a result, within a few days the media wave became a ripple and soon after, still water.

Would revealing to Ashley what he had done at The Loft be similar? Notoriety based on an inaccurate portrayal of his action? Would he have to fend off requests from other media? Despite these questions hanging in the air, the deciding factor was Ashley herself. He wanted to be interesting and not the dull interviewee he was years ago.

Right on cue, Ashley looks at him as if there could be nothing more interesting than what he had to say.

"So, Dr. Isaacson, when did you become aware something out of the ordinary was happening?"

Lenny sips his coffee to reorient himself. "I was listening to someone reciting poetry when I heard a commotion near the entrance."

"And then what happened?"

"An instant later, there were shouts and screams and what sounded like a car backfiring. Of course, it was gunfire, but because it seemed so improbable, it took a few seconds to register. I looked over to where the sound was coming from and saw this guy with a rifle. The whole place was in pandemonium, people dashing around in all directions, tables and chairs being overturned."

"And what did you do?"

"At first nothing. My perception of time and my ability to process what was happening had slowed almost to a halt. When it registered that a guy with a rifle was shooting people, I dove to the floor near an overturned table and tried to lay very still. I was scared stiff."

"Did anything else happen?"

Here was the moment of truth. *Am I going to tell?*

Speaking softly, Lenny says, "The gunshots seemed to be getting closer so I cautiously looked up and saw the guy heading in my direction. Since he seemed to be shooting people indiscriminately, I felt paralyzed with fear hoping he would not shoot me. As he came to where I was lying, he hesitated for a moment. I held my breath doing my best to play dead. When he started to move past, I grabbed his ankle and he fell."

Ashley's eyes get very big. "You're the one who made him fall?"

"Yes, but it was not a conscious act. Lucky for me, the combination of surprise, his momentum, and all the debris, caused him to stumble and fall into an overturned table which knocked the rifle out of his hands. As soon as that happened some brave people jumped on top of him and prevented him from doing further harm."

Ashley looks stunned. "You're a hero! Who knows how many lives were saved because of you."

"Hero?" He squirms in his seat. "Sorry, but it's a crown that doesn't fit. The heroes are the people who stopped him from hurting anyone else. I'm glad I was able to trip him, but as I said, it was done without forethought."

"I think you are being overly modest," says Ashley with admiration in her dark eyes. At least that's how Lenny interprets it. "Whether or not there was forethought is less important than what you did."

Lenny's mind is in overdrive. Part of him likes the way Ashley is looking at him, another part is telling him to dismiss this adolescent fantasy and focus on how he wants his words to be reported. Searching for a middle ground, he says, "I appreciate your praise, Ashley, and I don't want to overanalyze this. What happened, happened and I am grateful it helped. What I would like from you is to stick to the facts and not play it up as an act of heroism. Can you do that?"

Ashley's mouth turns down slightly. "I can, but I still think you are being too modest. Can you tell me about what you did next?"

"Once I knew the shooter had been subdued and the police had arrived, I got up and began looking around. The carnage was terrible. Injured people being attended to by paramedics. People in shock staring blankly at nothing. Moans and cries for help . . . and blood. I scanned the room for the daughter of a friend who I had seen earlier in the evening." He pauses, feeling emotion again infuse his voice like when he talked with Gifford.

"She was on the ground with paramedics working feverishly over her. I took out my phone and called my friend."

"What did you say?" asks Ashley, concern in her voice.

"I told him where I was, and that his daughter was also here." He looks away. "And . . . there had been a shooting, and he needed to come right away."

"Is she going to be alright?"

"I don't know."

"Did you speak with the police?"

"No. I was depleted and sore and just wanted to get home," says Lenny, deciding not to mention the injury he had sustained for fear it would embellish the hero notion. "Once my friend arrived, I left."

The rest of the interview was about the aftereffects of having been part of this horrific event and how he was dealing with it. Ashley also wanted to know if Lenny had thoughts about the shooter and what should happen to him.

Lenny downplayed his struggles and stated he was doing relatively well. "I've been trying to take it easy and not make many demands on myself."

With regards to Jeremy Larsen, he repeats his belief that

although Larsen is responsible for his actions, he feels sad our society produces people filled with such anger and hate that they are susceptible to extremist right-wing groups who preach violence.

"Do you think Jeremy Larsen is also a victim?" Ashley asks.

"I do, but that should not be equated with those who were injured or killed at The Loft."

Switching into academic mode, he continues. "We need to consider broader societal issues that provide the breeding grounds for these kinds of brutal acts. Causal explanations of these tragedies tend to be confined to the perpetrator as if what happened was an individual problem. A common way we do this is by blaming their actions on mental illness. This allows us to ignore contributing societal issues like the easy access to firearms and the glorification of violence. Unless we accept our collective responsibility and enact system-level changes, I'm afraid such violence will continue to increase."

Ashley seems captivated by Lenny's minilecture. "That's very interesting, Dr. Isaacson. It certainly puts the shooting in a different light. Thank you for sharing your thoughts. And thank you for agreeing to meet with me. You've given me much to write . . . and think about."

As she moves to turn off the recorder on her phone, Lenny realizes he doesn't want the interview to end. He reflects out loud. "Isn't it interesting how our context and audience influence what we say. I spoke with someone else recently—thinking of the psychologist, Stuart Gifford—about the same events, yet my story was not quite the same. Descriptions of events can include innumerable details. Including them all is impossible; we're always editing, consciously and not, deciding what to omit or add and what words to use. I am sure you experience this as a reporter."

"No one tells you everything," says Ashley. "What I try to do is get to the important aspects of the story."

"But how do you know what those are?"

"I usually have a general idea since that is the reason for the interview. Then it's up to me to show the person I am genuinely interested in what they have to say and I can be trusted."

"Is that what you tried to do with me?"

Ashley smiles demurely. "Yes, but with you it was easy. You are articulate, open, and likable."

Lenny hears 'likable' a little louder than the other words but does not react. Instead, he says, "The stories we tell shape our memories and become, in effect, the experience. Even more so when they're printed in a newspaper."

"Fascinating," says Ashley with a look of interest he's seen on his best students. In contrast, her movements suggest she is thinking about leaving.

Ok, time to end this, he thinks, resignedly knowing the chances of them meeting again are slim to none.

Putting away her phone, Ashley says, "Thanks again, Dr. Isaacson for your time. It was a pleasure to meet you."

"My pleasure, too. Do you think some of what we talked about will make it into print?"

She assures him it will, probably within the next day or so as this was current news and will be of interest to readers. Ashley stands and extends her hand. He takes it and says, "Goodbye, Ashley. If you have any questions, feel free to call me."

Stop it you fool, she's not going to call you, and even if she did, it would be strictly business or to ask you about gift suggestions for her grandfather.

"Will do," replies Ashley and leaves.

* * *

Lenny remains in the booth. *I should try to get out more,* he thinks glumly. After a couple of minutes, he gets up and goes to the counter for a refill of his coffee. Returning to the booth, he takes stock of his current state. Aside from his sophomoric fantasy about Ashley, speaking about his experience enabled him to further reflect on its impact. He thinks about the last thing he said to Ashley—*how our stories about our experience become the experience*—and wonders what it has become for him.

In the past, when dealing with difficult situations he found thinking out loud has been helpful. Since he is alone, he decides to do this by furtively recording his thoughts on his phone. He begins.

"Like many people fortunate enough not to have to worry about their basic needs being met, I have lived life assuming things will continue more or less as they have in the past. This is easier when you are young, but the longer you live the more likely you will experience unexpected events, good and bad. These events can be personal, like an accident, or impersonal like an earthquake ... or a mass shooting. In either case, these experiences unsettle us and threaten our assumptions of stability. It's why you'll hear people say things like, 'It made me realize we only have today,' often accompanied by a vow to 'live in present.' Unfortunately, these homilies and resolutions tend to fade over time and our old, familiar life rhythms reinstate themselves."

Lenny pauses the recording and plays back what he dictated. After further reflection, he adds:

"What makes the shooting at The Loft different is that unlike an accident or act of nature, it was a person deliberately targeting a specific group. Not only does it threaten assumptions of regularity and safety, but of justice; it's an incomprehensible, just-world shattering event.

"The literature on recovery from traumatic events emphasizes how finding meaning is crucial for moving on with your life. But what meaning could there be for people like poor Emily who was at The Loft for an enjoyable evening? Like I said to Jerry, meaning is not inherent in an event but by how we respond to it. How I live my life going forward will be its meaning. What seems necessary is coming to terms with uncertainty: accept that absolute predictability is a wish but a myth and not allow this acceptance to rule your life. I think that is what Ezekiel was getting at."

Lenny stops recording. *Ok, this was a start. What happens next?*

Chapter Fourteen

Lenny's phone is chiming with text messages every few minutes. He rubs his eyes and stretches. *What's going on? Am I on some spammer's computer-generated text algorithm?* He glances at his phone and recognizes some of the texters. Ashley's story was published. His heart beats a little faster as he opens the texts. Those from people he knew express shock he was at The Loft when the shooting occurred. Some praise his 'heroic' actions while incredulous he had acted how he did. 'You tripped the gunman? Holy shit!' Others express concern for his wellbeing with a few extending general offers of help and support. One colleague simply wrote 'WTF??' But the most surprising and moving text was from someone he did not know: 'Thank you for saving my son.' He stares at the words struggling to believe they are referring to him. A tear rolls down his cheek.

Needing some emotional space before deciding how to handle things, Lenny puts his phone aside and makes coffee. He turns on his iPad and finds the newspaper story. The headline, "Loft Shooter Taken Down by Retired Professor," was decidedly not what he wanted although it explained why he received so many texts. Ashley's article was faithful to what he had told her until he got near the end where, to his chagrin, she added "acting with disregard for his own safety, he tripped the gunman which led to his capture and saved many lives."

He feels foolish for allowing his enjoyment of their interaction to override his judgment. *I should have known she would write something like that.* The article ends with Ashley pronouncing him a hero. It felt fraudulent. How was he to continue dealing with the troubling impact of the shooting while being cast as an ersatz hero? He began dreading how to respond to the congratulations and accolades for what he had supposedly done. Praise felt good when it was deserved, something he did not believe was true in his case.

Hold on, protests another voice. *You're being too harsh. People cannot know your internal state at the time you stuck out your arm. They know what you did and the result. Of course, they will praise your action. Your discomfort has more to do with the discrepancy between your presumed attributes of a hero and how you think of yourself.*

Feeling like he doesn't have the energy for an extended self-analysis, he tells himself he'll eventually figure it out, but to let it go for now.

These things are like comets. They shine briefly and fade away. Doing nothing may be the best course of action.

* * *

A knock on his door sends Sisu into a barking frenzy. His anxiety resurfaces. *Oh no, what now?* Glancing through the peephole, he sees his neighbors from across the hall, Javier and Carol. Despite living near many people in his apartment building, Lenny, like many

Americans, knew few of them beyond a perfunctory hello when they happened to see one another. An exception was Javier and Carol, a couple in their early fifties, with whom he had developed a friendly relationship. Lenny first met them about a year ago when Carol knocked on his door to ask if she could borrow two eggs.

As he soon found out, Carol was quite gregarious and egg borrowing was a sufficient excuse to start a conversation. Before she left, Lenny had learned that Javier was from Guadalajara and she was from Minneapolis. They'd met as students at the University of Pennsylvania where they majored in romance languages. They had two grown children who lived nearby. Javier was a Spanish teacher at the local high school and Carol was a freelance editor. Before leaving with her eggs, Carol invited Lenny to drop by for coffee which after several prompts at chance encounters, he did. It was a good decision. Lenny found them to be bright, warm people who were pleasant to be around.

Opening the door, he sees the concern on their faces.

"Lenny," exclaims Carol with some alarm. "We just saw the story in the *Chronicle*. Are you ok? Is there anything we can do?"

"Thank you," says Lenny. "It was a terrifying experience, but I'm doing alright." He hoped that would be enough to avoid further discussion of what happened or how he was feeling but that vanished when neither Carol nor Javier made any move to leave.

"Is it true? Did you trip the gunman?" asks Javier with a look of disbelief.

Uh, oh. This is the question I am going to be repeatedly asked. "I guess I did, but it was just a reflex kind of thing. Nothing heroic about it," he adds trying to preempt any talk of heroism.

It doesn't work. "You should get a medal" Carol exclaims, as Javier nods enthusiastically.

Fighting the urge to hide in the bathroom or tell them he has an appointment somewhere, he says, "You're very kind, but I'm just happy it allowed others to stop him from hurting anyone else."

They stand facing each other at the doorway threshold for a long minute until Sisu, who is quite fond of the couple, comes up to them wagging his tail. This is enough to end the impasse and Lenny uses it to thank them for their concern.

Javier reiterates. "We just wanted to check in and make sure you were ok and let you know we admire what you did."

"Yes," affirms Carol. "And Lenny, *please* let us know if you need anything. We're here for you."

After assuring them he would, they leave.

Is this a portent of things to come and if so, how long will it last? He reminds himself most people will be well-meaning although some might be more interested in the 'juicy' aspects than his experience. He thinks again of how naïve he was to believe Ashley wouldn't play up his part in subduing the shooter. She's not only a reporter but an employee of a newspaper whose aim is to sell their product.

Did some part of me know this?

* * *

Alone again, Lenny resumes his morning routine. He showers and gingerly applies antibiotic cream to his still tender wound and rebandages it. Donning his typical attire of jeans and a pullover shirt, he begins looking at his texts.

Sisu's growl precedes another knock on the door.

Who now? Are texts not enough? He's starting to feel annoyed.

This time his peephole view reveals a man and a woman he does not know. Wary of opening the door, he says in a loud voice, "Can I help you?"

"Dr. Leonard Isaacson?" says the woman.

"Yes."

"We're from the FBI," she says holding up her credentials where Lenny could see them. "We'd like to speak with you about the recent incident at The Loft."

Jesus, the FBI? He half expected a visit from the local police, but not the FBI. "Ok," he says. "As soon as I put the dog away."

He carries Sisu into the bedroom. On his way to open the door, he grabs a sweatshirt from the couch and throws it on the bed. The agents enter.

"I'm agent Ben Gustafson and this is my colleague agent Lisa McGuire.

Do I shake hands? he wonders. Instead, he says, "Hello."

Lenny immediately feels self-conscious. He wonders if they're assessing his appearance and living conditions. Ironically, he does the same, trying to size them up while appearing natural.

Gustafson looks to be in his mid-to-upper-forties, dark-complexioned, about six-one, medium build, close-cropped hair with a few hints of grey, and wire-rim glasses. Agent McGuire is younger; Lenny guesses early thirties. She is fair-skinned, about five-eight, athletic physique, and short, cinnamon-colored hair longer towards the back. They are dressed in the conservative attire he associates with the FBI. Gustafson in a grey suit, blue shirt, and red and black striped tie, McGuire in a brownish pantsuit and lavender shirt with a rounded collar. Their badges are visibly displayed: Gustafson's on his belt and McGuire's on a cord around her neck.

McGuire repeats they are investigating the shooting at the Loft. "It has come to our attention you were there during the incident."

Lenny nods affirmatively.

"We'd like to talk with you about what you may have witnessed."

Trying to portray himself as a concerned citizen who wants to be helpful, although not sure what that looks like, Lenny offers them seats in his living room. As they settle in, Agent Gustafson takes out a pad and pen.

"Were you planning on contacting us or the local authorities?"

Gustafson's tone feels a bit provocative and Lenny can feel himself growing anxious. He tries not to respond defensively.

"I was severely shaken up and needed time to recover. Since I knew the person who had done the shooting was in police custody, I didn't feel any urgency to contact them."

"True," says Gustafson, "but for us to get a complete picture of what happened witnesses need to come forward."

Not wanting to get into a contentious interaction with the FBI, Lenny says, "Your right. I'm sorry. I guess I wasn't thinking clearly."

What Lenny doesn't know is that yesterday morning another agent had asked Gustafson if he had seen the story about the old guy who had tripped the shooter at The Loft. Gustafson had not, but since he did not like getting scooped by someone not assigned to the case, he said, "Yeah, we're following up."

After reading the article, he and McGuire had a brief discussion about whether they should talk with Lenny. Gustafson was hesitant. "What difference will it make? We already have the little shit in custody and tons of eyewitnesses."

"Still," countered McGuire, "he might have information that could be helpful toward establishing a hate crimes indictment." Gustafson reluctantly agreed and they decided to go there the next day.

McGuire asks Lenny if he had been to The Loft before.

"Yes."

Why he went that evening.

"It was open-mike night. I enjoy the local performers."

Did he notice anything out of the ordinary before the shooting?

"No."

She then asks him to describe what he observed beginning from when he first became aware of something unusual happening.

Lenny dutifully recounts what he saw and heard—not what he did—emphasizing that most of the time he was on the ground with limited visibility. When he finishes, Gustafson asks, "Did you hear the shooter say anything? Any racial, ethnic, or other types of slurs?"

"Not that I recall. All I remember hearing is shouting, screaming, tables and chairs being knocked over, and the sound of gunfire."

"What about the newspaper story that reported you tripped the shooter with your arm. Is that true?"

Lenny's body jerks involuntarily. He feels dumb for thinking the topic would not come up. Knowing he must answer, he gathers himself.

"Yes," he replies in a subdued tone.

"What led you to do this?" asks McGuire. "You put yourself at considerable risk."

He shrugs. "Maybe knowing my friend's daughter was there had something to do with it. I don't know. I just acted."

"Who was your friend's daughter?" asks McGuire.

"I'd rather not say. She was shot and is still recovering from her injuries. She and her family are struggling to cope with all that has happened."

"If she was injured and treated at the hospital, then we already have her name. Telling us will help us to be more sensitive to their situation when we talk to the family."

Conceding her point, Lenny discloses the information. Gustafson checks his notepad then asks a series of questions at once: Did he know the shooter? Had he ever seen him before? Does he know anyone who might know him?

"No to the first two questions. Regarding the third, if he was in the social services system then I might know someone who had worked with him, but I've seen no information about that."

"Why do you think he did this?" asks McGuire seemingly straying from a just-the-facts approach.

"I don't know. My understanding from reading the newspaper is he was associated with some extreme right-wing groups that condone violence." Deciding not to disclose he did some of his own research, he adds, "It wouldn't surprise me, although this is speculation, to learn he was a loner who might have been bullied or abused. It's a common profile of many perpetrators of this kind of act."

"How would you know this?" asks Gustafson.

"I am a retired professor of social work. It's part of my general knowledge."

They both nod and Gustafson makes a note.

"I'm curious," says Lenny. "Can you tell me what he is being charged with?"

"There's an array of charges being considered," says Gustafson, "but the possibility of a hate crime is why we're involved."

"Can you think of anything else that might be helpful?" asks McGuire winding up the interview.

"Not at the moment."

"Ok. If you do think of anything, please give me a call." She hands Lenny her card.

Both agents stand, shake Lenny's hand, and thank him for his time.

* * *

Lenny's armpits are damp. Speaking with police irrespective of the reason has always evoked anxiety. An unpleasant encounter with the law when he was fifteen set the stage for his reaction. It began when a blue Ford Galaxy pulled up to the street corner where Lenny happened to be standing. His friend Brad was driving.

"Hey, Lenny," Brad shouted through the half-open window. "Hop in."

Lenny hesitated. Wasn't Brad the same age as him? Too young to have a driver's license.

Seeing his hesitation, Brad yells, "Come on. It's ok. It's my mother's car."

Although car ownership had nothing to do with Brad's driver's license status, Lenny, not wanting to appear 'chicken,' got in.

At first cruising the neighborhood was fun. Then Brad made an illegal turn and a police car appeared behind them, lights flashing. Rather than pulling over, Brad panicked and floored the gas pedal. What ensued was a heart-thumping dash through city streets until the police car, now with sirens wailing, pulled alongside them, and ordered Brad to immediately stop the car.

It would be an understatement to describe the officers as not happy. "License and registration," barked one of them through the rolled down window. Since Brad didn't have a license, he tried to stall by asking Lenny to open the glove compartment and retrieve the registration. That was when they saw the gun!

Everyone was stunned.

Lenny's eyes grew impossibly wide, transfixed on the gun. He flattened his back against the seat as if it was radioactive.

"Get out of the car," the officer shouted while backing up and putting his hand on his holster. "Hands behind your head, feet apart."

Terrified, both boys immediately complied.

"Whose gun is it?"

Brad, now on the verge of tears, croaked, "I don't know. I swear. It's my mother's car."

"You're under arrest," was the response. They were handcuffed, put into the police car, and taken to the precinct.

Once inside, they were informed they we were in big trouble. If this was meant to scare the already terrified boys further, it worked. Lenny's anxiety was off the charts, and he was close to peeing in his pants. He felt like a criminal whose only future was within barbed wire-topped walls and an eight by ten cell.

Despite his doomsday catastrophizing, the drama ended when

Brad's mother, who the police had called, arrived with her boyfriend who claimed the gun was his and produced a permit. Just like that, Brad and Lenny were free to go with stern warnings about what would happen should either of them get in trouble again. Lenny never tested the validity of these warnings, but the experience had a lingering effect on his interaction with the police.

* * *

Returning to the present, Lenny reminds himself that he is neither an adolescent, nor has he done anything wrong. It was clear the FBI agents were looking for new information that might strengthen their case for a hate crime. Nevertheless, he's happy they're gone.

He sits in his favorite chair with the intent of relaxing when his phone buzzes. According to his caller ID, it was a local radio station. *Shit, here it goes, the fifteen-minute deluge. Well, I am not giving interviews.*

The call goes to voice mail. He feels the beginning of a headache. *Too much stress,* he tells himself.

Once again, however, his attempt at relaxation is cut short by the sound of his phone. *Is this what it's going to be like all day? Maybe I should shut the phone off.* Before doing so he glances at the caller ID. It's Jerry so he answers.

"Hi, Jerry. How are you?"

"I just read the story in the *Chronicle*," says Jerry ignoring Lenny's query. "Why didn't you tell me you tripped the shooter?"

Surprised by Jerry's abruptness, Lenny says the first thing that comes to his mind. "I don't know. You had enough on your plate and I didn't want to add more."

"I appreciate that, but this couldn't have been easy for you. Were you hurt?"

"Just a few scrapes, nothing serious." As he says this, he becomes aware of itchiness around the wound. *I think that means it's healing.*

"I'm glad but sorry I neglected to ask about you. I was so caught up in what happened to Emily that I blocked out everything else. Sorry for being such a jerk."

Thinking Jerry is beating himself up again, Lenny says, "Totally understandable. She was seriously injured and needed you."

"Yes, but I am sorry you had to go through this. I'd be happy to meet again if you want to talk about it."

"Thanks, Jerry, but you don't need to take time for me."

"I want to," counters Jerry. "Besides, talking will be helpful for me too."

Hearing that made a get-together more palatable. *And it will give me a break from sitting here and dodging calls from the voyeuristic media.*

"Ok, thanks. Let me know a good time."

"How about in an hour?"

Mmm, so soon? Oh well. "See you then."

* * *

Holy Grounds is about half full. Lenny turns towards their usual booth and sees it is unoccupied. He goes there to wait for Jerry. A few minutes later, Jerry enters. Lenny breathes a sigh of relief seeing that Jerry looks like his old self. He hopes it's a sign things are improving.

Jerry comes to the booth. They exchange greetings and proceed to the counter to order their coffees. Once re-seated, Lenny says, "You're looking better. How are things going?"

"We're managing, but first I want to hear about you," says Jerry thinking about their last phone conversation. "Your experience must have been terrifying."

"It was," he says honestly. "Like something out of a nightmare. You read about these things and imagine what it must have been like for the people involved, but it doesn't come close to experiencing it."

Jerry grimaces thinking of Emily. He says, "I'm sure that's true, but you acted bravely and limited the number of casualties."

But not for Emily, Lenny thinks. Although tired of responding to the same accolades, he feels compelled to set the record straight for his friend. "The truth is I was scared shitless, paralyzed, and trying to play dead. I was more surprised than anyone when I stuck my arm out. Even thinking about it makes me nauseous. Sometimes, I even wonder if I made it up or if someone else did it and I mistakenly got the credit. One of these days the real person will show up and I'll be exposed as a fraud."

Jerry looks skeptical. "You're being too modest. Circumstances bring out things in people they may never have thought possible. You know, like the stories about parents lifting the front of a car to save their child. Your instinct was to stop this person from hurting others. That's what matters."

Lenny lowers his eyes. "Thanks, Jerry. I can accept, in hindsight, that I did something helpful. I'm just not comfortable with the hero label. It was a one-off kind of thing and not representative of who I am, so accepting praise feels inauthentic."

"All the more reason why you deserve it," replies Jerry resolutely.

"It's not like you've lived your life performing heroic acts. None of us know how we will react in such situations, but we hope it would be like you."

Moved by Jerry's sincerity, Lenny says, "I hear what you're saying and I appreciate it. I guess I could analyze this forever and still not have answers. I'm glad that I did what I did. And since I decided to tell the reporter about it, I will have to deal with the reactions of others." He pauses. "I only wish I could have helped Emily," he adds sadly.

The muscles around Jerry's jaw tighten as a long-ago memory flickers and fades like a dying light bulb. "There's nothing you could have done," he whispers.

"How is she doing Jerry? How are you all doing?"

"It's been rough but we're managing. Emily continues to improve which is a huge relief. Danny seems to be getting on ok. Katie's been amazing. I know she's hurting, but she's able to stay focused and hold things together."

"And you?" asks Lenny.

"Me? I feel like I'm in uncharted waters. Like you, I couldn't know in advance how I would respond to what happened. Sometimes I feel like I'm handling things ok and other times not too well."

"I get it. Imagining a what-if situation and experiencing it are very different; it's like comparing a cardboard cutout of a person to a real human being. Also, it's not a one-and-done kind of thing. There's an unfolding in which your reactions become part of the situation, something a hypothetical discussion can't duplicate."

Seeing Jerry's puzzled look Lenny tries to clarify. "Think about how you, and for that matter, Emily, Katie, Danny, and the medical staff, reacted on the first day. Those reactions became part of the experience. Although what happened began with the shooting, its meaning is shaped by our interactions with each other and with subsequent developments."

"I guess," says Jerry still looking bewildered. "The way you describe it seems quite complicated—too complicated for me."

"Of course," he answers realizing he lost sight of Jerry's emotional struggles. "My timing is way off." Upset about his insensitivity, he says, "What I said wasn't meant to suggest you should be doing anything different. It's just my way of trying to understand difficult situations."

"I know," says Jerry. "And you may be right, but there's too much happening for me to go there."

"I have a talent for overcomplicating things," says Lenny contritely.

"It's ok. It might be helpful later on. Your way of looking at things is one of the reasons I like our talks."

Still uncomfortable about his lack of judgment, Lenny attempts to redirect their conversation. "The last time we talked it seemed like Emily's emotional struggles were as big an issue as the physical ones. Is that still the case?"

"It's hard to tell. The changes in her medical condition are more visible and measurable. The wounds are healing or they are not. You can stand up or you cannot. Her emotional struggle is less predictable and harder to manage. At her age, you feel invulnerable; I certainly did. So having to confront her mortality so abruptly and starkly must be devastating. She just wants her old life back . . . we all do.

"Me too, but I don't think that can happen. Not fully. Our lives have changed. Our challenge now is to figure out a 'new normal' and move on."

"Is there an instruction manual for that?" asks Jerry with some rare levity.

"I wish, but I'm afraid there's no one-size-fits-all solution. Nevertheless, if I wrote such a manual, I would advise patience and self-care, understanding we might cycle through a range of emotions in no particular order. And I would encourage staying connected to those who care about us. At least it's what I am telling myself."

"Sounds like good advice. I'll buy the book."

Something about Jerry's tone feels inauthentic to Lenny. Like he's acting in a way he does not feel. Uncomfortable about digging deeper, Lenny continues to play along.

"I'll let you know when it comes out."

"I'll be expecting the friend discount," says Jerry with a slight smile.

Maybe I'm overthinking this. He sounds good so best to leave on a positive note.

"You got it." He slides to the end of the booth. "Hang in there my friend and stay in touch. If there is anything I can do for you or anyone in your family, please let me know."

As he stands, Jerry says, "Have you heard anything about what's happening with that Larsen guy? Have they charged him with a hate crime?"

Lenny sits back down. "I believe they're still deciding. The FBI paid me a visit this morning about that very issue."

Jerry becomes very attentive. "What did they say?"

"They asked about my experience at The Loft and whether I

heard him shouting anything that might suggest he was targeting specific ethnic or racial groups."

"Did you?"

"No. I heard shouting but couldn't tell what was said. Then I heard gunshots and dove to the floor. Some hero, huh."

Ignoring this last remark, Jerry exclaims, "I'm sure it was a hate crime! Just look at his background and the groups he belongs to. I hope they don't let him off easy. You know, cave into some sob story about his troubled childhood."

Jerry clenches his fists and stares at Lenny. "The son of a bitch deserves to die!" Lenny recoils at the savagery of Jerry's words and tone. It's as if another Jerry, an evil doppelganger, has taken his place. Desperate to defuse the situation, Lenny says, "I'm sure he's not going anywhere but prison for the rest of his life."

"Not good enough," snarls Jerry, his voice low but threatening. "He needs to *die*."

Who is this man? Lenny wonders with alarm. He again tries to mollify Jerry's anger.

"I can understand why you would feel that way and it might seem like justice, but it's out of our control. Nothing can bring back the people who died or change what happened. We have to let the justice system run its course knowing he won't be able to hurt anyone else ever again."

Jerry hisses through clenched teeth. "No, nothing can bring them back" and suddenly he's crying, his anger replaced by anguish.

"I couldn't protect my D, D . . . Emily." He holds his face in his hands and closes his eyes while mumbling, "It's my job to keep her safe and I failed."

The depth of Jerry's suffering is heartrending. Speaking softly, Lenny says, "I think you know what happened to Emily could not have been prevented. We all want to protect our children just like our parents wanted to protect us, but that's not always possible. You and Katie have been great parents. You gave your kids love, you instilled them with good values, and provided for their needs. What happened to Emily was awful. But despite the difficulties you are facing now, I know in time you will all recover and find a way to move on with your lives. And I will say again, I am here to help in whatever way you would like."

Jerry looks depleted from his emotional outburst. The doppelganger has gone. With what appears to be great effort he gets up and says, "Thanks, Lenny. You're a good friend, but I should get back home now."

Lenny is filled with worry, but not knowing what else he can do, he says, "I understand. We'll talk again soon."

* * *

Outside the coffee shop. Lenny again reflects on how it's easier to give advice than apply it to himself. *Well, at least when we meet, I get to hear what I think. Time to go home and see if I can take some of my own advice.*

He spends the next hour with Sisu. *Poor guy hasn't gotten much attention lately.* They play 'fetch the toy' until he feels a twinge in his side. He goes into the bathroom to check his wound. It's still red around the edges. He applies some hydrogen peroxide which stings like hell. "Yeow!" he bellows. The pain evokes a memory of his mother applying Merthiolate to a cut when he was a child.

Merthiolate also stung, more than other available antiseptics, but his mother seemed to believe feeling pain meant it was working; those germs didn't die quietly. Later in life, he learned Merthiolate was banned by the FDA in the 1990s because of its potentially toxic effects. He manages a smile. *Those dying germs got the last laugh.*

Another stinging sensation from the peroxide brings him back to his current task. He covers his wound with a fresh bandage and resolves to call his doctor if there is no improvement over the next few days.

Time to check in on the status of my fleeting celebrity.

He plops onto the couch and turns his phone back on. There are several texts and voice mail messages. He scans the numbers and IDs of the callers. Some are familiar: his sister, friends near and far, and former colleagues. He deletes the rest. He listens to his voice mail. The first is from a radio station requesting to talk with him about his heroic act. He deletes it. Next, is someone from the AARP saying they might be interested in doing a story about him for their members' magazine, emphasizing they had millions of senior readers like him. *Don't think so,* but he does not delete. Third, is a former student asking if he had checked the Twitter feed #badassoldguy. "You're famous!" *Ugh,* he thinks, but since he had never used Twitter, he could easily ignore it. The rest are from people he knows expressing their concern or admiration, other media requests, and junk calls that evaded his phone's scammer screens: Did he want to extend his car warranty? Interested in lakefront property?

Two unrecognized messages get his attention. In the first, a male with a gruff and menacing voice says, "You will pay for what you did to Jeremy." The second is another male who warns. "We will finish what Hitler started."

A chill runs through him. That someone like this could call his cell phone and likely discover where he lived is frightening. His finger moves to delete the message when it occurs to him that he should share them with the FBI. He puts down the phone and stares into nothingness. *I should have thought about this possibility when I gave the newspaper interview. Am I now a target for the lunatic fringe?* A panicky feeling begins to swell. He tries to quell it by reminding himself this is what they want.

These groups thrive on fomenting fear and panic, I need to stay calm. His self-talk helps, but he knows the sense of being a marked man will keep him on edge.

Why did I reveal what I had done? he chides himself. *Because the adolescent in me wanted to impress a young, attractive woman,* came the embarrassing answer. After shaking his head in disgust at how easily his judgment became impaired, he gets up, goes to his desk, picks up Lisa McGuire's card, and calls her number.

She answers on the second ring.

"Hello, this is special agent McGuire."

"Hello, Agent McGuire. This is Lenny Isaacson. We talked earlier in the day."

"Yes, Dr. Isaacson. What's up?"

Lenny fills her in on the phone messages.

"Thanks for informing me. It's important information. Can you forward the messages to me?"

"Sure, should I use the number I just called?"

"Yes, it's a cell I use only for official business."

"Er . . . one other question. Should I be scared?"

McGuire answers matter-of-factly. "I know getting these messages can be upsetting, but it's rare they're acted upon. Most of these people get their jollies by scaring other people and spreading hate under a cloak of anonymity. On the other hand, I wouldn't ignore them completely."

He shivers. *I wouldn't ignore them completely?' What the hell does that mean?*

"What should I do?" he asks trying to keep the alarm out of his voice. "I can't barricade myself in my house."

"No, of course not," responds McGuire, her voice maintaining its dispassionate tone. "I would say for the time being don't go anywhere where you would be an easy target of harassment. You know, out of the way, desolate places. As long as you are where other people are around, you're probably safe. But if you do see anything suspicious or that concerns you, don't hesitate to call me."

Hardly comforted by this, Lenny says, "Ok, I will." He ends the call.

He turns to Sisu who has curled up next to him on the couch. "I wish you were 120 pounds instead of twelve. But here's the deal. Be on guard for anyone who looks or smells suspicious. And if there's any trouble, go right for the crotch."

I need a beer.

PART THREE

Chapter Fifteen

As Lenny hoped, and to his relief, media coverage of the shooting began to fade as more recent tragedies dominated the news cycle. Thankful to be out of the spotlight, he turns his attention to the messages that have been piling up. His first call is to his sister, Eleanor. Five years his junior, Eleanor lives in Iowa where she remained after graduating from the university with a degree in forest management. Their divergent career paths were a source of intrigue and playful jibes: "I talk to people; you talk to trees."

Lenny admired how she managed to have a successful career, as a conservation specialist for the state, and a loving family: her spouse, William, an electrical engineer, and two, now adult, children, Tyler and Martha. Although she and Lenny did not speak often, their connection was strong.

Eleanor is happy to hear back from Lenny. She had read about the shooting in Vermont and was shocked to see him identified as one of the people present.

"Are you ok? It must have been awful."

He assures her that despite being shaken up he was fine. "In fact," he tells her, "I feel lucky to be alive."

When she asks for details he provides a brief, first-person summary minimizing his role in taking down the shooter. Eleanor mentions she read about the shooter's connections to neo-Nazi groups and asks if he is worried that he might become a target of "those crazies." She goes on to suggest he might want to "get out of Dodge" for a while and visit.

Lenny thanks her for the offer. "It would be great to see you again. Some time away might be beneficial. Unfortunately, this is not a good time." *Not until I know Emily is out of the woods, Jerry is ok, Larsen is convicted, and my life has returned to some semblance of normality.*

Eleanor does not ask for a further explanation, but he still tries to soften his rejection of her offer by saying he will figure out a later time when he will be able to come. They promise to talk again soon.

* * *

Some of Lenny's messages were from people who were at The Loft thanking him for his courageous action. He appreciates the sentiment telling himself they are thanking him for what he did, not why he did it. *Just be gracious and accept it.*

One voice message, from a woman named Patricia Sullivan who had been at the Loft with her daughter, Diedre, was particularly moving. A sophomore in college, Diedre was planning to read a poem she had written. It would be her first public reading and her mother came along for moral support. However, it was not to be. Before her turn came around the shooter arrived and Diedre was killed.

How unfathomably horrible was all Lenny could think. Even in the voice mail, her grief was evident.

"I'm not sure why I am calling you and hope it is not an intrusion. I guess I'm still in shock and don't know where to turn. One minute Diedre and I are laughing and the next she is gone. I appreciate the condolences and well wishes of others, but as you know, they cannot understand what it was like to be present during the shooting . . . or to lose a daughter." Lenny hears a muffled sob. "Sorry for the long message but I'm feeling very alone and vulnerable. Again, I apologize for taking your time. I imagine you too are dealing with the repercussions of what happened."

There's a silence and Lenny assumes the message has ended; however, just when he is about to move on, he hears, "I wonder if you might be willing to speak with me. I realize this might feel like an imposition, so I will understand if you don't call me back. I hope you are doing ok and thanks for listening."

God, how sad. So much destruction and heartbreak from the actions of one deluded, angry man. He tells himself to return the call later in the day.

He notices a new text from Ashley Lee, the reporter. "Hope you liked the story. Based on our conversation, I decided to do some research on mass shootings and Jeremy Larsen. The piece should be in today's edition. Thanks for the inspiration." Lenny puts down his phone and searches for the article. He finds it with the byline, "The Making of a Killer: Individual Disorder or Societal Failure?" Per his conversation with Ashley, it discusses the tendency to pathologize the perpetrators of mass killings while paying little attention to societal issues that produce such people and enable them to carry out their deadly missions. It identifies poverty, discrimination, the glorification of violence, and the availability of guns as contributing factors. Jeremy's troubled past and his abuse are used to illustrate how these factors shaped his life. To Lenny's surprise, the article quotes him as saying alienation and social isolation when coupled with brooding anger, make people like Jeremy receptive to the messages of hate groups. Using Jeremy as an example, Ashley describes how such groups provide members with a sense of camaraderie, belonging, and justification for the expression of their anger.

Then came the shocker. Last evening, Jeremy attempted to hang himself in his cell. He would have been successful but for a guard who happened to be walking by and got him down. He sustained serious injuries and was taken to a local hospital where his condition was listed as guarded.

Lenny is saddened by this new development. He wonders if Jeremy is receiving any help beyond his physical injuries. *Likely only interrogation by FBI agents.* He feels the urge to reach out to him, but also a reluctance to make this his *cause célèbre* or to increase his visibility.

Another internal argument ensues. *I'd like to help but there are too many complications.*

Yes, but should I let that stop me from reaching out? Maybe having someone who was at The Loft showing some compassion instead of just anger and the desire for punishment would be helpful.

But I too am angry and want him punished.

Yes, but I also have sympathy for the shitty life he's lived.

Ok, but what can I do? He's going away for life. And what about the other victims? How would they react? Shouldn't I be reaching out first to them? What about Jerry? Would he see it as a betrayal? I just don't think I can, or should, take this on now.

The result is a stalemate, inaction, and a vague feeling of regret.

He texts Ashley telling her he was impressed by her story about Jeremy and glad the interview provided another perspective. He resists suggesting another meeting.

A chortling sound from Sisu draws his attention. He's near the front door alternating glances between Lenny and the door. "Good idea," says Lenny thinking a walk will grant some respite from the stress he's feeling and help him clear his head.

Stepping outside immediately feels therapeutic. The weather is perfect: low seventies with a few fluffy clouds in a serene, blue sky. Taking some deep breaths, he feels his tension receding. He heads toward the park seeking its restorative properties. Sisu senses where they are going and does his best to accelerate Lenny's pace.

Entering the park, Lenny notices others are taking advantage of the nice weather. Some are sedentary: sitting or lying on blankets, lawn chairs, and benches; others more active: throwing a ball or a frisbee, walking or jogging.

Observing the scene, he recalls how it is possible to predict what people will be doing just from knowledge of the setting they are in. Whether in a restaurant, sports arena, classroom, or park, the behavior of most occupants can be accurately described without knowing anything about them. He wonders. *How much of our lives are lived according to social mores? What percentage of our waking hours are we conscious of what we are doing? I guess this is what the mindfulness movement is trying to counteract. Good luck!*

Seeking to be more mindful himself, he tries focusing on the foliage and spring blooms of the park but is distracted by the feeling that people recognize him from the story in the Chronicle and are looking at him. Although the story did not include his photo, finding one on the internet and posting it would be easy. He tells himself to stop being paranoid, but the feeling doesn't go away. He tries focusing on Sisu who is blissfully darting here and there discovering new buffets of smells and places to leave his 'calling card' for other dogs. This helps, but uneasiness remains.

As they continue through the park, loud music draws Lenny's attention to a group of men and women up ahead. Scattered among them are American flags and posters he cannot make out. Drawing closer, he sees some are wearing MAGA hats and sporting various tattoos and decals on their clothing that he recognizes as representative of neo-Nazi groups. His mouth becomes dry and his body tenses. He hears agent McGuire's voice telling him he would probably be safe when he was around other people. *She forgot to specify which other people.* He reverses his direction and accelerates his pace, not stopping until he is outside the park.

Back in his apartment, which now feels safe instead of confining, Lenny decides to take another shower for sedative rather than hygienic reasons. For ten minutes, he stands motionless under steaming water with his eyes closed. He tells himself nothing has changed except his hypersensitivity and vigilance. Reality is equivocal. If he starts thinking danger lurks in every nook and cranny, he will see it. It's a dilemma. If he reacts to imagined dangers before they happen, he will never know if they were real thereby maintaining his fears. On the other hand, if his fears are not irrational, then some degree of caution is prudent. After mulling it over to the point where his skin is beginning to wrinkle, he concludes that since the current situation is not permanent, it is best to err on the side of caution until it blows over.

The shower performed its magic and he feels more relaxed. He picks up his phone and calls Patricia Sullivan. She answers on the second ring.

"Hello, Ms. Sullivan?"

"Yes," answers a soft voice.

"This is Lenny Isaacson. You left me a voice mail asking me to call."

"Oh, Dr. Isaacson! Thank you so much for calling me back."

"You're welcome. Please accept my deep condolences on the loss of your daughter. I can't imagine what you must be going through."

"Thank you. It's been very difficult. I feel scared and lost."

"That's understandable."

"Diedre was my only family." Her voice cracks at the mention of her daughter's name. "We were very close."

"How can I help?"

After a brief silence, she says, "I'm finding it hard to talk with people who didn't experience what happened. Then I read about you in the *Chronicle*. I know you might also be struggling, so I hoped we might be able to meet . . . for our mutual benefit."

Sadness envelops Lenny as he imagines the horror of seeing your daughter killed and trying to manage your overwhelming grief by yourself. "I'd be happy to meet," he says earnestly. *At least I can provide a compassionate presence.*

"Thank you so much. Would it be ok to come to my home? I'm not quite ready to go out yet."

Lenny agrees and they decide on tomorrow. Patricia texts him her address.

* * *

Lenny adjusts his blanket for what feels like the hundredth time. He likes to sleep on his left side, but his wound makes it uncomfortable. His thoughts keep returning to The Loft, the carnage, and the fear he experienced. He glances at the bedside clock: 2:20. Feeling too restless to sleep, he gets out of bed and walks into the living room. He looks out the window at the empty street. The silver maple trees lining the road stand like sentinels watching over the neighborhood. He watches their deeply toothed leaves turn gently in the breeze revealing their silvery undersides from which they derive their name. He imagines they are whispering to each other in a language humans have long ago forgotten. For a while, he loses himself in their communion before making his way back to bed.

Morning arrives too soon. He drags himself to the bathroom and splashes cold water on his face. He checks his wound. It's not healing as quickly as expected, and he chides himself for not seeking medical attention. *Why do I keep putting it off?* The question is not rhetorical. He knows the answer: his fear it could be something serious. He tries to rationalize his avoidance by telling himself he is meeting with Patricia Sullivan, but it's a flimsy excuse, and he knows it. A promise to himself to call tomorrow if it doesn't look any better buys him time.

Chapter Sixteen

Patricia Sullivan lives about eight miles away in one of the many small towns outside of Burlington. Her home is a typical New England rectangular-shaped, two story, wood colonial with symmetrically placed windows. There's a covered porch in front with two rocking chairs and flowers along the border. A one-car garage sits on the side with a Prius in the driveway. Lenny parks behind the Prius. As he walks toward the door, he glimpses a good-sized backyard with several trees.

Just as he is about to knock, Patricia opens the door. She appears to be in her early to mid-fifties, about 5'9", with a slender but solid build and shoulder-length, auburn hair. She's wearing jeans and a simple white top with some embroidery just under the oval neckline. Her eyes are a striking cornflower blue reminiscent of the famous oil painting *Girl with a Pearl Earring* by the Dutch artist Johannes Vermeer. But sadness is also present. '*Bluer than goodbye,*' thinks Lenny, reminded of a line from a song.

She greets Lenny with a modest smile. "Hello, Dr. Isaacson. Thanks so much for coming."

"Sure," says Lenny. "It's nice to meet you although I wish the circumstances were different."

This elicits a sad nod. "Please come in,"

He follows her into the living room. It is minimally but nicely furnished with a couple of comfortable-looking chairs and a couch. He notices a variety of artwork on the walls and some photographs on side tables.

"Have a seat," says Patricia. "Would you like something to drink?"

"Coffee would be nice."

While she goes to get the coffee, Lenny looks more closely at the photos. One that catches his eye is of a smiling, young woman with the same auburn hair and blue eyes as her mother. Based on her clothing, backpack, and the wooden walking stick she is holding, he assumes she is beginning or returning from a hike. How sad, he thinks, to have such a youthful, vibrant life snuffed out by a random and violent act. Another song line pops into his head. 'Lord, don't let the cold winds blow until I'm too old to die young.' That wish would not be realized for poor Diedre.

Patricia returns with the coffee and sits in a chair opposite Lenny. "Thanks again for coming over. As I said on the phone, it's hard to talk with people who didn't experience what happened. I'm still having trouble believing that Diedre is gone, yet, at the same time, it's crushingly real. Does that make sense Dr. Isaacson?" she asks as tears form in the corners of her eyes.

"Perfect sense," answers Lenny. "I've had similar feelings. And please, call me Lenny. What happened is so unimaginable, that our minds rebel against its acceptance, but the harsh reality cannot be wished away."

"No, it can't," Patricia whispers. "It's crazy, but I woke up the other morning thinking Diedre was home. I called her name only to have the silence jolt me back to reality. I so much want this to be a nightmare I will wake up from," her voice becomes tremulous, "but as you said, wishing doesn't make it so." Tears are now visible on her cheeks and sadness fills the room.

"What you describe is perfectly normal," says Lenny softly. "You've suffered a terrible loss and need to allow yourself to grieve. Would it be ok to tell me a little about Diedre? I assume that's her," he says pointing at the photo he'd been looking at.

"It is."

"It's a beautiful photo. She seems to have your hair and eye color." He realizes too late that he addressed her in the present tense.

"Yes, people often commented on how alike we look . . . looked." She takes a deep breath and wipes her eyes with a tissue she removes from her pocket. "Diedre was a sophomore at the University majoring in art. "She is, er, was, quite talented." Struggling with talking about her daughter in the past tense, Patricia stops abruptly as if the words are stuck in her throat. After some moments she says, "Would you like to see some of her work?"

"I'd love to."

Lenny follows Patricia through the house as she points out her paintings hanging on the walls. Most are nature scenes reflecting the waters, mountains, and boreal landscapes of Vermont. Although far from a connoisseur, Lenny can tell she was talented. He shares this with Patricia which elicits a wistful smile. As they walk, Patricia describes how Diedre loved to draw even as a young child. "I've even saved some of her crayon drawings," she says with obvious pride. Sadly, this uptick in mood vanishes when she realizes there will be no further creations.

They make their way back to the living room. Patricia talks more about Diedre's interests, her many virtues, and their relationship. Lenny senses talking about her daughter, although painful, is important, so he stays attentive and quiet only commenting briefly about what a fine person Diedre was and how her loss must be felt by many.

Patricia tells Lenny that Diedre lived at home to save on expenses but was considering getting an apartment with friends for her junior year. "That won't happen now," she says again wiping her eyes.

Lenny's face reflects her sadness.

Still needing to talk, Patricia describes how Diedre's birth changed her life. She was married at the time to Diedre's father, but they had been struggling. Dan, her ex, was ambitious in a way that Patricia felt compromised their values and led to lots of conflict. When Diedre was born, she naively thought it would bring them closer, but it had the opposite effect. Dan felt more tied down and frustrated and started drinking. Eventually, it got to the point where Patricia felt unsafe not only for herself but for Diedre. After a scary incident in which an inebriated Dan dropped Diedre, Patricia gave him an ultimatum: get help or leave. He took the latter option. Three years later he was killed in a car accident where it was determined he was legally drunk.

"I would have fallen apart if not for Diedre. My love for her was stronger than my self-recrimination and grief. I was determined to give her a good life. I had a degree in English and I went back to school and earned a teaching degree. I thought it would provide stability and would give me summers off to spend with Diedre. Luckily, I was hired by Burlington High School and have been there ever since."

"Do you have any children?" she asks Lenny.

"No. When I was married, we tried for a few years but were unsuccessful. The reason was never clear leading to guilt and subtle blaming on both our parts. Instead of children, we had dogs and immersed ourselves in our respective careers. So, no children, but I do have a niece and nephew in Iowa, my sister's children."

"That's nice." Then changing the subject, Patricia says, "Why do you think he did it?"

Lenny scratches the back of his neck. The sudden change of topic surprises him, but he goes with it. "My impression is he is a very troubled man caught up in Neo-Nazi and racist paranoia to the point where he believed certain people were a direct threat. Apparently, he thought such people were present at The Loft. What is not known is whether he did this on his own or was pushed into it by others of his ilk."

"It's so sad how we create such monsters. He didn't come into the world that way."

"No, he didn't," says Lenny noting the similarity to his own views. He thinks how different her reaction is from Jerry's who wants to kill Larsen and wonders whether gender plays a role. *Maybe some, but I'm guessing there's more to it.*

Then, in a barely audible voice, Patricia says, "I don't know what to do," reminding him that she did not ask him over to have an intellectual discussion.

In what he hopes is an empathic tone, he says, "There's no blueprint or roadmap for how to deal with this. It's still so raw. Most important at this point is allowing yourself to grieve, keeping expectations to a minimum, and practicing self-care."

"Good advice, but it hurts so much. I find myself sobbing half the day."

The heartache in her voice is palpable. He restrains himself from reaching out and holding her knowing that as a relative stranger it might be perceived as inappropriate. There is no quick fix.

"Of course. You suffered a tremendous loss under terrible circumstances. Although the sense of loss will likely always be with you to some degree, I believe in time you will find a way forward. I'm sure you have other supports, but if I can be helpful, feel free to call me anytime."

Patricia looks up. Her eyes are red and puffy. "Thank you, Lenny. It was kind of you to talk with me. Feeling alone with this was overwhelming. Despite how I look, I feel a little better." She laughs ruefully.

Lenny's glad he came. She's a good person, and he's pleased he could be helpful. At the same time, he knows the road ahead will be long and painful.

As he gets up to leave, Patricia says haltingly, "Can I give you a hug?"

"Sure," says Lenny. Expecting a somewhat perfunctory hug, he is surprised by the intensity with which Patricia holds him. *She must really need this kind of connection*, realizing after a few moments that he does too. About fifteen seconds into the hug, Patricia's hand touches his side where his wound is located. He grunts involuntarily in pain. Startled, she drops her arms and moves back.

"Are you ok? Did I hurt you?" she asks, concern in her voice.

"I'm ok," says Lenny trying not to wince. "During the attack, I fell and cut myself on my left side. Nothing serious, but it's still sensitive."

"Oh, I'm sorry. Have you had it looked at?"

"No, but I plan to."

Inside his car, his wound is still smarting, so he calls his doctor's office. Miraculously, they can see him later today.

"Just keep moving," he mutters as he drives away.

Chapter Seventeen

After a beautiful morning, the weather grows progressively unsettled. From his living room window, Lenny watches the trees do their wind dance as the sky darkens. It's an hour before his doctor's appointment, so he passes the time reviewing his remaining messages related to The Loft, politely but succinctly answering ones from people he knows and ignoring or deleting the rest. As he writes, he reflects on how contingent events and being in a certain place at a certain time can change your life. And once those events occur, our interpretations and responses shape what those changes will become. But what shapes those interpretations and responses? Sensing he's about to slide into another of his bottomless interrogatives, he shifts to the concrete example of The Loft and how that evening changed so many lives.

Was it chance, fate, karma, providence, a message from God, none of these? How do each of these explanations affect peoples' understanding and actions? He catches himself. *Not only 'people,' me!*

Why not be pragmatic? Choose whatever explanation will be most helpful.

Don't be naïve Lenny. What is most helpful will be influenced by past experiences and current beliefs including believing you can choose among explanations.

And don't forget relationships. When we talk about 'what happened,' we are, in effect, re-constituting the event. My conversations with Jerry, Patricia, Ashley, and Gifford all contribute to my understanding and theirs.

Whatever the reasons, chance works best for me. It is neutral, not implying what happened was a judgment or consequence of the kind of person I am.

On the other hand, it's not very grounding: anything can happen at any time . . .

Unaware that he failed to avoid yet another rabbit hole, he is rescued by the message tone from his phone reminding him of his doctor's appointment. Time to get off the couch and get ready. He goes to the bathroom and examines the wound. It looks about the same which confirms his decision to get it checked out.

* * *

Although never eager to see a doctor, Lenny has known his internist, Michael Lisman, for almost twenty years. In addition to his clinical practice, Dr. Lisman taught at the university medical school which made him Lenny's colleague. This relationship helped put Lenny at ease and made it easier to raise questions and express concerns.

After checking in, he is led forthwith by a cheerful nurse to an examining room. She checks his vital signs and asks some perfunctory questions about his visit.

A few minutes later, a soft knock on the door is followed by Lisman's entrance. He smiles and greets Lenny. Lisman is in his late-fifties, tall and lean with thinning brown hair. His round, boyish face and intelligent blue eyes belie his years. Eschewing the traditional white coat, he is dressed in a blue, button-down oxford shirt and tan corduroy pants.

They briefly exchange views on non-medical topics: university politics, Lenny's retirement, and Lisman's Fulbright application which he hopes will enable him to go to India. Then turning to the business at hand, Lisman glances at his assistant's notes. "So, you cut yourself. How did it happen?"

Lenny tells him about his experience at The Loft and how he fell.

"Wow," exclaims Lisman. "I didn't realize you were there."

He must not read the newspaper.

"What an awful experience. Well, let's take a look at your injury."

Lenny removes his shirt. "I tried treating it myself, but as you can see, it's not healing too well."

Lisman spends a minute peering at the wound and gently touching the surrounding skin. Lenny winces. "Sorry," says Lisman. "Have you had any fever? Chills?"

"No."

"Unusually fatigued?"

"I have been tired, but I think from being emotionally drained."

Lisman nods. "You have cellulitis, a bacterial skin infection. I'm going to prescribe an antibiotic that should clear it up. If you don't see any improvement after three days, or if it gets worse, or you develop other symptoms like chills or fever, let me know. I'll give you some sterile bandages you can use to keep it clean."

Lenny leaves the office happy to learn the wound is not serious. Walking towards his car he notices two guys on motorcycles at the far end of the parking lot who seem to be glancing his way. The phone message threat resurfaces. *Is this real or am I getting paranoid?* Fortunately, he does not have to go by them, so he exits without incident.

About halfway home he hears the rumble of motorcycles behind him. He looks in his rear-view mirror. It's the guys from the parking lot. His anxiety spikes. Without thinking he accelerates and makes a few unnecessary turns. He rechecks his mirror. No sign of them. Shaken, but relieved, he heads directly home.

I may be imagining things, but I think I'll call agent McGuire.

Entering his apartment, the ever-effusive Sisu is there to greet him. *What must it be like to feel such joy over the mere presence of someone? We can learn a lot from dogs.*

In the safety of his apartment with the perceived threat gone, he feels ambivalent about contacting the FBI agent but he calls. McGuire listens without interruption.

"I'm glad you called. It's better to be wrong than harmed," she says, echoing his thoughts. My guess is that even if they were following you, their goal was to frighten you. Typically, these guys get their jollies by intimidating people. Still, continue to be cautious and let me know if you have other sightings or experience any direct threats."

Talking with McGuire helps tamp down his frayed nerves, but he's still worried. After The Loft, his safety is a foreground rather than a background concern. *Am I letting these assholes get the better of me? Maybe, but it only takes one of these wackos to act on his delusions.*

He walks to his closet and takes out a long rectangular box.

Inside is a 20-gauge shotgun. He got it as a going-away present decades ago when he left his social worker job in rural Wisconsin. It was a strange gift since the only time he'd ever shot a gun of any kind was when a friend took him skeet shooting. He found it entertaining despite bruising his shoulder from the gun's kick but never considered taking it up as a hobby. Other than showing the gun to a former university colleague who was a hunter—hoping he might want to buy it—it had not been out of the box. Now he wonders if he should buy some shells.

Will life ever return to normal? I doubt it. Too much has changed that can't be erased. Maybe the more relevant question is what will life be like going forward? Despite the terrible things that have happened some good might come out of this. Evil and good are not mutually exclusive; they coexist. I need to keep that focus or I'll wind up a basket case.

* * *

Sitting at his computer, Lenny loads the file of a novel he's been puttering with for about a year. After years of scholarly writing, he enjoys the creative freedom of fiction and the challenge of expressing ideas in plain language through interesting storylines. Even when he was at the university, he questioned the ponderousness and inaccessibility of academic prose as if such qualities indicated erudition. What it did guarantee was the readership would be limited to other academics and even among this group only those interested in the topic.

Now in retirement, free from any pressure to publish, he looked forward to expressing his ideas in new ways. *Who knows? Maybe*

I'll write something more than ten people will read. He soon learned, however, that the idea of writing a novel and doing it were quite different. Confronting a blank computer screen with only your imagination, creativity, and life experience to draw on was daunting. As a result, his work pace was slow, but his commitment to seeing it through kept him plodding along.

So far, the story was about a computer scientist named Tobias Phillips who teaches at a small college in the Midwest. While attending an academic conference in Italy, he meets Dr. Carolina Gutiérrez, an educational consultant and independent scholar from Spain. They wind up spending a lot of time together both at the conference and outside of it. In a short time, their relationship becomes more than collegial. When the conference ends, she asks him to extend his stay at her home on the Costa del Sol in southern Spain. Quite infatuated with the brilliant and exotic Carolina, Tobias agrees. After a few days of enjoying the breathtaking landscape and each other, Carolina tells him about her involvement in a secret society, simply called The Group which seeks to disrupt what they see as oppressive, corrupt systems of power in the world. Drawing on their talents as scholars in different fields, they engage in what Carolina calls the resistance tactics of the powerless. Mostly, this entails publishing letters and articles, often under pseudonyms, in newspapers, social media, and the popular press, and in supporting websites and organizations that critique various global trends and promote progressive ideas.

Their agenda and the opportunity to shake up the system are attractive to Tobias who sees himself as politically progressive. Along with being swept up in the romance with Carolina and wanting to please her, he welcomes adding a little spark to the tedium of his academic life. With little urging from Carolina, he allows himself to be conscripted into their ranks.

Lenny rubs his chin as he thinks about how to continue. Although nothing specific comes up, he starts to write :

> Returning to the U.S., Tobias energetically tries to advance The Group's mission by writing opinion pieces for various social media outlets about the neo-liberal plot to convert higher education from its traditional goals of education and critical thinking into an institution guided by corporate ideology and economic needs. He even critiques his own field of computer science, under a pseudonym, for its complicity with the anti-democratic surveillance practices of the government.
>
> A significant personal benefit of these activities is it keeps him connected with Carolina. She is profuse in her praise of his writing and her feelings about him. Life is tinged with excitement and Tobias feels more alive than he can remember.
>
> Six months into his involvement with The Group, Carolina invites him again to her home. Romantic fantasies blossom and he eagerly accepts. However, those fantasies fizzle when he arrives and learns he is not the only guest; another man and woman are present. They introduce themselves as Marcos Estrada and Audrey Williamson. Marcos' firm handshake fits his muscular physique. Tobias guesses him to be mid-forties.

He's about 5' 10" with light brown skin, black hair, and intense, penetrating dark eyes. Audrey is around the same age, about 5' 4" with a medium build. Her pale-complexioned face and brown eyes are framed by short, chestnut-colored hair. She conveys an air of friendliness and intelligence that softens the blow of not being alone with Carolina. Both are casually dressed in jeans, comfortable shirts, and sandals.

Tobias learns Marcos and Audrey are co-founders and de facto leaders of The Group. Like Carolina, they complement him on his recent activities and commitment to their cause. Audrey says, "You have shown an unusual talent for articulating our issues in a compelling way. Your contributions will be rewarded." She turns to Marcos who informs him he has earned the privilege of learning about other lesser known but core activities of The Group. At this point, Carolina, who had been brewing coffee, joins them and sits by Tobias.

He listens as they explain that while his current activities are important, they are peripheral to The Group's primary purpose of stopping global corporate hegemony. More radical actions are needed. However, because such actions carry greater risk, only a small subset of The Group's members—those who are exceptionally talented and dedicated to the cause—are invited to become involved in what they call their blueprint for transformative change. Tobias shifts in his seat intrigued but a little anxious. Sensing his unease,

Carolina moves a little closer and takes his hand.

Marcos and Audrey explain that select members of The Group—the inner circle—are involved in more formidable activities designed to disrupt and subvert existing systems ranging from educational institutions to governments. This destabilization, they stress, is a prerequisite for real change to occur. Their interest in him becomes clearer when he learns a primary activity involves hacking into the computer networks of governments, financial institutions, arms manufacturers, private militias, and chemical companies. Some of this information is leaked strategically to the public. Occasionally, information is changed to create uncertainty, lack of trust, and a general disruption of operations. Carrying out these activities requires The Group to develop alliances with certain radical political factions some of whom are engaged in other illegal activities including isolated acts of violence.

At the mention of violence, Tobias' body goes rigid and his eyes open wide. He stammers, "You . . . you kill people?"

Marcos answers in a neutral tone. "No, but there are occasions, very rare, where drastic action is necessary to save the lives of others. You know, acting for the greater good."

Marcos' justification does little to alleviate Tobias' growing alarm. *What have I gotten myself into?* He begins to question whether Carolina's feelings for him are real or a recruitment task she was carrying out for The Group. *And what will happen if I refuse to get further involved? Can they allow me to leave with the knowledge I already possess? How far would they go to stop me?*

He struggles to keep an impassive look and tries to ask what he thinks are reasonable questions from someone hearing these things for the first time. Hoping there has been a misunderstanding that will let him off the hook he says, "My computer work is somewhat esoteric and not very applicable to what you describe, so I am not sure how I can be helpful."

Audrey smiles. "You underestimate yourself, Tobias. Your technological expertise and knowledge of social issues would be of great value to our efforts." Pausing to let her words sink in, she adds emphatically, "We would be honored to have you as part of the team."

A queasy feeling arises in the pit of his stomach. At the same time, Carolina leans over and whispers in his ear, "It will be fine. You will do great work. I am sure of it." Her reassurance, however, does not stem his growing unease.

As if prescient, Marcos says, "I realize this is a lot to process Tobias. Take some time and think it over." Then, changing the topic he enthusiastically declares, "Enough of this serious talk. Let's get some dinner and have some fun!"

His declaration lightens the mood, and they spend the rest of the evening dining, drinking, and talking as if the previous conversation never occurred. Marcos is in good spirits regaling them with humorous stories from his childhood to the delight of Audrey and Carolina. Tobias plays along trying to hide the precarious web he feels descending over him.

When the evening winds down, Carolina leads Tobias to her bedroom telling him how proud she is of him and how much she missed him. For the rest of the night, his misgivings are forgotten.

* * *

Lenny stops writing unsure how the story will develop from here. Since this is his first attempt at a novel, he is learning by doing. He's discovered that his style of writing is to allow the story to unfold as he writes rather than to follow an outline. Writing this way is not easy, there are many dead-ends, and he often struggles with 'the critic in his head' who tells him he has nothing interesting to say. He counterbalances these messages with stubbornness and determination.

As he reflects on his work, he muses aloud, "This is not so different than what is happening in my life. Is it happenstance or another way of working through stuff? Either way, I hope it helps the novel and my life."

FINDING LENNY

Chapter Eighteen

The next couple of days are spent in a futile attempt to reinstate a sense of normalcy to his life. Worries and uncertainties demand his attention: his relationship with Jerry, the response to his role in the shooting, anxiety about his health, and threats to his safety. But it was the enigmatic Ezekiel that raised the most questions. Who is he? Will I see him again? Is he even real? Is there a message in his words I should be paying more attention to? He counsels himself not to dwell on him, that doing so embellishes weirdness and coincidence with meaning. But he cannot shake some unnamable feeling that these encounters are important.

Putting these questions aside, he decides to check in with Jerry, hoping the anger he witnessed when they last met is under control. After four rings, his call goes to voicemail. He leaves a message that he's been thinking about him and would be happy to get together. Fifteen minutes later Jerry returns his call.

"Hello, Lenny. I've been letting calls go to voice mail to avoid nuisance calls. Once your name is public you become a target for people's exploitation: People trying to sell us home security equipment or wanting to interview Emily. Stuff like that. Anyway,

I'm glad you called and would like to meet. How about instead of the coffee shop you come to my home and have dinner with us?"

Lenny is surprised but pleased by Jerry's upbeat mood. "You're sure it won't be too much trouble? You have a lot going on."

"No. Katie and the kids would love to see you."

"Ok then," says Lenny. "I'll see you tonight."

"Great. Come about six."

* * *

Through his living room window, Lenny watches some fluffy clouds retreat from inclement weather moving in from the west. Feeling lethargic, he settles into a chair and closes his eyes. He could stay like this for a long time but a paw on his leg tells him that Sisu has other ideas. He looks down into his beckoning eyes and says the magic word, "out," which instantly elicits ear-splitting yips as Sisu runs to the front door.

"You're right," says Lenny. "We should get out before the weather gets any worse."

Once outside he can feel the movement of the oncoming front. He has always liked storms and usually enjoys being out in unsettled weather. Now, however, the unsettledness is also internal as he finds himself scanning his surroundings for anything out of the ordinary. After walking two blocks he turns back towards home. "This needs to stop," he mutters as he enters his building.

He checks the news for any follow-up stories related to The Loft. As he expected, with each passing day the newsworthiness of the event diminishes and the two pieces he finds require some searching. One story is about Jeremy Larsen. He's expected to be charged with a hate crime at his formal arraignment after his discharge from the hospital. The other focuses on the victims, their devastated lives, and how they are trying to put them back together. The story is by Ashley Lee and much of it focuses on Emily, how she and her family are dealing with her recovery, and the emotional fallout from the shooting. She describes how the shooting shattered the family's sense of safety and how they are struggling to come to terms with their new reality. He feels that the piece is sensitive and well done. *I guess I'll learn tonight how they feel about it.* Gratefully, he finds no mention of himself.

His phone chimes alerting him to new texts from Agent McGuire and Patricia Sullivan. The FBI agent is checking in on whether he's encountered any new situations where he felt threatened. He texts back that although some people seem a bit too focused on him, there have been no direct threats. Then feeling like he may be overreacting or becoming paranoid, he deletes the first part of the sentence and thanks her for her concern.

Patricia's text reiterates that she enjoyed meeting him and asks if he would be interested in getting together again. He writes that he would be happy to meet. It's strange, he thinks, how most major life disruptions are related to loss, yet the process of trying to put your life back together generates new experiences and opportunities. Within a few minutes Patricia messages back asking if he's free tomorrow and if so, could he come again to her home and perhaps have some lunch. Lenny smiles. *Well, whatever happens, at least I won't starve.*

* * *

Lenny arrives at Jerry and Katie's home a few minutes before six. It's located in a quiet, upper-middle-class neighborhood of Shelburne, a small town about seven miles south of Burlington. Situated at the end of a fifty-foot driveway, their colonial-style home is typical of the area: gray with white trim, covered front porch, two-car garage in front, and a half acre yard in back. Lenny notices that the lawn could use mowing which given Jerry's fastidiousness surprises him. He knocks on the front door and is welcomed inside by Katie and their golden retriever, Chester, who sniffs Lenny's pants legs undoubtedly smelling Sisu. Katie escorts Lenny into the living room, a large rectangular space with two huge windows facing the front opposite a gas fireplace. There's a comfortable-looking, beige couch on one side and two, gray, accent chairs on the other. A wooden coffee table with a vase of flowers sits in the middle.

Jerry is sitting in one of the chairs. He rises, shakes Lenny's hand, and tells him he's glad he could come. Katie asks Lenny if he would like something to drink: beer, wine or something else. Lenny goes with a beer. She turns to Jerry who says he will have the same.

"It's been a while since you've been here," says Jerry.

"A couple of months, I think," replies Lenny noticing that Jerry looks more relaxed than when he left him at the coffee shop.

Jerry says, "so tell me what's been happening in your life. Has there been much reaction to the news stories?"

Lenny wonders if Jerry is trying to be a good host or hoping to direct the conversation away from himself. "I've had many texts and calls since the story appeared in the *Chronicle*. They range from well-wishers, concerned friends and acquaintances, to salesmen and supporters of Jeremy Larsen."

"Jeremy Larsen? The gunman?" says Jerry.

Lenny describes the threats and the 'sightings' of people he thought might be targeting him. Immediately, he regrets doing so. Jerry's jaw tenses and he clenches his fists, his calm demeanor from a moment ago gone.

"What the hell is this world coming to?" he says, his volume rising. "If you ask me, we've been far too lax in our responses to this kind of stuff. These people are scum, and they should be dealt with in that manner. Wrapping themselves in the flag is such bullshit. They desecrate the flag!"

Jerry's outburst sets off alarm bells in Lenny who recalls his rage when they last met. He tries to defuse Jerry's anger by reframing the situation. "I agree. No one should feel threatened because they disagree with another's beliefs. I think—"

"This is more than disagreement," interrupts Jerry with shocking intensity. "They're like a virus that should be eradicated like any dangerous disease."

Wow. What has happened to him? He's like nitroglycerin. One shake and he explodes. Ironically, he seems unaware that his position is a mirror image of the people he is raging against. What should I say?

Before he can formulate a response, Katie appears. If she heard Jerry's outburst, she's not letting on. Instead, she calmly tells them to come to the dining room. They rise and silently follow her.

Entering the room, Lenny is surprised to see Emily seated at the table. He smiles while walking towards her.

"Emily, it's so good to see that you are up and around."

Emily returns his smile. She stays seated but extends her hand. "Hi, Lenny. Nice to see you too."

Her handshake is restrained. The youthful robustness he associates with Emily is markedly diminished, replaced by sadness or fatigue. *I hope this is temporary.* Not wanting to linger on Emily, he turns to Danny, their teenage son who has also entered the room. "Hi, Danny. Good to see you. How's soccer going?" he asks as if this was a normal visit.

"Ok," he answers in a monotone voice. Like many teenagers, his expressionless expression is hard to read.

There's an uneasiness in the room as if everyone is trying to figure out how to behave in contrast to how they feel. It's a difficult balancing act. Katie tries to elevate the mood or at least keep it from getting worse.

"Danny's being modest. He's doing great. He scored the winning goal in their last game," she says proudly. From the look on Danny's face, she could have been talking about the weather. When no one else in the family comes to the rescue, she moves on.

"Drinks anyone?"

The meal proceeds uneventfully. Attempting to make conversation, Lenny asks Emily how her recovery is going. She tells him that she's still sore, but each day is a little better. She adds that she hopes to return to school when the next semester begins. "I hope so too," says Lenny. He briefly considers asking about the interview with Ashley Lee but decides against it not wanting to risk worsening what feels like a volatile situation.

Katie thanks Lenny for calling Jerry when he saw that Emily was injured. She also asks how he is doing. Before he can answer, Danny says, "That was very cool what you did, Lenny. You should get a medal" (echoing Lenny's neighbors). Katie and Emily nod their heads in agreement. Jerry seems somewhere else.

In typical fashion, Lenny thanks them but downplays his role.

The conversation, minus Jerry's participation, remains cordial but stilted as if they are reading from a script entitled 'everything is ok despite what happened' while ignoring the obvious elephant in the room. When the meal ends, Jerry rises and without a word leaves the room, threatening the emotional status quo. Lenny wonders what he is trying to communicate, or whether he is too wrapped up in himself even to be thinking that way?

After an uncomfortable silence, Emily and Danny look at each other and ask Katie if they can be excused. They turn to Lenny, tell him it was nice to see him, and leave.

* * *

Katie and Lenny are alone in the dining room, a cloud of discomfort from Jerry's distress and abrupt departure hanging over them. Katie gets up and picks up a plate as if starting to clear the table then turns to Lenny. "I'm worried about Jerry."

Playing dumb, Lenny says, "He did appear out of sorts. Is something else going on?"

Katie puts down the plate, concern etched on her face. "I'm not sure. He's not telling me much which is unusual, He's struggling with anger, mostly at the guy who did the shooting, and guilt about his inability to prevent what happened to Emily."

"It's hard to predict our reactions to such extreme incidents," offers Lenny. "Even though there was obviously nothing he could have done, he might still feel that he failed in his role as Emily's father."

"But that makes no sense," says Katie, exasperation creeping into her voice. "Why can't he see that?"

"Sometimes the things we struggle with don't make sense from an intellectual perspective," replies Lenny sympathetically. "We get stuck between a view of ourselves, that we may not have been aware of, and what we are experiencing."

"You mean like seeing himself as someone who keeps his children from harm no matter what and the reality that Emily was harmed?"

"Yes."

Tears form in Katie's eyes. "Jerry's always been so even-keeled. I don't think he knows how to handle these feelings. He tries not to show it, but as you saw tonight, it's not working. I'm scared for him . . . and for us. What can we do?"

"Your continued support is probably most important even if it looks like he's trying to push you away. I can also try talking with him. I'll call tomorrow and ask him to meet."

"Thanks," says Katie lightly touching his forearm. "I think that could be helpful. He respects you and values your friendship."

"And vice versa," says Lenny as he stands. "Let me help you with the dishes."

When the task is complete, Lenny prepares to leave. Jerry has not made an appearance and Lenny decides to let him be. As he gets into his car, he glances down the street and notices what he thinks is a motorcycle. There's a tightening in his chest. *Am I being followed?*

He takes a deep breath. *Don't run away with this, Lenny,* he counsels himself. *People own motorcycles. If you continue down this path, you'll start seeing potential assailants behind every bush.*

Struggling not to panic he starts the engine and drives home; however, he can't help glancing repeatedly in the side and rear-view mirrors.

* * *

The next morning is slow in coming. Dreams of encounters with bad dudes on motorcycles and discomfort from his wound, leaves Lenny feeling exhausted. He gets up and checks his side. There's still redness. *Have I been taking the meds every day?* he asks himself, unsure. *I'll call Lisman.*

He also reminds himself to check in on Jerry. What he observed last night was worrisome. It's like he was struggling with an alternate self, an angry and guilt-ridden Jerry that had been buried and out-of-awareness until awakened by his daughter's injury.

Lenny wonders how many others not listed among the injured have had their lives thrown into turmoil, uncertainty, and fear, unable or unwilling to seek help because of guilt or shame at their self-perceived weakness? He has a new appreciation for how the casualties of wars go well beyond the combatants.

His thoughts turn to Patricia Sullivan and how alone and alienated she feels. He finds himself looking forward to seeing her this afternoon. He enjoys the human contact and is comfortable being in a helping role. And yes, he acknowledges, she is an attractive woman, although at this point in his life he feels that romance is more a fantasy than anything else.

He commences his morning routine of eating, showering, dressing, and walking Sisu. Although he sometimes questions how routinized his life has become, he finds comfort in it. *Besides this day is different. I'm checking in with Lisman and Jerry and going to see Patricia. I might even answer a text from my sister asking whether I decided to visit. Who knows what adventures await,* he tells himself with a mocking grin.

Time to get moving. He calls Lisman's office and speaks with one of his nurses. He describes the situation with his wound and also mentions a cough that's been hanging on for some weeks. *Might as well cover all the bases.* She puts him on hold to consult with the doctor. After a few minutes of annoying pop music, she returns and tells Lenny Dr. Lisman can see him in two days. *Two days? So, he doesn't think it's serious. Good.* However, the nurse adds, if the wound gets worse before then, or if he experiences symptoms like chills or fever, he should call or go to the ER. *That's comforting,* he thinks sarcastically, his concern reinstated. He makes the appointment.

He texts his sister again thanking her for her offer to visit and reiterating that matters at home require his attention. He assures her that once they are taken care of, he will contact her about a time he can come to Iowa. She responds immediately with an 'ok' and an offer to talk with him about 'those matters' if he thinks it might be helpful. She ends with, 'Take care of yourself, Lenny. After all, you're an old guy now,' followed by a winking and grinning emoji.

* * *

Driving to Patricia's home he's relieved no one, real or imagined, followed him. Patricia greets him warmly informing him lunch will soon be ready. In the meantime, they have some coffee in the living room.

"Our previous talk was helpful," says Patricia. "Although every day is a struggle, it reminded me that it will take time to find a way to live with my sorrow."

"Yes, and as I said, you are in an acute phase of grief. Allowing yourself to experience it, despite how painful it feels, is healing."

Lunch consists of a salad with a variety of fresh vegetables and what looks like homemade bread still warm from the oven. After taking a bite, Lenny asks, "Did you bake this?"

"Yes. I like to bake. I find it calming."

"And I find it delicious," he says, while helping himself to another piece.

Patricia smiles. "Glad you like it."

As they eat and talk Lenny becomes aware that despite Patricia's grief, he is enjoying their interaction. *Maybe I'm lonelier than I thought.*

When they finish, Patricia says, "Would you like to go for a walk? There is a nice trail not far from here."

"Great idea. It will be good to be outside."

"Do you mind if we take Monet?"

"The artist?" says Lenny with a mock smile.

"Oh, I forgot, you haven't met him. Monet is our . . . my dog. A friend was caring for him since . . ." her voice trails off. "He's in the back now, but he always loves walking on the trail."

"Sure, bring him along," says Lenny. He'll have to meet my dog sometime. He also loves to walk."

"It's a date," says Patricia.

A date? Is that what she said?

The day is gorgeous: pale blue sky, mild temperature, and a light breeze. Lenny is happy to be out and moving. From the looks of Patricia and Monet—a small, wire-haired terrier mix with a constantly wagging tail and a sweet face—they are too. They walk through the neighborhood for about ten minutes before reaching the trail. There is a wooden sign at the front with *Bouchard Trail* at the top and a map below showing a three-mile loop. It looks well maintained and inviting.

Lenny says, "Let me guess, Bouchard was the person who donated his land for the trail."

"Good guess," says Patricia. "This whole area used to be part of a farm. The family must have decided there was more money and less work in housing than farming."

"Probably true," responds Lenny wistfully. "It reminds me of a song. 'There's houses in the fields. And the last few farms are growing out of here.' Have you ever thought about what the land around here was like before it was settled? People come, cut down the trees, clear the land, and build their houses. Before long, the original landscape is forgotten. I find it ironic that often these same people, and I'm one of them, decry the destruction of the natural environment for development; development that comes *after* them. Our starting point shifts depending on when we arrived on the scene."

"I guess we're all guilty of that," replies Patricia. "But people have to live somewhere. Maybe the key is *responsible* development, finding a way to exist in harmony with nature rather than dominating it."

"Yes," he concurs. *I like how she thinks.* "And that would include population control so there would be less pressure on continual development."

They continue in silence, aware of each other's presence while enjoying the peaceful setting. Patricia stops and points to some lavender wildflowers. "They are bluebells. Aren't they beautiful?"

"They are," agrees Lenny, happy to be looking at wildflowers instead of the inside of his apartment.

They're about to resume their walk when a large, portly man with dark hair and a scraggly black beard emerges from the bushes on the side of the trail about fifteen feet in front of them. At first glance, Lenny thinks he might be a homeless person who has been camping out. That impression changes as the man turns toward them. He's wearing an old army jacket with an American flag patch near the left shoulder and the name Henderson on the right. Tattoos are visible on his neck including a small swastika under his right ear.

Fear grips Lenny. He stops walking and takes Patricia's arm to halt her forward movement. She looks at him questioningly.

"I think this guy might be trouble," he says under his breath.

'Henderson' walks slowly towards them until a few feet away. Sneering at Lenny, he says in a voice rife with derision, "Hello, Isaacson. Out for a stroll with the lady? Must be nice to enjoy your freedom while Jeremy sits rotting in jail."

Oh shit, he's one of them.

Looking confused, Patricia whispers, "He knows you?"

Lenny can feel the adrenaline coursing through his veins. The flight or fight phenomena that ethologists talk about with animals has become painfully real. *Think Lenny!* he shouts to himself. He glances at Patricia. She's watching the guy without much expression. *She must be terrified. I have to keep her from getting hurt.*

In as calm a voice as he can manage, he says to Henderson,

"Jeremy is in jail because of what he did, not because of me. There was no way he was not going to get caught." As he is speaking, he doubts that a rational argument is going to be effective.

Henderson takes another step towards them. "Bullshit," he shouts, his face getting red and spittle landing on his beard. "If you hadn't tried to play hero, he would have walked out of there."

Lenny's knees begin to buckle. *Why, oh why did I tell Ashley Lee that I tripped Larsen? Now it's going to get me killed.* As a teenager he would talk his way out of potential fights or dangerous situations; and when that failed, he was a fast runner. In the present, fast running, even if he was alone, was no longer an option. Talking, it seemed, was his only alternative.

"Look, Henderson. We don't want any trouble. I know you're angry about what happened, but let's not make the situation worse."

As he feared, Henderson is not appeased. He moves closer which causes Lenny to take a few steps backward. Patricia, however, has not moved nor has Monet although his tail continues to wag.

Oh no, she must be frozen in place with fear. He whispers, "Patricia" to get her attention, but she remains in place—her gaze fixated on Henderson.

In a menacing tone, Henderson says, "Things can't get worse for Jeremy, only for you. People like you are what is wrong with this country. Jeremy is a patriot and you . . ." his lips curl in contempt, "you slimy, money-grubbers are the enemy."

The derogatory Jewish stereotype intensifies Lenny's fear. Given their relative isolation on the path, he cannot see how they are going to get out of this unscathed. His heart thumps like a bass drum and his body trembles. He considers rushing at Henderson thinking the element of surprise might allow Patricia to run away and get help.

While engaged in his frantic, self-deliberation, Henderson takes a few steps toward Patricia. "Hey, honey," he says in an oily voice. "What's a cutie like you doing with this loser? Is he paying you?"

Responding with a composure that surprises Lenny, Patricia says, "As my friend said, we don't want any trouble, but if you don't leave you will be sorry."

Henderson laughs. "How brave, protecting the helpless Jew." He spits on the ground. "I'll tell you what, honey, come with me and no one will get hurt. Plus, you'll get to be with a real man." As he talks, he inches closer.

Lenny's mind is racing. *What is Patricia thinking? Fear can make you do strange things. Should I attack? Should we run? Plead?* Henderson is now only a foot away. He extends his left arm toward Patricia. *Enough*, thinks Lenny, *I need to strike before he gets to her.* He says a silent prayer as his body tenses in anticipation. But before he can act there's a blur of movement at his side. He turns and sees Patricia has pivoted to the right and grabbed the outside of Henderson's wrist. Using her body as leverage, she simultaneously raises and twists his extended arm while seizing the other side of his hand with her left arm. Then, applying her body weight she bends his wrist backward while also exerting pressure downwards. Henderson screams and bends at the waist, his arm being held as a fulcrum. Patricia sweeps her leg across his ankle sending him to the ground. Still holding his outstretched arm and bent wrist behind his back, she says, "Ok, asshole, you move, I break your wrist. Got it?"

"You bitch," he screams. "When I get up, you're both dead."

"Except you're not getting up," says Patricia, using her foot to slam his head against the ground knocking him unconscious. She releases his arm which drops limply by his side.

Lenny is having trouble believing what he just witnessed. In a voice filled with awe, he says, "Where did you learn how to do that?"

Patricia brushes herself off and looks at Lenny with a mischievous smile. "I've practiced martial arts for many years. Used to teach self-defense for women although I never had the opportunity to use it in an actual situation. What I did was pretty basic. You know that old saying, the bigger they are, the harder they fall? Well, there's some truth to that if you know what you're doing."

"Pretty basic?" repeats a still incredulous Lenny. "That was amazing! Remind me never to get into a fight with you."

Patricia says, "Maybe you should call Lisa McGuire before this jerk wakes up." Another surprise.

"How do you know about Lisa McGuire? I don't recall telling you her name."

"You didn't. I know Barbara McGuire, Lisa's mother, from my school. I learned from her that Lisa was working on the case."

"I guess after living in Vermont all these years, these 'small world' connections shouldn't surprise me." Lenny takes out his phone and calls McGuire. He explains what happened and where they are. McGuire says she will be there in five minutes and to be careful.

"Don't worry," he says. "Patricia has things under control."

McGuire and her partner, Ben Gustafson, arrive just as Henderson is regaining consciousness. They sit him up, tell him who they are, and handcuff him while telling him that he is being arrested for assault. They read him his rights. Henderson seems disoriented and mumbles something about protecting the purity of rightful U.S. citizens. His speech is slurred and since he might have suffered a head injury when Patricia slammed his head on the ground, they decide to call for an ambulance. While waiting, they learn that Henderson is not his name; it's Jeffrey Wingate. McGuire calls it in and learns he's been arrested several times for crimes ranging from carrying an unlicensed firearm to simple assault. Not surprisingly, she also learns that he has a known association with the same neo-Nazi group as Jeremy Larsen.

After the ambulance leaves with Wingate and Gustafson, she says to Lenny, "I'm glad that you called," adding with a wry smile, "and that Ms. Sullivan was with you. I'll need to get full statements from both of you about what happened."

"Certainly," says Lenny as Patricia nods in agreement.

"Can we do this back at my home?" asks Patricia.

"That would be fine."

They assemble themselves around the dining room table. Patricia offers coffee, tea, "or something stronger," but all opt for coffee. Before they begin, McGuire turns to Patricia and tells her how sorry she is about Diedre.

"Please let me or my mother know if there is anything we can do to support you during this difficult time."

"Thanks. Your mother has been a big help, as has Lenny. And kicking that guy's ass felt pretty good too," she adds with a twinkle.

McGuire asks if it's ok for her to record their statements and they consent. In their statement, they note Wingate's use of ethnic slurs. Turning to Lenny, McGuire asks, "Do you think he targeted you for being Jewish?"

"I think that may have been part of it. He blamed me for Jeremy's arrest and used ethnic slurs when he confronted us."

Patricia adds, "He did refer to Lenny as a Jew and characterized Jews as the enemy."

McGuire asks more questions trying to get them to reconstruct verbatim the entire incident. When satisfied she has what she needs, she gets up to leave.

Lenny asks, "What now? It appears that I am in greater danger than you thought. Is there anything I should do?"

"Don't stray too far from Patricia," says McGuire with a deadpan expression followed by a smile. Then more seriously, "It's hard to predict if there will be other incidents. I don't want to downplay what happened. It could have ended badly, but my feeling is that this guy took things further than others are likely to do. Also, once the incident is reported, I am hoping it will serve as a deterrent to others who might have such inclinations. My suggestion is to continue living your life as you have been, being reasonably cautious and getting in touch if you observe anything that makes you uncomfortable."

Once again, McGuire's words do little to bolster Lenny's sense of security; however, realizing there can be no guarantees, he expresses his appreciation for her help and support. Concealing his anxiety, he turns to Patricia, "I guess I will have to follow orders and hang around you."

"Fine with me."

McGuire departs.

Lenny stays a while to process with Patricia what they've been through. "I think I am ready for a beer now."

"Me too." They sit quietly drinking their beers until Patricia says, "I know you were kidding before, but you are welcome to stay if you don't feel safe at home."

"Thanks. I am ok for now, but I will keep the offer in mind."

Patricia seems a little disappointed by his response (*or is that what I want to see?*). He's attracted to Patricia, but the timing feels off. *We are both needy and vulnerable. Not the best time for jumping into a romantic relationship. Better to keep this as a developing friendship at least until our situations become more stable.*

"I'm sorry I brought this additional trouble into your life," he says apologetically. "You have enough to deal with."

"It wasn't your fault. That guy was a loose cannon who was going to confront you somewhere. I'm glad I was there to help. And, it turned out to be a bit therapeutic for me, so maybe I should thank you." Patricia's words are accompanied by a kindly half-smile.

Lenny feels a lump in his throat. "In that case, I'll look for another right-wing extremist that you can save me from."

Patricia laughs. Then catches herself, as if it is too soon to feel cheerful.

Also seeing this, Lenny says, "But seriously, without your help who knows what might have happened. It was an impressive display of bravery and skill."

"Thanks," Patricia says softly. "If there's anything I have learned from my work with women who have been assaulted, it's that bad things not only happen, but they can happen to anyone. It keeps me from the inaction of disbelief and ready to act if the situation calls for it. That's partly why what happened to Diedre is so difficult. There was nothing I could do."

Her comment strikes Lenny as similar to what Jerry has

expressed, and he wonders if it would be helpful for them to meet. He puts the thought aside for now. "Parents want to protect their children from harm, whatever their age. When bad things happen to them, even when they are beyond our control, we feel that we failed."

He looks into her eyes. "I can't know what you are going through, Patricia, only that your grief must be profound. In time, you will find your way toward reconstructing your life. It will not be the one you had before, but it can still have meaning and worth."

Patricia places her hand over his. "Your support means a lot, Lenny. I'm sorry if my offer to stick around seemed too forward. It was just my way of saying I like you and appreciate your company."

Her touch elicits sparks and anxiety. He wants to stay but thinks he should leave. "I like you too and I wish I could stay longer but my friend whose daughter was injured at The Loft is having a tough time. I need to check in with him."

Patricia withdraws her hand. "That's good of you and I'm sure like me he appreciates your support. But before you go, I need to ask, are you also taking care of yourself?"

Lenny is touched by her caring. "I am. For me, supporting others is a form of self-care. When I talk with you and Jerry about how to cope, I am also talking to myself."

They stand and hug, Patricia conscientiously avoiding his injured side.

"Let's get together again soon," Lenny whispers.

"I'd like that."

Chapter Nineteen

As Lenny pulls into his parking space, he receives a text alert. It's from Jerry asking him to call. Still unsettled from the previous night's encounter, he's anxious about the reason for his request but tells himself that whatever it is he needs to be there for his friend.

After greeting Sisu, he phones.

"Lenny, thanks for calling. I want to apologize about the other night. I'm not sure what got into me, but I shouldn't have acted as I did. I hope you will forgive me."

"Of course," says Lenny relieved. "You've been dealing with some tough issues. There's going to be ups and downs."

"I know, but . . . would you still be interested in getting together at our usual spot? I promise to be better company."

"I'd be happy to, and no promises required. When would you like to meet?"

"Er . . . Is today too soon?"

"Let me check my social calendar," replies Lenny tongue-in-cheek. Pausing for a few moments, he says, "You're in luck. The governor's ball was canceled, so I am free."

***

This is becoming my second home; Lenny thinks as he enters the Holy Grounds coffee shop. This time Jerry has arrived first and is in their usual booth.

"Hi, Jerry. Did you order yet?"

"No, I just got here."

"The usual?" asks Lenny.

"Sure."

Lenny gets their coffees. He notices that Jerry is looking more typical than recently. *Of course, I've observed that before.* He hands Jerry his coffee and settles into the booth. "How are you feeling?"

"Better, thanks. You caught me in a dark place," says a Jerry eyes downcast. "It's embarrassing."

"There's nothing to be embarrassed about. As I said on the phone, you've been dealing with stuff most people could never imagine. I know it's easy for me to say but be gentle with yourself."

Jerry sips his coffee. He puts the cup down and takes a deep breath as if trying to compose himself. "You're right, but lately I get overwhelmed with anger and thoughts of revenge."

Lenny decides on a more direct approach. "There was no way to know, or even suspect that going to The Loft posed a danger for Emily. You're a good dad who wants to keep his children from harm. But it's not always possible. Despite this, it is not surprising you would feel like you somehow failed to carry out your responsibility. These are deep emotions that do not often respond to rational arguments."

Jerry is looking at him attentively, so he continues.

"What can you do with these feelings? One option is to focus on the perpetrator, rechanneling your guilt into anger, hurt those responsible as if it would make amends for not protecting your daughter. It may seem justifiable, but as you recognize, not helpful."

Jerry cringes as if in pain from Lenny's words. *Have I gone too far?* Lenny worries. *His anger is explosive. Who knows what he might do?* However, when Jerry speaks, his voice is heavy with remorse.

"I'm afraid I have not been handling things very well. You are right about me feeling like a failure to protect Emily." Jerry shuts his eyes to suppress the image of Daniel that appears in his head. Silently struggling to keep his composure, he continues. "I know I could not have prevented what happened but seeing her gravely injured overwhelmed me."

Lenny repeats what is beginning to sound like a mantra. "There's no magic bullet that will make everything ok. Healing will take time."

"You keep saying that, but I can't just sit around and hope things will someday improve. I need to be doing more. The problem is I don't know what to do. If, as you say, believing I'm responsible for what happened to Emily is irrational, then who *is* responsible? I considered God but can't accept He would allow this to happen to someone like Emily. Then I realized it was simple. It's that Jeremy guy and all those like him. They're responsible and need to be held accountable."

As soon as he mentions Jeremy's name, Jerry's demeanor changes. It's as if he swallowed Dr. Jekyll's transforming potion. His eyes flash with anger, his mouth forms into a snarl, his body tenses, and his voice assumes a threatening timbre. Lenny's initial, favorable impression of Jerry's appearance has evaporated and once again he sees the haunted, enraged person he encountered at last night's dinner. He feels tongue-tied doubting that in Jerry's current state anything he could say would have an impact. *On the other hand, it was Jerry who asked to meet, presumably for help, so I shouldn't abandon that responsibility.* He continues cautiously.

"I agree what Jeremy Larsen did was horrendous and the hate that he and his ilk preach is offensive, but if you were to take revenge on them how would that help you or Emily?"

Jerry does not respond, at least not verbally, but the pulsing vein on his forehead leads Lenny to think there's an intense internal struggle going on. He decides to wait it out. A couple of minutes pass and Jerry's shoulders gradually slump and the tension in his face and body subside.

Mr. Hyde is transforming back again.

Looking tired and vulnerable, Jerry says, "I know that focusing on revenge is stupid, but it seems like the only thing available."

Sensing an opening, Lenny says, "That's an important insight. When we're in a situation where we feel helpless, it makes sense to focus on something tangible toward which we can direct our energy. In this case, however, acting on that focus would make things worse."

When Jerry doesn't respond Lenny continues. "As I said, you're understandably angry at the perpetrators, but since you cannot directly act on that anger, you're left feeling like you are still failing her. In a way, this becomes the problem. Emily's suffered terrible injuries, but she's recovering. This is your injury."

Jerry remains silent and expressionless. *Am I reaching him? Is he processing anything that I am saying?*

FINDING LENNY

Finally, in a barely audible voice, he says, "I bought a gun."

Lenny stares in disbelief, not sure what he heard.

Jerry continues. "I told myself I was doing it to protect my family, but I was also thinking about how I could kill the guy that hurt my Emily. It's like I'm caught between two sides of myself. One side pushing me to do something terrible and the other side trying to restrain me from doing so. I'm scared Lenny."

Jezzuz, Are we all arming ourselves? "Where is the gun now?" he asks, struggling to project calm.

"It's hidden away in my closet."

"Is it loaded?"

"No. I haven't taken the bullets out of the box."

"Good. Does Katie know?"

"No. I was afraid if I told her she would get upset."

Lenny nods at what seems like a gross understatement. "Look Jerry, I think I know you well enough to believe that buying a gun has you feeling like a foreigner to yourself. It isn't you.

"Here's a practical suggestion. Either get rid of the gun—return it, donate it, destroy it, whatever—or if you are not ready to do so, make it difficult to retrieve and use. Frankly, you're in too volatile a state to have access to something so lethal. The last thing you want is to do something you will wind up regretting."

Neither seeing nor hearing any agreement from Jerry, Lenny tries another approach. "I know you know this, Jerry, but I'm going to say it anyway. You're suffering, sure, but so are the people you love—Katie, Emily, Danny—who love you too. They worry about you, whether you want them to or not, just as you worry about them. They need you and you need them. This is a collective struggle.

Separating yourself from them, whatever your reasons, makes it harder for everyone. You might feel trapped in remorse and guilt, but rather than feeding those feelings with self-recrimination and anger, you need to focus on healing. There is a lot you can do for your family and they for you. Caring for those you love is a way to care for yourself."

While Lenny has been talking, Jerry has been aimlessly stirring his coffee. Lenny is tense, feeling like the situation can go in many directions.

Jerry slowly lifts his head, sighs deeply, and looks at Lenny. In a voice suffused with despair, he says, "I could never have imagined being in this situation. I remember you once saying that we are multiple beings and new situations may bring out selves that we have not even been aware of. I guess this is one of them."

"Right," says Lenny, relieved that his anger has dissipated. "And it can be disconcerting especially if that self contradicts the person we believe ourselves to be. The sense of disconnection, of not feeling in control, can leave us feeling adrift and afraid."

"That's very much how I feel."

"Yeah, it sucks, but that recognition gives us choices. Rather than give in to the fear and self-recrimination, you can begin to explore other options that will enable you to put your life back together again."

Jerry appears lost in thought so Lenny decides to get refills of their coffees thinking it might help to give Jerry some time to reflect. When he returns, neither Jerry's body position nor facial expression has changed. Lenny settles back into the booth, places Jerry's coffee in front of him, and waits.

Lenny drinks half his cup before Jerry says, "I've been thinking about the kinds of things I would do if I was lost in the woods. I would try to get my bearings by looking around, noticing the sun, things like that. Then I would use that information to consider where I started from and how I got to where I am. Where did I take a wrong turn or get turned around? I would also take stock of what resources I had like food, water, and matches. Then I would start walking in the direction I thought would take me back to familiar territory."

"That's an insightful analogy of your situation," says Lenny. "Maybe the next step is to apply it to your current feeling of being lost."

"Yeah," says Jerry. 'I've been wondering how to do that."

An idea comes to Lenny. "I recently met a woman who was at The Loft with her daughter during the shooting. Tragically, her daughter died."

Jerry shrinks back in the booth as if he hadn't considered that others had more devastating experiences. His lips move, but no sound emerges. Worried that he just made things worse, Lenny quickly adds, "I'm telling you this because I think it might be helpful for the two of you to meet. If anyone can understand what you are going through it's her. I found her to be easy to talk with. If you want, I'd be happy to set it up."

"I don't know," says Jerry, his voice shaking. "I'm not in a place where I could be helpful to anyone."

"Maybe, but this is someone who knows, firsthand, what happened and is dealing with all the things you are dealing with and more. You would be meeting just to share your experiences and struggles. I think it's worth considering."

"Ok."

"Her name is Patricia Sullivan. I'll contact her and get back to you. In the meantime, please promise me, as your friend, that you will not do anything that could harm yourself or others."

When Jerry does not respond, Lenny repeats what he said enunciating each word. "*Promise me,* Jerry. You can get through this. You *will* get through this so long as you don't do anything rash. Promise me."

"I promise," Jerry mumbles.

Although his lack of inflection did not inspire confidence, Lenny feels it's as good as he's going to get right now.

Chapter Twenty

Lenny calls Patricia to inform her about the suggested meeting with Jerry. She readily agrees and suggests a few times over the next couple of days. He texts these to Jerry who, to Lenny's surprise, writes back that he could meet tomorrow. Great, thinks Lenny, happy this is happening quickly. He sends Patricia Jerry's contact information.

The rest of the day is spent attending to mundane but necessary tasks he has been neglecting: cleaning, washing clothes and the like. He also spends time with Sisu. Despite some anxiety, he goes to the park where they can play fetch. We can both use the exercise he tells himself, although Sisu does most of the running. To his relief, there are not many people around, and he sees nothing suspicious.

Back in his apartment, Lenny decides to resume his writing project. He spends a few minutes staring at the dreaded blank page—in this case, the computer screen—while thinking about where the story should go next. When nothing comes to him, he returns to what he has recently written hoping a recap will spawn some ideas.

The main character, Tobias Phillips, an academic, computer

scientist, is recruited into 'The Group,' a clandestine organization of intellectuals committed to countering the influence of what they see as a global network of multinational corporations and their institutional allies. Tobias was introduced to The Group by Carolina Gutiérrez, a brilliant and vivacious Spanish woman he met at a conference and with whom he soon became romantically involved. On a visit to Carolina's home, Tobias meets Marcos Estrada and Audrey Williamson, cofounders of The Group. Through them, he learns of an inner circle of members who engage in radical activities including occasional violence. Although disapproving of these tactics, his relationship with Carolina and a general malaise with his life leave him ambivalent about what to do.

"Ok, so now what?" he says to the computer screen. Getting no answer, he reminds himself that the cardinal commandment of a writer is to write. Simple in concept, difficult in execution. *Trust emergence*, he tells himself. *Stop thinking and start doing.*

He begins:

> Tobias slowly awakens to the sounds of birds and the warm, naked body of Carolina cuddled up beside him. Although in a different context this might be his idea of paradise, the revelations of the previous evening hover like a dark thundercloud. He slowly inches himself away from Carolina and gets out of bed. He walks into the adjacent bathroom and splashes water on his face. Gazing at his tired and worried image in the mirror, he thinks, *Is this how the others see me? I need to regain some control over the situation, but how?*
>
> A faint sound behind him causes him to turn. He

sees a brown scaled lizard with large eyes skitter across the floor. The strangeness of the creature brings an acute awareness of where he is and what he has gotten himself involved in. He pivots back to the mirror and whispers to his reflection, "What am I going to do?"

* * *

Lenny pauses. He wonders how much his current situation is influencing what he is writing. All so-called fiction is grounded in what we take as real. Otherwise, how would we know it was fantasy? *So what if my story is influenced by what is happening in my life? Maybe it will provide some useful insights. The important thing is not to let this distract me from continuing. Remember Lenny, writers write.* He continues:

Later that morning after a delicious breakfast of tomato bread, fruit, and baguettes with Iberic ham, the four of them—Tobias, Carolina, Marcos, and Audrey—get together to discuss in more detail the plans of The Group. The day is warm and clear, so they meet on the outdoor patio. Marcos asks Tobias if he has had a chance to think over what they discussed the previous night, adding with a mischievous grin, "or perhaps you were otherwise occupied." This comment elicits a playful slap on Marcos' arm from Carolina who says in Spanish, "y lo que estaba ocupando tu atención?" (and what was occupying your attention?) In response, Marcos assumes a bewildered look. "Estuve dormido toda la noche" (I was asleep the whole night).

Despite his poor Spanish, Tobias gets the drift of their exchange.

Audrey ends this good-natured teasing by saying, "Seriously Tobias, what are your thoughts about what we discussed?"

Hoping to buy a little more time, Tobias tries to extend the jovial atmosphere. "I will need at least one cup of coffee before I can intelligibly answer that."

"Fortunately, I just made some," says Audrey without laughing. "Help yourself in the kitchen." The others follow suit, and in just a few minutes, they are re-seated. Tobias feels like he's expected to say something and struggles to find a position between rejection and commitment. He sips his coffee to collect his thoughts. Choosing his words carefully, he says, "There was a lot to think about and I'm not sure I can jump in with both feet without giving it further consideration. But what I can tell you is that I agree in principle with the need to bring about transformative change and that such change cannot come about solely by working within the system."

At this juncture, Lenny is tempted to add some lines from a Leonard Cohen song: 'They sentenced me to twenty years of boredom for trying to change the system from within,' but decides that would make Tobias too much like himself, so he leaves it out. Instead, he has Tobias say,

"What I am still mulling over is how to best go about this. I understand the desire to take more radical actions as the pace of change can seem maddeningly slow. Obviously, the power structures of this world will not be easily dislodged and the effort it takes to create even a small change can consume enormous amounts of energy and resources." Then taking a deep breath he adds, "I just don't want my desire to bring about change to lead me to become like the very people who are part of the problem."

Marcos responds, "I'm glad that you are giving this serious thought, Tobias. We want thoughtful people. So let me ask you this. Do you believe that corruption, greed, and the lust for power have infiltrated the highest levels of government? And that the actions being taken by governments and their corporate masters have led to, and continue to lead to, the suffering and dying of untold numbers of people?"

Tobias nods.

"Well then, isn't it ethically justified to do whatever we can to try and change this? Yes, your caution about becoming like our oppressors is important. But with the stakes so high we sometimes need to travel down these perilous paths. That is why we need people like you to help make sure that we do not lose our way."

"Thank you," says Tobias. He looks at Carolina who turns to him. Her dark eyes hold him in a way that makes his heart beat faster. Realizing that his involvement with her is inextricably tied to this situation, he asks himself how he would feel if she were not in the picture. He also again questions why such a beautiful woman would be so enamored with someone like him. His mind drifts to those espionage exposés where a man is seduced by a female spy and manipulated into turning over government secrets. Would he only learn the truth of her affection after it was too late? But what if that isn't the case and her feelings are genuine? He might be throwing away a unique opportunity for happiness because of his . . . his what? Cowardice? He feels between a rock and a hard place and fears there is no risk-free solution.

The room has become quiet save for the birds whose melodic songs are unaffected by the weighty conversation. Finally, with considerable trepidation, Tobias says, "I agree, as the saying goes, that desperate times require desperate measures; however, I'm not sure I am up for the task."

Instead of the expected reprisal, Audrey surprises him with a sympathetic response. "That is perfectly reasonable, Tobias. At one time, we felt similarly. What we were asking of ourselves was beyond anything we had ever done. How could we know if we could carry out such acts even if we believed they were justified? And what if we got caught? Then we realized our support of each other was critical. And that goes for you too. No one is going to ask you to do something alone that you had not imagined doing." She hesitates. "Well, maybe you had imagined it, but never thought it could go beyond that. All of us were brought along slowly and without pressure. We trust you will let us know when the time is right."

"That's true my love," adds Carolina. "I felt just like you, believing in the cause but unsure and afraid of how I could be part of this. Eventually, however, I decided that the stakes were bigger than my fears and that I would have to risk trusting these people who seemed so much like . . . what is the English term? . . . kindred spirits? I did so, and I am glad that I was able to find the courage. At some point, I hope that you can also make that leap of faith."

Then, perhaps trying to lighten the atmosphere in the room, Carolina says, "Look at me, using all these English idioms. Maybe your presence is already rubbing off on me!"

Marcos and Audrey chuckle. Tobias manages a half-smile, but his mind is turning over the various ramifications of committing to The Group. Somehow what started as an unexpected romantic encounter has turned into his potential involvement in a radical network committed to causing upheaval by means that he did not know if he could, or should, accept. He also had the feeling that if he did become more involved, extricating himself from The Group would not be easy or even possible. With these thoughts swirling around, and not knowing what to do, he asks, "Are you planning any new projects?"

"We are," says Marcos.

* * *

Lenny stops writing. He's not sure what he wants The Group's new project to be, or how dastardly. For a few minutes, his mind wanders among various possibilities ranging from minor infractions to assassination. His musings return to the possible parallels between what he is writing and experiencing in his life. Is he using his novel to express his anger through violence? Years of self-analysis and occasional psychotherapy have led him to acknowledge that anger is an emotion he's harbored much of his life. In hindsight, this realization made sense having grown up in a home where physical punishment was seen as the appropriate response to misbehavior. Although fear kept him from striking back, the anger remained.

He thinks about the recent encounter with the Neo-Nazi guy on the path with Patricia; how he experienced that familiar feeling of being suspended between fear and anger. Now as an adult, the fear was not only about incurring physical harm, but about the harm he wanted to inflict. Despite being an avowed pacifist, in his darkest moments he worried that if he ever let go and attacked, he wouldn't be able to stop. The thought terrified him. And yet when Patricia unleashed her astounding display of martial arts skills, he felt emasculated.

So maybe I am using the novel to express the anger I feel about my current situation. Even if that's true, it's a lot better outlet than actually being violent. Besides, isn't that what writers do, live vicariously through their characters?

* * *

That night Lenny dreams he is on an airplane flying to some unknown destination. Without warning, what has been an uneventful flight changes with the appearance of a small missile flying parallel with the plane. Someone screams, "we are under attack!" At first, Lenny thinks the person must be mistaken, there must be some benign explanation for what he thought he observed. But then another missile appears and the pilot begins taking evasive action, banking right and left, and engaging in steep climbs. His stomach lurches with each maneuver and the prospect of imminent death seeps into his consciousness. The plane shudders violently and Lenny sees smoke billowing from one of the engines. Through a staticky intercom, the captain announces, "We've been hit! Assume the position for a crash landing." There's a pause before the captain adds, "And if you are so inclined, you might say a prayer."

As they descend, the plane becomes eerily quiet save for the laboring sound of the one engine still functioning and someone murmuring the twenty-third psalm.

Lenny looks around. He's the only passenger on board! The cockpit door opens and the pilot comes out. It is Ezekiel.

Lenny says, "Ezekiel, are you also a pilot?"

"You might say that," he answers.

Aware that the descent is continuing, Lenny screams, "What's going to happen to us? Are we going to die?"

"We might, but don't we all?" says Ezekiel calmly.

"How can you be so nonchalant? We could crash at any moment!"

Ezekiel comes closer. "Haven't you contemplated death?"

"Well, yes," Lenny stammers, "but that was just intellectual stuff. This is real!"

Ezekiel smiles ambiguously. "Would that be real with a small r or a capital R?" This gives Lenny momentary pause until the catastrophic nature of the situation overwhelms his ability to contemplate Ezekiel's query.

Abruptly the plane dives. Lenny feels like he's in a plunging skyscraper elevator. His stomach lurches and his ears fill with the screeching of the dying remaining engine and the screaming of passengers who have reappeared. Terrified, he looks out the window at the fast-approaching ground. The terrain is mountainous, and he sees nothing that looks like a place to land.

Bracing for the inevitable impact, a movement outside the plane catches his eye. He lifts his gaze and is startled to see Ezekiel now standing on the wing doing some kind of dance. A *Twilight Zone* episode from 1963, "Nightmare at 20,000 Feet," appears on the TV monitors. An airplane passenger, played by a pre-Captain Kirk, William Shatner, sees a frightening creature out on the wing.

"I got it!" Lenny yells in a flash of insight. "I'm in an episode of the *Twilight Zone*. Any minute now, I will hear Rod Serling's soft, omniscient voice narrating the scene. 'Lenny Isaacson along for a ride . . . to the twilight zone.'"

He breathes a sigh of relief. "I'm ok," he tells himself. "I'm in the twilight zone," as the plane crashes into a mountain top.

* * *

Lenny jerks awake. His muscles are tense and his T-shirt is soaked in sweat. He turns his head towards his bedroom window and sees the sun beginning to filter through the curtains. Conscious that he is in his bed, not on a crashing plane, he says out loud, "Oh God, what a dream!" He sits up and holds his head in his hands trying to excise the last tendrils of fear. *What does it all mean? And what about Ezekiel? Could he have somehow been communicating with me?*

A wet nose on his leg grounds him in the present. Sisu to the rescue. *Was he sensing my distress, or needing to relieve his bladder?* Whatever the reason, it gets Lenny out of bed. He throws on some clothes and takes Sisu for their morning walk.

Being outside further distances him from his nightmare. *I'm alive and safe,* he reassures himself. Sisu completes her local olfactory census and evacuation routines and turns towards home knowing that what comes next is breakfast.

After a long shower and coffee, Lenny checks his messages. He is pleased to see that inquiries and comments about his presence at The Loft have diminished. *Thank goodness for short attention spans and the competition of other news.* He wouldn't mind recognition if it was deserved. Accolades for his book, should he ever finish it, would be welcome, even a little celebrity, but not for an unconscious act borne of fear.

Thinking of fear, he hopes there will be no further encounters with the Jeremy Larsen sympathizers. The need for constant vigilance is wearing on him. Not that he's a stranger to vigilance. It's a handy sixth sense for anyone growing up in New York City. His training began at an early age with incessant warnings from his mother: be careful, don't touch that, look both ways. For her, the world was a dangerous place and you needed to be on guard against its ever-lurking dangers. Over time and repetition, this mantra became internalized and part of his everyday orientation. How might his life have been different had he not adopted this worldview? What actions would he have taken or not taken to avoid some imagined danger? Not much I can do about the past, he reasons, other than not let it rule the present. Maybe I should hire Patricia as my bodyguard. No one is going to mess with her!

He hopes her meeting with Jerry goes well. *Poor Jerry. He's so lost; his world unexpectedly and abruptly upended. How will he rebuild his life? How will any of us?*

A twinge in his side reminds him of his doctor's appointment later this morning. He's worried about what Lisman might find. *What if I have developed sepsis or have contracted those flesh-eating bacteria I've read about? That is not how I want to die.* He starts to feel panicky but catches himself. *Stop catastrophizing Lenny! Just go to the doctor and get it taken care of.*

Chapter Twenty-One

The waiting room at Lisman's office is about two-thirds full. Lenny checks in and finds a chair in a relatively unoccupied corner. He picks up a health-oriented magazine from one of the ubiquitous piles always present, checks the date to see if it's from this century, and begins leafing through it. An article on the health benefits of laughter catches his eye. He's always believed that laughing was good for you. Laughter produces endorphins, the hormones associated with feelings of well-being. It also tamps down the body's stress response. In the long term, it can enhance the immune system, improve mood, even alleviate pain. *All benefits I can use.* What Lenny didn't know is that laughter can produce these positive effects in the absence of humor.

According to the article's authors, there is no need to wait until we find something humorous in order to laugh; we should laugh without prompting, long and hard, every day. Looking at the somber faces of the people waiting to see the doctor, he wonders if he should share the article.

The image evokes a childhood memory of a television cartoon. There were two groups of characters, the happy ones and the sad ones. The sad ones wore dark robes with hoods, shuffling along grumbling and chanting a dirge that sounded like

> I'm happy when I'm sad.
> I'm always feeling bad.
> How are you?
> Terrible.
> That's fine.
> I'm happy when I'm sad.

The diminutive happy characters emanated sunshine. When confronted by the gloomy bunch, they poured bottles of a magical elixir over their heads transforming them into happy creatures.

Their dirge was replaced by a new song, sung in a higher-pitched voice.

> I want to be happy and glad
> and never again be sad.
> The sun will shine,
> everything will be fine
> 'cause I want to be glad.

The song was accompanied by everyone holding hands in a circle, smiling broadly, and doing a merry jig.

"Leonard Isaacson?" calls a nurse. Jerked back to the present, Lenny is unsure whether he has been singing the happy song aloud. His cheeks turn red as he glances around the room. He sees, or imagines, subtle smiles on some of the faces of the people sitting nearest to him. *Oh well, maybe I brought them a few moments of relief from their worries.*

He follows the nurse into one of the examination rooms where she checks his blood pressure and pulse, asks him about medications he is taking, and whether he has any particular concerns.

Does she even know why I am here? He tells her about the wound and his recurring cough. She makes a few notes, tells him to undress, and to put on one of those nondescript hospital gowns with ties in the back that he can never reach.

"Dr. Lisman will be in soon," she says as she leaves.

Lenny dons the gown and sits in a chair near the examining table. After a few minutes, there's a knock on the door and Lisman enters.

"Hi, Lenny." His greeting, as usual, is cheerful as if Lenny is there for a social visit. He almost expected him to say, "Nice hospital garb. I'll have to get me one of those." This time, however, he gets right down to business.

"So, how's that wound doing?"

"Not great," answers Lenny. "Take a look." He drops the front of the gown.

Lisman puts on a pair of disposable gloves from a box on a shelf and examines the wound. Lenny grimaces as he lightly touches the area.

"Sorry," says Lisman.

Although his expression is one of concentration, Lenny does not have a good feeling about this.

Similar to his last office visit, Lisman asks a bunch of questions about possible symptoms: fever? chills? vomiting? confusion? Lenny responds in the negative to all.

Lisman says, "The good news is that I don't think you have anything life-threatening like sepsis or toxic shock syndrome. However, it is healing slower than I thought it would. Let's try a different antibiotic cream. Once I'm sure there's no infection, we might want to put in a few stitches."

Lenny is relieved that he does not have any of the horrible conditions he imagined. But to make sure he says, "So no flesh-eating bacteria?"

Lisman chuckles. "None that I can see." He takes a minute to look over Lenny's chart. "Your last tetanus shot was about three years ago which should take care of any concerns in that area."

He puts down the chart and asks, "Tell me about this cough you mentioned to the nurse."

"It's nothing terrible but I've had it for a couple of months and can't seem to get rid of it."

"You don't smoke right?"

"Not anymore. Stopped about twelve years ago."

"For how long did you smoke?"

Lenny pauses to think. "Around fifteen years."

"Anyone in your family smoke when you were growing up?"

"My father."

"Is he still living?"

"No he died twenty year ago of . . . ," *oh no,* "lung cancer."

Lisman listens to his heart and lungs. "I don't hear anything obvious, but as a precaution, you might consider a scan. We now have low-dose CT scans that are safer than traditional x-rays."

Surprised by Lisman's suggestion, Lenny says, "Do you think it's necessary?" while thinking, *Great, something else for me to worry about.*

"It's up to you, but given your cough, your smoking history, age, family history, and the fact that lung cancer is often asymptomatic until it is fairly advanced, I think having the screening might be a good idea. I'll put in an order at the clinic near the university. When you're ready to have it done you can call and set up an appointment."

Lung cancer? Often asymptomatic? "Thanks," says Lenny although that's not what he feels like saying. Rather, he would like to tell Lisman his timing sucked. That he's dealing with all the stress he can handle and even the hint that something else could go wrong is not something he wants to hear.

Returning to his car he thinks about how everyone has their standpoints—different positions from which they see the world. Which are dominant will depend, in large part, on the context. For Lisman, as a physician, the salient context is the health of the body, or more accurately, the treatment of diseases and injuries. That's why talking with Lenny about getting a cancer screening, even if it was not urgent, superseded concern about other aspects of Lenny's life.

What are my standpoints? he asks himself. He thinks about how he perceives Jeremy Larsen from the standpoint of a social worker and how it conflicts with the standpoints of those who were victims of Larsen's rampage. *What about the guy that attacked Patricia and me? I could try to see his actions from his standpoint, although that would be my standpoint of his standpoint. Still, it might help me to understand how he justified what he did. But would it change my condemnation of his actions or his beliefs? No. Understanding is not acceptance. There are boundaries that you don't cross.*

Before he can conjure up counterarguments, Lenny hears the sound of a child's laughter. He turns and sees a woman with a girl of maybe six or seven engaged in a playful interaction while walking to their car. *Ah, to be a child again,* he muses nostalgically. *Maybe sometimes ignorance, or naivety, is bliss.*

His self-deliberation interrupted; Lenny starts his car. *I'd better shift my standpoint to one of a safe driver if I want to get home in one piece.* He exits the parking area while making a mental note to come back to these thoughts when he can do so safely.

About halfway home, he realizes he is passing by Patricia's neck of the woods. *I wonder how her meeting with Jerry went?* Impulsively, he pulls over to the side of the road and texts her.

'Hi, How did it go with Jerry?'

'We had a good discussion. I can fill you in the next time we get together.'

'On my way back from the doctor's office. Passing by your neighborhood. Would it be convenient to drop by?'

'Yes.'

His mood instantly improves, but he cautions himself not to read too much into her receptivity. Patricia is vulnerable and needy for obvious reasons. And while her friendliness feels good, he doesn't want to risk violating her trust by presuming anything more.

* * *

As he pulls into the driveway, he sees Patricia weeding around some flowers along the front of the house. She waves and approaches. "Glad you were nearby. Come on in."

They settle in the living room. Conscious of his self-counsel, Lenny sits in an armchair rather than on the couch. Patricia offers him coffee which he happily accepts. They engage in a few minutes of small talk.

"Beautiful flowers," says Lenny. "You looked very content tending to them."

"Thanks. I find it therapeutic. But tell me, were you at the doctor for the wound on your side?"

Lenny summarizes Lisman's assessment, assuring her that it is nothing serious and leaving out the part about the scan.

"It's good you had it checked out," says Patricia. "I was concerned that it might be more serious than you were letting on."

"Yeah, I'm good at denial when it comes to things like that. Not always the healthiest response." Not wanting to dwell on himself, Lenny changes the subject.

"Thanks again for taking that guy out of commission."

"You're welcome. I didn't know what to think when he emerged from the bushes."

"There's no preparing for something like that, but you were amazing."

"I guess my training came in handy," says Patricia modestly. "Never thought I would have to use it as I did."

Lenny feels an urge to be self-effacing and say something about how useless he was but restrains himself. Instead, he says simply, "And I'm grateful."

Patricia smiles demurely. "It did shake me up though. You know how you can do something on automatic pilot, but when you think about it afterward your feelings about what could have happened surface?"

"Definitely," he replies thinking about The Loft. "Sometimes we need to shut down our emotions, especially fear, so we can respond in a self-preserving manner. That's also where muscle memory from all your martial arts practice came in. You knew what to do without thinking about it."

"I guess so. Was your reaction to the shooter similar? Not the muscle memory part, but the emotional rush after realizing what could have happened to you?"

Lenny's anxiety barometer rises. "To be honest, I have kept my emotions at bay by addressing things intellectually. Maybe I'm afraid of where it might take me."

"I understand. But, if you ever want to explore it further, I'm here."

"Thank you," says Lenny moved by Patricia's sincerity, although unnerved by the possible ramifications of opening a Pandora's box of emotions. Once again, he redirects the conversation to a new topic.

"So how did it go with Jerry?"

"Umm . . . I think it went ok. He's a nice man, but clearly struggling."

"He is."

"Our conversation started somewhat guarded. We shared our incredulity about what happened and how such violence has become increasingly common. We also talked about you and how your action saved many lives."

Lenny squirms at this remark but does not comment.

"He seemed very nervous which I later learned was more about what I had experienced than him." Seeing Lenny's puzzled look, she explains. "He felt ashamed that he was hoping to be helped when his daughter lived and mine had died. However, when I explained to him that we both experienced terrible tragedies that night and sharing our struggles might be mutually helpful he seemed to relax some."

"You seemed to have approached him in just the right way."

"I hope so." Patricia looks away as if thinking. She straightens her back and turns toward him. "I have a confession," she says solemnly.

"Ok," says Lenny not having any idea what is coming next.

Looking chagrined, Patricia continues. "I mentioned the incident with the guy on the path assuming you had shared it with Jerry. He was shocked and said he didn't know anything about it. I think hearing what you experienced made him more upset about how he acted toward you at his home. I'm sorry, Lenny."

Lenny breathes a sigh of relief realizing he was preparing for something much worse. "No need to be. There was no way you could have known."

"Yes, but I should not have presumed without first checking with you," she says contritely.

Thinking their conversation might devolve into apologies and pardons, he asks, "Did you talk about anything else?"

"After a while, we got around to talking about our own experience, then and since. Jerry was very sad about my loss of Dierdre, and I was moved by the sincerity of his condolences."

"How about his experience?"

"It was hard for him to talk about his struggles, but he did share how he was haunted by the 'irrational belief'—his words—that he should have prevented his daughter from being hurt."

"I think he's conflating the intellectual with the emotional," says Lenny.

"What do you mean?"

"I mean that intellectually he knows he couldn't have prevented what happened, but the guilt about it somehow being his fault, well, that's coming from a different place. I would guess from his love for his daughter and a primal sense of responsibility for her wellbeing, although sometimes I get the feeling that he's struggling with something from the past."

"I can understand," says Patricia looking pained. "What we know and what we feel can be very different. I sometimes struggle with that too."

Now it's Lenny who looks pained. "I'm sorry Patricia. I should have been more sensitive. We don't have to continue talking about this."

"No, it's ok. The truth is that I hear and see things all the time that remind me of Diedre and what happened. It's something I'm going to have to learn to manage. Please, go on."

Hesitantly, Lenny says, "I'll tell you what I told Jerry. There are no definitive answers or fixes for what happened. You need to let yourself grieve and recognize your other feelings without necessarily acting on them or punishing yourself. Although you might feel a sense of alienation, avoid isolation and stay connected with others. It's what I was hoping to encourage Jerry to do when I suggested you meet."

"You're right about staying connected," says Patricia brightening. "You've done that for me."

Never good at accepting compliments even when he wishes for them, Lenny tilts his head slightly downwards. "Thanks," he says softly. "You've been helpful to me as well."

Patricia smiles affectionately. It's an expectant moment. Lenny feels like he should move closer. He *wants* to move closer. *Hic!* He feels a slight spasm in his chest. *Oh, no. Am I regressing to my adolescence?*

Fortunately, Patricia doesn't seem to notice. Before the next hiccup surfaces, he tells himself that it is too soon to risk complicating their relationship. *She's in mourning and I'm struggling. Better to support each other as friends and not complicate things.* He shifts the focus back to Jerry. "Are you going to meet with Jerry again?"

"We didn't make any specific plans, but I think we will," says Patricia without revealing whether she shared his sense of the moment. "Jerry's in a fragile place right now, and he's going to be cautious about opening up. I didn't want to push him."

Lenny asks, "Would it be ok if I mention to Jerry that we met and talked about your meeting with him?"

"I don't think he would mind, but you know him better than me."

For some reason, Lenny feels antsy. He wonders if it was a mistake getting them together, or if he's taking too much on and not attending to his own needs, or maybe he's anxious about what might be happening between him and Patricia. Whatever it is, he wants to leave. He tries to end things on a light note.

"Well, I'm glad I was able to drop by on the spur of the moment, but if I don't get back and walk my dog Sisu, I fear that I will return to a puddle on the floor."

Patricia smiles. "I'm also glad you came by. You know it's ok for you to bring Sisu the next time you visit. I bet he'd love running around the yard with Monet."

"I'll do that."

The next time I visit. Good . . . I think.

* * *

Driving home, Jerry is on his mind. He was hoping, unrealistically in hindsight, that meeting Patricia would leave Jerry not feeling guilty about Emily or so angry. How ironic that the orderly, conformist way that Jerry has lived his life makes what happened so difficult for him to deal with. He thinks about times when his own life seemed to be falling apart and he wished he was more like how he perceived Jerry: structured, in control, certain of who he was and where he was going. Now he thinks that maybe Jerry's surface demeanor hid a more molten inner life. His way of living served him well when things were going relatively smoothly, but not for handling a catastrophe like this. But who could?

He decides to check in with Jerry later today. *Who knows, maybe his view of meeting with Patricia will be very different.* Turning into his designated parking space he notices a woman sitting in a car two spaces to his left. She turns towards him and he recognizes McGuire. *What is she doing here?* He gestures with a wave. She gets out of her car and walks toward him. He rolls down his car window.

"Hello, Dr. Isaacson," she says, maintaining her formality.

"Hello, Agent McGuire. What brings you here?"

"I wanted to check in and update you on some developments. Can we talk in your apartment?"

"Sure, but I probably should allow my dog to relieve himself first."

"Alright. I'll wait down here, and we can talk while you walk him."

A few minutes later, they are walking down the street. Sisu, who generally is reserved around strangers, seems comfortable around McGuire and after a few sniffs at her ankles turns his attention to the ground.

"Sorry about the run-in with that guy on the trail," says McGuire. "I didn't expect anything like that to happen."

"It was scary, but thanks to Patricia it turned out ok."

"Yes, she's quite a woman," offers McGuire admiringly. "My mother once suggested that she consider applying to the Bureau, but she told her she had other interests."

"I'm sure she would have been an excellent agent."

"How are you doing?" McGuire asks. "The recent incident couldn't have helped."

"I'm hanging in there, although I am more watchful and cautious than usual. Knowing there are people out there who would seek to do me harm feels a bit like living under the sword of Damocles."

"Understandable," says McGuire seeming genuinely concerned. "I wish I could guarantee you that nothing like that will happen again but I can't, and under the circumstances telling you that it is unlikely is not going to sound credible."

Lenny shrugs. "I know you can't make guarantees, but maybe you should take these threats more seriously."

McGuire doesn't respond. After walking a little further, she says, "I wanted to update you about what's happened since we arrested Jeffrey Wingate. He's been charged with simple assault and is being arraigned tomorrow."

"Not a hate crime?" asks Lenny.

"No. It was decided that the incident was retaliation for what you did at The Loft, not an attack based on your actual or perceived race, color, religion, or national origin as stated in the hate crimes statute. Still, given his priors, I am hoping he'll see some jail time."

"Is he likely to be released on bail?" asks Lenny, his worry evident.

"I don't think so. His history of violence will not work in his favor. But of course, it will be up to the judge."

Lenny tenses. Even the small chance Wingate might be released scares him.

Reaching the midpoint of his usual walk, Lenny turns back towards his apartment.

"There's something else I want to tell you," says McGuire. "You would probably find out in a day or two, but I wanted you to know before it became public. Jeremy Larsen, the shooter at The Loft, is dead."

"Dead? What happened?"

"As you know, he tried to hang himself and because of that was on a suicide watch. However, he somehow got hold of a sharp object; I believe a piece of glass that had broken off from something and used it to cut his wrists. He bled out during the night and was found dead this morning."

Although McGuire delivered the news without emotion, Lenny is stunned. He feels a sense of anomie about the breakdown of civil society and the violence it has spawned. Jeremy committed an unspeakable act, but his life was tragic. An old song by the singer-songwriter Phil Ochs surfaces.

> *Show me a prison, show me a jail*
> *Show me a prisoner whose face has gone pale*
> *And I'll show you a young man with so many reasons why*
> *There but for fortune, may go you or I.*

We are born into circumstances over which we have no control.

How different might I have been if I had been born into an environment like Jeremy's? It's impossible to know. Then, thinking about Jerry and Patricia, he says to McGuire, "I wonder how this will affect the people who were at The Loft and the families of those who died."

"Hard to say. My guess is it will vary. Some will feel glad he is dead, others will feel angry he escaped punishment, and some won't care." Seeing Lenny's melancholy expression, she asks, "What's your reaction?"

"I feel sad," he admits. "Not just for Jeremy Larsen's death, but for his life . . . for the shooting at The Loft, for those who will feel like he escaped justice and deprived them of closure, for a society that produces hate groups. I even feel sad for you."

McGuire raises her eyebrows in surprise. "Sad for me? What do you mean?"

"I mean we live in a society—a world—that requires organizations like the police and the FBI to enforce laws and keep order. So bright people like yourself who could be contributing in many positive ways, spend their time investigating potential wrongdoers and arresting people."

"It's a dangerous world and as you experienced, you ignore it at your peril," says McGuire sounding a bit defensive. "I'm proud to help make it safer for law-abiding people."

To Lenny, McGuire's statement is begging to be interrogated; however, he also realizes that her occupational choice is highly personal, and it would not be wise to question it further. Plus, he is relying on her to keep him safe. "I appreciate what you do, Agent McGuire. You've been a great help to me. I just wish things were different."

This appears to appease McGuire who responds in a softer tone. "Don't we all."

Lenny asks, "Do you know when and where they are burying Jeremy Larsen?"

"Not sure, but I could find out if you are interested."

"Yes, I'd appreciate it."

Nearing the parking area, Lenny says, "Agent McGuire, thanks again for looking out for me."

"It's my job," she responds matter-of-factly. "Call me if needed."

* * *

Lenny gazes out his bedroom window barely taking in the scenery or activity below. His mind is elsewhere. *So much has happened in such a short time. I feel like I'm treading water, not drowning but getting nowhere. How do I step back and gain a broader perspective?*

He wonders if anyone will be at Jeremy's burial. It would be another sad commentary on his life if he was interred with no one present but the gravediggers. He decides that if McGuire gets him the information he will try to go.

Chapter Twenty-Two

Meeting with Jerry is no longer predictable. Lenny's usual anticipation about spending time with him has been replaced by apprehension about which Jerry will show up. Now waiting in 'their booth' at the Holy Grounds coffee shop, he drums his fingers on the table.

Jerry walks in five minutes later. Lenny does a quick appraisal of Jerry's appearance. His clothes are clean and wrinkle-free, he is clean-shaven, and his demeanor seems calmer than when they'd last met; hopeful signs bolstered by the friendliness in Jerry's voice when he greets Lenny.

Maybe he's turned a corner. I'll soon find out.

After getting their coffees and reseating themselves, Lenny tells Jerry that he is looking better. Jerry responds with a simple "Thanks."

"I hope you are also feeling better," adds Lenny.

"Sometimes," says Jerry halfheartedly.

Deciding against digging deeper, Lenny says, "As I mentioned in my text, I talked with Patricia. She enjoyed talking with you."

Jerry nods and shrugs at the same time.

This is going well, Lenny laments. Hoping to draw him out, he asks, "What was your impression?"

Jerry remains succinct. "She's a nice person and I appreciate you getting us together."

Ok. Maybe my initial assessment was wrong. He tries to elicit more dialogue without sounding provocative. "Did you find it helpful?"

"Helpful?" Jerry repeats. "Not too much. She's suffered a tragedy far worse than mine. If anything, I hope I was the helpful one."

"Yeah. Losing her daughter was awful, but also to witness it . . . I don't know how she is managing as well as she is."

"She's strong," says Jerry. He looks out the window adjoining their booth. "Not like me," he adds dejectedly.

"I don't agree. Everyone's experience is their own. There's no basis for comparison."

"Easy for you to say."

Detecting a bit of hostility, Lenny is not sure how to go on. He sips his coffee to buy some time.

Jerry continues. "Sitting with her and hearing her story left me feeling embarrassed to be there."

His comment stings. *Did my attempt to help only make things worse?* He counters, "Well, if it's any consolation, I don't think that was Patricia's view. She was glad to meet with you and hopes to see you again."

Jerry grimaces in a way Lenny cannot decipher. An uncomfortable silence ensues.

Then, in a resolute tone, Jerry says, "To lose your child in such a senseless and violent manner is horrid and to witness it is beyond comprehension. The death and injury perpetrated by that sicko must be avenged." His last sentence is said with chilling intensity.

Uh oh, is Mr. Hyde reemerging? In an unsteady voice, Lenny says, "That's what the courts are for."

Jerry waves his arm in a dismissive gesture. "Come on, Lenny. We both know the so-called justice system is a sham. With plea bargaining, overcrowded prisons, corrupt police, and judges, there are no guarantees what might happen. And besides, there is no death penalty in this state."

"I always thought that was a good thing," offers Lenny immediately thinking this wasn't the time to voice his opinion.

"Please, spare me your bleeding heart, liberal philosophy," says Jerry, his tone now mocking. "It doesn't work in this case. Since torture is technically illegal, it's the only punishment that fits the crime."

Lenny is appalled by Jerry's thinking, but he continues to try and reason with him. "I guess if our courts were based on the *Code of Hammurabi* in the *Old Testament* an eye for an eye would apply, but for better or worse, we have a secular system of jurisprudence."

Jerry looks at him coldly. "Sometimes you have to take justice into your own hands."

This remark is so extreme that at first Lenny thinks he's being facetious. But there is nothing about his tone or facial expression that suggests this.

Jesus, I'm not even sure who I am talking to. It's like he's being channeled by some demon. This is not a person who should own a gun. But how do I reach him?

He tries combining empathy with a reality check. "I can

understand your feeling that way, but even if there was a death penalty, it would not apply in this case. Jeremy Larsen is dead."

Jerry's body goes rigid. His eyes bulge. "What?" he shouts. "What are you talking about? I read about his cowardly suicide attempt, but he was recovering."

"True," says Lenny, "but he tried again, this time cutting his wrists, and was successful. I just found out this morning."

Whatever was left of Jerry's composure evaporates. "No!" he screams slamming his fist on the table with enough force that some coffee spills from his cup and a few patrons turn their heads.

Lenny startles. "Jerry, Jerry . . . are you ok?" he says with urgency, although it is clear that he is not.

"That fucking coward," says Jerry now seeming to waver between anger and despair. "He should not have gotten off this easy. He deserved to suffer like the rest of us. How could this have happened? Wasn't he on a suicide watch?"

"He was. They haven't figured out how he got the piece of glass."

Looking beyond distraught, Jerry mumbles, "I need to go," and gets up to leave. "Jerry, wait," says Lenny forcefully, alarmed by Jerry's abrupt termination to the conversation and emotional state. "Listen to me. You are in a bad place and need to get help."

Jerry pauses and turns toward Lenny.

Feeling like he's running out of options, Lenny quickly checks his contact list and writes Stuart Gifford's name and number on a napkin. "Here, call this person. He's a psychologist that I have seen myself. He can help."

Jerry makes no move to take the napkin.

"Jerry, you're my best friend and I'm telling you to do this because I care about you. You're struggling but going at it alone is not the wisest course of action. Please take this and call him."

Jerry hesitantly accepts the napkin and puts it in his jacket pocket.

"Tell me that you will call," implores Lenny not willing to let him leave without some commitment.

"Ok," mumbles Jerry as he walks away, his voice barely audible.

* * *

Lenny is not convinced Jerry will follow through. He continues sitting in the booth trying to reconcile this version of Jerry with the person that he knew, or thought he knew. *Jerry's in a dangerous place where he could do something that would generate what he fears, hurting himself or someone else to stop his imagined hurting of his family which, of course, will hurt his family.* It's a pattern Lenny has seen often, including in himself.

What should I do? Should I speak with Katie? Would that make things worse? Christ! What a mess!

A deep voice interrupts his thoughts. "Mind if I sit, Lenny?"

He turns toward the source. The speaker is a very tall black man, around mid-sixties, He has a friendly face—short dark hair, a greying mustache and goatee, and large, bottomless brown eyes.

Puzzled that he knows his name, Lenny says, "Do I know you?"

"Maybe," is the ambiguous response. "I was sitting nearby and couldn't help but overhear some of the conversation with your friend. You're upset and I thought you might want to talk about it."

"Thanks for your concern," says Lenny thinking he will politely dismiss this kindly but presumptuous stranger, "but I don't—"

And then he sees his eyes. *Holy shit. It's Ezekiel! No, it can't be. Wrong height, wrong age, wrong skin color. But he's a shape shifter so maybe* . . . Needing to know more, he says, "Ok, have a seat, Mr. ?"

"You can call me Ezra," says the man moving into the booth.

Lenny feels like he is in a liminal space between fantasy and reality. It would not surprise him to suddenly find himself at home in bed thinking, *Wow, that dream was so realistic!* But something tells him he's not dreaming.

"What did you hear?" Lenny asks.

"I heard a person terrified that he no longer knew who he was and another person, although also feeling lost, trying to help his friend find a way forward."

Ezra's countenance and intonation emanate warmth and tranquility. Lenny feels it like an invisible wave gently sweeping over him. He sits quietly basking in the calm. Then he hears himself saying, "I'm scared."

"Fear is like a hydra," says Ezra. "It has many faces—fear of failure, fear of harm, fear of loss, fear of fear—are some you may recognize. When we acknowledge and name our fears, they begin to loosen their paralyzing grip."

"But how do I do that?" asks Lenny, a slight quaver in his voice.

"Trust and courage," answers Ezra. "These are faces of life."

There's a hypnotic quality to Ezra's words. Lenny closes his eyes and is transported to a room where he is standing before a huge mirror. But rather than seeing his reflection, he sees kaleidoscopic versions of himself in familiar and unfamiliar settings ranging from the bucolic to the threatening. In each setting, his face and body show different emotions: dancing with happiness, sobbing with grief, trembling with fear, flagellating himself in remorse, glaring in anger, and longing in envy. As he watches, the images begin to rotate faster and faster until in a wisp of smoke they disappear.

He opens his eyes and is relieved to see that he is still sitting in the booth. He looks across the table to ask Ezra what the hell just happened, but no one is there. A quick scan of the coffee shop reveals no sign of him.

How did this weirdness enter my life? he thinks, now visibly trembling. Once again, he wonders if he might be experiencing some kind of breakdown from stress or some organic brain disease.

Too shaken to dwell on such possibilities, he gets up and leaves. He feels disturbed and numb at the same time not knowing how to even begin processing what happened. About two-thirds of the way home, a thought resounds. *I am the hydra.* Without intention, he starts singing, 'I am the Walrus,' by the Beatles.

He recalls that John Lennon said it was a nonsense song without any particular meaning, more like the singing of a dream. Yet, interpretations proliferated with various phrases in the song being given different connotations. Was the walrus like a hydra, an object upon which we project our hopes and fears? And was the mirror a manifestation of those projections?

Every time he encountered Ezekiel—and he was certain that Ezra was Ezekiel—he left with more questions than answers. At times it frustrated him, not because the questions were less valuable, but because the desire for answers increases when life is scary and uncertain. *I need to not allow my fears prevent me from exploring the questions he raises.*

Questions, he often contended, were most important, particularly those that seem unusual or naïve. They're the ones that lead to new insights because they don't conform to what is assumed thereby constraining what we can discover.

Maybe the key is not just to ask questions but to live them as the poet, Rainer Maria Rilke, advised the nineteen-year-old, Franz Xaver Kappusto, in his Letters to a Young Poet.

What are my questions? And what would it mean to live them?

Another internal dialogue begins.

In the broader scheme of things, there are the big metaphysical questions like what is the meaning of life?

But doesn't asking this question presuppose there is a meaning, waiting like a buried treasure to be discovered?

Still, that doesn't mean seeking the meaning of life is fruitless since you can't predict with certainty where it will lead. Hasn't my exploration of this question led to new understandings and a different, more volitional, phrasing of the question itself? What are the meanings—plural—I would like my life to have and how can I pursue them? Might this be closer to what Rilke meant?

Or is this rephrasing still too directive, cutting off some yet unknown possibilities? Maybe I should simply accept questions as—

The whining sirens of a passing ambulance jar him from his thoughts. He blinks rapidly reorienting to time and place.

I did it again, he thinks shaking his head. *Lost in my internal dialogue. Have I created a möbius loop where my cognitive journey leads back to where I began? All very interesting, but there are more immediate, pragmatic questions I need to address, like how to help Jerry.*

He leaves the coffee shop and heads home.

* * *

A text from McGuire informs Lenny that Jeremy Larsen will be buried two days from now. She will text him again when she knows the time and place. He's ambivalent about going. Someone should bear witness to the other tragedy that was Jeremy Larsen's life. But there are many people, particularly the victims of his rampage, who would not condone such a choice. Indeed, several, like Jerry, would want to spit on his grave. *Should I go?* For now, he decides not to decide.

Chapter Twenty-Three

Lenny wakes the next morning feeling groggy. His body is leaden and getting out of bed feels like a Herculean task. He has a vague memory of a disturbing dream but is unable to recollect what it was about. He stares at the ceiling for a few minutes before pushing through his lethargy and age-related body aches to an upright position. "Good work," he says aloud, congratulating himself on this small accomplishment. He chuckles and continues talking. "Is this what is meant by the circle of life? I now compliment myself as I would an eight-month-old achieving the same developmental milestone. Well, I'm on a roll, so I'd better keep going." He instructs himself on the next steps: "Splash water on my face, pee, brush teeth, drink coffee, and walk Sisu."

Morning tasks completed; he decides to re-enter the world of his novel. He sits down at his computer and opens the file. Although to this point the story is not exactly uplifting, it still provides a temporary escape from his multiple real-world concerns.

He reviews what he last wrote. Tobias Phillips was struggling with his deepening involvement with The Group especially after learning they are involved in questionable activities. Complicating the situation is his romantic attachment to Carolina, the woman who recruited him to The Group. In the last scene, Tobias is talking with Marcos and Audrey, The Group's co-founders. While he tries to buy time so he can figure out what to do, Marcos discloses that they are planning a new project that they would like him to consider.

Mulling over ideas for the new project, Lenny remembers hearing about a little-known society made up of powerful people within government and industry who met annually to discuss and influence matters of import to them. Speculation has it that their topics include manipulating current and potential future economic and political trends, addressing global developments, and assessments of government leaders who they might support or oppose. He decides to create a fictitious version of this group for his next chapter.

> Marcos asks Tobias if he's heard of the Rendenhall Collective. Tobias has not. Marcos describes it as a group of extremely wealthy and politically powerful individuals who meet each year at different, unannounced locations.
>
> "What's their purpose?" Tobias asks.
>
> Audrey answers. "Succinctly put, it's to determine the fate of the world."
>
> "Modest goal," says Tobias with a dead-pan expression.
>
> "Quite," responds Audrey, playing along for a moment before adding, "joking aside, they are formidable and influential."
>
> "And you know they exist, how?"

"Let's just say we have our sources."

"Ok, but secret groups trying to change the world?" Tobias says in a doubting tone. "With all due respect, it sounds a little like UFO sightings."

"It's not as farfetched as it might seem," says Audrey. "Have you heard of Davos?"

"Yes. It's the place in Switzerland where billionaires and government big wigs get together for an economic conference."

"Right," replies Audrey. "But although much of it is conducted like a typical conference with presentations on various topics, it is well-known that a lot happens outside of the formal sessions; what might be called backdoor diplomacy."

"I've heard that," Tobias concedes. "But how much do we really know about what goes on?"

"Interestingly," says Audrey, "they are quite transparent about their aims. If you go to their web site . . ." Audrey holds up her hand as a signal to wait. She takes out her phone and presses some keys.

"Here it is. Their aim," and I quote, "is to engage the foremost political, business, cultural and other leaders of society to shape global, regional and industry agendas."

Tobias says, "I'm surprised by how blatantly ambitious they are. It says something about the world we are living in that a group like this can announce such an aim with impunity. Is the Rendenhall Collective similar?"

"Yes and no. They share a similar aim; however, Rendenhall is more secretive and ambitious. When they gather there is no pretense of holding a conference with presentations. If there is an agenda, it is not made public. It's been alleged, with some credibility, that they function like a shadow global government whose decisions are instrumental in determining who gets to rule and how."

"But how do they do that?" asks Tobias.

Audrey turns to Marcos who responds. "We believe it's done through multiple forms of influence, some visible, some not. Remember, these are the people who control a disproportionate amount of wealth and power in the world. Everything they do is in the service of retaining, or increasing, their position. Based on their assessments of the current situation and global trends, they formulate an action plan."

Still skeptical, Tobias asks, "What kind of plans?"

"In our view," says Marcos, "they operate in three primary ways: by manipulating elections, by influencing government policies, particularly economic policy, and through instigating, sponsoring, or carrying out acts of violence. Of course, they are careful not to leave their fingerprints on these latter activities, making it look like the work of terrorist organizations or governments they oppose. And some are never reported or are called something else like accidents."

Tobias is finding this far-fetched. However, not

wanting to appear disrespectful, he asks, "Sounds a bit conspiratorial, don't you think?"

"It does," agrees Marcos, "but that just makes it easier for them to carry out their agenda."

"I'm not sure what you mean."

"In the current political climate calling something a conspiracy is equated with a kind of paranoia that allows the claim to be easily dismissed. Ironically, this lack of credibility makes conspiracies more likely to be successfully implemented."

Carolina, who's been quiet, interjects. "Wouldn't it be interesting if the situation you describe was itself a conspiracy," eliciting smiles from the others.

Audrey looks at Tobias. "All we're saying is that before dismissing something on the grounds that it cannot be a conspiracy, look at the available evidence. The kinds of activities we are talking about—regime change, election tampering, even assassinations—require clandestine cooperation among several major players."

"And that's why," says Carolina with a tone of finality, "the Rendenhall Collective must be stopped."

"Stopped?" Tobias asks anxiously. "What does that mean?"

Marcos looks him in the eyes. "Without going into specifics, it means that we need to disrupt their plans. Please understand that we can't say more until we know that you are committed to being part of our team."

Tobias feels like he is walking into something that

he will regret. He looks at the three people in the room. They all seem confident and committed to their cause. Maybe too committed. Although his sympathies lie with their general desire to make this a more just world, he is troubled by the measures they believe are necessary and are willing to take towards this goal.

He debates himself. *The means do not always justify the ends. Ethics and consequences need to be considered. Also, the forces they are trying to disrupt are imposing and impenetrable. Their resources and reach are unlimited and their ability to enact retribution frightening.*

Yet isn't doing nothing a form of doing something? At what point is it necessary to act even at the risk of retaliation? How will things ever change if I merely toe the line?

"You look deep in thought," says Carolina interrupting his debate.

Aware that the others are looking at him, Tobias tries to explain his uncertainty, carefully choosing his words to appear thoughtful rather than rejecting. "Aren't other forms of protest and resistance like those you first told me about sufficient without resorting to measures that risk hurting others or having one's life ruined?"

Marcos is the first to respond. "Yes, these are valid forms of dissent, but let's be candid, they wouldn't be tolerated if they had the potential for real system change. They're just another form of domestication; a way of duping the masses into thinking they are being responsible citizens bringing about a better way of life, kind of like thinking recycling is going to save the planet. But nothing ever changes—the poor stay poor and the rich get richer."

Audrey adds, "Marcos and I invited you to join us because of Carolina's recommendation. Her confidence in you seemed borne out by our initial interaction. You understand the necessity for systemic change and the measures that need to be taken to bring it about. But please understand our need to be cautious even though we think you would be a great asset to our cause. Inviting you to join us entails considerable risk. What if we are wrong and you turn against us? The results could be devastating to our efforts."

As Audrey is speaking, Tobias detects a menacing subtext that increases his unease. He voices his concern. "Do I have the option to refuse?"

Instead of answering, Marcos tries to lighten the atmosphere. "Oh, this is sounding so serious! Tobias my friend, as Audrey said, our dear Carolina spoke glowingly of you—your intelligence, your politics, and your commitment to the cause of justice. For us, there can be no stronger recommendation."

Tobias notices Carolina inching closer. She takes his hand and he turns to her. Her smile and the radiance of her eyes envelop him in a way that threatens to evaporate all his misgivings. He squeezes her hand.

Turning to Audrey and Marcos, he says, "I understand the need for caution. But it's hard for me to commit to a specific action when I know so little. Can you tell me what you are planning?"

The three look at each other and Marcos nods toward Audrey. She clears her throat and says, "Unlike Davos whose very name is their location, the Rendenhall Group never meets in the same place twice nor do they publicize the location of their meetings. Also, whereas the Davos Forum takes place each year at the Hotel Seehof, a five-star hotel with easy access to the ski slopes, Renndenhall meetings are held at venues that belie their elite participants."

Marcos continues. "We've learned that their next meeting will be in about two months at a location in or near Salisbury, England. We believe that it will take place at a small religious-oriented college that will not be in session during this time. This type of venue is typical. It provides a perfect cover for their deliberations. If they follow their usual modus operandi, there will be no limousines driving into town or people with visible entourages. Attendees will arrive by rented cars, taxis, trains, and busses. If you attempted to contact them at their home bases during this time you would be told they are unavailable for some reason having no connection to the meeting."

"One other thing," adds Carolina. "These locations are chosen not only for their accommodations but for their historical significance that aligns with the group's agenda for that year. For this meeting, it's the Salisbury Cathedral, the highest cathedral spire in England and the home of one of the four remaining original copies of the Magna Carta, considered by many as a foundational document for the development of individual liberty and democracy."

"Yes, I know about the Magna Carta," says Tobias. "What do you think is the message they are trying to send?"

"Who knows," responds Carolina. "Are they saying they are the guardians of individual freedoms and democracy? Or are they mocking these ideas? The symbolism is ambiguous and open to many interpretations, but that's how they operate."

The room again becomes quiet. Finally, Marcos says in a soft, but serious tone, "That's all we can share for now. We don't want to be overly dramatic, but we hope you agree that before we disclose the details of our plans, we need your solemn oath that you are one of us. Once we tell you, there is no going back."

No going back. The phrase reverberates through Tobias' soul as if he was being asked to make a deal with the devil. Is he?

* * *

DING DONG, DING DONG!

Lenny is ejected from his world of danger and subterfuge back to the familiar and mundane setting of his bedroom. As if emerging from a dream, it takes him a few moments to recognize the sound of his doorbell. He notices that he is sweating. *Maybe I was a little too absorbed in the story.* He takes a few calming breaths, rises from his chair, and walks to the front door.

He looks through the peephole and sees it's Javier and Carol, his somewhat nosey but well-meaning neighbors from across the hall. Javier waves at the peephole and Carol is holding what looks like a cake. *Their ticket to ride,* Lenny thinks, borrowing a line from the Beatles' song. He opens the door and is greeted by two smiling faces.

"Hi Lenny," says Carol. "We thought we'd just drop by to see how you are doing, and if you'd like to share this coffee cake I made. Is this a good time?" she asks already halfway into his apartment.

Although the timing isn't great, Lenny appreciates the gesture and invites them in. They promptly make themselves at home taking seats around his kitchen table. Carol places her cake in the middle.

"Shall I put up some coffee?" he asks trying to be a considerate host.

"That would be great," says Carol as Javier nods. "After all, she adds with a giggle, "what's coffee cake without coffee?"

Lenny forces a smile to keep himself from groaning.

Still, not completely extracted from his book, Lenny contrasts the last scene he was writing with what is happening in his apartment. He imagines Marcos and Audrey interacting with Carol and Javier. The former trying to save the world with stealth and cunning, the latter trying to be good neighbors by baking a coffee cake. He laughs softly. Luckily, Carol and Javier think he's responding to Carol's last remark which saves him from having to explain himself.

After some idle chit-chat, Lenny serves the coffee and distributes napkins, plates, and forks. Carol has brought her own knife to slice the cake. The portions are served and there is a brief silence as they eat. About halfway through, Carol says to Lenny, "We hope we're not keeping you from anything."

"Not really," Lenny lies. "I was working on a novel I am writing but was about to stop when you rang the doorbell."

"A novel?" exclaims the loquacious Carol. "How exciting!" She glances mischievously at Lenny. "Am I in it?"

Playing along, Lenny replies, "Well, it's a work of fiction so the characters are imaginary, but you never know where someone resembling you might show up. Maybe a woman who makes delicious coffee cake."

"Great idea!" says Carol. "Don't forget the brown eyes . . . hint, hint."

Javier asks, "Can you tell us what the book is about?"

Not wanting to say too much about his unfolding story, Lenny evades the question. "I'm still in the early stages. The story is evolving so there's a good chance it may become something very different from what I am writing now."

Javier looks disappointed, but says, "I understand. Maybe sometime later when the storyline is set."

"Sure," says Lenny, "when I am further along."

"Remember Lenny," Carol reminds him, "I'm an editor so if I can help, call me."

They spend the next twenty-minutes talking about different things going on in their lives. Lenny avoids disclosing anything that has not been made public. He isn't sure about the encounter with the guy on the path, but since they don't bring it up, he doesn't mention it. Finally, after about half the coffee cake has been consumed, Carol gets up and begins gathering the dishes. Taking his cue, Lenny also stands and carries some things into the kitchen. Noticing that Carol is about to wash the dishes, he says, "Thanks Carol, but I'll take care of it."

"Ok, but let us leave you the rest of the cake."

"Great," says Lenny thinking that refusing might be interpreted as an insult. Although he initially felt aggrieved that they disrupted his writing, he now feels grateful for the pleasant break it provided. In contrast to the weighty and somber discussions he's been having, their light banter was refreshing.

* * *

Alone again, he considers going back to the book, but it feels like too much effort. He's tired. He goes over to his couch, sits down, and closes his eyes. His mind wanders to recent events: getting attacked, Lisman's recommendation to get a chest scan, talking with Jerry, Patricia, and McGuire and his encounters with Ezekiel in his dreams and real life, although he's not certain of the latter.

His thoughts turn to the Lewis Carroll poem, *The Walrus and the Carpenter*, which was supposedly a muse for John Lennon's song. In the poem, the elder oysters resist the invitation of the walrus to go for a walk mindful of the danger of leaving their oyster bed home (especially since they do not have legs!). However, some young oysters, enticed by the promise of "A pleasant walk, a pleasant talk, Along the briny beach," excitedly agree, soon to be followed by others. After being led far from their home, they are eaten by the walrus and carpenter although the walrus weeps while doing so.

Am I like the walrus? Lenny wonders, *feeling remorse for actions that I tell myself were justified?* He recalls an essay by Allan Watts, the English author known for his writings on Eastern spiritual practices, about eating meat. As he remembered it, Watts argued that to live was to kill other living things. Even Jainists who are devoted to *ahimsā*, the practice of non-violence to any life form, breathe in and kill living organisms. Once you accept Watts' premise, it's not a huge jump to argue that we are justified in killing other life forms that we consume.

Although Lenny is aware that there are counterarguments, one point Watts made always stuck with him: If we are going to eat the flesh of other creatures, we should do so with a kind of reverence. As Watts put it, eating should be an act of love, consciously making another being a part of me. He recommended ritual meals as a way of expressing our veneration for the once-living thing that we have killed, or more likely, others have killed for us, and we are consuming.

Returning from this tangent back to Carroll's poem, Lenny thinks, *maybe I am not the walrus but more like the elder oysters, afraid to venture far from home or wisely seeing through the disingenuousness of those whose alluring promises are actually self-serving lies.*

And then there is Jeremy. Was he a young oyster? Lured into the path of his own and others' destruction, only to be remembered for the terrible violence he committed. Although it feels like a lot of effort, he decides to go to the cemetery. *Someone* needs to show up.

He wishes he had the energy of the younger oysters coupled with the wisdom of the elders. He recalls the adage that 'youth is wasted on the young.' *Somewhat true, but only from the perspective of the old. Maybe it would be just as true to say that old age is wasted on the elderly.*

A vibration in his pocket alerts him to a text message. *How did this become such a normative part of my life?* he thinks disapprovingly. Nevertheless, he checks and seeing it's from McGuire, opens the message. She informs him that Jeffrey Wingate took a plea deal that will keep him off the streets for at least a year. It also means, she writes, that Lenny and Patricia won't have to testify. *That's a relief.*

She also confirms that Jeremy Larsen will be buried tomorrow at 10 a.m. at a municipal cemetery with the euphemistic name of Lakeside Gardens. *Unfortunately, the residents won't be enjoying the view,* he thinks a bit mordantly. He looks at their website and learns that there is an area of the cemetery known as the 'free ground' where indigent and unidentified people are buried, many with only numbers on their simple grave markers. *Faceless in life, faceless in death.*

Despite his infamy, he hopes that Jeremy's marker will bear his name. *Like it or not, his atoms will merge with the universe so best not give them a negative charge.* "Ha, ha," he laughs soberly at his grim attempt at humor.

PART FOUR

Chapter Twenty-Four

The morning is partly cloudy with a light breeze out of the west. Lenny is driving to the cemetery where Jeremy Larsen will be interred. It's northeast of Burlington towards the mountains. As the elevation rises, he notices many trees showing early signs of fall, their green leaves turning shades of yellow and red. He's always loved this time of year when nature puts on its kaleidoscopic foliage show. About forty-five minutes into his trip, he sees the sign for the Lakeside Gardens cemetery. He drives through the entrance towards a parking area stopping as far away as possible from the other cars. Various signs direct visitors to different parts of the cemetery. He locates the one labeled 'The Free Grounds' and follows the gravel path indicated. In contrast to his colorful drive, the trees here are evergreens, beech, and yellow birch.

As Lenny walks, he thinks about his life only a few weeks ago. If he were asked to sum it up in a word he might have said 'uneventful.' Well, that was no longer the case. If only the event had been something uplifting instead of what brought him here today.

The path opens to a field dotted with numerous burial plots, all with modest markers. About thirty yards ahead and to his left, he sees a small gathering of people. It's a little past ten o'clock so he wonders if they might be here for Jeremy Larsen. His question is answered when he notices some motorcycles parked in the grass off to the side. *So, I'm not the only one who came to pay their respects.*

Now that he knows others are attending the service, he considers leaving but nixes the idea. *I'm already here and I'm curious to know how this will go.* However, since the mourners would likely not welcome his presence, he decides it would be best for him to observe from a distance. He finds a place about forty feet away among a copse of beech trees he hopes will allow him to hear what is going on without being seen. Lenny counts eight people at the graveside: six men and two women. A wooden coffin sits next to a dug grave. The people stand in a semi-circle around the grave with one person, a male, in front. He's older, sixtyish, wearing dark, formal attire, and holding a small, black book. Lenny assumes he is a clergyman who will officiate. The others are dressed in jeans and the leather jacket uniform of the bikers he has encountered.

The man opens the book and begins speaking. Unfortunately, at that moment a breeze rustles through the trees making it difficult to hear what is being said. Lenny does make out a reference to Matthew 6:14: 'For if you forgive other people when they sin against you, your heavenly Father will also forgive you.' He wonders whether this is directed toward Jeremy's victims or those at the graveside.

A few more biblical references complete the formal part of the service. Nothing Lenny has heard suggests that the clergyman knew Jeremy. Closing the Bible, he looks at the people surrounding the grave and asks if anyone would like to speak. At first, no one says anything, then a tall, burly fellow with a long, red beard, sunglasses, and a black bandanna steps forward. The deep resonance of his voice carries easily to Lenny. "Jeremy was a patriot who could no longer tolerate the threats to our American way of life. Despite how he is being portrayed by the Jew-controlled media, he was a true martyr, sacrificing himself to protect the God-given rights of white Christians. He will be remembered and his death avenged."

Lenny hears murmurs and sees nods among the others. It's a chilling display. When no one else comes forward, the clergyman gestures to the man who spoke prompting him and three others to lift a strap that had been placed under the coffin. They raise it off the ground and slowly lower it into the open grave.

Lenny shudders. Feeling unsafe and exposed he recedes further into the surrounding bushes. While debating when and how to surreptitiously leave he notices a woman he hadn't seen approach the bearded man. She talks with him for a few minutes while writing in a small notepad. When she turns to go, he recognizes Ashley Lee, the reporter from the *Chronicle*.

He continues watching as she walks from the gravesite in a direction that will take her near his hiding place. As she passes, he whispers, "Ashley." She stops and cocks her head, a puzzled expression on her face. Lenny repeats, "Ashley." This time she turns toward his location. He emerges from his shelter just enough to be visible while whispering, "It's me. Lenny Isaacson."

Ashley startles, but recognizing Lenny regains her composure. "Dr. Isaacson!" she exclaims. "What are you doing here?"

Lenny puts a finger to his lips and motions for her to come closer which she does. He explains why he came, but after seeing the attendees didn't feel safe. "If you'd like to talk further let's meet somewhere."

Ashley nods in consent.

"How about the restaurant in Morrisville called Kathy's Kitchen?" asks Lenny, choosing a town not far from the cemetery.

Ashley whispers, "ok," and begins walking toward the parking lot. Lenny waits a couple of minutes and then stealthily makes his way to the path leading to his car. About halfway to his destination, he hears the rumble of motorcycles and steps off the path so as not to be seen. Crouching behind some bushes he watches as the bikers roll slowly by.

* * *

Lenny arrives at the restaurant and spots Ashley waiting outside. He hadn't thought he would see her again and this unexpected encounter stirs up some of the emotions from their previous interactions which he quickly shelves. She sees Lenny and approaches him. They walk inside together.

They sit at a small wooden table with a red checkerboard tablecloth. Lenny orders coffee and a croissant and Ashley tea.

"I was surprised to see you there," says Lenny.

"Likewise," replies Ashley, "especially hiding among the trees."

"When I saw the motorcycles, I thought it best to stay out of sight. Then when I heard the guy with the red beard speak, I decided to become even less visible. I hope I didn't scare you when I called your name."

"When you first whispered my name, I wasn't sure if someone was calling me. Being in a cemetery feeds the imagination. When

I saw you, I was puzzled why you seemed to be hiding, but then I thought about what the bearded guy had said and understood. I think the minister was shocked."

"I noticed you talking to 'Red Beard.' How did it go?"

"I tried to get him to be more specific about what he meant by his remarks, but he wouldn't go there. He would only say, 'Make of it what you will.'"

Lenny shakes his head. "They're scary folks. You probably heard about my encounter with one of them a few days ago."

"I did. It was shocking. You must have been quite shaken."

Lenny reads her expression as concerned and sympathetic. It would be easy for him to pretend there was more to this, but he reminds himself that she's a reporter and while her reaction might be sincere, building rapport is the means to disclosure and an interesting story. Treading cautiously, he says, "Yes, it was a harrowing experience. Luckily, my companion was skilled in martial arts and able to subdue him."

"I read about that," says Ashley. "It was quite amazing. The article mentioned her daughter was killed at The Loft. How tragic. Did you know her before then?"

"No, I met her as a consequence of us both being there."

"Oh. As you know, I have been talking with some of the people who were there and the families of those who were killed or injured. The devastation this one man inflicted was enormous."

"Yes, it was," Lenny agrees. "But as we saw today, his delusions are shared by others."

Ashley nods. "So, what are your views on the service?"

Lenny notices she has taken out her notepad. "Listen, Ashley,

I asked if you wanted to meet so we could catch up on events and process what went on at the cemetery. I do *not* want my presence there to be reported. It would only further complicate my already complicated life and possibly place me in danger."

"I would never want to do that," says Ashley looking upset. "I was thinking your decision to be present at the funeral would be of interest to our readers, but I will respect your wishes." She puts her pad back in her bag.

"Thank you," says Lenny relieved at avoiding a conflict. "To answer your question, I went because I did not know if anyone would show up and despite what Larsen did, I thought he deserved someone to acknowledge his tragic life. Other than the FBI agent who told me about the burial, no one knew I was going. How about you? Why did you go?"

"It was a natural extension of my previous reporting on The Loft. Also, like you, I was curious to see who, if anyone, would show up. I was more surprised to see you than the others."

Is she subtly encouraging me to reconsider not reporting my presence? He decides to ignore it. "What will you be writing?"

"I'm not sure yet. I need to think about how best to report what I observed."

"If you are referring to Red Beard, why not just quote him verbatim?"

Ashley pauses as if considering what he said. "Hmm, I did write it down word for word."

Their conversation lapses until Ashley asks, "Are you doing okay, Dr. Isaacson? You've been through so much. I've thought about you often."

She's thought about me often? Before he can formulate a response that will encourage her to elaborate, he reminds himself that to her he's still Dr. Isaacson and not to embarrass himself by assuming her concern is anything more than compassion for what he's been through.

He smiles and says, "Thank you, Ashley, for your concern, but I'm ok. I'll just need to be observant of my surroundings for a while and careful about where I go."

"I understand," she says sympathetically. "It's unfortunate, but a wise course of action. The increased activity of these hate groups has upset many people in the community. I recently learned of a newly formed organization, the Alliance for Peace, that hopes to counter this trend. In contrast to dividing people and encouraging violence, they advocate tolerance, respect, and peaceful protest. Have you heard about them?"

"No, but I am glad to learn of their existence. The current administration's unwillingness to condemn these hate groups is seen by them as tacit approval for their racist, antisemitic, and xenophobic agendas. We need visible alternatives."

Ashley perks up at these remarks. "Do you think the administration is responsible for what happened at The Loft?"

"Not directly, but I believe their rhetoric and inaction have emboldened those who hold these pernicious beliefs. Promulgating fear and division among people are time-honored methods of control. Couple that with an armed citizenry and you have the conditions for violent conflict or worse."

"Worse?" says Ashley riveted by what Lenny is saying.

"The unthinkable: civil war."

"Wow," exclaims Ashley. "That puts what happened at The Loft in a whole new light." Clasping her hands together under her chin, she asks, "Can I quote you as an unnamed source?"

Lenny smiles. "How did we get from this conversation being off the record to quoting me as an unnamed source? You're not secretly recording me, are you?" Although his inflection is lighthearted, his words are serious.

"Oh no," says Ashley, looking somewhat abashed. "I would never do that without your explicit permission. I'm sorry if you think I am being manipulative. I just thought what you've been saying would be informative and of interest."

Seeing Ashley's discomfort, Lenny tells himself he should be more sensitive to how differences in their age, gender, background, and roles play out in these interactions. He tries to assuage Ashley. "No need to be sorry. You're just doing what good reporters do: getting their sources to feel comfortable and disclosing their views. And it doesn't take much for me to go off on tangents and begin talking about things I hadn't anticipated."

"Thank you, Dr. Isaacson. I work hard at being a good journalist, but I wouldn't want you to think unkindly of me."

"Not a chance." Feeling like their conversation has come to an end, Lenny says, "I look forward to reading your story, Ashley, and to seeing the public's reaction. Making these disturbing trends explicit is an important duty of the press. In contrast to Bob Dylan's lyrics, some people do need a weatherman—or a reporter—to know which way the wind is blowing."

Ashley tilts her head and squints slightly.

"Oh," says Lenny. "You're not a big Dylan fan?"

"Not so much. Is that from 'Blowing in the Wind?'"

"Good guess. It's from 'Subterranean Homesick Blues.' In the song, the line goes 'You don't need a weatherman to know which way the wind blows.' Seems obvious, but I think he underestimates peoples' ability to screen out what they don't want to know."

Ashley nods. "Well, thanks for your comments, Dr. Isaacson. I hope my piece makes readers more sensitive to the weather," she adds with a smile.

As they exit the restaurant, Ashley says, "Would you be interested in attending the Alliance for Peace meeting? I was planning to go and interview some of the members. It's next Thursday evening at the downtown Unitarian Universalist church."

Lenny likes the idea of being around kindred spirits with youthful idealism. It would be a nice change, whether or not Ashley was there. "Sounds interesting. I'll plan on it."

"Great," says Ashley with a buoyant smile. "I'll see you there."

Chapter Twenty-Five

Lenny is spent. Hiding at the cemetery, hearing the pledge of vengeance for Jeremy Larsen's death, and constant vigilance are emotional anchors doubling the effort necessary to get anything done. *Is this what it feels like to be old?* He sits on his living room couch and allows himself to succumb to his weariness. Before long, he drifts into a troubled sleep.

Opening his eyes about an hour later, he's disoriented, suspended in the viscous medium between sleep and wakefulness. For a moment he thinks he's in Spain at the home of Carolina. He feels trapped. Panic rising, he shouts, "STOP!" and focuses on his surroundings: the couch he is lying on, his books on his coffee table and Sisu, head tilted to the side, looking at him quizzically. He takes a few calming breaths.

Wow, that was weird. I seem to be blurring the lines between reality and fantasy. But is it really a dichotomy? Every character in my book, no matter how similar or different, is an expression of me, of my reality. Could the story be a kind of self-analysis, a way of telling myself I need to take more control of my life? I'll need to revisit this.

He gets up and shuffles to the bathroom. After splashing some water on his face, he stares at himself in the mirror. "Am I really this old?" he asks his reflection. It answers, "Nothing that grows ever grows old."

"I hope I'm still growing."

Aging is multidimensional. Our bodies, minds, and hearts do not age at the same rate. The disconnect among them can be disorienting, like when he tries to reconcile his self-image with his physical reflection; or embarrassing, when he forgets how he appears to others who are much younger.

He takes off his shirt to check his wound. It hasn't been bothering him as much. Removing the bandage, he sees the redness has subsided. *Thank goodness, one less thing to worry about.*

His cell phone rings. Unable to localize the sound or remember where he left it, he darts around the apartment, a spurt of energy returning. Just as it goes silent, he spots it on the floor near the couch where it had fallen when he dozed off. He checks the caller ID: 'Katherine Finner.' *That's Jerry's spouse. Why would she be calling me?* He sees there's a voice mail message and with a sense of foreboding, opens it.

"Lenny. It's Katie. Call me as soon as you can." The message ends.

He immediately calls. She picks up on the first ring. "Hello, Katie," he says trying to sound calm.

"Jerry's in the hospital," she says, her distress evident.

"The hospital?" Lenny repeats. "What happened?"

"There was an accident."

Lenny's first thought is that Jerry intentionally hurt himself. *Please don't let that be true.* "What happened?" he asks again.

Stifling a sob, she says, "He was going to the supermarket to buy some food. I had suggested a backyard picnic might lift his spirits. He was out a long time and I began to worry. I called him but it went to voice mail. I was about to go out and look for him when I got a call from the police saying he had been in an accident."

Katie stops speaking and Lenny can hear her heavy breathing. He waits so she can compose herself sufficiently to continue. Then in a voice choked with emotion she says, "They said his car had gone off the road and hit a tree and that he was on his way to the ER at the university hospital."

A pang of fear courses through Lenny. "Do you know his condition?"

"It's uncertain. When I got to the ER several people were working on him trying to determine the extent of his injuries." Another pause. "It's like reliving what happened with Emily . . . It's too much!" She sobs.

Knowing there is nothing he can say to ease her anguish and wanting to avoid platitudes, Lenny says, "I'll be there shortly."

He goes across the hall and knocks on his neighbor's door. Carol answers and he explains a friend has been in an accident and is in the ER. Could she watch Sisu until he returns? She readily agrees, so he brings Sisu along with his food, water bowl, and some treats. Fortunately, Sisu is fond of Carol and barely notices when Lenny rushes down the stairs to his car.

* * *

The sights and sounds of the ER feel all too familiar. *As Yogi Berra said, 'it's déjà vu all over again.'* He texts Katie and lets her know he is in the waiting area. She appears about fifteen minutes later looking haggard and stressed.

"Thanks for coming, Lenny."

"Of course," he replies taking her hand. "How's he doing?"

"Hard to say. The biggest worry is a head injury. They're going to do an MRI."

"Did his airbag deploy?" asks Lenny.

"It did, but he wasn't wearing a seat belt and was thrown from the car." She hesitates. Her voice trembles. "Why would he not have buckled his seatbelt? That's so unlike him. Do you think . . ." Tears well in her eyes.

Given Jerry's recent emotional state, Lenny doesn't dismiss this unsaid but obvious possibility. However, he says, "We'll just have to wait until we can speak with him. We know he's been struggling with guilt, although unfounded, about not being able to prevent what happened to Emily, but has anything else happened the past few days?"

Katie thinks for a moment. "After he spoke with you at the coffee shop, he was very upset. I think he was mortified by how he acted."

Lenny is distressed. "Oh, I'm sorry if I made things worse."

"No. You didn't do anything wrong," Katie reassures him. "Learning that the guy who did the shooting committed suicide set him off. He started ranting about all the evil in the world and how everyone just stands around and lets it happen. It was so out of character. The kids noticed it too. We were all concerned, but he seemed so wound up and distanced from us that we found ourselves tiptoeing around him."

The sounds of the ER have faded from Lenny's ears replaced

by a heavy silence between them. He grieves for them all. Taking Katie's hand again, he says, "Your family has been through so much. I'm so sorry."

She gives him a tight smile of acknowledgment. "I need to get back. I'll let you know when we hear something more."

Lenny watches her go through the doors leading to the treatment rooms. Not knowing what else to do except wait for further news, he finds a coffee machine and gets himself a cup. He returns to the waiting room and texts Carol to see if Sisu is ok and to let her know he might be a while. She texts back that he should take all the time he needs and that Sisu is being spoiled. At the end of the sentence is an emoji of a yellow face with one eye closed and a tongue sticking out the side of its mouth. Despite his distress, Lenny finds himself smiling.

Sensing a presence, he looks up and sees Danny, Jerry and Katie's son, standing by him.

"Hi Lenny," he says grim-faced.

"Hi, Danny. How's your dad doing?"

Danny shrugs, but his lower lip quivers. "He doesn't look too good. They've taken him for some tests. We should know more after that."

Responding to Danny's distress, Lenny says "You've been through a lot in a short time. First Emily and now your dad. How are you holding up?"

Danny takes a seat next to Lenny. "Ok, I guess. It's just, I don't know, crazy." He shakes his head in disbelief.

"Yeah," says Lenny. "There's no way to make sense of it. What happened to Emily has been very hard for your dad."

Danny nods in agreement. Lenny knows Jerry and Danny are close so Jerry's struggles must be particularly painful for him to witness.

Danny says, "My dad seemed upset that the guy who did the shooting at The Loft killed himself, but I thought that was a good thing. You know, he got what he deserved."

"I think your dad didn't like that he got to decide his own fate."

Danny squinches his face. "I don't know how he could have gotten a worse punishment than dying unless maybe he was tortured."

Lenny doesn't respond.

Danny stands and says, "I'm going to head back to see if there's any news about my dad. It was nice seeing you, Lenny."

"You too, Danny. Hang in there."

"Yeah."

Poor kid. This must be overwhelming. I hope he'll be ok.

Lenny's not sure what to do. Should he continue to wait? He came to the ER to be helpful, but maybe now's not the time. He decides to stay a bit longer to see if anything develops. Some minutes later a text arrives from Katie:

'Concussion but no brain damage. Some broken bones and lots of bruises, still assessing. Will likely be transferred upstairs to a regular room. I'll let you know when you can visit. Thanks for talking with Danny. It's been hard on him.'

Lenny breathes a sigh of relief that Jerry's injuries are not life-threatening and his brain intact. He returns to his other worry. Was this truly an accident? *He seems so lost. Can I, or anyone, provide him a lifeline?*

He exits the ER with a heavy heart.

Chapter Twenty-Six

Lenny texts Patricia that Jerry had a car accident and is in the hospital. A minute later she calls.

"Oh no, that's terrible," she says, her voice filled with anguish. "What happened? Is he going to be ok?"

Lenny fills her in on what he knows and braces for what he is expecting will be Patricia's next question.

"Do you think it was an accident?"

"If you mean was he trying to kill himself, I hope not, but given his emotional state, it's hard to dismiss the possibility. The police report might shed some light and, of course, Jerry himself when he is conscious and able to talk."

"You don't think one of those Nazi guys might have come after him, do you?

Lenny hadn't considered this but thinks it is unlikely and conveys that to Patricia. The next thing he hears is Patricia's muffled sobs.

"Are you ok?"

Another sniffle. "Yes. Ever since . . . I just get overwhelmed with emotion. I'll be doing a routine task or even just sitting in the yard or listening to music and I find myself crying."

Lenny tries to normalize her reactions. "You've suffered a devastating loss. Being emotionally fragile is expected."

Silence. Then in hushed tones, Patricia says, "And I saw it happen," before choking up again.

Lenny is not sure what to say.

"I'm sorry, Lenny," says Patricia. "I know you called about Jerry, not me. I, I don't think I can talk now."

She disconnects.

Lenny continues to hold the phone to his ear as if willing Patricia to say something more. His heart goes out to her, and he is filled with remorse. He walks away from the ER toward the street. The act of moving and distancing himself from the hospital grounds helps center him. When it's out of sight he stops. Since he's near the university, there are several young people he assumes are students walking among the buildings. Occasionally, someone older or carrying a briefcase appears. Faculty or administrators he guesses depending on how formally they are dressed. He muses on the different worlds of the university and hospital existing in such close proximity. One concerned with intellectual matters the other with life and death.

Life is complex but our experience of it is fleeting and partial. So many things occurring concurrently, dramas of triumphs and tragedies, large and small, playing without end.

His phone vibrates. A text from Katie.

'He's awake! Come by in about an hour and I will meet you in the lobby of the main entrance.'

Learning Jerry regained consciousness is a huge relief. A spring returns to his step, and he spends the time until he can visit walking some more and getting something to eat.

* * *

The main lobby of the hospital is an immense open area spanning the entire length of the building. Its recent construction is reflected in its modern architecture: huge glass facades allowing for abundant natural light and visible courtyards with greenery and trees. He notices the abundance of art—paintings, photographs, a few sculptures—and mellow background music. Everything is carefully designed to counteract the stress and anxiety of those entering this space.

On the entrance side of the building, there are several comfortable-looking chairs, some arranged in semi-circles and others scattered about. Opposite them is an information desk, a gift shop, and various medical check-in stations. At the far end is a hallway that leads to the different wards.

Typical for this time of day, many people come and go. He identifies three groups. Patients wearing the standard hospital gown, walking or in wheelchairs, a few pushing IV stands alongside them. Medical personnel in green scrubs or with a stethoscope around their neck. And visitors like himself, here to see patients or for other reasons. Lenny assumes Katie will be coming from one of the wards, so he finds a chair near that end of the lobby and texts her his approximate location. A short time later he sees her turn the corner and head his way.

Katie's appearance shows the stress of recent events. Typically well-coiffed and vibrant, she looks drawn and tired. Lenny greets her and asks how Jerry is doing. Katie's expression is pained, and he braces for bad news. It turns out to be mixed.

"The good news," says Katie, "is that he is going to survive.

Besides what I told you before, they discovered some internal bleeding which they believe is under control."

Lenny lets out a breath he didn't realize he was holding. "That's a relief . . . and the not so good news?"

"His blood-alcohol level was above the legal limit," says Katie flatly as though she's used up her emotional resources.

"That doesn't sound like Jerry."

"No, it doesn't. And it makes me wonder what was happening and whether this was an accident." Speaking these words aloud restores her responsiveness and her eyes grow puffy.

Lenny puts a hand on her arm. "I'm so sorry, Katie. You've been shouldering so much."

His acknowledgment dissolves Katie's remaining self-composure. Her face contorts with grief.

"I don't know what to do. All my energies have been focused on Emily. My God, she almost died! And now this." She pauses to wipe her eyes.

"What happened to Emily was beyond belief. We were shell-shocked and scared. We felt like we were walking down a treacherous passageway in total darkness unsure of our next step. But even though the tension was enormous, Jerry and I knew, or I thought we knew, we could turn to each other for support. But strangely as Emily began to get better, Jerry began to slip away."

"I saw the change in him," says Lenny. "Although one part of him knew he had nothing to do with what happened to Emily, another part couldn't stop blaming himself. And as Emily improved his remorse transformed into intense anger and vengeance toward the shooter."

Katie nods in agreement. "I watched him go from shock to concern, to guilt, and then anger. I tried to reach him, but he just withdrew into himself. It was like he didn't want, or couldn't accept, my help. I told myself to be patient and let him work it through in whatever way he needed." She wrings her hands. "I should have done more."

"Don't blame yourself, Katie. Hindsight is 20-20, but you couldn't have known where this would lead." He thinks back to his last conversation with Jerry. "As you mentioned to me, he became enraged when I told him the guy that did the shooting had committed suicide."

"But why? I can't understand it. I thought he'd be relieved."

"That's what Danny said. I also thought that, but instead, he grew agitated. He said by killing himself Larsen had evaded punishment by the courts even though just before he told me he believed the court would be too lenient. He wasn't thinking straight.

"Did you know he bought a gun?"

For a moment, Katie looks at Lenny in disbelief. Then her eyes grow wide with terror. "What?" she shrieks.

Now, it's Lenny who feels he should have done more, like telling Katie earlier. "He told me about it the last time we met. From how he acted, I had the feeling it scared him, like he was becoming a stranger to himself. He assured me he put it somewhere where no one could find it and that it wasn't loaded."

"My God," says Katie, her alarm not eased by Lenny's words. "Where is it?"

Lenny tells her what Jerry had said. "Obviously, I was very worried by this and suggested he might need to talk with someone. I gave him the name of a psychologist I knew and made him promise he would call him."

"Did you think about telling *me*?" says Katie now sounding a little angry.

"I did, but he was adamant I not tell anyone. I was afraid if I betrayed his confidence, it would make things worse."

"Well, it did get worse."

"I'm sorry," says Lenny feeling chastised.

They sit for a while without speaking, Katie unable to grasp that the man she loved and thought she knew, had purchased a gun, gotten drunk, and crashed his car; Lenny alternating between feeling numb and overwhelmed.

Katie changes the subject.

"Jerry seemed pretty calm when I left his room. It may be the pain meds, but I think it would be ok for you to visit. Why don't we go upstairs."

Without waiting for a reply, she turns and walks towards the hallway where the elevators are located. Lenny dutifully follows. He's anxious about seeing Jerry. What will he look like? How will he react? He fights the urge to rehearse what he is going to say, telling himself he needs to respond authentically to whatever he observes.

* * *

They get off the elevator on the third floor. Katie continues to lead the way down the ward. Lenny's senses are inundated by the mélange of sights, sounds, and smells: Smiling people bringing flowers, physicians huddled together reviewing charts, laughter at the nurses' station, someone in distress, the odor of illness. Hospitals make him uneasy possibly because he's had the good fortune to never have been a patient in one.

He attempts to distract himself from his discomfort by going into academic mode. He thinks about how the hospital is an instantiation of what the French social theorist Michel Foucault would call medical discourse. For Foucault, a discourse encompasses the beliefs, practices, and organizations that embody an area of knowledge at a particular historical period. From this perspective, medical discourse generates hospitals, doctors, nurses, and patients. It provides rules for ways of talking and relating: their identities, their responsibilities, and privileges.

"Here we are," says Katie breaking into his intellectual sanctuary.

He swiftly reorients. *Ok Lenny, time to focus on your friend.*

Katie knocks softly and they enter. Jerry is lying with his eyes closed, an IV attached to one arm and monitors tracking his heart rate and respiration. His right eye is visibly swollen and surrounded by an ugly, purple yellowish bruise. Stitches run along his jaw on the same side. A bandage is wrapped around his head. His complexion is pallid. Although Lenny expected him to be banged up, seeing the extent of his injuries is nevertheless distressing.

For a minute they just stand there looking at Jerry. Then he opens his eyes, mostly the left one, but they seem unfocused. Eventually, his gaze settles on his visitors. "Hello," he whispers.

Lenny feels Jerry's discomfort. In a soft voice he says, "Hello Jerry. How are you feeling?" unhappy with the banality of the question but not knowing what else to say.

"I've been better," answers Jerry with an expression between a smile and a grimace.

"Hi, sweetheart," says Katie. "I told Lenny he could see you. He was very concerned."

Lenny notices Jerry is averting Katie's gaze. "Thanks for coming, Lenny," he says weakly. "It's not Holy Grounds, but I hear the coffee's okay."

His comment surprises Lenny who worried he would be consumed with self-reproach. Must be the drugs, he thinks.

Before he can respond, Katie says, "I'll give you guys some time to chat. I'm going to meet Danny in the cafeteria."

"See you soon," she adds, trying but failing to sound upbeat.

Once alone, Jerry's cheerful demeanor vanishes. "What have I done?" he whispers, tears threatening to emerge from his bruised and swollen eyes.

Lenny moves closer, glimpsing the depths of Jerry's emotional pain. His own tears begin to blur his vision but he manages to keep them contained. "Sometimes when we are struggling and feeling lost, we make decisions that are not in our best interests. I know you feel great regret but beating yourself up about what you've done will only dig a deeper hole. The best thing you can do is to focus on getting well."

Tears are on Jerry's cheeks. Talking ceases, the only sounds the beeping monitors and muffled voices outside the room. A good two minutes pass. Then Jerry asks for a tissue that with effort he uses to wipe his eyes, the movement causing him to grunt in pain. Using the hospital bed's remote to raise his head, he talks about his rage and the urge to find the people he blamed for what happened at The Loft.

"I wanted to hurt them, even kill them. It was crazy, I know, but I couldn't stop myself. When Katie would ask what was wrong, I was afraid to tell her so I withdrew. I started thinking my family was in danger. Maybe these people wouldn't stop with Emily but come after Katie and Danny. I couldn't fail again. I had to protect them. So I bought the gun."

Lenny wonders what Jerry meant by "I couldn't fail again," but before he could ask, Jerry continues.

"It felt like my life was crumbling and I couldn't put it back together. Everything I tried to do seemed to make things worse. Eventually, the pressure in my head got so intense it felt like it was going to explode. I didn't know how to get relief, but I knew I could not be around my family. I was a negative presence. I told Katie I was going out to the store, and I intended to, but when I got into my car, I drove aimlessly. I passed a bar and thought a beer might help calm my nerves. It was not something I would normally do, but I was desperate. I went in and started drinking. After a few drinks, I felt a little better, numb really, so I drank some more. I shouldn't have gotten back into the car. After that, all I remember is driving and waking up in the hospital."

So, he didn't try to kill himself, at least not consciously.

"I am so sorry, Jerry, for what you have gone through. I can only imagine the hell you were experiencing, but thankfully you're alive and have a second chance."

Jerry's expression is inscrutable.

"I don't know what you're thinking now, but I am going to tell you honestly what I believe. You are a good person who was abruptly thrown into a horrific situation for which you were not, nor could have been, prepared. You were driven by the noble desire to protect Emily and to fix things. When you couldn't do so in a way you thought you should, things started to unravel and now you are here."

Lenny pauses to gather his thoughts. Sweat seeps from his armpits and dribbles down his sides. He's not sure how Jerry is taking this but decides being candid is the best he can do. "You can recover Jerry, but it's not a journey you can travel alone. It will only happen if you stop punishing yourself and begin accepting help from your family, friends, and others. Remember, accepting help is strength, not weakness."

Jerry's mouth moves as if he wants to speak but cannot. Lenny waits. Finally, Jerry murmurs, "Thank you, Lenny. You're a good friend and I know your right. I just don't know if I can do it."

"That's why we're here for you," says Lenny trying to hide his apprehension.

Jerry closes his eyes and is still.

"I'll see you again soon," whispers Lenny.

* * *

Waiting for the elevator, Lenny hopes what he said was helpful. *At least I was honest,* he consoles himself.

As the elevator doors open, he sees Katie and Danny about to exit. He remains in the hall.

"How did it go?" asks Katie as the doors close.

"Pretty well."

Sensing there is more to learn, Katie says, "Danny, why don't you go see Dad while I talk with Lenny for a few minutes."

Danny departs and Katie says, "There's a lounge at the end of the hall where we can have some privacy."

They sit at a small round table in chairs facing each other. Katie looks expectantly at Lenny.

He relays their conversation emphasizing he doesn't think Jerry was trying to commit suicide. Rather, he believes it was a confused attempt to dull the pain he was feeling combined with an alcohol-fueled lapse in judgment. He shares that Jerry was very remorseful and it is critical to direct this remorse toward constructive action. "What we don't want is for this incident to exacerbate his guilt or hopelessness, but for it to be a wake-up call that he needs help."

"What about the gun?" asks Katie. "What should I do?"

"As I said, I believe he bought it out of fear further harm might befall your family and a misguided sense it would protect you. I don't think he believes that anymore, but as a precaution, I would get rid of it."

Katie nods. Her hands tremble and her shoulders slump. Seeing this, Lenny says, "You know Katie, it may not be a bad idea for you to also consider getting some help. You're an incredibly strong person, but everyone has limits."

"Thanks, but I need to focus on my family."

"I understand," says Lenny thinking she sounds a bit like Jerry. "But the two are not mutually exclusive."

"Where would I even go?" asks Katie.

He considers also suggesting Patricia but recalling their last meeting he nixes the idea. Instead, he says, "You could see the psychologist I recommended to Jerry."

Her response is less than enthusiastic. "I'll get the information from Jerry, but as I said, for now I need to focus on my family.

Rising from the chair, she says, "I'd better get back to Jerry, Thanks so much, Lenny, for your support."

"Don't hesitate to call if you need anything," says Lenny also rising while thinking she is not going to follow through.

They stand facing each other, weary and afraid. Spontaneously, they hug, both needing the palliative of human contact.

"It's going to be alright," Lenny murmurs.

"I hope so."

* * *

Lenny returns home. He retrieves Sisu who is decidedly blasé about leaving the attention and treats he has received from Carol. *So much for loyalty*, he thinks with a smile. Drained from the emotional intensity of the hospital visit he feels the need to chill out for a while. Plunking down into his most comfortable chair, he puts on his headphones, goes to the music app on his phone, and selects his Leonard Cohen playlist. Within minutes, he begins to feel sleepy. The last thing he hears just before nodding off is Cohen's sonorous voice.

> Show me the place, help me roll away the stone
> Show me the place, I can't move this thing alone
> Show me the place where the word became a man
> Show me the place where the suffering began

Lenny awakens about an hour later to the same voice, different song. He stops the music and removes his headphones. He feels a headache coming on and takes some ibuprofen to head it off. While he waits for the pills to kick in, he scrolls through the news. Not trusting the integrity of a mainstream media largely owned by a few politically right-leaning people, he relies on alternative, independent news sources, the one exception being the local newspaper.

Regardless of the source, there is not much to feel good about. The global rise of right-wing populism, often accompanied by xenophobic oppression of 'the other' is a scary development. Nationally, these trends are visible in the increasing activity of extremist militia groups encouraged by an administration and his political cohort who are unfailingly subservient to his wishes, and a so-called opposition party impotent to the point where Lenny wonders if their interests might be aligned with those with whom they allegedly disagree.

He's intrigued by how language is used to justify and manipulate public sentiment by framing events to evoke fear and legitimize the solutions they offer. Recently, the conjured-up specter of lawlessness from subversives and revolutionaries, which could be any group opposing the administration's policies, and the so-called threat of immigrants and refugees, has been used to increase government surveillance and the inhumane treatment of people whose only crime is desperation to escape from unbearable circumstances and make a better life for themselves.

Yet, in spite of the devastating effects of the administration's policies on the lower economic rung of society, the president has managed to make himself a hero of the downtrodden, portraying himself as a symbol of opposition to the intelligentsia and privileged classes although his own life was and is one of privilege. Lenny shakes his head thinking how easily people can be manipulated to vote against their own interests.

What might be mere academic reflection becomes personal

when Lenny considers the similarities between the president's inflammatory and divisive rhetoric and previous autocratic regimes we now condemn. Particularly chilling is that he is preaching to a population that is armed and ready to use their weapons. And as Lenny's recent experience has frighteningly shown, his community is not immune to these trends. To Lenny, the shooting at The Loft, being assaulted, and the overt threats are indicative of the loosening of civic bonds. He's glad to hear organized opposition is beginning to form and looks forward to attending the meeting Ashley told him about.

Despite the less than uplifting news, his headache has been reduced to a mild, dull ache. He decides to continue his novel noting with a chuckle that the world it depicts is not very different than the one he inhabits. *Next time, I'll write a comedy.* He goes to his desk, opens his most recent file, and reviews the last few paragraphs to avoid being redundant or inconsistent. Reoriented to the storyline, he begins.

The Rendenhall Collective.

Tobias informs the members of The Group he will give them his answer by the afternoon. He tells Carolina he would like to be alone for a while to think things over. She displays a mock pout but says she understands. The weather is clear, so he retrieves his laptop and searches for an out-of-the-way spot where he can consider his options without being disturbed.

He repeats to himself the questions that trouble

him. *Is this a real choice they are giving me? What happens if I refuse? How could they ensure their secrets are safe? Would I be considered a threat?* These last thoughts make his blood run cold. *Maybe I'm already in this too far.*

He tries to learn more about the Rendenhall Collective, but as he suspected, he finds little of substance or credibility. There is even some question whether such an organization exists or if it's a creation of factions like The Group used to stoke the flames of resistance. Several internet sites hold Rendenhall responsible for a myriad of events ranging from stock market fluctuations to coup attempts, even alien abductions. Tobias views the proffered evidence as flimsy and unsubstantiated. Nevertheless, given the global political climate, he's hesitant to conclude Rendenhall, or something like them, does not exist. There might be a modicum of truth, abductions aside, in some of these claims.

"Ok," he asks himself. "Let's suppose Rendenhall is up to no good. Does that justify my engaging in illegal acts to disrupt its activities? And, if so, just how far should these acts go?" He brings his hand to his forehead hoping some answers will be jarred loose. When that doesn't work, he gazes at the pink and white blossoms of the almond trees and the purple-flowered jacaranda. He is struck by the contrast between their vibrant beauty and the dark, colorless place in which he finds himself. Shutting his laptop, he closes his eyes and tries to meditate on the moment. After a few minutes, a thought, which quickly becomes a conviction, takes hold. *I need to distance myself from these people.* He realizes he has his passport and wallet with him, leaving only his clothes in the villa. Without further thought, he picks up his laptop and begins jogging in the direction of Marbella, the nearest town.

Tobias covers the three miles into Marbella in about thirty minutes. His phone buzzes. It's from Carolina, no doubt wondering where he has gone. He doesn't answer. His heart thumps and sweat soaks through his shirt. Striding through the streets he locates a taxi that will take him to the Málaga airport about thirty-five minutes away. During the ride, he considers his next move. The first is obvious. Leave the country. Although it will probably cost him a small fortune, he is hoping to book flights that will get him back to the U.S. *I'll figure out the rest after it feels safe, or at least safer than here.*

At the airport, Tobias is able to get a flight to London leaving in one hour with a connecting flight to the U.S. Stationing himself in what he hopes is an inconspicuous location, he scans the small terminal for signs of danger although unsure what that might look like. He considers texting Carolina but decides to wait until he is in London. Time passes tortuously slow, but finally he boards. In the safety of his seat, his tension subsides and exhaustion sets in. He sleeps most of the way.

Arriving at Heathrow, he has a two-hour layover.

Still vigilant, he tries not to broadcast his nervousness lest he attract unwanted attention. Just blend in, he tells himself. He buys coffee and sits at a crowded gate waiting for a flight to Ankara. He takes out his phone and composes a text to Carolina.

'I am on a flight to the U.S. Sorry for my sudden, unannounced departure, but what The Group was asking of me would be life-changing and I need some time and distance to think it through. I hope you and the others will understand.'

A short time later he receives another call from Carolina. He doesn't answer and a text soon follows. He's torn about whether to read it now or wait until he's safely on the plane. He knows it would be safer to shut off his phone, but his desire to know her response to what he's done wins out and he begins reading. Surprisingly, Carolina's message seems warm and supportive, even apologetic.

'Dearest Tobias,

We are sorry for putting so much pressure on you to make a binding commitment to our cause. In hindsight, we should have realized this was a decision needing considerable deliberation. We regret placing you in a position where you felt it necessary to leave without informing us.'

Until the last sentence—

'Is there any possibility we could still make contact before you are too far away?

With love, Carolina'

Alarm bells go off in his brain. Why would they think he's still close enough for them to make contact? Is he being observed? Was the first part of the text a way of keeping him from leaving the country?

Tobias can't get on the plane soon enough. His thoughts are racing. They would assume London is the most likely place to get a connecting flight to the U.S. Could someone from The Group he would not recognize be looking for him right now?

His gaze swivels across the terminal, but he detects nothing unusual. He tries to calm himself. *I'm overreacting. Heathrow is huge and there are people and security everywhere. I'm like a grain of sand in the desert. Besides, The Group is not an international cabal. Stop blowing this out of proportion. I'm ok.* But he's not. He finds his departure gate and paces while waiting for boarding to begin.

Sick with worry, Tobias manages to return home without incident. After a few days of wariness without any sign or contact from The Group, his life begins to resume its typical rhythms. He tries convincing himself it's over and he won't hear from them again. It doesn't work, but he does his best to act like it did.

Exactly two weeks after his arrival in the U.S., his period of relative calm abruptly ends when he receives a text from Carolina asking him if he's made up his mind about their offer. She adds that she is not trying to pressure him, but the meeting of the Rendenhall Collective will be happening soon, and they need to know if they can include him in their plans. She reiterates how in hindsight they realize they were asking too much of him too soon; however, they would hate to lose him. As a concession, they will modify their initial expectations.

'If you truly believe in our cause and want to remain involved, we will limit your role with Rendenhall to an observer.' She closes with 'I miss you' and a heart emoji.

His defenses crumble. Swirling thoughts and emotions return. He wants to interpret the text as an apology of sorts; trying to make amends for pushing him too hard by easing up on what they expect from him, at least for now. But what hasn't changed was their insistence, albeit velvet-gloved, that he needs to make a decision. And then there are Carolina's expressions of affection tugging at his heartstrings.

He wonders if this is merely a ploy to secure his involvement or a way to insure he cannot compromise their plans. *Can they allow me to exist with the knowledge I have about them? What if I simply do not answer? Will it flush out their intentions?*

Inaction wins out and as time passes without further contact, he again begins to think he is out of the woods. The time for the Rendenhall meeting comes and goes. He searches the news for any mention of the meeting or The Group's involvement but finds nothing. He concludes his fears led him to make The Group into something more powerful than it is.

After all, what evidence do I have they are not just the three people I met? In all likelihood, I will never hear from them again. He breathes a sigh of relief that it is over.

Then he is kidnapped.

* * *

Lenny stops writing. He is surprised by the direction the story is taking as if it's writing itself. He returns to the idea that personal events are shaping what he writes. *Is this my vicarious way of living or rehearsing an alternate life?* Although curious about how the story will unfold, he decides to let it sit for a while.

Sorry, Tobias. You'll have to hang in there a little longer.

Chapter Twenty-Seven

Lenny calls Patricia. He's upset that he underestimated how much she is struggling, his judgment clouded by her prowess at dispatching the guy who had threatened them. *The woman saw her daughter, her only child, shot and killed! And here I am talking to her about my problems. What was I thinking?* A wave of guilt sweeps over him as he smacks his forehead with the heel of his hand.

His call goes to voice mail. He leaves a brief message saying he wanted to see how she was doing and to contact him when it's convenient.

A few minutes later his phone rings. Assuming it is Patricia, he's surprised to hear his sister's voice. "Hi, Lenny. It's Eleanor. I've been thinking about you. How are you doing?"

Not wanting to worry her or get into a discussion about the issues he's dealing with, he expresses appreciation for her call and assures her he's ok.

Eleanor doesn't sound convinced but lets it go. The conversation gravitates towards, "What's new?" and she tells him about work and what's happening with her kids. As the call winds to an end, she repeats her offer of having him visit.

"A week or two away might be relaxing. Plus, it would be nice to spend some time together."

"I agree and promise I will come. I *want* to come. But now is not a good time." Feeling he should be more specific. He appends his last statement. "How about if we tentatively plan something for a month from now?"

"Sure. And I'm not going to let you wiggle out of it, so be prepared to travel."

"No wiggling. You have my word."

The call ends. He's grateful for Eleanor's presence in his life and vows to make good on his promise.

He feels the rumblings of another headache coming on. *Only a couple of hours since I last took ibuprofen. I'll have to tough it out for a while. Maybe some fresh air will help.* He ambles toward the front door. Sisu, always alert to the possibility of a walk, is there before he can call his name.

Being outside feels restorative. They stroll around the neighborhood taking in the sights of everyday life. He watches people walking by. *What are they thinking? Feeling?* He reflects on how we are connected and separate at the same time. We reside within shared culturally and socially produced realities, yet experience our lives privately within our own subjectivity, a sphere of existential separateness that ironically is a product of our connectedness. He shakes his head at the complexity of it all. *This is probably not the best way to deal with my headache.*

"Come on Sisu. Let's go home."

* * *

A few minutes after returning to his apartment, the doorbell rings. Peering through the peephole, he is surprised to see Patricia. He opens the door. "Hello. This is a surprise."

"A good one I hope."

"Definitely. Please come in."

Patricia is dressed smartly but casually in a white, v-neckline shirt with a floral print and jeans. Lenny had not been expecting a visitor and feels self-conscious about his wrinkled, rather shabby attire. He tells himself not to apologize about his appearance as it will only draw attention to it, but he does so anyway.

"You look fine to me," says Patricia, leading to a silent beratement for bringing it up, but also relief he is not being judged.

Moving on, he says, "To what do I owe the pleasure of this unexpected visit?"

"I was out doing some errands when I heard your voice mail. I was moved by your concern and since I wasn't too far away, I thought I would take a chance and drop by." She lightly touches his arm. "I hope it's ok."

"It's great," he says aware of her touch. "Can I get you anything to drink? Coffee or tea? Something stronger?"

"Tea would be nice."

"And this must be Sisu," she says looking down at the little dog sniffing her shoes. She bends and pets him, receiving a lick in return.

"It looks like you passed the Sisu test. Good thing since he has the final word on who can visit."

"I'm so relieved," says Patricia swiping her hand across her brow.

Lenny takes a sideways glance at the living room and is grateful that except for a tee shirt draped over a chair, it's passable. "Please, have a seat," he says while deftly removing the shirt. "I'll put up the tea. Herbal, ok?"

"Perfect."

After serving the tea, they sit for a bit in silence, Lenny in a chair and Patricia on the couch. For the first time he's aware of his pedestrian décor. *I must really like her.* Patricia says, "I appreciate you reaching out to me. I usually don't mind being alone, but this is a different kind of alone."

"Yes, it is. I'm glad you took a chance and came by. After we last spoke, I realized I had been overly focused on myself and should have been more sensitive to what you are going through. I'm sorry."

"No need. We're all trying to deal with what happened. Sometimes when I am with other people, I adopt a guise of being all right even when I'm not."

"I do that too. Please know you don't have to do that with me."

Patricia leans forward and looks into his eyes. "Thank you, Lenny."

A flutter wings through Lenny's chest. It feels like another intimate juncture where they might get up and hug. He likes Patricia and misses this kind of human connection, but his fear of misreading the moment overrides his desire for closeness.

Patricia remains seated. He tries to read her expression but cannot disentangle what he wishes from what is real.

Why do I always complicate things? Have I lost the ability to be spontaneous? He feels irritated at himself and wonders whether his inaction is due to a fear of rejection of the very intimacy he craves. Instead of revealing his feelings to Patricia, he says, "Would it be helpful to talk about how you are doing?"

"It might be."

Patricia proceeds to talk about the emptiness of her home without Diedre, how much larger and quieter it feels. "I considered moving until I realized I would be leaving all my memories of Diedre that are connected to the house."

With tears in her eyes, she describes her nightmares of that terrible evening, of holding her daughter's lifeless body, and her feelings of helplessness. She confesses her fear that because of the suddenness of Diedre's death it has not completely registered, and she has yet to experience the enormity of her loss.

"I think what you heard in our last conversation was the cracks beginning to form in the façade I've erected to keep from fully facing what has happened. What will happen when I do?"

Lenny listens, his heart breaking. "Grief is not an all-or-nothing affair," he offers. "Sometimes protecting ourselves from the full force of our loss until we are better prepared to deal with it is best."

Patricia sips her tea and takes a deep breath. "I've always thought of myself as the kind of person who can handle stressful situations while maintaining my cool. It was something I was proud of, and I liked that others thought of me in this way. Now I realize adopting this persona left me unprepared to deal with what happened."

Again, Lenny wants to move closer and put his arm around her. Instead, he stays where he is and says, "There is no preparation for something like this. But as your realization demonstrates, tragedy can also provide an opportunity for greater self-awareness."

"You mean wanting to see myself as a person who can handle every stressful situation?"

"Yes. Maintaining your cool can be useful in certain situations, like when we were confronted by that guy on our walk, but at other times expressing grief or fear might be best."

"I agree, but it's hard to reverse a way of being for which I strove for such a long time. When my marriage ended, I needed to be strong not only for myself but for Diedre. To me, it meant being able to handle demanding or tense situations without getting too distraught."

"And you were successful," says Lenny. "But now you need to expand being strong to include being vulnerable and accepting help from others. Remember the Beatles song, I get by with a little help from my friends?" Patricia nods. "Well, they were right."

Lenny's words open a spigot and tears trickle down her cheeks. This time Lenny does get up and sit next to her. He put his arm around her shoulders. Patricia leans her head on his chest and they stay that way until her sobbing subsides.

She moves her head and looks at him. "You're a good person Lenny Isaacson. Thank you for being my friend."

"And you mine."

He hiccups and puts his hand to his mouth, embarrassed. But Patricia laughs and then he does too.

They kiss.

And it feels right.

STANLEY L. WITKIN

Chapter Twenty-Eight

After several reminders from Dr. Lisman's office about the CT scan, Lenny finally goes to the clinic. He thinks it's unlikely anything is wrong—*I stopped smoking more than ten years ago*—but he's uneasy. *I do have this cough.* Like many people, he struggles with the tension between knowing the benefits of early detection and the fear of learning he has a dreaded disease. And it's the fear that makes it easy to rationalize avoidance: I'm too busy, I'll get around to it, What if it's a false positive, etcetera, etcetera.

The clinic is located near the university which is convenient but increases the chance he might encounter someone he knows, something he'd prefer to avoid. He checks in and is directed to the waiting area. Although several people are there, he's relieved they are all strangers. He wonders what brought them to the clinic. *Does that overweight guy fidgeting with his phone have heart problems? Is he trying to lose weight? And the young woman thumbing aimlessly through a People magazine. Did the appearance of an abnormality shatter her sense of invulnerability and now she anxiously awaits the results of a diagnostic test? Is that tittering couple expecting good news or are they trying to conceal their apprehension from each other?* So many stories and this is only one clinic. We live in worlds within worlds.

His diversion is ended by the sound of his name. A friendly-looking young woman in a white, medical coat leads him to the room where the procedure will take place. He blocks out his fears and stoically goes through the procedure. At least this one is painless, he tells himself. In a short time, it is over. He jokes with the technician asking if he gets a lollipop for being so cooperative. He gets a smile instead. Good enough.

Checking out, he asks when he will be contacted about the results and is told it depends on how busy the radiologists are, but hopefully not more than a week. Feeling relieved it's behind him, he decides to spend the rest of the day taking it easy and avoiding, at least for a while, further stressful events.

* * *

As hoped, the day is uneventful. Katie texts him in the evening that Jerry is doing considerably better. The doctors feel he is out of danger and might benefit more from convalescing at home. She suggests he check on his status tomorrow and see if a visit might be ok. Lenny is buoyed by the news.

That night he sleeps fitfully, his cough keeping him awake. The frozen pizza he ate for dinner didn't help either. He vows, as he often has, to eat healthier. Morning arrives too soon. If it wasn't for Sisu needing to go out, he would have stayed in bed. He drags himself from under the covers and goes into the kitchen to brew his wake-up cup of coffee. Sisu, having witnessed this routine numerous times, waits patiently for it to progress to the almost-out-the-door stage at which point he begins to turn in increasingly tighter circles, his way of saying "let's get going."

The morning is clear and crisp and once outside Lenny rallies. Other than commuters and a few joggers, the streets are quiet. They walk a few blocks and Lenny again finds himself thinking about how his life has changed over the past few weeks and how it will affect his life going forward. Change is part of life, he thinks. We assimilate what happens into our dominant narratives in ways that preserve the basic storylines. But sometimes we encounter events, like at The Loft, that cannot be assimilated. Instead, we need to accommodate them which may require substantive changes in our foundational beliefs. When we can't, it precipitates a crisis, a feeling of being unmoored, of not knowing who we are.

In our individualistic society with its pull yourself up by your bootstraps mentality, we often try to resolve this crisis by ourselves making a difficult situation more challenging. He remembers learning the word 'crisis' in Chinese is written as two characters combining danger and opportunity. How does this representation affect how Chinese people respond to crises? Do they view it more constructively? As always, Lenny has more questions than answers.

He pauses, glances up, and sees his building. *How did that happen?* He looks at Sisu. "It was you, wasn't it?

Sisu wags his tail.

* * *

Later in the day, he calls Katie to check on the status of Jerry. "Good news," she tells him. "He had a restful night and was discharged a couple of hours ago. He's still quite sore and will need bed rest for at least a few more days."

"How's his mood?" asks Lenny.

Katie pauses thinking about how to answer. "Hard to read, maybe because of the pain meds. I would say subdued but glad to be home. Seeing Emily seemed to bolster his spirits. He slept for about an hour but now is alert and talkative."

"Sounds like real progress both physically and psychologically," says Lenny encouraged by Katie's report. But then cautioning, "You probably know there could be some downswings. Recovery is rarely linear."

"I agree. The doctors mentioned that plus we've seen it with Emily. The last thing I want to do is put pressure on him to heal. Anyway, I was thinking if you wanted to stop by for a short visit in a couple of hours, he might like that."

"You don't think it's too soon?"

"No. He told me how much he appreciated your visit at the hospital so I think he would welcome seeing you. It might even be therapeutic."

"Ok. I'd be happy to come by. Say about four?"

"Should be fine. If anything comes up before then I will let you know."

* * *

Lenny is greeted by Danny who seems in a better place, literally and figuratively, than when he saw him at the hospital. He walks inside and is surprised to see how orderly things appear in contrast to the upheaval in their lives. *I guess people deal with stress in different ways. I sure do.*

Katie thanks him for coming. She tells him Emily is with Jerry but expects it will only be a few more minutes. They wait in the living room. Lenny asks, "Has the day continued to go well?"

"The same as when we spoke. Mostly, Jerry's been resting. He's experiencing a lot of discomfort although he is not complaining. I think for the next couple of days the focus will be on recuperation. There'll be time to process other stuff when he's feeling better."

"That sounds wise. You will know when he's ready to talk."

Emily enters the room. She's wearing jeans and a green University of Vermont sweatshirt. At first glance, she looks like a typical college kid, but then Lenny notices her drawn appearance and halting gait, evidence of the ordeal she's been through.

"Hi, Lenny," she says.

"Hi, Emily. It's good to see you up and around. How are you feeling?"

"A lot better. All my working parts seem to be functioning," she says with a weak smile that vanishes when she adds, "It's my dad I am worried about."

"How's he doing?" Lenny asks, interested in hearing her take on Jerry.

Echoing Katie, she says, "He seems happy to be home and I think seeing me out of bed gave him a lift." Then with concern she continues, "But he keeps apologizing to me like it's his fault for not preventing what happened."

"How did you respond?"

"I tell him what happened could not have been prevented and that I love him and want him to get better." She chokes up as she says these last words wiping away a tear with the sleeve of her sweatshirt.

"Perfect," says Lenny. "He loves you and I think the possibility of losing you overwhelmed him, but that same love is going to get him through this."

Together, Emily and Katie nod and whisper, "Yes."

"Would you like to see him now?" says Katie.

"Sure."

"I'll let him know you're here."

* * *

Lenny taps on the bedroom door. "Jerry, it's Lenny," he says poking his head into the room. Jerry turns his head on the pillow in his direction and manages a half-smile.

"Hi, Lenny. Come on in."

Lenny enters a spacious room, brightly lit, and tastefully decorated. He notices a multi-colored 'Welcome Home Dad!' sign hung on the wall. *A much better place to recuperate than the antiseptic hospital room with its endless beeps and chirps.*

He seats himself in a chair by the side of the bed. "Hi, Jerry. How are you feeling?"

"Like I've been in a car accident," says Jerry with a deadpan expression.

Lenny follows suit. "Yeah, I've heard it's bad for your health. You could use a shave; that might help."

With some effort, Jerry touches the stubble on his chin. "It might, but I'm thinking of going for the 'Lenny look' so I'm gonna let it grow."

"I'm flattered," says Lenny, "but you should realize my beard is just there as a counterbalance to the few hairs left on my head."

This time Lenny's remark is met with silence and closed eyes. Has their banter already exhausted him? Lenny leans closer. "Do you need to sleep?"

At first, Jerry doesn't answer and Lenny wonders if he is already asleep. He considers leaving when Jerry opens his eyes and says, "It's nice to see you, Lenny," as if he just walked into the room.

Ok, we'll start over. "Nice to see you too. It must feel good to be able to leave the hospital and return home."

"It does. The food was terrible."

"Are you in a lot of discomfort?"

"Only when I breathe."

Who is this comedic Jerry? Is it the drugs? If so, maybe I should try them. He says, "Hey Jerry, whatever meds you're taking, I'd like some too."

Jerry smiles wanly. A few moments pass in silence. Then Jerry starts talking as if they were in the middle of a different conversation.

"It's hard to explain. Seeing Emily so wounded . . . I felt impotent, then guilty, then agitated like I had to do something to make things better. When I realized I couldn't, I felt all that was left was for me to enact revenge on the person who did this. But again, I was stymied. I began to feel angrier and angrier. And at some point, I lost control."

Jerry's face and voice are infused with emotion. "It took me a long time, too long, to take your advice and stop beating myself up, but with the help of a car accident and Emily, I think the message finally penetrated my thick skull, no pun intended."

"What did Emily say?"

"She said I had nothing to do with what happened to her and I am a great dad. She also said she loved me and what would help her more than anything is if I would stop blaming myself and appreciate all the good things we have in our lives, especially our family." Jerry wipes away a tear with the back of his hand.

"She's right," says Lenny. "Just remember to be patient and kind to yourself even if there are setbacks and you will be fine."

Jerry nods and shifts his position which causes him to wince in pain. "I wish it didn't take a car crash to wake me up, but since I didn't kill myself, I'm determined to make the best of the opportunity I've been given."

Lenny is amazed by his friend's turnaround. Like so many others, he thinks, Jerry had to hit bottom to see a way forward. *Thank goodness he gets a second chance.* They sit together in silence feeling a closeness that comes from gratitude, vulnerability, and trust.

* * *

Lenny has another restless night. Dawn is breaking when he finally starts drifting off. Too soon, his phone rings. "Now what," he grumbles out loud. He groggily takes the phone from the bedside table. It's from Dr. Lisman's office which triggers instant wakefulness. The caller tells him Dr. Lisman would like to see him as soon as possible to go over his test results. Lenny tenses. *He wants to see me ASAP? This can't be good news.* He says he can come in today and an appointment is made for the early afternoon.

The possibility of any further sleep now gone, he tumbles out of bed and gets ready to take Sisu on her morning walk. Although he would like to curl into a fetal position, he is grateful Sisu's needs keep him from doing so.

When he returns, he takes a long, hot shower remaining under the water until he feels some of his tension dissipate. He tells himself not to catastrophize about the scan. *Whatever it is I will deal with it.* Despite this, he starts thinking about his will and if he needs to make any changes.

This is not helpful. Breathe Lenny, Breathe!

Lenny has always struggled with transitional or in-between spaces, whether it's waiting to board a plane or, like now, anticipating a test result. To distract himself, he tries working on his novel but cannot focus long enough to write anything. He tries playing his guitar, usually a relaxing activity, but finds himself playing songs that under the circumstances are not very uplifting.

'If life is like a candle bright, then death must be the wind.

You can close your window tight but it still comes blowing in.'

Even reading doesn't work. Resigning himself to mindless activity he turns on the TV, something he rarely does unless it's to watch a movie or a sporting event. Flipping through channels reaffirms his view that most of it is junk.

Time creeps along. He remembers reading the book, *Einstein's Dreams*, a fictional story of the young Albert Einstein during the time he was working in a Swiss patent office while laying the groundwork for his special theory of general relativity. Each chapter is devoted to a different conceptualization of time. In some chapters, time moves very fast, in others it moves at a crawl, even stopping or stuttering. Not only does time's velocity vary, but also the very nature of time itself, being circular, repetitive, or even reversible. Some of these variations are tied to different locations, but all have implications for the kinds of events that occur and how people think and behave.

Lenny imagines what life would be like if time always moved like he's currently experiencing it. *Would the pace of life be slower? Would life seem longer or shorter? Would we be endlessly anticipating what might happen next, or would we be more ensconced in the present? Of course, if this were the norm, it wouldn't seem slower. Rather, what we now consider normal time would seem fast. But what is normal time anyway? Can anyone know how someone else experiences time? Usually, we're not aware of time unless, like now, events bring it to the fore. And what about how we measure time, what impact—*

Ha, Ha, Ha! Loud laughter from the TV intrudes on his latest contemplation. He looks up and sees a commercial about a fast-food restaurant chain. Two people are sitting in a car eating grotesquely mammoth meat sandwiches and slurping carbonated drinks. When they pause for air, they squeal as if this is an orgasmic experience. *Yup*, Lenny thinks, *here's one reason obesity and heart disease are so prevalent in this country. If I were in charge, these kinds of ads would be treated like those for prescription drugs with the mandatory inclusion of all the possible negative side effects.*

He looks at the time and sees it's only an hour before his appointment. *Finally!* A thirty-minute walk with Sisu and he'll be ready to go.

*   *   *

He signs in at Dr. Lisman's office. After two or three minutes, a young nurse—they all look young these days—carrying a clipboard and scanning the room, calls his name. He gets up and walks toward her.

"I'm Lenny Isaacson."

"How are you today?" she says cheerily like he was checking into a hotel.

"Ok," he answers, "considering I am at my doctor's office."

She smiles—*Is smiling part of their job description?*—and guides him into one of the exam rooms. As is standard procedure, she measures his blood pressure, temperature, and pulse. All okay. She asks if he is experiencing any problems. He tells her he is there to follow-up on some tests Dr. Lisman prescribed. She jots this down, smiles again, and tells him the doctor will be with him shortly.

Five minutes pass until the signature soft knock on the door. Dr. Lisman enters. After greeting Lenny, he dispenses with pleasantries. "I received the results from your imaging procedure." He brings up the pictures on the computer in the room. "There's a shadow on your right lung that we need to look at further," he says while pointing to a white-gray area.

A tremor ripples through Lenny. *A shadow on my lung?* He's having trouble believing Lisman is talking about him. He hears himself say "ok" in an emotionless voice while feeling an eruption of emotions could occur at any moment. He manages to ask, "What do you think it can be?" fearing he knows the answer.

Lisman's mien remains amiable but professional. "It could be a tumor. If it is, we want to catch it as early as possible. It's imperative we know what we're dealing with."

Suppressing his fear, Lenny forces himself to ask the dreaded question. "Could it be cancer?"

Lisman is matter of fact. "It could be, but I don't think we should get ahead of ourselves." Then, more sympathetically, "I know this is hard to hear Lenny, but we need to take it one step at a time. The first step is to find out what this is, and once we do, we can decide how to proceed."

Lenny thinks, *why does he keep saying we as if this is happening to us both. It's my life that may be in jeopardy, not his.*

Lisman continues. "I'm going to set up a more sensitive imaging test that should help clarify what is going on. I'd like you to do this within the next week." He hands Lenny a paper authorizing the test.

"Do you have other questions?"

"Not at the moment," answers Lenny to numb to think straight. "It's a lot to take in."

"It is, but we're going to figure it out. In the meantime, take it easy . . . no marathons," he adds with a smile.

His attempt at levity falls flat. Lenny continues to sit in the exam room. He tries to calm himself with some deep breaths, but it's not working. *What should I do now?* He can't decide if he wants to be alone or around other people. By default, he returns home.

* * *

Once home Lenny, starts researching reasons for the 'shadow.' It could be a benign tumor or an abscess, but other credible possibilities are much worse, especially when combined with his cough. There's a knot in the pit of his stomach. He halts his search.

What good is this doing? Whatever I learn will be speculative and probably only make me more anxious than I already feel.

Stop putting your head in the sand. Ignoring potentially bad news won't make it go away. Figure out your options. Your time may be short.

It's a standoff. He feels like talking to someone about it but who?

He considers Eleanor but decides he doesn't want to upset her with his conjectures about what may or may not be the case. His head begins to throb. As he rises, vertigo causes him to steady himself against the wall.

Did I get up too quickly or is this a symptom of a malignancy that has metastasized to my brain?

Whoa. You're being a little extreme, don't you think?

Perhaps, but isn't that what most people think? No one believes anything terrible can happen to them, but if I've learned anything from recent events it's that it can and does.

Enough! You need to slow down or you will self-combust. You will find out soon enough. Now stop torturing yourself and try to relax.

This time the calmer voice prevails. As is his practice when feeling stressed, he sits in his favorite chair and puts on his noise-canceling headphones. W*hat I need is thought canceling headphones.* He opens his music app and selects his relaxing classical music playlist.

Beethoven's moonlight sonata begins to fill his senses. The piano in the first movement is meditative and peaceful. He remembers reading the name came from a German music critic's characterization of the piece as like moonlight shining upon a lake although to Lenny the original name, *sonata quasi una fantasia*, or sonata in the manner of a fantasy, was apt as well.

The music works its magic and by the middle of Richard Stoltzman's rendition of Mozart's *Clarinet Concerto*, he dozes off. He dreams he is floating at a great altitude looking down at the earth. When he gazes at a particular part of the globe the area comes into sharp relief allowing him to observe and hear in vivid detail the goings-on below. He floats over his neighborhood. All looks typical.

He moves closer to his apartment and sees himself sitting in his living room holding a calendar and looking distraught. Sisu appears and he hears himself say to him, "How many more days?"

Looking plaintively at Lenny, Sisu replies, "It depends."

"You mean on how sick I am?"

"No, on how you use the time. You're in Einstein's dream, Lenny. Look at me. Does my time move at the same rate? Are my days equivalent to yours? I live in the present while you focus on your past and future."

Lenny says, "I don't know how to do that. I feel like I've been given a death sentence."

"We've all been given death sentences, Lenny," says Sisu. "Did you think you would live forever?"

"No, but now I'm compelled to think about it."

"What about your *life* sentence. Are you going to live it out in prison?"

"Are you saying I have a choice?"

"Woof," barks Sisu wagging his tail. And Lenny awakens.

He searches for Sisu and spots him curled up on a throw pillow he managed to push onto the floor. Lenny says to him, "Did you channel, Ezekiel?"

Hearing Lenny's voice directed towards him, Sisu gets up and tilts his head right and left. When Lenny doesn't say anything more, he walks over to him and licks his hand.

"I don't know if you had any part in what I dreamed," says Lenny, "but you deserve a treat." Sisu responds to the word 'treat' with high-pitched yips.

Lenny feels better after his nap. He remembers The Alliance

for Peace, the new progressive political group, is meeting tonight. He had been wavering about whether to go but thinking about his dream and how he will live with whatever time he has left; he decides to check it out. *Even if it's a bust, it will provide a temporary distraction from obsessing about my possible diagnosis. In the meantime, I'd better get back to my novel while I can.*

* * *

Lenny looks at his last sentence: Then he is kidnapped. It was not something he had planned to write nor does know what will happen next. He stares at the computer screen for several minutes hoping for inspiration. When none comes, he decides to try a free write, writing without stopping for a brief time. The key is to think via writing—no editing, no contemplation—just nonstop writing. If you get stuck, then you write 'I am stuck,' as many times as it takes to move on. If your internal editor complains what you are writing is crap, then write 'this is crap' until you can proceed to something else.

He sets the timer on his phone and begins.

Five minutes and two pages later he stops and reviews what he has written. As often happens with stream of consciousness writing, it's haphazard and not all relevant. However, within the stream he discovers a few nuggets to further explore.

Ok, let's find out what happened.

> Tobias hears a knock on his door. Thinking it's the pizza he ordered he nevertheless asks, "who is it." Receiving the expected reply of "Dominoes," he grabs his wallet and opens the door. Instead of a delivery person, two

large men burst into the room knocking him to the floor. Before he can react, a dark cloth bag is placed over his head and his hands secured behind his back with a plastic tie. Then he is stood up and told if he struggles or makes a sound he will be killed. With each man holding one of his arms, he is hustled outside and into what seems like a van and driven away.

Tobias is numb with fear. Everything happened so fast and with such force that he is unable to process it. As he sits in silence, he begins to regain his senses. His thoughts turn to The Group. This must be their doing. *Oh God, I was so wrong about them and it might have been a fatal mistake.*

He can sense the presence of the men in the van, but neither speaks. After what he judges to be about thirty minutes, he musters the courage to ask, "Who are you? Why did you do this? Where are we going?" All his questions are met with silence.

Another five minutes pass. He feels the van speeding up. *Are we on a highway?* He tries to guess where they might be taking him. Some remote spot where they will kill him and dump his body? *I have to escape, but how?* He pushes against his bindings but they are secure. *Maybe when we stop, I will be able to reason with them. Offer them money. Tell them I have a seriously ill child.* His racing thoughts at a dead end, he returns to a state of numbing fear.

The silence is interrupted by the clicking of a turn

signal followed by the vehicle slowing. It resumes a moderate speed for another fifteen minutes or so until the road becomes rough like dirt or gravel. They make several left and right turns. Believing his demise is at hand, Tobias desperately tries again to think of a plan that will keep him alive, or at least buy him time, but to no avail.

The van decelerates to a crawl and stops. *Oh God. This is it.* The side door slides open and he is taken out. Tobias tenses in anticipation of the lethal blow. Instead, his hood is removed and one of the men says, "Welcome home."

Tobias blinks rapidly trying to adjust his vision to the abrupt change in light. He looks around. In front of him is a sizable log cabin sitting in a clearing of dense forest. It has a gray slate roof with a stone chimney on its left side where wisps of smoke are wafting from the top. An open porch area dotted with Adirondack chairs extends across the front. In different circumstances, he might have thought this to be a vacation hideaway, but this was no vacation. He finally gets a good look at his abductors. As he suspected, both are formidable men whose hard expressions underscore his dire straits. Yet, the site of the cabin stirs a faint hope that he will not be summarily killed. They motion for him to walk to the house.

He's ushered through the front door into a large, wood-paneled room circled by windows. A long, wooden table with four chairs on each side sits in the middle.

At the far end of the room, in contrast to the rustic décor, are three comfortable-looking beige accent chairs arranged in a semicircle. However, it is not the chairs that capture his attention, but their occupants: Marcos Estrada, Audrey Williamson, and Carolina Gutiérrez.

"Hello, Tobias," says Marcos. "You're a hard person to get a hold of."

None of them are smiling. Tobias is silent. He turns to Carolina hoping for some sign, however subtle, of connection, but her face is impassive. *I'm a dead man.*

Marcos continues. "Your disappearance was puzzling, then disturbing. Initially, we did not know if something happened to you. Then we learned you were ok. When we tried making contact, you didn't respond or were uninformative. You placed us in a difficult position. Were you friend or foe? Since we did not know, we had to divert precious time and resources to finding you and bringing you to us."

All three turn to Tobias. Too traumatized and scared to formulate a response he thinks will save him; he remains silent. Minutes pass. Then Audrey says, "Would you care to explain?"

Knowing he has to offer some explanation if he is to have any chance of saving himself, he utters in a trembling voice, "I'm sorry for the trouble I caused. When we were in Spain, I realized I was in over my head. Although I was, um, am, sympathetic to the views of The Group, I wasn't ready to participate in the kinds of actions being proposed. It was too big of a jump for me, but I was scared that I had already gotten too involved to back out. I felt trapped. I wanted to talk with you about how I was feeling, but I panicked and ran." His voice takes on a pleading tone. "Again, I'm very sorry, but you should know I didn't say a word about this to anyone, nor do I plan to."

The three glance at each other. Carolina says, "And what about me, Tobias? Was that too just pretend?"

"Not at all," says Tobias, his volume rising as he turns towards her. "My feelings for you were, and are, genuine. I wanted to reach out to you, but by then I was questioning everything and not thinking clearly."

He looks at her beseechingly. Carolina shakes her head sadly and turns away. Marcos speaks again. "It's too bad you chose to act on your fear by running and hiding instead of talking with us. Not knowing where you were or what you were up to put us all in potential danger. What we do, our cause, is bigger than any of us, so we had to track you down. And now we need to decide what to do about you."

"But I'm on your side," Tobias pleads, his voice tremulous with fear. "As I said, I agree with your goals. I just wasn't ready to go as far as you in pursuit of them. I guess I'm a coward."

Audrey asks, "But what about when we reached out and said you could just be an observer at the Rendenhall site? Was that still too much?"

Tobias tries to explain but feels like he's being redundant. Marcos interrupts him and says sternly "Enough! We get it. The problem now is you have information about us that could be damaging and your past actions suggest you are not trustworthy."

Tobias's insides are churning. He again fears for his life. *Would they go that far? Surely, they know I am not their enemy.* He looks again to Carolina begging with his eyes for her to intervene, but her expression is unreadable. Trying hard but unsuccessfully to keep the panic out of his voice he reiterates his promise to never reveal anything about The Group. "I am on your side," he repeats.

Marcos looks unconvinced. Out of options, he closes his eyes preparing for whatever might come.

The next voice he hears is Carolina. "I agree Marcos. What Tobias did put us all in possible jeopardy, and we have reason not to trust him. But I think it's fair to say I know him better than any of us and despite his actions, I believe him to be a man of honor. Part of this situation is our fault, mostly mine. He seemed to fit so well with our cause and brought such valuable skills that we were over-enthusiastic in our recruitment. He tried to tell us, indirectly, that he was not ready for what we were asking of him, but we could not, or did not, want to hear it."

Although Tobias did not like being talked about in the third person when he was present, he couldn't recall hearing a sound as sweet as Carolina's voice. He opens his eyes and looks at her. She briefly meets his gaze.

"So, what do you suggest we do?" asks Audrey.

Carolina says, "Tobias understands the importance of keeping information about The Group secret. I also accept he believes in our cause. I propose he remain a member of our organization with the understanding that for now, we ask nothing of him except a pledge that he not divulge information about us or our activities to anyone."

"Are you willing to do this?" Audrey asks Tobias. "Understand there will be no second chance."

For Tobias choosing between staying silent and staying alive is a no-brainer. He agrees.

Marcos says, "I'm ready for a beer."

* * *

Lenny sits back in his chair and stretches his fingers.

I guess love wins in the end.

Chapter Twenty-Nine

Lenny arrives at the Unitarian church a few minutes before the 7:00 p.m. starting time of the Alliance for Peace meeting. The front door opens into a spacious corridor. A sign announcing the meeting points to an open door at the back of the building. At the entranceway is another sign stating in bold, capital letters, NO GUNS, KNIVES, OR WEAPONS OF ANY KIND. Below these words is a circle with a handgun inside and a diagonal red line going over it.

Entering the room, he sees twenty-five to thirty people, most young—which to Lenny means under fifty—milling around. The room itself is nondescript: large and rectangular with white walls adorned with a few prints of nature scenes, some black and white photos of buildings he assumes are related to the church, and a few cork boards to which an assortment of papers is thumbtacked. Fluorescent lights are embedded in the ceiling at three-foot intervals giving the room an almost daylight brightness. Four, long, narrow tables against the far wall hold various signs and papers. Two people sit behind each table.

Lenny walks over to one of the tables and picks up a brochure.

The cover consists of the words Alliance for Peace, a red, orange, and green peace symbol, and underneath, 'Working towards a socially just world in which all people can live in peace, dignity, and respect.' A thirtyish-year-old man with curly, red hair is sitting at the table.

"Hi, can you help you with anything?" he asks in a friendly voice.

"Hello. I was pleased to hear about this meeting. What are you hoping to accomplish tonight?"

"We want to increase awareness about the growing threat of extremist groups peddling hate and division among people. We also want to encourage greater community involvement in activities that promote social justice and human dignity, and to make Vermont a welcoming place for all people."

"Noble goals," says Lenny. "Is your organization new? I hadn't heard of it until a few days ago."

"We formed a couple of months ago. We were motivated by the need to provide a visible alternative to the hate groups that have been receiving so much attention. The violence in this country is becoming an epidemic. Look at what happened at The Loft."

Lenny twitches involuntarily. He hopes it wasn't noticed. "Yes," he says, "a terrible tragedy. Are you one of the meeting organizers?"

"I am." He extends his hand. "Ethan Weinstock."

"Lenny Isaacson." He shakes the proffered hand.

Ethan tilts his head as if trying to remember something. He says, "Do you teach at the university?"

"I did, in social work. I'm retired now."

"Right," says Ethan becoming animated. "I took a course from you!"

Lenny tries to remember this person from the thousands he has taught over the years but comes up blank. Perhaps sensing this, Ethan saves Lenny from having to admit he does not remember him. "It was many years ago and there were about forty students."

"What was the course?" asks Lenny

"It was called human behavior and the social environment. What I remember is that you introduced us to something called social constructionism. It was kind of mind-blowing at the time."

"I hope in a good way," says Lenny.

"Many of us found the ideas challenging and interesting, but others were freaked out."

"Freaked out?"

"They expected the course would be different. Some complained it was like a philosophy course; others were uncomfortable with how you questioned everything. And, of course, some were just worried about their grades." He shrugs. "I guess you can't please all the people all the time."

"Nor should you try," says Lenny. "Which group were you part of?"

"Oh, the first one. I loved the course. It influenced the direction of my life."

"Really? How so?"

Without missing a beat, Ethan says, "It made me more aware of how our beliefs are shaped by our history and culture. Also, I liked your view that everything needed to be looked at with a critical eye. Even ideas we value or assume are true should be examined critically, not to bash them, but to understand their origins and how they are used. When I started applying these ideas to my life and what was happening around me, I began to see things in a new light. You might even say it was partly responsible for where I am sitting tonight," says Ethan with a smile.

"I'm impressed," says Lenny. "You've done just what I hoped for when I taught the course. So, besides the work here, what do you do?"

"I teach social studies at Burlington High School. I guess it's another way I was influenced by your course. It helped me realize that as a teacher I could make a difference. It's been very fulfilling."

"Good for you," says Lenny admiringly. "I'm sure you are having an impact."

"Thanks."

"Did you start the Alliance for Peace by yourself?"

Ethan shakes his head. "No, it was me and a few like-minded friends; two of whom will be speaking tonight. We found ourselves increasingly sharing our concerns about what was happening in this country: the vitriolic, hateful rhetoric, the increasing violence, and the tacit, sometimes overt, encouragement of right-wing extremist groups from government leaders. Those venting sessions evolved into forming the Alliance, but it was the shooting at The Loft that spurred us to do something more. So, we decided to hold this meeting to mobilize the community."

As Ethan is talking other people begin congregating at the table. Not wanting to monopolize Ethan's time, Lenny says, "I'll let you get to some of these other folks. Thanks for the information and good luck with your organizing efforts. We can chat again later if you're free."

"I'd like that," says Ethan. "It was great seeing you again,

Professor Isaacson. But before you go, can you tell me how you heard about the meeting? We're trying to determine the best ways to get the word out."

"Yes, but only if you call me Lenny," he says with a grin. "I heard about it from a reporter at the *Chronicle*, Ashley Lee. She was planning to come tonight and I'm sure she will want to speak with you about the group and give you some press coverage. I'll send her your way if I see her."

"That would be great."

* * *

Lenny strolls around the room curious to see if he might know any of the attendees. His previous impression, that most are of an earlier generation, is borne out. He thinks about how quickly time passes when considered in retrospect. *Yet, I clearly remember when I was one of those youthful people. When all things seemed possible. In a way, I still am one of them. I've just been younger longer.* He smiles in self-amusement until another thought intrudes. *Other than this body wearing out.* His mood darkens as his thoughts drift back to the terminal diagnosis he believes will come next.

People begin putting out folding chairs in preparation for the meeting. As Lenny is deciding where to sit, he notices Ashley Lee entering the room. He walks in her direction. She sees him and waves.

"Dr. Isaacson, I'm so glad you came."

"Me too," says Lenny, aware she is still calling him Dr. Isaacson. "Thanks for telling me about it. By the way, I met one of the Alliance's organizers who you might like to interview. He's the guy with the red hair at the back table," he says pointing to the table where Ethan is sitting. "His name is Ethan Weinstock. I mentioned you were coming to the meeting and might like to speak with him."

"Thank you," says Ashley. "I am interested."

The room begins to grow quiet as people start taking seats. Ashley and Lenny find two empty chairs and sit down. Lenny guesses there are now thirty-five or so people in attendance. Ethan and two other people walk to the front of the room. He is holding a small, portable microphone which he uses to greet everyone and thank them for coming. This settles down the audience and brings the remaining stragglers to their seats.

Ethan introduces himself and his two companions—Azad Rahaim Noorani and Latisha Underwood—as co-founders of the Alliance. He explains why they formed the organization and expresses the hope they will be able to offer people a constructive alternative to the growing specter of bigotry and divisiveness and encourage the growth of caring communities.

He passes the microphone over to Azad, a slim man of Middle Eastern descent wearing a red and blue scotch plaid shirt and jeans. He appears to be about the same age as Ethan. His dark hair is cut short as is his neat beard and mustache. Mahogany brown, full-rimmed eyeglasses are perched on his prominent nose. After adding his welcome, Azad talks about the philosophy of the group and some of the people that have inspired them: Mahatma Gandhi, Martin Luther King, and Shirin Ebadi. Assuming most would not recognize this last name, Azad tells them she is an Iranian attorney, author, and activist who started the Defenders of Human Rights Center in Iran among other activities. In 2003, her work received global recognition with the awarding of the Nobel Peace Prize, making her the first female laureate from the Islamic world. "Sadly," he informs the audience, "in 2009, this honor was rejected by the conservative Iranian government, her Nobel medal confiscated, and her bank accounts frozen. She was forced to live in exile in the UK where she still resides."

Latisha is next to speak. Like the others, she looks to be in her early to mid-thirties. She is tall, with a dignified bearing. She has rich brown skin, compelling chestnut eyes, and short, dark hair cut close above her ears, accented by gold hoop earrings. Her attire consists of a white V-neck shirt with magenta embroidery down the front on each side and jeans.

After thanking the audience for their support, she expresses concern about the increased boldness of extremist groups, asserting that the view of Vermont as a bucolic oasis from the troubles of the rest of the country is a dangerous fantasy. She also talks about government complicity and the danger to vulnerable people such as those who are black, brown, or of an ethnic minority.

Returning to the Alliance, Latisha lists the general aspirations of the group: awareness of the increasing threat posed by hate groups and those who support them, educating people about their rights, generating opposition to oppressive policies and corruption, and promoting an alternative vision for the future. She follows this with several extemporaneous examples of the kinds of activities the Alliance for Peace hopes to carry out in support of these aspirations: holding regular meetings, organizing vigils in public places like parks and downtown areas, expressing their views on social and local media, giving talks to civic and educational groups, supporting other like-minded organizations, working for progressive political candidates, and engaging in peaceful resistance.

Her delivery is eloquent and impassioned. There are numerous nods among listeners as she is talking and sporadic shouts of "Yeah," and "Right on." Lenny is impressed. To him, these people are beacons of hope in an otherwise dreary and threatening landscape. He's glad he decided to attend the meeting. At the same time, he's sad that he probably won't live long enough to contribute to their mission.

He pushes this last thought aside as Latisha turns to the challenges they face. She stresses the need for allies and alliances to counter how the government and the media instigate divisions among groups by categorizing people in simplistic, homogeneous ways that emphasize their differences and by presuming they only care about one issue.

Eyeing the audience, she says resolutely, "Fighting among ourselves only serves the powers that be and weakens our efforts to bring about change. The differences among progressive groups are trivial compared with those who would seek to divide us and maintain the status quo."

She pauses to let her words sink in. Then building on her momentum, she stresses that people in solidarity engaging in non-violent resistance can make a difference. "Although we are angry, violence only serves as a rationalization for further violence from the hate groups and the authorities and turns public opinion against us." This is borne out, she claims, by the presence of infiltrators who pretend to be part of their movement, but whose purpose is to instigate violence to justify retaliation.

In a softer tone, Latisha talks about how peace work can be

scary and exhausting, and their hope The Alliance can provide support for those who commit their time and energy to the cause.

Concluding on a personal note, she describes how her participation in The Alliance has emboldened her to face her fears as a woman of color and to find kindred spirits who are now among her dearest friends.

The audience is moved by Latisha's talk and responds with enthusiastic applause. She is rejoined by her two colleagues who open the floor to questions. This goes on for about twenty minutes after which everyone is encouraged to interact informally and visit the signup table if they wish to volunteer. Lenny walks to a table with some coffee urns set up and pours himself a cup. There's a buzz among the crowd and a synergistic vibe he guesses comes from being with others 'fighting the good fight.'

He watches small clusters of people intermingling, their gestures and facial expressions animated. He hears snippets of introductions and entreaties to organize and act. Observing these interchanges summons memories of when such gatherings would inflame his desire to right the wrongs of the world. *We were so hopeful,* he thinks wistfully. Standing here now, so many years later, he would be hard-pressed to say things are better. It would be so easy, reasonable even, to become jaded and depleted, and he feels grateful for the positive energy in the room.

His reminiscences are cut short by the intrusion of thoughts about his upcoming diagnostic tests. A shroud of sorrow settles over him as he contemplates his future, or more precisely, the lack of a future. *How long will I have? Not just of my life but my viability. I don't want to live in a vegetative state.* He realizes it's not dying that he fears, although he would prefer it not happen, but the debilitating pain and indignities that might precede it. He reminds himself to get his affairs in order while he still can. Then, as often happens, another part of his brain offers an alternative. *Slow down, Lenny. Yes, this is scary, but you're getting ahead of yourself. You don't know what the tests will show. There are a lot of other possibilities besides a terminal disease.*

Yeah, maybe only a debilitating one. His mood darkens and he considers leaving when he hears "Dr. Isaacson?" He turns and sees Ashley Lee and Ethan Weinstock approaching. They're both smiling.

"Hi Ashley," says Lenny, also nodding at Ethan. "I see you found each other."

"We did," replies Ashley brightly. "And Ethan told me he had you for a course when he was a student at the university."

There's something in Ashley's tone and their body language that leads Lenny to think this is not the last time they will be talking. "That's true," says Lenny. "So how did the interview go?"

"Great!" they answer simultaneously. Ethan shuffles his feet and Ashley examines her shoes.

Yup, thinks Lenny trying to hide his smile. *There's more than business happening.* Veering the conversation in a different direction, Lenny says to Ethan, "I was impressed by your remarks and those of your colleagues. I wouldn't be surprised if you gained some new members tonight."

"Thanks. I hope you're right. We can use all the help we can get."

"And hopefully, my story about the group will generate even more interest," adds Ashley.

"I think you've made a convert out of Ashley," says Lenny, hoping he's not revealing too much.

"I'm not sure she needed converting," says Ethan hastily adding, "but I'm sure her reporting will be objective."

Ashley nods in agreement.

"I look forward to seeing the piece. Any idea when it will appear?"

"Probably the next couple of days."

Suddenly heads are turning toward the room's entrance. Four men, each wearing identical black jackets with an American flag on one side and a patch with the words American Liberation League on the other, are gathered by the door. The tallest of the group has a long red beard. Lenny immediately recognizes him as the person who promised revenge at Jeremy Larsen's burial service. "Uh-oh," he whispers under his breath.

Ashley also recognizes him. Her eyes widen and her hand comes to her mouth like she is trying to stifle a scream. Before either of them can say anything, Ethan says, "Stay here," and strides towards the entrance.

The room has gone from bustling chatter to eerie quiet as though an emotional circuit breaker was tripped. A palpable sense of unease permeates the space as if each person is frantically assessing the situation.

All eyes turn to Ethan as he approaches the newcomers, joined en route by his two colleagues, Latisha and Azad.

Ashley turns to Lenny, alarm written on her face. Lenny says what they both know. "It's that guy from the cemetery." Then hoping to allay Ashley's distress, he adds, "They probably just want to scare us and disrupt the meeting."

The four men turn towards the organizers. Ethan says matter-of-factly, "Can I help you?"

Red Beard steps forward closing the gap between them. In a voice loud enough for all to hear, he says, "We're here for the meeting. It's open to the public, right?"

Maintaining his calm demeanor, Ethan says, "Yes, it is, but the meeting started more than an hour ago and things are winding down. You must have gotten the time wrong."

"No problem," says Red Beard. "We're here to let y'all know about our group, the American Liberation League."

"That wouldn't be appropriate," says Ethan.

"Oh, no? Why not? Afraid of a little competition?"

When Ethan doesn't answer, he says, "Well, if we can't talk, we'll eat. We heard there was free food, *kosher* food, and we're starving." His three companions snicker.

This remark provokes a woman in the back of the room to shout, "We know who you are. Why don't you just leave!"

The big man grins sardonically. "That's not very hospitable." Looking directly at Ethan he says, "I thought you were into free love and acceptance. You should talk to that person." And in a more menacing tone, "But either way, we're not leaving until we've had our fill."

The atmosphere is like being trapped in a room with a ticking explosive device and praying the bomb squad will arrive in time to defuse it. People are glancing around nervously, wringing their hands, and murmuring to those around them. Some inch toward the exit but stop when they realize they will have to pass by Red Beard and his pals.

Watching this unfold, Lenny has a flashback to The Loft. He

feels an admixture of anger, fear, and the preternatural vigilance that often accompanies situations hovering on the brink of violence. He begins to question what he said to Ashley. *Are they here just to intimidate or do they mean to do us harm?*

Latisha, undeterred by Red Beard's thinly veiled threat, steps forward. Although relatively tall, the big man towers over her. She says, "What's your name?"

Red Beard, showboating for his companions, says in a mocking tone, "You can call me Massa, sweetheart."

Without hesitation, Latisha says, "How about if I call you a racist asshole."

For a moment, there is a shocked silence as if time itself is suspended while everyone digests what just happened.

Then all hell breaks loose.

It begins with people in the room moving forward and shouting at Red Beard and his cronies to leave. A group surrounds Latisha forming a protective wall. Someone shouts they are calling the police, while others are asking for calm. A few simply cower.

Lenny has not moved. Repulsed but not surprised by the crude racist slur, he is encouraged by the responses of Latisha and the others. These guys are bullies and if you kowtow to them things will only get worse. Still, he fears this is not over. Unlike The Loft, however, where he was paralyzed by fear, he feels calm. Paradoxically, believing he's already been given a death sentence gives him a sense of invulnerability. *What can they do to me?* There's no longer an impulse for self-preservation or a need to seek shelter or hide. *I never realized the benefits of a terminal condition,* he thinks somberly.

The four men exchange uncertain looks and begin to retreat. However, when they are a few feet from the exit, Red Beard suddenly reverses direction, reaches behind his back, and pulls out a gun. He waves it toward the encroaching crowd and shouts, "You know if you people threaten us, we have the right to defend ourselves. It's in the Constitution." And then in a threatening and booming voice, "So back off motherfuckers."

This development ratchets up the situation to a level few are prepared to confront. With the memory of The Loft still an open wound in the community, the bravado of the crowd collapses and devolves into panic. Some who were moving forward freeze mid-step, while others cringe and seek shelter.

Red Beard and his friends sneer derisively as if confirming their loathsome view of the people at the meeting. Now brazenly confronting the group, Red Beard snarls, "What's wrong? Don't you believe in the second amendment? We're not going to hurt anyone as long as you don't try to hurt us. But I have an idea. Let's say a prayer for Jeremy Larsen, a true patriot who was driven to desperate measures to bring attention to the Zionist conspiracy and racial apologists threatening our country. Good people cannot stand by while our White Christian principles are defaced and defamed."

He steps forward and takes a petrified young woman by the arm. "Come on honey, you can lead us in prayer." Except for the tears on her cheeks, the woman appears catatonic.

Anger rises in Lenny. Although not sure what he can do, he knows he can no longer stand idly by. He starts walking towards Red Beard and the woman. When he gets within about ten feet, Red Beard notices him.

"What do you want, old man?"

Without fear, Lenny moves closer. In an even voice he says, "For starters, I want you to let the woman go."

"Oh, you do, do you," Red Beard jeers. Looking at Lenny more closely, he squints and his lips tighten as if trying to remember something. Then, in a flash of recognition, he blurts out, "Wait a minute. I know you. You're the guy who tripped Jeremy at The Loft!"

Heads turn.

"And you're also the Jew who called the FBI and got my buddy Wingate arrested."

He points his gun at Lenny. "You must think you're a real hero. Well, I got news for you, asshole. Your heroics end here."

A tidal wave of dread threatens to overrun the room, yet Lenny is calm. He's aware this situation would previously have him terrified, but it's like he is watching what is happening from a distance. It's almost laughable. This guy acting tough and threatening his life when it is already on the brink of ending. He feels more in control of his fate than he can ever remember.

Lenny looks at Red Beard, his demeanor serene. Red Beard's bravado begins to waver replaced by confusion. This is not the way the script is supposed to play out. Lenny should be quivering and pleading for his life, not standing there like he doesn't have a worry in the world.

Trying to conceal his uncertainty, Red Beard turns to his companions and says with a smirk, "The little Jew thinks he can stop us so everyone can tell him how brave he is. Let's see where that gets him."

They all snigger but there's a nervousness about it. Red Beard glares at Lenny. "Get out-of-the-way, Grandpa, or you're a dead man."

Lenny coolly stands his ground. "How did you know?" he asks.

Lenny's inscrutable question elicits a flicker of indecision on Red Beard's face. He tries to regain his composure by exclaiming, "You are one fucked-up dude."

"And you are angry and hurting," responds Lenny. "Why else would you be doing this. I'm giving you a chance to act on your better nature. These people have not done anything to you. There is no need to threaten them. Just leave in peace."

The room has again become tomb-like quiet as if people cannot quite believe what they are witnessing. They are shocked to learn Lenny is the person from The Loft that they read about and some wonder if he has a death wish or is crazy. Most are fixated on the gun and the threat it poses to their safety.

Lenny is unaware of any of this, even the quiet. It's as if he is participating in a transcendental, coming-to-grips-with-death ritual inspired by the belief in his imminent demise. Ironically, it's this death warrant that inures him against Red Beard's threats.

Suddenly, Ethan steps forward and says forcefully to Red Beard, "Put the gun away and leave. Now!"

In response, Red Beard points his gun at Ethan. "You got it wrong. You're the one who's going to leave."

Lenny quickly moves in front of Ethan.

A shot rings out.

People scream and chaos erupts.

But for Lenny, all is silent and dark.

Chapter Thirty

Lenny is hiking up Mount Mansfield. At 4393 feet, it is Vermont's highest peak, a mere hill relative to mountains in the West whose summit exceeds two miles. But it's early fall and the variegated beauty of its forests and foliage, changing with increasing altitude, is unmatched.

Lenny walks through an arboreal canopy of white birch, beech, and sugar maple interspersed with colorful and delicate wildflowers and other groundcovers. He stops and lets his senses reach out to the terrain: the earthy scents of flora and fauna, the faint rush of a brook, the songs of birds, and the scamper of animals moving through the brush. Through an opening in the canopy, he watches a redtail hawk circle effortlessly on invisible air currents. Walking further he spots a clump of lion's mane mushrooms on the side of a dead beech tree and gingerly touches its long spines. Carefully removing a mushroom, he takes a small bite savoring its bitter taste in contrast to its crustacean-like flavor when cooked.

His trek has no particular destination or timetable. He feels very much in the present moment, moving with rather than through time. As he gains altitude he notices more evergreens—balsam fir and red spruce—as well as heart-leaved paper birch. A faint sound to his left draws his attention. He turns and sees a deer, a doe, about thirty feet away watching him with large, serene dark eyes. Her upright ears twitch and her tail flicks from side to side. Their eyes meet and they stand connected in quiet communion. What passes between them feels to Lenny both earthly and sublime, a oneness existing in the material and the transcendent. Then she is gone, enveloped in her forest home.

Continuing his ascent, he comes to a cloud spanning his path. Curious, he leans into its feathery whiteness. There's movement within, a dizzying blur of rapidly revolving images. Worried he might fall, Lenny steps away and leans against the grey-brown bark of a red spruce for support. He closes his eyes, but the spinning continues. Not daring to move, he waits. Eventually, the revolutions start to slow and the images begin to come into focus. He thinks they might be people, but it is like they are behind an opaque screen and he can barely make them out. As he tries to discern the murky figures, he also becomes aware of muffled sounds, multilayered at different pitches and volumes. By degrees, they morph into a single voice repeating one word over and over. A heavy fatigue descends on him.

I need to sleep, he tells himself while sliding down the trunk of the tree. Just before drifting off, the word becomes clear.

"Lenny."

* * *

In the meeting hall, pandemonium reigns. Within seconds of the gunshot, people start screaming and searching for a way to escape.

Those who saw no way out huddled behind overturned tables, throw themselves on the ground, or stand frozen like deer caught in headlights.

Some take more offensive actions. Ethan pounces on Red Beard knocking the gun out of his hands. Azad appears and immediately scoops it up. Inspired, others rush forward to help. Red Beard's companions seem stunned by the turn of events, the angry crowd dashing any thoughts they might have about assisting him.

Missed in the pandemonium was that simultaneously with the gunshot, Lenny had crumpled to the ground. Amidst the chaos, he looked like one more person diving for cover. It wasn't until Ashley spotted him and screamed, "He's been shot. He's been shot. Call 911!" that several people could be seen punching numbers on their phones.

Ashley drops to the floor next to Lenny. There is an oval-shaped wound on his forehead with some blood around it. Although the bleeding is not profuse, it's obvious his injury is grave. Lenny's eyes are closed and he appears unconscious. Still, Ashley says, "Lenny, Lenny, can you hear me?" over and over, beseeching him to respond.

If Lenny can hear her, he shows no sign of it. Feeling helpless and panicked, Ashley looks around for help. A woman emerges from the frenzy and kneels next to them.

"My name is Jane. I'm a nurse. Can I examine him?"

"Yes, please," says Ashley with obvious urgency. "He's badly hurt."

Jane begins assessing Lenny's condition: checking his breathing, pulse, pupils, and head wound. She gently turns him to the side to examine the back of his head. Another wound is visible.

Turning to Ashley, she says, "He's still breathing although his respiration is shallow. There's a wound on the back of his head that I'm guessing is an exit wound. If so, it suggests the bullet passed through which may be a good thing. What's critical now is that he get to a hospital."

Ashley says, "I'm sure someone called 911."

"Let's hope they get here soon."

Jane's last few words are drowned out by the wail of sirens followed by police in riot gear, guns drawn, rushing into the room.

Ethan yells, "This is the shooter," instantly drawing two policemen to the prone Red Beard. They handcuff him and bring him to his feet. The other members of American Liberation League put up no resistance and are taken into custody.

As they begin leading Red Beard away, he can be heard shouting, "It was an accident man. I was just trying to scare them." And then, "They were threatening me." One of the officers shouts, "Has anyone seen the gun?" Latisha steps forward and hands it to him. Another officer comes to where Ashley and Jane are sitting with Lenny.

"What happened?" she asks.

"He has a gunshot wound to the head," says Jane. "There's an entrance and an exit wound so the bullet may be somewhere in the room. He needs to get to a hospital right away."

The officer nods grimly as if she's seen this kind of wound before. "An ambulance should be here any minute."

Ashley is sitting on the floor by Lenny. She looks at his ashen face. "Dr. Isaacson . . . Lenny, this is Ashley. I don't know if you can hear me, but you've been hurt. An ambulance is on its way. They're going to take care of you and make you better."

A sob escapes, but she continues. "Hang on, Lenny. Help is on the way."

Finally, after what feels to Ashley like an interminable amount of time, another siren announces the arrival of the ambulance. Two EMTs enter the room. Jane reports what she has found regarding the gunshot wounds, Lenny's respiration, and pulse rate. She repeats that he needs immediate transport.

One EMT asks his name which Ashley gives him. He turns to Lenny. "Lenny, can you hear me?" When there is no response, he says, "My name is Bill. I am an EMT here to help you. If you can hear me but can't talk, do anything you can to let me know you are hearing me: lift your finger, blink, move your lips, anything."

They all look closely but detect no movement. Without comment, the EMT administers oxygen while the other EMT starts an IV. They go back to the ambulance and quickly return with a stretcher bed on which Lenny is carefully placed.

As they are wheeling Lenny out, Agent Lisa McGuire arrives. She looks at Lenny as he passes and her face falls. She does an abrupt about-face and walks beside the EMTs.

"What's his status?" she asks showing them her badge.

"Gunshot wound to the head at fairly close range. Critical. Sorry agent, but we need to move."

McGuire nods and watches them load Lenny into the back of the ambulance. She can see he is not conscious.

"Shit, shit, shit!" she screams under her breath. After taking a few deep breaths she returns to the meeting hall. She goes up to an officer who looks to be in charge, identifies herself, and asks for an update on the situation. He recaps what he knows. Four males, members of a group called the American Liberation League, entered the meeting looking to frighten and intimidate the attendees. Things got out of hand and there was a confrontation between the gun-wielding assailant and one of the organizers. The victim stepped between them as the gun went off and received a gunshot wound to the head. All four have been taken into custody and the victim transported to the hospital.

McGuire recognizes the attackers as belonging to the same group as Jeremy Larsen and Wingate. She thinks about her previous conversations with Lenny, his concerns about his safety, and her reassurances they would protect him. *Well, that didn't happen*, she tells herself. Although they met only a few times, Lenny struck her as a kind and considerate person, someone who thought deeply about life. *And now that life might be over because I didn't take the threats seriously enough.* Sadness and a twinge of guilt threaten to overwhelm her.

Struggling to maintain equilibrium she surveys the crime scene. She walks over to an officer taking statements from two men and a woman. She learns they are the leaders of the group: Ethan, Azad, and Latisha. All were actively involved in trying to stop the perpetrators from disrupting the meeting and hurting anyone. They are badly shaken and attempt to support each other as they give their statements. She listens as Ethan describes the sequence of events. He recounts how after Red Beard drew a gun and grabbed a female attendee, "Dr. Isaacson stepped forward and tried to get him to stand down. When Red Beard recognized Dr. Isaacson as the person from The Loft, he became incensed and threatening."

Ethan pauses, straining to retain emotional control. "People were freaking out, but Dr. Isaacson was amazingly calm. Then the bearded guy told Dr. Isaacson he was a dead man and Dr. Isaacson said, 'How did you know?' I was puzzled by this but then thought it might be his way of trying to defuse the situation, you know, saying something unexpected. But Red Beard got more agitated. I tried to intervene and he pointed the gun at me. That's when Dr. Isaacson jumped in front of me and was shot."

Ethan wipes his eyes. "He probably saved my life." He swallows hard. "What happened next is a blur." Latisha jumps in and tells how Ethan tackled Red Beard after the gun discharged keeping others from possible harm.

McGuire leaves it to the city police to take statements from people in the room. She goes outside and heads toward her car to give herself a quiet place to collect her thoughts, report her findings, and request additional forensic assistance at the scene. The press and the media have begun to converge on the parking area outside the church. She ignores their shouted questions and makes a beeline to her vehicle. She sits down and shuts the door. The car windows are tinted and given the time of night and the absence of many lights; it would be difficult for anyone to see inside. This modicum of privacy allows her to set aside her professional demeanor. Although she has seen her share of violent crime scenes and has learned how to keep the images at bay, it doesn't make her immune to experiencing feelings, especially when she knows the victim.

Poor Lenny. Another good person whose life may be over for no reason other than having the courage to stand up to hatred.

She thinks about their previous conversation where he expressed sadness about the level of crime and violence in society, and how, if things were different, she might be lending her talents to another vocation. While she believed in the importance of her work, she liked that he saw her in such a positive light. "And now he's fighting for his life," she mutters as her eyes grow moist.

A knock on McGuire's car window shatters her sense of privacy. It's a reporter whom she knows from his presence at other crime scenes. Another person, she thinks, whose life revolves around the awful things humans do to each other. *He must have watched me go to my car.* Not feeling ready to talk, she pretends to not hear him despite knowing this is implausible. Instead, she starts her car and drives to a remote section of the parking area to await the arrival of her colleagues.

Chapter Thirty-One

A fierce wind buffets Lenny as he trudges through empty streets. Trees are bending unnaturally, and he hears sporadic cracks as trunks succumb to the relentless pounding. Little eddies of swirling winds lift litter from the ground into revolving carousals of detritus. Even the birds seem to have decided not to chance the turbulence as none are visible save for a few huddled together in the interior of some large trees.

Lenny leans into the wind feeling its unrelenting power with the strain of each step. "I need to keep going," he shouts at the wind as if an adversary. He does not have a destination. Rather, this is a journey *away* from somewhere he does not want to be. *As long as I keep moving, I'll be safe.*

Tiny particles of salt sting his face. He wonders if he is nearing the ocean. No matter. "Keep moving, keep moving," he repeats like a mantra, trying to distract himself from the fatigue that grows with each step. Soon every word of exhortation is met by a counter plea from his muscles to rest. "We're depleted," they tell him. "Pause for a while and recharge." His lungs join in. "We need more oxygen if we are to continue."

"Not much longer," he urges. "We can make it," although in truth he is not sure.

The wind has a strange sentient quality. Amid its unrelenting buffeting, a presence dances at the edges of his consciousness.

"My exhaustion is causing me to imagine things," he tells himself. But no sooner has he spoken than he hears the indisputable sound of someone calling his name. He knows the voice. It is Carolina.

"Lenny, Lenny," she calls. "I have been waiting for you to return to me."

I must be going crazy. "You're a character in my book. You can't be real."

"You are not crazy, Lenny. Love is transcendent."

He becomes aware that his eyes have been closed. *Aha, that's the problem. I've blocked out visual stimuli.* He blinks them open and stares into an opaque whirlwind. He tries to focus. At first, nothing is visible, then he sees her, translucent and ethereal. Her smile is beautiful and beckoning, just as he remembered writing about it.

So, this is how you look in real life, he thinks, but catches himself and shakes his head to dispel the mirage. The image, however, doesn't waver. He says to her, "How can you be here?"

Carolina gazes at him with loving eyes. "I'm here because you're here, Lenny. It's time to finish the story."

* * *

At the hospital, Lenny is hurriedly but thoroughly examined as it is clear his wound is life-threatening. A neurologist is brought in and after a CT scan, a decision is made to prep him for emergency surgery.

In the meantime, word of the incident has gotten out via local news and other media outlets. The community is stunned by a second violent event in less than two weeks. Also shocking is that the person shot, Dr. Leonard Isaacson, is the same person who tripped the gunman at The Loft leading to his apprehension. This seems more than coincidental and fuels speculation this was a revenge shooting.

Patricia is at home when she hears the news on TV. She listens in disbelief, the information not quite registering. Once it does, however, she gets up, sprints out the door to her car, and heads for the hospital.

A similar scene plays out for Jerry. He's lying in bed channel surfing when he comes to the local news. He lingers long enough to hear there has been another shooting. Like Patricia, he is stunned to hear Lenny's name. He yells for Katie who rushes in thinking something is wrong with him. He points to the TV, his face ghostly, and they watch the news. "We need to go," he says and without another word gets up and prepares to leave. Katie hastily tells the kids what has happened and where they are going. They too are shocked and ask her to contact them as soon as she knows more. She promises to do so.

When Carol and Javier hear the news, they call the building manager to get access to Lenny's apartment and take care of Sisu. They enter and call his name, but he is nowhere to be found. Eventually, they find him under the bed. Carol is sure he senses something is not right, so she calmly coaxes him to come out. Javier grabs his leash, food, and water bowl, and they bring him to their apartment.

As soon as Ashley and Ethan are finished with the police, they too head to the hospital. Both are very shaken and find comfort in each other's presence.

A friend and colleague from Lenny's old department at the university calls the hospital to get an update on his condition. Although he does not learn anything new, he is connected to a nurse who asks if Lenny has any immediate family who should be contacted. He remembers the name of Lenny's sister, Eleanor, and the town in Iowa where she lives and shares the information.

*　*　*

It's almost midnight when the phone rings in Eleanor's home. She and Ted are sound asleep. After a few seconds of disorientation, Ted grumbles, "Who could be calling now?" He turns and picks up the phone located on his side of the bed. Eleanor, still half-asleep, but feeling the tension that accompanies a middle-of-the-night call, hears him say, "What is this about?" which is enough to keep her from turning away. Ted listens for a few moments then says, "Yes, she is here." From his tone, Eleanor knows something is wrong. Sleepiness is replaced by alarm.

"It's about Lenny," he says handing her the phone. "He's been injured."

Eleanor's shaking hand fumbles with the phone. She listens while the situation is described. Having turned on his bedside lamp, Ted sees her biting her lower lip. This is very bad, he thinks. Eleanor asks some questions about Lenny's condition and what is being done. She ends the call with, "Yes, I will come as soon as possible."

"What happened?" asks Ted.

At first, Eleanor is too paralyzed with shock to answer. She opens and closes her eyes as if hoping to awake from a nightmare. Then, barely able to get the words out, she says, "Lenny's been shot. I need to go there right away."

* * *

Lenny has been in surgery for five hours. Patricia, Ashley, Ethan, Jerry, and Katie are gathered in the waiting room. Although they had not all met before, within the first hour they figure out they're all there for Lenny. They briefly share information about how they know Lenny and what happened. Then resume their vigil.

The night drags on. By 4 a.m., they are alternately dozing and talking in whispers. Around 6:30, Agent McGuire arrives. She spots Patricia and walks over to her. "How's he doing?" she asks.

"He's been in surgery for several hours. It's very serious," says Patricia tearing up again.

McGuire is grim. "I arrived at the meeting hall just as they were taking him to the ambulance. At least they got to him quickly."

Aroused by the newcomer, the others inch closer and introduce themselves. McGuire informs them that all the perpetrators are in custody and will be arraigned today. She adds it was fortunate there were no other casualties.

"Thanks to Lenny," says Ethan. They all nod in agreement then lapse into silence, the weight of exhaustion, anxiety, and dispiritedness settling on the group. Without another word, they shuffle back to their previous places.

Another hour passes. Then a middle-aged male with short white hair wearing green hospital scrubs enters the waiting room.

Everyone is instantly awake. He asks who is here for Leonard Isaacson. They all stand. He introduces himself as Mark Saunders, the surgeon who operated on Lenny. He asks if any of those present are family. Patricia tells him Lenny's only family is a sister who lives in Iowa and it is her understanding she has been called.

Jerry, unable to contain himself, blurts out, "How is he? Was the surgery successful?"

Saunders responds in a neutral voice. "As you know, Mr. Isaacson suffered a gunshot wound to the head at close range. It was a perforating wound which means the bullet exited the skull so we did not have to deal with an embedded bullet or fragments. However, the CT scan revealed a hematoma, a blood clot, so we performed an emergency craniotomy, opening a small part of the skull to remove the clotted blood. There was also considerable swelling, not uncommon in this type of injury, which is a major risk factor. To reduce pressure buildup and lessen the chance of restricted blood flow to the brain and additional tissue death, we did not replace the bone flap."

Anticipating their next question, Saunders adds, "The skull fragment is frozen and can be replaced at a later time."

This update does not placate a still agitated Jerry. He asks, "What are his chances? If he lives, will he have brain damage?"

Saunders rubs his eyes, his fatigue after hours of surgery apparent. He patiently answers. "I don't want to make any predictions at this time. The good news is he survived the surgery; however, his condition remains precarious and critical. The brain can continue to swell for several days so we hope to know more when it subsides."

Seeing their puzzled looks, he continues. "Do you remember

Gabrielle Giffords, the congresswoman from Arizona who was shot in 2011?"

They nod.

"Mr. Isaacson's injury is similar. I believe in both cases a 9-millimeter passed through the skull. Like Gifford, Mr. Isaacson has been put into a medically induced coma and given different medications and solutions to reduce the swelling and draw fluid from his brain. He has also been put on a respirator to help his breathing and keep his brain cells oxygenated.

"Gifford survived," says Patricia.

"And although she had some brain damage, she's made almost a full recovery," Ashley adds in a hopeful tone.

"That's true," says Saunders, "but she was the exception, not the norm. We will do everything possible to achieve a similar outcome but keep him in your thoughts and prayers. For now, I suggest you get some rest. You can check on his condition later today when he is out of recovery and in the ICU. When and if his condition stabilizes, we can see about visits. Now if you'll excuse me, I too will get some rest."

Given a temporary reprieve from their vigil, the group slowly begins to leave. Before exiting, they exchange contact information and agree to keep each other informed of any news.

* * *

Jerry and Katie walk to their car in silence. Katie is worried Jerry will start blaming himself for what happened to Lenny, replaying the self-destructive pattern he did with Emily.

"I can't believe this is happening," he keeps repeating while shaking his head from side to side. "First Emily and now Lenny."

"I know," says Katie. "Our lives have been turned upside down, but for the sake of our kids and ourselves, we need to find a way to maintain our stability."

To her relief, Jerry nods affirmatively and mumbles, "We do. I'm just not sure how."

Sensing a moment of vulnerability, Katie stops, takes Jerry's hand, and looks him in the eyes. "For starters, we need to stay connected. We have each other to help get through this. There is no need to navigate these waters alone. I love you Jerry and I'm here for you."

Jerry's eyes grow moist and his lips turn slightly upwards into what looks to Katie like a mournful smile. "And I will try to be there for you," he says collapsing into her arms.

They remain bound together, eyes closed, wrapped in the warmth of their connection, their communion more powerful than words. After a minute, Katie gently extracts herself from his embrace and takes his hand again.

"Let's go home."

Jerry's bond with Lenny and the gravity of his condition jolts him from any remaining preoccupation about his own ordeal. He needs to be there for his friend and, as Katie rightly pointed out, for his family. As Katie drives toward their home, he gazes out the window. What he sees resembles any other day, but he knows life will never be the same. He wonders if Lenny gazed from his car window at the same surroundings when he came to visit him at the hospital. Did he have the slightest inkling they would soon be changing places? That his life would be hanging by a thread?

Life can turn on a dime, he thinks, something he has experienced more than once. He reflects on how the death of his brother Daniel led him to seek orderliness and predictability, hoping it would protect those he cared about from harm. He now understands it created a false sense of security and set himself up for undeserved self-recrimination and blame when the unexpected happened.

It's time to change. We do the best we can in a world that doesn't always bend to our wishes. As Lenny would say, we construct our realities in relationship with others. I have been blessed with many loving relationships and it is those I will focus on.

* * *

Eleanor arrives later that afternoon. She rents a car at the airport and heads straight for the hospital. On the way, she hears a news report about what happened the previous evening. Leonard Isaacson, a retired professor at the university, was shot and is listed in critical condition. She presses harder on the accelerator. Despite not seeing each other often, their bond is strong. To lose him at any time would be difficult, but for it to happen so suddenly and brutally feels heart-wrenching.

Eleanor's thoughts turn to memories of their childhood. Depending on where they were in their developmental journeys, they could be tender or callous towards one another. As they grew into adulthood, they rediscovered their kinship and came to appreciate each other's struggle to develop an identity and find their pathway through life. Now in their later years, with the hindsight and wisdom of age, their gratitude was deeper than ever.

Pulling into the hospital parking garage, Eleanor readies herself for what she might hear and see. She stops at the information booth to find out where Lenny is located. The pleasant 'candy striper' consults her computer and informs her he is in the ICU but visiting hours are restricted. Without another thought, she goes up to the floor. She introduces herself at the nurses' station explaining she has just flown in from Iowa to see her brother, Leonard Isaacson. A nurse tells her that she will need to consult with the attending physician before she can permit her to visit. Frazzled from lack of sleep, travel, and stress, Eleanor is about to argue when she hears someone say, "Are you Lenny Isaacson's sister?" She turns and sees a tall, middle-aged man dressed in a blue, button-down shirt and tan chinos.

"Yes. I'm Lenny's sister, Eleanor," she answers wondering if this might be a friend of Lenny's.

"Hello. I'm Michael Lisman," he says extending his hand, "Lenny's primary care physician."

She shakes his hand. "I'm glad you were able to come, Eleanor. I just came by to check on Lenny."

Eleanor asks if he can tell her about Lenny's condition. He suggests they go to the lounge at the end of the hall where it will be easier to talk. She agrees while trying to detect anything in his expression or tone that might presage what he will say.

Two other people are in the lounge, but it is large enough for them to converse in private. Eleanor spies a coffee machine, and needing a caffeine boost, helps herself to a cup. Once seated, Lisman tells Eleanor he has been Lenny's physician for about twenty years as well as a colleague at the university where he is a clinical instructor. He has talked with the surgeon who operated on

Lenny and had just come from Lenny's room when they met. He describes Lenny's injury, the surgery, and the current treatment. As Eleanor listens, the gravity of Lenny's condition becomes more real. The weight of her sorrow threatens to submerge her. After a brief silence, she summons the courage to ask the dreaded question: "Is he going to live?"

Lisman crosses and uncrosses his legs. "It's touch and go. I'm not going to sugarcoat it; survival rates in such cases are not high . . . but he's made it through the first step, the surgery, and he's a fighter."

Lisman is aware he is not telling her about Lenny's recent visits and the possibility he could have cancer. Why add to her already heavy emotional burden, he reasons. Since Lenny never got the additional tests, there is no way to know definitively what the diagnosis would be.

Eleanor interrupts his thoughts, asking him when she will be able to see Lenny and if he will be aware of her presence.

"It's up to the attending, but I think it will be ok for you to see him for a short while. As to whether he will be aware you are there, it's hard to say. Generally, people in medically induced comas don't recall specific conversations, but some report glimpses of awareness. I would assume he could hear you despite not being able to respond."

Eleanor thanks him for the information and his concern for Lenny. They walk back to the nurses' station where Lisman checks in about a brief visit. He gives Eleanor the ok and they go to Lenny's room.

Upon entering, Eleanor hears the beeps of the monitors and

the metronome-like 'breathing' of the respirator. She looks at her brother. He appears small and fragile. Multiple tubes attached to his body and a bandage covering his head distort his appearance, but it's still Lenny. His eyes are closed and he seems peaceful. Eleanor feels tears forming and struggles to hold them at bay. *There will be a time for tears. Now I must be here for Lenny.*

She pulls a chair to his bedside and takes his hand. It is limp and warm to the touch. She sits without speaking willing Lenny to feel her touch while observing him for any signs of awareness. Not detecting anything she says, "Hi, Lenny. It's your sister, Eleanor. When we heard you were injured, I came right away."

She pauses and takes a deep breath to maintain her composure. "I'm so sorry about what happened, but you're in good hands. I met with your doctor, Michael Lisman, and he says the surgery went well and for the next few days they need to keep you sedated to give your head time to heal. I plan on staying until I know you will be ok."

As she talks, Lisman quietly checks the readings and the latest entries in Lenny's chart. He tells Eleanor Lenny's vitals are stable and they will continue to treat the swelling and pressure. He says although the bullet exited Lenny's skull which is better than being lodged in his brain, the tract taken by the bullet was deep which makes the outcome guarded.

Eleanor thanks him for the information and asks if she can stay longer.

"Sure," says Lisman. "How about another fifteen minutes."

"Ok," Eleanor whispers.

"I need to get back to the office, but feel free to call me if you have any questions or would like to talk." He hands her his business card.

"I'll do that," responds Eleanor, glad to have a credible source of information.

Turning back to Lenny she says, "Hi, Lenny, it's Eleanor again." She takes his hand. "I don't know if you can hear me or not, but I will assume you can. I hope you are comfortable and not in pain. I don't know if you realize you were shot, but it's why you are in the hospital. There's a machine doing the breathing for you and you're getting different medications to help with your injury. Also, I am sending you loving and healing thoughts. I hope you can feel them."

Watching him intently as she speaks, Eleanor thinks there may have been a slight fluctuation of his eyelid. Her heart beats faster. Is Lenny giving a sign that he heard her? If so, it was too subtle and fleeting for her to be sure.

The moment vanishes when the door opens and a nurse enters. "Sorry to interrupt, but we need to check on some things and turn him."

Taking her words as a hint that it's time to leave, Eleanor gets up from the chair and leans close to Lenny. "I need to go now, Lenny, but I will return later this evening. Wherever you are, dear brother, be at peace and know you are loved."

Chapter Thirty-Two

Lenny is at the Holy Grounds coffee shop sitting in his favorite booth near the back. The place is almost empty except for a few people at the counter. *I've come at a good time.* A thin spiral of steam rises from his mug of coffee. He takes a sip enjoying its flavor and smoothness. Out of habit, he looks around for Jerry. *I wonder if he will show up? He's been having a difficult time, but I think he might be turning the corner. What happened to Emily shredded his implicit sense of homeostasis sending him into a tailspin. He hit bottom but got back up and now seems to be finding a new equilibrium that will serve him better in the future.*

Lost in thought, he is surprised when he sees Jerry sitting across from him. There's something different about him. More contemplative? Determined? Maybe a touch of broken heartedness? It's hard to tell, but what is familiar is Jerry's smile and the transparency of his friendship.

"I'm glad we have this opportunity to meet," says Jerry. "We are both on uncharted journeys, so I'm grateful our paths have crossed."

"Me too," says Lenny. "I'm happy to see you looking so well. I've been worried about you."

"I'll be fine," says Jerry, "thanks in part to you. Your friendship has meant a lot to me. Now it's my opportunity to be there for you."

Although they hadn't moved, Lenny feels himself wrapped in Jerry's warm embrace. Lenny returns the embrace and they merge, a transcendent union filling Lenny with gratitude and joy.

Hearing a familiar voice at the counter, Lenny looks over and notices the serving person is his sister, Eleanor. He is comforted by her presence. *I'm glad she is here with me.*

As he is thinking this, she turns in his direction and smiles. "Remember how you loved pecan pie as a kid?"

He mouths the word "yes."

"Well, I saved a piece for you."

Inexplicably, tears slowly wind down his cheeks.

* * *

Over the next two days, Lenny's condition remains unchanged. He is allowed a few visitors for brief periods. They talk to him reverently as if he can hear them although they often find themselves mouthing cliches like 'you're strong,' 'you're a fighter,' and 'you can get through this,' because his unresponsiveness is awkward and they are unsure how to be helpful.

For some, seeing Lenny evokes memories of their own or others' hospitalization. Ashley thinks of her father. He too was in an ICU hooked up to a ventilator. In his case, it was chronic obstructive pulmonary disease commonly known as COPD. As an eight-year-old, she remembers how her father gradually withered to a feeble caricature of the strong and vibrant man she knew. She didn't understand much about his disease, only it was like a savage beast decimating its prey. Sitting with her mother by his bedside in a room like the one she was now in, she remembers her disbelief that the frail and unresponsive person lying in the bed, the person she assumed was invulnerable, was her father. And then one day he was gone, devoured by the beast who left only his ashes in a ceramic urn.

Ashley realizes she is crying. She has an urge to tell her story to Lenny but suppresses it. How could she even think such a thing? She scolds herself. There is no happy ending to share. To do so would be a selfish act, her personal catharsis at Lenny's expense. She composes herself and assumes what she considers a more appropriate persona, expressing good wishes and other sincere platitudes.

Other visitors disclose thoughts and feelings they never before shared with him while alternating between hoping he can hear them and hoping he cannot. They want Lenny to know they too suffer or have suffered, or that they are flawed human beings who deserve to be lying in the hospital bed instead of him. For those who think he can't hear them, it becomes an opportunity to talk to themselves about experiences or feelings lurking in some nether region of their consciousness. As they speak, they watch him carefully for signs of responsiveness: a blink, a facial twitch, the movement of a finger. When they cannot detect any response, they tell themselves it's ok to go on.

There are different variations on these themes. When Jerry visits, he finds himself talking to Lenny as if they were at Holy Grounds. He's not sure why, but a part of him knows it allows him to avoid dwelling on the real possibility Lenny won't survive, or if he does, that he may no longer be able to participate in their coffee and conversation rituals. It's also a ploy that lets him talk about things on his mind. Since Lenny doesn't respond, he takes on the role of both interlocutors. As Lenny, he says things like "I see your point Jerry but have you thought about it this way?" or "I read about this philosopher who argues that . . ."

He feels self-conscious about doing this and keeps glancing back at the door to the room to make sure no one has entered. Given his recent history, he could see how his behavior might be construed as a sign he is relapsing. Still, he finds it comforting. As Lenny has said, sometimes just expressing your thoughts out loud can clarify things or provide a new perspective. Like the other visitors, he doesn't know if Lenny can hear him, but if he can he thinks he would be amused and perhaps find added incentive to keep fighting. Before leaving, he whispers. "I love you, Lenny."

Eleanor visits twice a day. Holding Lenny's hand, she reminisces about their past, experiences they shared, or she assumes they remember about each other. She tells him he was a positive influence on her growing up, a role model of sorts, and how she liked how protective he was of her even when she complained it was an intrusion.

She talks about her present life: the ups and downs of her job, what her children are doing, and her relationship with her husband. She assures him everything is ok at his apartment. Sisu is with his neighbors and seems happy. His apartment is clean and ready for his return at the appropriate time.

Eleanor's monologues are interspersed with words of encouragement and bromides about how well he is doing despite how difficult his struggle is. Looking optimistically toward the future, she says that once he is discharged, she and Ted would welcome him to rehabilitate at their home.

And she cries. With their parents gone, the thought of losing Lenny feels like the end of something precious, leaving her the only remaining scribe of their family narrative.

Patricia tells him how meaningful their relationship is to her. "You've helped me with my grief about Diedre. I appreciate how you listened without prescribing how I should or should not be feeling. As you know, I'm still struggling so you're going to have to get well so I can lean on you some more."

She tries to joke. Recounting their encounter with the guy on the trail near her home, she tells him he'll need to work on his self-defense skills in case they're accosted again. However, as soon as she says it, she wants to take it back, feeling she was trivializing his dire condition.

Embarrassed and trying to recover, she mumbles to herself, "Listen to me, making dumb attempts at humor when you're fighting for your life." Then to him, "I'm sorry, Lenny. I guess I'm feeling overwhelmed by all that has happened. What I want to say is that I look forward to seeing, talking . . . and kissing you again, however long it takes."

She stands and moves to the bed, gently squeezing his hand while wiping away her tears, she says, "I'll be thinking of you and holding you in my heart." Then she turns and leaves the room.

* * *

Another day passes without any change in Lenny's condition.

The doctors are concerned, but there is not much more they can do. In the meantime, Lenny's reality alternates between timeless stretches of nothingness and vivid dreams as real as anything he has experienced. Although externally he appears to be in stasis, his adventures continue.

STANLEY L. WITKIN

Chapter Thirty-Three

Lenny is in an ethereal dreamscape of gently rolling hills and woodlands interspersed with open meadows. An alabaster sun sits prominently in a cerulean sky. Each time Lenny looks up, the sun's location changes between east and west as if unsure whether it is rising or setting. He enters a forested trail, adorned with yellow, white, and orange flowers he does not recognize. Plants with huge fronds of teal, emerald, and malachite bend across the path their leaves fluttering like diaphanous curtains parting soundlessly before him. He feels like he's in a Rousseau painting and wonders if the artist had been inspired by such landscapes.

A large shadow across the ground accompanied by faint rustling draws his gaze upward. A ginormous kaleidoscope of butterflies is swooping and darting about creating swirling palettes of colors against the blue background of the sky. At first, their movements appear chaotic, but soon he discerns a patterning to their flight, a kind of aerial ballet, beautiful and mesmerizing.

A single, huge butterfly descends from the swirl. In contrast to its multicolored companions, it is dusky white except for some gray scaling along the edges of its wings. It stops in front of Lenny at eye level, its knobbed antennae bending slightly forward, its wings undulating in a steady rhythm that keeps it in place. As it holds its position, Lenny has the impression it is attempting to speak to him. He listens closely for a message without success. Uncertain what to do, he says, "Are you trying to speak to me?"

No recognizable response comes from the butterfly. *What now?* he thinks. *Should I wait? Move on?* Then from somewhere outside the whirling vortex of beating wings, he hears a male voice. "It's called a West Virginia white or, more formally, *Pieris virginiensis*."

The names strike a familiar chord, like a faint echo from his past. Lenny says to the voice, "I remember as a youngster reading about different species of butterflies in school, but I had forgotten their names."

The voice answers. "Or maybe the connection has atrophied."

"Well, just the same," says Lenny, "it's beautiful."

"Yes, it is," agrees the voice. "The people known as the Blackfoot, *Siksika* in their language, believe white butterflies can travel between the physical and spiritual world. I hear it's a fascinating journey."

Lenny considers this. "I have the impression the butterfly is trying to speak to me, but I can't seem to hear it."

"Not speak," corrects the voice, "communicate. You are listening for words, but that is not its medium. Stop listening with your ears and open yourself to whatever channels it might use."

Ignoring the weirdness of conversing with a disembodied voice, Lenny takes the advice and clears his mind. He gazes at the butterfly still suspended in place its antennae now alternating forward and back. At first nothing happens. Then Lenny feels a pulsing vibration followed by an eruption of multicolored light. For an inestimable time, he merges with the butterfly host, gliding with them in near-weightless, choreographed synchrony. When it ceases, the white butterfly turns and reemerges with the others.

As he watches it go, Lenny realizes either the swarm has changed, or he is seeing it differently. No longer an amorphous horde, it has assumed an elliptical shape. Curious, he continues to observe. Suddenly, there's a furious beating of wings and the form begins to elongate and narrow. Butterflies of the same color coalesce in horizontal bands while others group at one end creating a dark area that resembles a head with orbs corresponding to rudimentary eyes. In a flash of recognition, he exclaims, "Wow. It's a caterpillar!"

Awestruck, his gaze remains transfixed on the 'caterpillar' as it twists its upper body right and left as if surveying the sky. Then a change in the humming sound of wings signals another transmutation, this time into a monochromatic pale green 'j' shape resembling a leaf.

Sensing what is happening, Lenny identifies the new form as a chrysalis. The butterflies comprising the form are motionless with wings outspread as though held aloft by an imperceptible breeze. Silence reigns as the chrysalis hangs quiescent in the sky. Lenny can feel its retreat from the external world as it prepares for transformation.

Minutes pass or maybe hours or days, when a barely perceptible ripple flows through the form soon followed by others. Slowly, they increase in frequency and intensity until the entire configuration pulsates.

Lenny can see as well as feel the energy. The chrysalis begins to swing from its invisible perch, its hull straining from the powerful undulation. A bright flash fills Lenny's field of vision momentarily blinding him. When his sight clears, the chrysalis is gone. In its place is a colossal white butterfly with gray borders, a new multi-being actualized by thousands of butterflies interacting in perfect unison.

Enthralled by this drama of metamorphous and transformation, Lenny watches the butterfly slowly unfold its enormous, translucent wings and descend to about five feet above him. Regarding Lenny with huge, luminescent, blue eyes he feels a beckoning, to what or where he does not know. Before he can process this further, a vigorous whoosh of its wings propels the magnificent creature into the sky, soaring through the incandescent air until absorbed into the sun's radiance.

Stillness returns. Lenny breathes deeply consumed by the incredible drama he just witnessed. A primal stirring portending a transfiguration of major proportion dances on the edge of his consciousness, an existential epiphany that he too is undergoing a metamorphosis and transformation.

Closing his eyes, he drops to his knees overwhelmed by the revelation of the white butterfly's message.

"I see you were able to communicate," says the disembodied voice.

This time he recognizes its source. He opens his eyes.

Ezekiel is in a clearing about ten feet away. He's sitting in a rattan chair at a round white table. Lavender chrysanthemums stand in a glass vase at the center. Behind him is an expansive lake whose placid waters seem to stretch into eternity. Above is a clear blue sky accented with some high-altitude, feathery cirrus clouds. Gentle light filters through trees bordering the clearing creating flickering shadows that give Ezekiel the appearance of being in an old movie where images fluctuate in and out.

He is decked out in a white suit over a dark purple shirt. Completing his outfit is a white, Panama hat with a black band above the rim, sunglasses, and high-top basketball sneakers.

"You look dapper," says Lenny. "What's the occasion?"

"It's your death day," says Ezekiel with a smile.

Lenny squints in confusion. "You must mean my birthday, but I'm afraid you're mistaken. It's not for several months."

Ezekiel looks at Lenny with a kindly expression. "Your birthdays, many of them, already happened. Today we are celebrating something new. The butterflies were just the beginning."

Still puzzled, Lenny seeks clarification. "I'm not sure what you mean. If I am going to die today, why would we celebrate? Shouldn't we mourn or be afraid?"

"That's up to you," replies Ezekiel getting up from the table. "It's a beautiful day. Let's walk by the lake. Maybe it will help you decide."

Without waiting for a reply, Ezekiel turns and begins walking.

Bewildered but curious, Lenny follows. They continue in silence. A gentle wind rustles the leaves among the trees lining their path.

As the leaves turn in the breeze, their undersides produce a strobe-like shimmer accompanied by a faint, melodious sound. Lenny stops, closes his eyes, and listens as he has learned, with his whole being.

Subtly, the sound begins to transform from the arboreal melody to a barely distinguishable whisper with the familiar, gravelly voice of Leonard Cohen.

Listen to the hummingbird
Whose wings you cannot see
Listen to the hummingbird
Don't listen to me
Listen to the butterfly
Whose days but number three
Listen to the butterfly
Don't listen to me
Listen to the mind of God
Which doesn't need to be
Listen to the mind of God
Don't listen to me

Cohen's syncopated rhythm blends harmonically with the music of the trees in a manner reminiscent of the beat poets of the 1960s who would read their poetry to jazz accompaniment in the dusky clubs of Greenwich village. To Lenny however, Cohen's words feel like a personal invocation.

"What is happening?" he says to Ezekiel who is gazing out across the lake. Ezekiel turns toward Lenny. "You are beginning the process of return."

"Return? Return to what?"

"To existence without borders."

"Must you always be so enigmatic?" asks Lenny despite feeling a straightforward answer could never capture what is happening.

In response, Ezekiel begins to chant.

"I speak the language of magic and dreams
a lexicon of spirit and rhythms
creating and being created in a dance of relation

> *like snowflakes in the eddies of a winter wind.*
> *I speak the language of secret lives*
> *transcending time and forever*
> *where hopes, fears, passion, and longing*
> *tumble together in melodic images of tears and laughter.*
> *I speak the language of canyons and mist*
> *borne in the interstice of day and night*
> *floating ghost-like toward beauty wherever it exists*
> *and however it is worshiped.*
> *I speak the language of the heart*
> *existing in the echoes of longing and transcendent love."*

Ezekiel's chant, the graceful rhythms, and the dancing light merge into a radiating presence. Lenny feels in a transitory state of disassembling and emergence. Lost in this rapturous awakening, he is startled by the touch of something warm and moist against his hand.

"Sisu!" he exclaims in delight at the sight of his little dog pushing his nose up against him. "How did you get here?"

He reaches down and rubs his hand through Sisu's soft coat feeling a connection that fills him with joy and then, unexpectedly, melancholy.

"He was wondering where you were," says Ezekiel. "But I sense sadness. Is that true?"

"I am saddened by the ending of this life," says Lenny. "I enjoy being alive. And I'm worried about Sisu. Will he be ok?"

"He'll be well taken care of. Of course, he will miss your physical presence, but like the poet Rumi he understands, 'Goodbyes are only for those who love with their eyes. Because for those who love with their heart and soul there is no such thing as separation.'"

Lenny looks down at Sisu. His brown eyes reflect their deep bond. In his mind, Lenny hears him say, "Hold on to this moment."

He scratches Sisu's ear feeling its velvety smoothness. "Thank you for being such a loyal friend and companion."

Sisu responds with another nuzzle and lies down.

* * *

Ezekiel is again staring out at the lake. Lenny walks over to him hoping to discover what he is looking at but sees only the gentle motion of the water. He notices the sun has moved from its midway position and is now lower in the sky creating a new mosaic of light and shadow. The breeze too shifts directions producing a tranquil arpeggiated melody through the trees. He feels the press of an arm around his shoulder. He assumes it is Ezekiel but is uncertain. *It doesn't matter*, he tells himself.

"The water is beautiful," says Lenny.

"Yes, it is," he hears Ezekiel say although he's no longer can tell where the voice is coming from. An all-encompassing, intuitive knowing fills Lenny; a *weltanschauung* of the interconnectedness of everything. He realizes his various strivings to gain an understanding of existence, whether mystical, artistic, or academic, were different ways of conceptualizing and responding to the call of this infinite fusion. Divisions fall away as the borders of separation dissipate. The ineffable becomes clear and death's mystery a kind of freedom. He is infused with radiance and love, the latter not an emotion but a state of being.

A banyan tree appears on the nearby bank. Its tall, expansive canopy and broad leaves cover him like a blanket of stars. Inside its primary trunk is a spacious hollow. Lenny enters. It is dark but even as his eyes adjust, he cannot see any walls, ceiling, or even a floor. It is as if he has become weightless or incorporeal. However, he feels neither frightened nor disoriented. *Where am I going?* he wonders.

"Follow me," comes a voice that sounds like Leonard Cohen but seems to be coming from the tree. It begins to sing.

Going home without my burden
Going home behind the curtain
Going home to where it's better than before
Going home without my sorrow
Going home sometime tomorrow
Going home without this costume that I wore

The verse repeats and Lenny joins in. As he sings, the sound transforms into a boundless, vibrational ocean. Its undulating waves embracing and subsuming the being that was Lenny Isaacson.

* * *

Within Lenny's hospital room an alarm goes off and a light just outside the door starts flashing. A nurse rushes into the room, glances at the monitors, checks Lenny's vital signs, and pushes a button. Immediately, an intercom voice announces "Code Blue. Room 135," repeating it several times. Within a minute, medical personnel are by Lenny's side assessing his condition and administering what they hope are lifesaving measures. However, after several minutes of strenuous effort without any change to the flatline of the heart monitor, they cease their efforts at resuscitation. A physician in the group states the time of death.

Epilogue

At 6:00 a.m., Eleanor's phone rings. Even in her groggy state, she knows what it's about. Hearing Dr. Lisman's voice, confirms her fears. Lenny has died.

Dr. Lisman explains that Lenny went into cardiac arrest and despite their best efforts, they were unable to resuscitate him. The damage from his injury was too extensive for him to recover. He assures her Lenny did not suffer.

"I am so sorry, Eleanor. Please call on me if there is anything I can do."

Despite knowing Lenny's condition was extremely critical, Eleanor had clung to a thread of hope that he might defy the odds. The severing of that thread was devastating. She grieved for her loss and for Lenny's life ending in violence. She prayed Dr. Lisman was right and he did not suffer. *If only he had taken me up on my offer to visit,* she couldn't help thinking.

When she called her husband, she sobbed convulsively. He offered to fly to Vermont which she gratefully accepted. Notwithstanding her grief, she knew it was her responsibility as Lenny's only surviving family member to make arrangements regarding his body and any memorial service. From previous conversations, she knew Lenny wished to be cremated and where his will was filed. Somehow, she found the reserve to cope sufficiently to attend to these matters.

* * *

It is two days after the cremation. The morning is calm. A light breeze blows in from the west off Lake Champlain. Sunlight filters through high clouds creating different shades of green on the sward outside of the Ira Allen Chapel on the University campus where people have begun to gather. Built in the 1920s, the Chapel building is an exemplar of colonial revival style architecture, its most distinctive feature a gold-domed bell tower rising 170 feet above the ground.

Although named for the university's founder, Lenny had more in common with a venerated graduate of more than a century ago, the philosopher John Dewey, whose gravestone stood just outside the north side of the building. A quotation from Dewey was displayed prominently in Lenny's university office and relocated to his apartment after he retired.

"Each individual that comes into the world is a new beginning; the universe itself is, as it were, taking a fresh start in him and trying to do something, even if on a small scale, that it has never done before."

* * *

About forty people and one small dog wait for the memorial service to begin. The day before, an article by Ashley Lee with the heading, 'Dr. Lenny Isaacson, Scholar, Humanitarian, and Friend.

In Memoriam' appeared in the *Daily Chronicle*. Besides providing some factual details about Lenny's life and accomplishments, Ashley wrote about her brief, but meaningful relationship with Lenny, highlighting her initial interview about the events at The Loft and learning of his part in apprehending the gunman, their unexpected meeting at Jeremy Larsen's funeral, and their final encounter at the Alliance for Peace meeting. She wrote about how she expected their first meeting to be a typical question and answer type interview, and her surprise when it turned into more of a dialogue with Lenny also asking her questions.

'As we talked, it became clear Dr. Isaacson was someone who thought deeply about the state of society and cared about the welfare of others. That he should die in such a violent way is a sad testament to the very issues that concerned him. He believed we could do better and if nothing else, perhaps his death will spur some of us to act in accord with his vision of a better world.'

Lenny left instructions for his memorial service in his will. He had an agreement with his friend, Dennis, who lived in the Midwest that whoever lived longer would officiate at the other's service. Dennis was intelligent, compassionate, and had a great sense of humor, qualities Lenny believed would create a balance between thoughtful solemnity and celebration.

True to his word, Dennis had come and although hurting from the loss of his friend, he brought his usual brand of respectful irreverence to the remembrance. He spoke about how Lenny 'won' their bet about who would wind up officiating at the other's memorial service. He also reflected on how their friendship had grown over the years despite residing 1300 miles apart and its meaningfulness to him.

"Here's a secret I can share now that I'm retired," he says with mock surreptitiousness to the people gathered. "Lenny and I used to meet at academic conferences, not because we were enamored with the presentations, but so we could have a few beers together and catch up on things. So, on his behalf and mine, I thank the University of Vermont."

Concluding his remarks Dennis says, "As many of you know, Lenny loved Leonard Cohen's songs and poetry." Then putting his hand by the side of his mouth as if commenting to someone else, he adds in a lower voice "A bit too gloomy for me. Give me vintage Leslie Gore singing 'Sunshine, Lollipops, and Rainbows' and I'm good to go."

Turning back to the crowd, he continues. "Nevertheless, I found a short verse from a Cohen song that I think Lenny would approve.

>"So come, my friends, be not afraid.
>We are so lightly here.
>It is in love that we are made
>in love we disappear."

"Lenny, my friend, our love for you transcends the flesh. I'll miss our repartee and your crazy way of looking at things. See you *mañana*."

Following Dennis's talk, others spoke, as people do at these events, of Lenny's positive qualities and how his memory and ideas will live on in others. A few spoke passionately, some tearfully, sharing anecdotes and reminiscences. There were even a few humorous stories, a nod to Lenny's fondness of satire, irony, and absurdity.

Eleanor talked about Lenny as a boy, his love of music and poetry, and how as he matured, he tried to find a way to combine his artistic sensibility with his intellectual interests. She shared memories of their early years. How when she was sad Lenny would cheer her up by creating wacky, impromptu theatrical performances, sometimes enlisting her, that would invariably change her tears to laughter. "We had our childhood spats, but I always knew he loved me." Her final words expressed gratitude that although their life pathways diverged, they remained connected and maintained a closeness she will cherish and miss.

Patricia spoke of how, like Ashley, her relationship with Lenny was brief but meaningful. In particular, she related how he helped her manage her trauma and grief after the death of her daughter.

"Lenny quickly became someone I regarded as a friend for which I will always be thankful. But for the same reason, I am heartbroken he is gone and our relationship will not have the opportunity to grow deeper.

"Dear Lenny, you appeared in my life at a time of need. And despite your own struggles with what you experienced at The Loft, you showed me warmth and caring. Although our time together was short, I hold you in my heart."

Last to speak was Jerry. As he rises, Katie squeezes his hand. His gait is unsteady as he walks slowly to the front of the gathering. "I can do this," he repeats to himself. Unfolding a paper gripped tightly in his hand he speaks of how his friendship with Lenny might have seemed unlikely given their differences in backgrounds, career choices, and lifestyles, but how it was precisely these dissimilarities that made their relationship special.

"On the surface we were like Jack Lemmon and Walter Matthau

in the movie, *The Odd Couple*. But unlike those characters, neither of us attempted to change the other. Rather, we respected and appreciated our different perspectives." He pauses to remove a handkerchief from his pocket and wipe his eyes. After a deep breath, he describes how these qualities were critical in helping him cope with his daughter's injury at The Loft.

"I was a mess and making unwise decisions, but Lenny was like a counterweight keeping me from falling off the cliff . . . Well, I did fall a little, but I never doubted he would be there to pick up the pieces. And he was."

He drops his paper and looks at the sky.

"Hey, Lenny. I'm already missing our regular meetings at the Holy Grounds coffee shop, but I want you to know I will always carry the lessons learned from our friendship. As you know, the last time we were there I was feeling down and struggling with how to go on. You looked at me and said, 'I know sometimes it's hard to maintain hope that things will get better. When I feel that way, I try to remember that no matter the circumstances, the world is always turning towards the morning.' I think that was a line from one of the countless songs residing in your head. But you know what? It helped."

His composure gone; Jerry manages to croak, "I will never forget you."

The service ends and people began to disperse, each carrying the relational realities they had constructed with Lenny. How those realities will be remembered would be as varied as their relationships: in a humorous anecdote, a quotation, a song, an act of kindness, or the bark of a dog.

ACKNOWLEDGEMENTS

Writing a book is never an individual achievement. Yes, I am the one who lays down the story lines and ultimately chooses the words that are read, but the finished product reflects numerous relationships, past and present.

Although many deserve mention, space limits me to a small number of active supporters. The amazing cover, which I am sure drew many of you to the book, is original art by my talented spouse, Frannie Joseph, who was also my first reader. My sister, Lynne Burley, read multiple drafts that were always followed by insightful suggestions. Katherine Tyson McCrea provided encouragement and useful advice for making the story more interesting. Allan Irving was an ongoing supporter and graciously allowed me to borrow some of his own written lines. Neil Abell, Pat Cook, Erik Moreau, and Noriko Martinez kindly waded through clunky early drafts and gave me useful feedback. The book is better for their efforts.

My exceptional grandsons, Micah and Isaiah Witkin Frishman, kept my motivation high with their frequent requests for updates on my progress and exclamations of "whoa!" in response.

Jeff Schlesinger of Barringer Publishers provided support and guidance throughout the process of putting the manuscript into publishable form.

Last, I want to acknowledge and thank you, the readers of *Finding Lenny*, for your patronage. There would be no authors without readers. Imagining you reading this book was a strong motivator to continue during challenging periods of writing.

I hope you found *Finding Lenny* interesting and enlightening. As you probably know, in the publishing game reviews carry a lot of weight, so if you liked the book, I would greatly appreciate it if you would consider writing even a brief review.

If you are interested in hearing Gideon's song about Leonard Cohen, check out my YouTube video at: https://www.youtube.com/watch?v=n0xE-A5WoV4.

Feel free to contact me at stanleylwitkin@gmail.com if you would like to share any comments or questions about the book, or want to be notified of future publications and activities.

Lightning Source UK Ltd.
Milton Keynes UK
UKHW020711051022
409964UK00019B/1319